W9-AFT-074

HER HIGHNESS'
FIRST MURDER

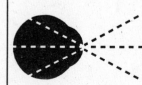

A SIMON & ELIZABETH MYSTERY,
BOOK 1

HER HIGHNESS'
FIRST MURDER

PEG HERRING

THORNDIKE PRESS
A part of Gale, Cengage Learning

GALE
CENGAGE Learning™

Detroit • New York • San Francisco • New Haven, Conn • Waterville, Maine • London

GALE
CENGAGE Learning™

LIBRARY OF CONGRESS CATALOGING-IN-PUBLICATION DATA

Herring, Peg.
   Her highness' first murder : a Simon & Elizabeth mystery / by Peg Herring.
     p. cm. — (Thorndike Press large print clean reads)
     ISBN-13: 978-1-4104-2540-9 (hardcover : alk. paper)
     ISBN-10: 1-4104-2540-1 (hardcover : alk. paper)
     1. Elizabeth I, Queen of England, 1533–1603—Fiction. 2. Women—Violence against—Fiction. 3. Large type books. I. Title.
PS3558.E7548H47 2010b
813'.54—dc22   2009051915

Published in 2010 by arrangement with Tekno Books and Ed Gorman.

Printed in the United States of America
1 2 3 4 5 6 7 14 13 12 11 10

For John

PROLOGUE

February 1546

The landlord of the Ox with Flowers glanced up as Mathilda hurried through her duties, her pert face for once serious as she worked. "Got an appointment, Tildy?"

The pretty wench grinned impishly, perfect front teeth showing white in the rushlight. "What do you care, John, with that wife o' yours always keepin' her eye on ye?"

Throwing a sodden rag into a bucket in the corner with a splash, Mathilda surveyed the room, nodded satisfaction, and pulled her cloak from a peg on the wall.

"It's a cold night out there," John warned.

"It is that." She gave him a saucy wave as she closed the door behind her with a firm thump.

Outside, the girl hardly noticed February's cold bite, though the wind lashed her heavy skirts around her ankles and fought to tear the woolen scarf from her head. When her lover proposed a private supper tonight, his accompanying look and warm touch had promised more.

Although a country girl until recently, Mathilda was not backward, and things were not so different in London as elsewhere. She knew what was expected of girls like her and accepted that it was why men came to them. Sometimes they were rough, tearing her clothing and leaving bruises on her otherwise flawless skin. The lover she hurried to meet tonight was different. Well dressed and well spoken, he treated Tildy, a runaway from Lincolnshire, like a lady, bringing ribbons for her heavy mane of hair and stockings finer than any she'd ever owned. Lately he had hinted that he might set her up in a small house. A girl like Tildy could ask for no more. She hated life at the Ox and would leap at the chance to be a kept woman, secure and pampered by any standard she'd ever known.

As the landlord had warned, the night was cold. Stars appeared to hang directly overhead, their light adding no warmth, only breathtaking beauty, which the girl chose to ignore. Hurrying out of the inn's dimly lit courtyard and down the dark, winding street, Tildy felt sharp gusts of wind as she navigated buildings set higgledy-piggledy, making the way sometimes wide, sometimes narrow. Coming around a poorly built wall that leaned over her like an eavesdropper, she saw him ahead. Wrapped in a long, dark cloak, her lover waited at the entrance of an alleyway. His eyes shone hungrily at the sight of her, his burning gaze warming the air between them.

Knowing better than to touch him first, the girl simply stopped within reach of his arms, smiling self-consciously. "Little Mathilda." His voice was hoarse with desire. His gaze swept the street full circle: no one. *Afraid he'll be seen by his fine friends,* she thought, *caught with his doxy from the Shambles.* A moment's bitterness marred the meeting. Even if Tildy got her little house, he would always be ashamed of their liaison.

The thought faded as her lover's arms went around her, drawing Tildy into the shadows of surrounding buildings. He kissed her with all the fire that had burned in his eyes moments before, hands caressing her pale throat gently. *I'm only his doxy, but I'll see that he is mine forever.*

It was the last pleasant thought she had, for the hands on her white throat tightened in the darkness, squeezing until she fought to be free of them, uselessly, fleetingly. Her scream was choked to silence and there was only the brief rustling of her fruitless struggle. As Tildy sank to the ground, lifeless, the same hands pulled her farther into the alley, where her body suffered such indignities that death had been a mercy after all.

CHAPTER ONE

Simon heard the cries as they climbed the steep hill to the castle. Screams vibrated with pain and panic, fluctuating between wordless shrieks and "No, don't!" repeated several times. His father, striding ahead with his soft bag over one shoulder, seemed unaware, but Simon cringed. Despite daily encounters with people in pain, the physician's son could not become inured to it.

Head down, Simon followed in his father's wake. A familiar tightness in his chest signaled that he would not breathe deeply again until their work was finished here. Every task required of him Simon performed with precision, but afterward his chest was wracked with long bouts of coughing as normal function returned to his lungs. If Jacob Maldon noticed his son's discomfort, he saw no reason to comment on it.

The fact that Hampstead Castle was three

hundred years old was discernible from both its crenellated walls and the thick moss that covered them to a height of at least ten feet. Father and son entered through a bailey no longer fortified but stout enough, the gate a good ten inches thick. Inside was a courtyard with several outbuildings on the right, uninhabited for the most part. They crossed to the castle itself, of defensible design with a large set of double doors, now propped open, and an inner set that opened with a minor groan as they approached. Above were the narrow windows common to fortresses, designed to make poor targets for archers. The heavy glass placed in these slits in more modern times would not let in much light, so the place would be dim. Since moss signaled damp as well, Hampstead's overall impression was unwholesome. Simon wondered who would want to live in such a place.

A slight sound of what he thought was impatience from his father made Simon break off his inspection and hurry along. Knowing he was a disappointment to his father, the son tried to furnish efficiency where he could not offer enthusiasm. His aversion to the medical arts aside, Simon admired his father above all men.

Apparently the physician had no inkling

that his manner signaled displeasure. Sharply efficient in his habits, Jacob was unaware that he often made those around him feel inadequate by comparison. Neither had it occurred to him to tell Simon where they were headed, or to whom.

Inside, they entered the hall, a room with almost no furniture. A fireplace took up one wall, its stone face blackened with years of use. Though it blazed and crackled inside the yawning expanse, the fire had not yet warmed the place much. Stone stairs to the right led both up and down. Below was a small room that housed the all-important well. Up the other stairway would be chambers for the family, probably provided with more comfortable trappings. Somewhere at the back would be the bake house, the kitchens, and servants' quarters. Simon heard a single peal of laughter from that direction, but otherwise the house had fallen quiet, no more pain-wracked screams.

They were met by a morose-looking woman, her face so white it seemed unnatural. Strands of hair visible around the coif she wore were dark, the face unlined. She was young, then, despite her grim expression. "Here." She gestured up the spiral stairs and turned a rigid back as she led the way. Even her voice was odd, sounding as if it came from deep inside her, weakened and quavering by the time it fought its way out.

Jacob Maldon ascended the stone steps calmly but with good speed. Long practice as a physician had inured him to panic in such situations, and he responded quickly, with tacit empathy for everyone involved. The old castle was cold, and there was a bad smell. *Mold,* Simon thought with a twitch of his nose. The silent, tight-faced woman led the way down a corridor and into a room moderately warm compared to the rest of the place.

Inside, two women stood beside a low wooden pallet where the patient lay, quiet now. Evidently moving her there had caused the screams. The right leg, propped on a soft blanket, lay at an odd angle. The limb had swelled, bulging in the middle till the skin looked shiny. Unaware of their arrival, the patient moaned once, but the other two looked up, relief registering on their faces.

"What's happened, then?" Jacob squatted beside the bed. He had little interest in the injury's cause, but it helped somehow for those involved to tell it.

One of the women, a striking blonde, made as if to speak but stopped, looking at the girl who stood, pale but composed, at the patient's side. She was younger than Simon, no more than fourteen. Although no beauty like the blonde, an air of assurance about her made a stronger impression. She looked squarely at Jacob with a directness Simon had seldom seen in women. Neither challenging nor inviting, her manner was simply honest, no hauteur but no false subservience either.

"Mary fell from a horse," the girl said in a clear voice. "She had not ridden before and thought to surprise me with her skill. The mount was poorly chosen and we found her on a hillside, among the rocks."

Jacob knelt and touched the leg, broken halfway down from the knee. Jagged ends pushed against the skin in opposite directions but fortunately had not split it open. Still, it was bad, not a clean break. Such an injury could heal poorly, leaving the victim lame for life and plagued by constant pain. The women had been right to call for a physician who had even been consulted on the king's health, which everyone knew was failing fast.

"What is your name?"

The patient was more fearful now, aware of the strangers present and their purpose. About thirty, she was stout and plain-faced, with smallpox scars like pebbles under her skin. Large brown eyes were her most attractive feature, but tears seeped out their sides and slipped into her hair as she shivered. "Mary, sir. Mary Ward." England was awash with Marys, Catherines, and Williams. Ward added little individuality.

"Mary, we must set your leg. It will hurt but you must be brave. My son here will pull it straight, which will send the bones back to their accustomed place." No use mentioning other possibilities at the moment. "I will bind it tightly so that it may heal good as new. We have done this many times and know how to accomplish it quickly. Do you understand?"

"Y-yes." Tears fell faster now, but the woman calmed somewhat at the sound of Jacob's voice. He purposefully spoke in low, soothing tones, telling clearly what would happen to remove her dread of the unknown. He had said it would hurt, and she knew it would. Now that it was spoken, Mary was as ready as she could be.

Jacob looked up at the women circling the pallet. The somber one and the fragile blonde looked away. Instinctively, the physician turned to the girl with the gray eyes. Although young and slight, she seemed accustomed to taking control. "Are you strong enough to hold Mary's shoulders and keep her still?"

The young face grew pale and the thin lips compressed. "Yes." She said no more but moved to the head of the pallet. Briefly caressing the older woman's hair, she murmured something that Simon did not hear, and Mary responded with a weak smile. Taking off the girdle that cinched her loose housedress at the waist, the girl looped it several times for fullness and placed it between the woman's teeth. Taking a grip under Mary's arms, she stood ready to lean back and put her weight against any movement of the patient's upper body.

Jacob chose what he perceived to be the braver of the other two, the somber one. "Hold the other leg still so that Simon is not kicked senseless." The pale woman took her place with obvious reluctance, not daring to demur since the girl had taken her part without hesitation.

Simon took the foot of the misshapen leg under his right arm and, at his father's signal, pulled gently but firmly, as he had been taught, until the bones started to move. Even muffled by the makeshift gag, the patient's screams were terrible to hear. Beside Simon the dark-haired woman turned away and gasped once, but she held on. The blonde ran from the room, a hand pressed to her lips. The girl held on fiercely, focused on the task at hand.

Jacob deftly placed wooden splints along the leg and secured them with tightly wrapped bandages. When finished, he sat back and nodded. The three assistants relaxed, and screams turned first to moans and finally to choked sobs.

The girl, white-faced but subtly triumphant, patted Mary's hand and told her she'd been brave. Turning to the dark woman beside her, she spoke formally. "You were a great help, Margot." The response was a slight nod in acknowledgment of the compliment, no more.

Pulling a packet from his bag, Jacob directed the dour woman to mix it with warmed wine for the patient. "She will sleep then, which is the best thing for her." Margot left the room as if she had escaped hanging.

"You did very well." Simon was surprised when his father, not one to hand out compliments, spoke to the girl.

"Someone had to do it."

"You have your father's sense of responsibility," Jacob commented. He paused for a moment and added with deliberate emphasis, "— and your mother's spirit."

Simon gazed at the girl in surprise. The

gloomy castle and the lack of finery notwithstanding, he faced Elizabeth, Princess Royal
of England, declared bastard in 1536, over
ten years before. Now he understood the
girl's youthful dignity, the deference from
others, and the red hair so like King Henry's
before age and disease had caught up with
him.

CHAPTER TWO

Elizabeth's face showed first surprise, then confusion at Jacob's direct mention of her mother. She glanced down at the patient to judge the woman's awareness of the conversation. Shock had done its work, and Mary Ward's eyes were glassy and heavy-lidded.

"You knew my mother?" The voice was carefully devoid of color, and she clasped her arms around herself as if to forestall any unconscious signal of interest.

"Before she married your father, I was physician to the Lady of Aragon. Anne was then of her household."

And caught the eye of the king so that he turned the whole of England upside down to have her, Simon added silently. When Spanish princess Catharine had borne no sons, Henry had discarded her for Anne Boleyn. She too had failed to have a son; only this self-possessed girl remained of their union. Jacob had always spoken of the matter with regret, although he never criticized the king.

Muscles beneath the skin of the pale face moved, and Simon could almost hear the questions that tumbled into the girl's mind about the mother she had hardly known. When Anne went to the block, convicted of adultery and accused of other heinous crimes, her only child had been three.

"Did you like her?" Simon would have asked about guilt: had Anne committed adultery with many men — her own brother — as had been claimed?

"She loved life very much, and I was saddened at all she bore at the end," Jacob answered candidly.

Elizabeth looked directly at Jacob, gauging his honesty. "I thank you for telling me," she finally said formally. "Few speak of my mother, and of course she is best forgotten. Still, a daughter may be glad to know something of the woman who bore her." Her tone was still carefully flat, but her expression was a bit defensive.

Jacob looked up as both attending women returned, one with the posset. An odd smell wafted toward them, earthy and thick. "I am pleased to be of assistance," he replied, which could have referred to either the bone-setting or the information. Jacob took the two attendants aside to give instructions for care of the patient.

Simon stared at Elizabeth, impolite but unable to help himself. The thin lips curved in an ironic smile. "Have I grown a second head in the last two minutes?"

"I'm sorry, Your Grace." He hoped it was the correct term, since Elizabeth's title changed depending on the king's attitude at the time. "Father never mentioned whose home we were called to. I do not mean to be rude."

She ignored the apology and followed her own thought. "Will you be a physician like your father, Simon?"

He blushed. A princess of England had called him by name, had remembered it despite the situation. An honest answer burst from him: "God shield it. I have no inclination for the work. In fact, I hate it."

Glancing at the semi-conscious woman between them, Elizabeth admitted tartly, "That was hardly enjoyable."

Simon was candid. "I can't bear their pain. My father is able to view patients as objects that need fixing, but I see their fear and it causes me to feel sick."

"But you did what had to be done." He sensed approval in the comment.

Surprising himself, Simon revealed the other reason he would never be a physician, one that he usually hid for as long as possible. "There is this as well." He held up his left arm almost challengingly. From the elbow down it was half the size of a normal arm. "It can grasp lightly, but most tasks I must do with one hand."

Looking calmly at what was Simon's greatest shame, the princess said only, "You hide it well. I had not noticed." With those few words and her calm acceptance of his infirmity, Elizabeth won Simon's affection forever.

"It has been this way since birth." Elizabeth required a sort of honesty that most people did not. Outright lies she might tolerate, but hypocrisy seemed alien to her character.

"My mother was born with an extra finger," she said, touching her left hand absently. "She had her dresses made with very long sleeves to hide it, I'm told."

"Who told you that?"

"My sister Mary." Elizabeth's voice hardened slightly at mention of the name. "She is often glad to tell me about my mother." Her tone conveyed that Princess Mary's confidences caused more pain than comfort.

Jacob ended his instructions to the women who must serve as Elizabeth's ladies-in-waiting. Although not often welcome in her father's palace, as a princess she required a certain level of care, and it seemed these three provided it. From the gentry or lesser nobility, they would be glad to have any position with the court, even companion to a child declared bastard.

England's king had married six times: Spanish Catharine of Aragon was Princess Mary's mother. Anne Boleyn had come second. The third wife, Jane Seymour, died shortly after bearing Henry's only son, Edward. The last three had no royal children: the marriage to Anne of Cleves was annulled when her looks displeased Henry, and Katherine Howard met the same end Elizabeth's mother had. Present wife Catherine Parr was mainly a comfort in the king's old age and very bad health.

Having given the necessary nursing instructions, Jacob returned his attention to Elizabeth. Simon marveled at his father's confidence. Being a sought-after physician, he sometimes gave commands to those around him without consideration for their station. Imagine ordering a princess of the blood to help with a bone-setting!

"Your Highness, I have made Mary comfortable and given instructions for her care. We shall not bleed her unless the blood overbalances the other humors, causing fever."

"As you say, Master Maldon."

Jacob rubbed his cheek, a gesture Simon knew signaled that he was getting an idea. "Any weight applied to the break over the first week may disturb it and ruin the chance of the bone healing correctly. Therefore I will send my son tomorrow with a crutch for her use."

Elizabeth nodded with a quick glance at Simon, her manner showing neither pleasure nor reluctance to have him visit again. "I thank you."

Although she need not explain herself to them, Elizabeth seemed compelled to, and she gestured at the dark structure around them. "Hatfield is being cleaned and repaired, so I must reside here for several months. In addition, my governess carries her first child with some difficulty and requires complete rest. My father provided Mary Ward, a good and faithful friend, as substitute."

Elizabeth spoke as though her father was solicitous of her welfare when everyone knew he barely noticed her existence. Perhaps sensing the girl's need to justify her state, Jacob politely kept his thoughts to himself.

Father and son made their way out, escorted by the princess herself. The day had warmed nicely, and contrast with dour Hampstead made the sunlight even more vivid and welcome. About to take his leave, the physician had an apparent last-minute thought. "Since you are separated from your home and friends, Your Highness, Simon could provide diversion for you. He is well taught, if I may boast my own instruction, and an amiable companion. My son excels at mathematics and the sciences, and he speaks and reads several languages."

Simon tucked his chin into his chest in horror. His father was pushing him at a princess of the blood, offering him like a toy for her amusement.

Elizabeth, though young, was well aware that her acquaintance was sought for all sorts of reasons unconnected with her personal charm. Eying the elder Maldon shrewdly, she considered the offer then turned to Simon.

"Do you read Greek?"

"Yes, Your Highness, if it please you, and Latin."

"Shall we practice with each other afternoons, then? I would like especially to practice Greek before my new tutor arrives in the fall. I have books that you may borrow if you like." Typically of royalty, she had no thought that he might have other things to do.

Her presumption did not occur to Simon, speechless with joy. He was to have the pleasure of the princess' company, and she would lend him books. "I, um, I would be most gratified to read Greek with you, Your Highness, and I would be most grateful for a book or two." He wondered how many he would be allowed to have. Everything his father owned, no matter what its language, he'd read twice already.

"Good, then I shall look for you tomorrow afternoon." The door closed behind them with a wooden thud, and Simon stared at it for some time in amazement before hurrying after his father.

Some distance southeast of Hampstead two men stood over the body of a young woman. The younger stepped away and was noisily sick after seeing the headless corpse they were called to deal with. His father, more accustomed to such things, stared in grim acceptance.

The younger man returned, his eyes drawn to the horror despite his stomach's objection. "Who would do such as this?"

"One of Satan's own," was the reply. "This

crime is beyond our scope, boy. Look at the hands." Here the old bailiff turned the palm of one dead hand upward. "She's done no labor in her life, this one."

"You mean she's noble?" the youth asked, incredulous. "Why would she wear such things?"

"I don't know," the father muttered, "but those above us should hear of this." Using his cap, he dusted off his son's clothing as much as possible. "You must look proper when you go to Whitehall to tell what you've seen." The older man considered the mutilated corpse on the muddy ground. "Much good it will do her, poor thing."

CHAPTER THREE

By the fireplace of their comfortable home that evening, Mary Maldon questioned her husband and son closely about their encounter with the princess, at the same time attacking the ever-present pile of mending that any mother of four must deal with. She demanded details of the girl's looks, the house's furnishings, even the attendants' clothing. As much as Simon loved his mother, he knew her faults, and snobbery was the greatest of them. Tomorrow she would report to anyone she met that Jacob had attended at the princess' home, tossing in bits of description as proof. An avid follower of news of the royal family, Mary had never forgiven her husband for being so truthful about the king's declining health that he was dismissed.

"Hampstead! Why, the place is moldering away." Mother sputtered with indignant shakes of her head. The cap worn loosely tied under her chin didn't follow the movement, making a comical picture. By tacit consent, husband and son omitted details of the castle's condition. If she knew of the suspicious odors inside Hampstead, Mary Maldon would have even more to say. *Her* house was aired and swept clean weekly, foul weather or no, and sweet-smelling herbs boiled in a pot on the fire. *She* would have no ill humors and miasmas collecting in corners or infecting the bedchambers.

A plump woman of middle age, Simon's mother was the opposite of his father, short where he was tall and round where he was spare. Jacob's hair was thin and straight while his wife's was abundant and spun in all directions. Their personalities were also opposite, Mary talking without much thought while her husband thought much more than he said.

"It is temporary." Jacob polished and honed the tools of his trade, the soft scrape of steel against stone underscored the discussion. "Hatfield is quite suitable. Besides, it is wise to keep royal children separate lest they catch some disease and all die at once."

"But Elizabeth reminds Henry that he threw away his good name and gained only a daughter. When he let 'his Nan' dictate the future of England, the king became the laughingstock of Europe."

"Elizabeth is of royal blood," Simon argued.

"Good English blood, not half Spanish or other foreign taint." Mary's lips pursed with righteousness. "An Englishwoman would be a more suitable queen than Princess Mary, who is half Spanish and Catholic to boot." Mary Maldon didn't approve of female rulers, but one had to be practical. "If young Edward dies of his many illnesses, I'd sooner see this princess on the throne than the other."

"It's not our affair in any case. God will decide it." Jacob put away the stone and returned his tools to the bag with a musical clank of conclusion. The subject was dropped and the family made their way to bed.

The man waited outside Hampstead impatiently, his pacing unconsciously metered: fourteen steps and a pause, then fourteen in the other direction. The Stations of the Cross. Finally, a soft scraping at the locked gate froze his movement. Forcing outward calm, he stepped toward the peephole, checking as he went. The bag sat nearby, accessible but out of sight, the required tools inside it. The night was perfect, only a metallic sliver of moon and cool enough to make the cape he wore seem natural.

A slit of light from a shuttered lantern shone through the gate's grated window, and the woman's face appeared in its glow. She was lovely, beautiful enough to be one of the saints pictured so masterfully by the great Raphael. Seeing him there she whispered apologetically, "It will be impossible to leave for a while. I must stay with her nights for at least a week."

Anger rose in him, mighty, righteous anger, swelling his chest and moving up to his head, making it hot, making him almost say the wrong thing. But years of training took over automatically. The man gripped the cold metal of the grate for a moment, letting it cool his heat. Smiling, he found comforting words, as he had been taught to do. "Don't fret, love. I will wait for you." He touched the warm fingers she slipped through the grate. In the darkness he pictured but could not see the wide, flat thumbs, her only physical imperfection.

The woman smiled in relief. "I'm glad," she said, her femininity reaching through the metal to entrap him.

"I will wait at this hour every night until you appear," he told her, "and I will count

32

the minutes."

She smiled again at the ardor in his voice, lowering her eyes flirtatiously before shuttering the lantern to hide her return to the house. He stared after her, although it was too black to see, his anger ebbing slowly. Taking up the bag from its hiding place, he turned and slid silently into the night. Preparations would have to be made again.

When Simon went next to the castle, he prepared himself to be a royal companion, dressing with care and combing his black hair neatly as he hummed an original tune. Although there was little choice in clothing, he cleaned his brown galligascons, loose-fitting breeches, thoroughly with a brush and topped them with a muslin undershirt and a green tunic his mother had recently made for him. Simon was neither handsome nor ugly, with a plain face and the same long upper lip and deep-set eyes that his father had. His height distressed him, well below his sister Annie's, although she was two years younger. Mother had assured him that with boys growth came later, but at fifteen he despaired of ever reaching normal size.

Other than his arm, which he hid with a full sleeve, Simon was robustly healthy.

"The boy can run all day," his mother boasted to the neighbors. He had learned to swim in the Thames despite the dirty water, his withered arm, and his parents' orders otherwise. Since pastimes requiring two strong arms were denied him, Simon's efforts focused on his studies with his father as tutor. There his arm was no hindrance, and he felt confident and whole.

Although he had prepared clever ways to let the princess know of his better-than-average education, Simon did not see her at all the second day. When he arrived, taciturn Margot met him with a cold stare and no word of welcome, leading the way in silence to the room where Mary Ward lay dozing on the same pallet. She woke when he set the crutch beside her and laid a warm hand on his arm.

"It's the physician's boy, isn't it?"

"Simon Maldon, lady. I've brought a crutch to use if you must walk, but it is best that you stay quiet."

Mary's plain face shone with momentary humor through her grogginess. "I could have told that, and I'm no physician. I won't go dancing at the king's."

Simon felt glad that the princess had such a companion, warm as silent Margot could never be. Margot herself stood behind him,

34

her flat gaze taking in all that he said and did. Conscious of Simon's nervous glance around the room, she said with a look that subtly relished his disappointment, "The princess has gone a-visiting."

"Oh." Simon's carefully planned conversational initiatives vanished into the air. The princess had forgotten her invitation to him.

As he left the room, Alice, the attendant who had run from the bone-setting, caught up to him on the stairs. Although eighteen or so, she appeared much younger when she spoke. "Young Master Maldon, how good you are to help poor Mary," she lisped in breathy tones.

Alice looked very much like his sister's favorite poppet, Simon thought, beautiful in the face and daintily made, but with an expression that showed no more intellect than the doll's. Blonde hair framed her face, emphasizing blue eyes and long lashes surprisingly dark for one so fair. A more sophisticated male might have suspected cosmetics, but Simon had no experience with such things.

Despite his ingenuousness, the boy soon sensed that Alice was practicing the only art she knew: captivating men. Following Simon to the landing, she thanked him to an embarrassing degree for his help and apologized several times for leaving the room during the bone-setting. In the process she managed to brush against him twice on the narrow stair.

As he stood, embarrassed at the attention, she tilted her head to one side so that her eyes showed to their best advantage. The linen dress she wore, neither rich nor elegant, fitted the curves of her obviously feminine body, and she instinctively arched her back to accentuate her shape. "I should have been more help to you," she piped. The combination of womanly charm and childlike behavior was designed to attract, and Simon felt the pull even though he had no interest in that particular feminine type. Alice's eyes showed that she understood her attraction and reveled in it.

"It was nothing."

"I wish I were strong-minded, as Elizabeth is," Alice lisped. "She is wise as any man and writes poetry most clever. I have heard the king's verse read at court, but Her Highness writes every bit as well, and only a girl."

Here Alice's admiration for Elizabeth overcame flirting and she spoke honestly. "I did not understand all the words, but I've asked Margot to teach me so that I may read them myself one day. Her Highness will say, 'Why, Alice, I did not know you were so bright.' She shall say that." Her blue eyes shone at the prospect of Elizabeth's admiration, and she smoothed her hair with both hands, as if determined to look her best when such a thing occurred.

At Alice's gesture Simon noticed that she had large, flat thumbs. Catching his gaze, the girl quickly hid her hands in the folds of her skirt. Simon blushed: who was he to note flaws in others? Alice went on in her childish way, "Margot says she will teach me, but not today."

At the outer door Simon took polite leave, sorry for Margot, who would try to teach this woman-child what was probably beyond her ken, and also for Elizabeth, kept in a cold castle with attendants who, however kind or efficient, were no stimulus for a girl with a lively intelligence and a passion for life and learning.

CHAPTER FOUR

The next day Mary Ward was able to move the leg without grimacing and declined further medicines, saying they made her dream "most oddly." The day was bright, and Simon helped her to a sunny window where she could crochet in good light. "Her Highness is with her drawing master," Mary reported, guessing that his glance sought Elizabeth. "His Majesty doesn't stint on her education, I'll give him that." Her tone suggested that she gave him credit for little else. "She will study in the autumn with Master William Grindal himself, from Cambridge." Looking about for eavesdroppers, Mary lowered her voice confidentially. "They give her the smallest accounts, no household to speak of, and no money to spend. It's sinful, I say. The girl is a princess, and most times, a sweeter girl never lived."

Simon did not know how to answer. To agree was critical of the king, to disagree was impolite as well as hypocritical. Elizabeth was kept meanly, because she was an embarrassment, a reminder of Henry's folly with Anne or his betrayal of her, depending on which side one took. "I'm sure the princess is grateful for your care of her," he replied diplomatically.

Outside the gloomy walls of Hampstead was a day that made the promise of spring specific. The air seemed to envelop Simon in softness. The sky was a deep blue, and the joy of being out-of-doors, drinking in the sensation of true warmth, was irresistible.

A few early crocuses sat in a sunlit turn of the wall, and he couldn't resist bending to touch the silky white petals. Straightening, he saw Elizabeth approaching, a sketch pad and drawing utensils in her hands. She wore a muslin slop over her plain dress to protect it from damage, and her red-gold hair was tied back with a ribbon to keep it out of her way, but it curled down her back, asserting the power of its strength and hue. Simon thought she looked charming.

The princess greeted him cordially, indicating the crocus. "The first of spring. I stole the bulbs from Hampton Court the last time I visited there."

"A beautiful place, Hampton."

"It is, and the flowers remind me of Katherine. To speak truly, I had permission to take them."

He tried a joke. "Her Highness is honest, then."

Her delicate face took on a pensive look. "I suppose I am as honest as one can be with the world as it is."

He did not know what to say to that. In his world honesty was required to gain peace from his mother and respect from his father. He took a different direction. "The queen likes flowers, Your Highness?"

Elizabeth dropped her gently pointed chin. "I spoke of Katherine Howard, not the present one. She was my cousin as well as my stepmother, and very like a flower, fragile and beautiful. She was kind to me." *And she lost her head, as Anne Boleyn did.*

Simon was embarrassed. What comment for a now dead and disgraced woman who had been the king's wife but never his queen? "They say she was lovely."

Elizabeth's pale eyes saw his discomfort and even paler brows rose as she spoke briskly. "I know she had grave faults. A queen must be above reproach. The present Catherine is most kind to me and is a comfort to my father the king. I am grateful for that."

"We are sorry to hear of His Majesty's illness, Your Highness. Without health, life is ever more difficult."

"True. The king was athletic as a young man, Kat says. She speaks of him playing tennis and besting all the others at tests of strength and skill."

Simon wondered if anyone would defeat a king at sport even if he could. Where would be the profit in that?

The present situation made Simon hesitate. A conversation was developing, and his neck reddened as he tried to decide what was proper for him to do. Should he offer to carry her things inside even though she had not invited him to stay? Commend her looks, although she was obviously dressed for leisure and not company? Stick to the safest of all subjects — the weather?

"Your Highness, Mary Ward is in good spirits and claims the leg does not ache so much."

"Yes, she seemed more comfortable when I visited her this morning," Elizabeth replied, and Simon chided himself. Of course she knew as well as he the condition of her household. As he wondered how best to take his leave, she said without preamble, "But we have Greek and Latin to practice, do we not?" Typically of royalty, the princess made

41

no apology or explanation of her absence the day before. Simon would serve at her pleasure, his presence required but hers at her leisure in the way of the ruling class. Simon had no objection, especially if she kept her promise about the books.

So began a strange relationship between Simon and the Princess Royal. At first he was shy, and understandably so. He was unused to such lofty company, ashamed of his arm and intimidated by Elizabeth, who had an authority about her that belied her years and trumpeted her Tudor heritage.

The second day, after he stammered "Your Highness" three times in one sentence, she demanded, "Simon, stop stumbling about and talk to me."

It was not easy, but he relaxed somewhat after that, gradually discarding stilted phrases for useful conversation. A routine developed in which he came to Hampstead Castle most afternoons where he and Elizabeth read aloud and conversed in various languages if she was not otherwise occupied. Simon's Greek was better than hers, but he knew no French. She taught him the rudiments, which he picked up easily.

Within a few weeks the crumbling old castle had become Simon's second home. If the princess was occupied or out, he visited with the staff. Soon the household women pampered him with sweets and fresh baked goods, and the guards ignored him. The only suspicious frowns came from Hampstead's guardian, Sir George Blakewell, a crusty knight of what Simon thought to be extreme age, at least forty.

He couldn't blame the man for being careful. If anything ill befell Elizabeth, bastard daughter or not, Sir George would be ruined. He and his buxom wife Bess worried when the princess rode for fear she would fall, when she studied late lest she ruin her eyes, and most of all, Simon suspected, when she spent time with the physician's boy.

Bess Blakewell stayed nearby whenever Simon was with Elizabeth. She said little, but sounds made as she knitted recalled his mother's broody hens guarding their nests: low, wordless lamentations for future grievances.

There was no cause to fear impropriety between the two young people. Both his station and his withered arm made Simon unlikely to seek physical contact. For her part Elizabeth seemed naturally indisposed to overt expressions of affection. Beyond the reassuring caress that first day when Mary Ward lay terrified and hurting, Simon seldom saw Elizabeth touch anyone.

The princess spoke of several people with affection, and it was odd for Simon to hear them mentioned casually: "Anne of Cleves gave me this book in German," or "The queen showed me this stitch." She often mentioned Robin Dudley, her trusted friend, and Kat Champernowne, now Ashley. Kat's pregnancy and Robin's trip to Scotland with his father had caused the loneliness that made Elizabeth take note of him, for which Simon felt lucky.

When the princess spoke of those she admired, her greatest respect was for her father. Though he ignored her and skimped on her care, it was apparent that she considered Henry an ideal man and the greatest ruler in Europe. Beside such lofty figures, Simon felt small, and Elizabeth's world seemed a great bubble that he could peer into but not touch.

So despite the Blakewells' fears, there was no experimental kissing in the garden, no touching hands as they chatted in foreign tongues. The two young people argued conjugations under budding cherry trees, discussed history as the fragrance of the blossoms built toward its finest days. Simon adored Elizabeth chastely, as a pilgrim adores the likeness of a saint. For her part,

Elizabeth seemed to look forward to his company. She called him Simon and he soon fell into casually calling her "Highness."

Simon walked briskly toward the castle early one morning in April, free of his duties for a day. He always felt lighter at such times yet a little guilty, since he knew his father released him knowing that he hated acting as physician's assistant. His brother William was far more interested in practicing medicine than he was, but at ten years old was a little too young. For the thousandth time Simon promised himself that he would try harder tomorrow to be content with what his father needed him to be.

Simon and Elizabeth were preparing a fete for her household in celebration of May Day. Excited by the prospect, he arose much too early and arrived long before the princess would arise. His plan was to slip into the bake-house and help with morning chores, which often led to an invitation to break his fast with the servants.

Heading for the castle with head bent, Simon strode along, considering how to arrange the furnishings of Hampstead's hall so everyone might view the entertainment. His feet automatically traced the way as his mind tried different ways to use the space available.

It had become his habit to enter through the garden gate, a small, arched doorway in the castle's west wall. Locked at nightfall, this entrance was opened at daybreak for the convenience of the household. The front gates, though imposing, opened away from the city and the market road. Elizabeth had shown him the smaller gate and suggested it would save him steps when he came to visit. He wasn't sure it would be unlatched so early, but the iron-bound plank door opened with its customary rasp as the hinges rubbed on the pins that held them together.

Dawn had broken, but the air was gray with fog as he entered the garden. It had become more welcoming lately, and flowers bloomed on all sides. While there were no gardeners hired for Her Highness' use, the garden had once been someone's pride. Elizabeth and her ladies had worked to repair years of neglect and make the place less dreary. Like any good Tudor or any good Englishwoman, the princess loved flowers. However, Simon thought with some animosity toward Henry, the king merely ordered flowers and they appeared while his daughter had to coax them out of the ground herself.

As the gate closed behind him with a click, something just off the path brought Simon out of his reverie. A sick feeling pulled at his stomach as his disbelieving mind took in the sight before him. With grim fascination he edged toward the spot where lay the body of a woman.

Her limbs had been carefully placed to suggest peaceful repose, feet together and arms crossed on her chest. She was dressed in robes that would identify her as a nun had that profession not been outlawed in England years before. The peace of the pose was shattered by the fact that the corpse had no head. Where it should have been, blood congealed on the rocks and soaked into the ground.

Simon stood frozen for a few moments as thought gradually returned. Elizabeth! He had to prevent her seeing this horror. It was said she suffered nightmares of her mother's beheading. One who had borne that should not be exposed to this. Hurrying past the corpse and up the walk, he knocked loudly on the heavy wooden door.

In a few moments Sir George answered, grumbling at the insistent pounding. At this early hour his hair, streaked with gray, stood up at the crown like a rooster's comb. The man seemed somewhat out of his time, like Sir Pellinore in stories of King Arthur. Although his beard was silver, his full, bushy eyebrows remained dark, giving him a stern appearance at the best of times. Upon acquaintance Simon had concluded that Sir George's frowning gaze came less from disapproval than from myopia.

"What is it, boy?"

"Sir, there's a dead woman in the garden —" Simon gulped before he could add, "— with no head."

Blakewell's brows, joined as he frowned at Simon, now flew toward his hairline. "No head? Boy, are you sure?"

"Yes, sir."

Cantankerous as he might be, Sir George was no fool. He called up the stairs, and Margot appeared with her usual blank expression. "Stay with the princess, lock yourselves in, and open the door to no one but me, do you understand?"

A look of curiosity passed over Margot's face, but she went off without asking the question that had seemed imminent. Sir George turned back to Simon and laid a meaty hand on his shoulder. "Fetch your father with all speed. Then go to St. James and tell the captain on duty what has happened. I will lock the gates and wait for your return."

Simon nodded compliance and took off at a run, feeling both purpose and relief to be away from the hideous scene. As he went, thoughts tumbled through his mind. Who was the woman? Who could have done this? And what would Elizabeth's reaction be when she heard, as she must?

CHAPTER FIVE

Of course his father was not at home, and Simon spent precious minutes locating him at a local merchant's house. Jacob wiped a lancet and returned it to his bag as Simon burst in. The coppery odor of blood mingled with the scent of fresh flowers placed in the room in the belief that they aided recovery. A departing maidservant carried a basin of blood, and the patient's inner arm was bound with cloth. Glancing into the basin, Simon saw the bodies of ants floating in the dark liquid. When held to a wound, the creatures bit down on the skin, pinching the edges together. The doctor then cut off their bodies, leaving the heads as sutures until the cut healed.

The boy imparted his message in a few whispered sentences. Checking his patient, pale and sleepy from the bloodletting and the drugs given, Jacob finished cleaning up.

His patient's recovery was up to the stars now.

"Fetch the Captain of the Guard at St. James, as Blakewell said. Bring him to Hampstead yourself, and tell no one else. He will know what must be done."

"Why keep it secret, Father?"

"It's murder, boy, in the princess' garden. The king must know before it is gossiped in the streets. Now go."

Again Simon ran, although this time he paced himself. The residence at St. James, Henry's shining new jewel, was some distance from Hampstead. Simon barely noticed as the houses became larger and more modern, the streets better cared for, and the congestion more dense. He ignored the babble of morning tradesmen crying their wares, slowing no more than necessary and weaving his way through the crowd as best he could. At St. James, gasping for air, he collected himself before speaking to a soldier at the gate. It would not do to be deemed a prankster and refused entry.

The guard wore the uniform of the Yeomen, a royal red tunic with purple facings and stripes on which gold lace ornaments were scattered. Red knee-breeches, red stockings, and a flat hat added to the striking outfit, and black shoes decorated with white rosettes completed the effect. The tunic's ornaments were Tudor symbols, a crown and the Lancastrian rose with Henry's initials woven in. By tradition all Guardsmen wore the same uniform, so Simon did not know if he addressed officer or common yeoman.

"I've come from the physician Jacob Maldon," he began. "He says I am to speak to the Captain of the Guard."

"What is it about, then?" The soldier looked bored and very likely to refuse to move.

"I have news for the captain, who will want to take the message to the king straightaway."

The weathered face looked doubtful. "You have a message for His Majesty?"

"Not I, my father, once a royal physician. The captain will recognize the name Jacob Maldon."

Evidently his assurance convinced the man, for he called over his shoulder to someone within, "Ask the captain to step out here, Calkin."

Within a few minutes, a man appeared at the gate. He was so tall that he walked with his body tilted a little forward, possibly from the habit of ducking through countless doorways. Brown hair had retreated on his oversized head so that the brow, which had undoubtedly always been high, extended still farther. The man's face was oblong, with flat cheekbones and thin lips. His pale blue eyes were piercing but not unkind. He studied Simon carefully before he ever said a word.

The guard spoke quietly to the newcomer for a moment. After a second study of the boy he announced in a calm, almost monotonous voice, "I am Captain Hugh Bellows. What is Jacob Maldon's message?"

Simon quickly related the facts. Bellows' intelligent face reflected concern, distaste, and something else as the story developed. "Calkin," he said, raising his voice only slightly, and there appeared at the gate a young soldier with sandy-red hair and freckles on every visible section of his skin. "I need three horses, yourself, and one other who can keep his own counsel here with all speed." Calkin disappeared immediately. "Boy — what is your name?"

"Simon, sir."

"Simon, I must leave you here briefly. Stay where you are, and speak to no one of this, understand?"

"Yes, sir."

Calkin appeared again very soon, and Bellows returned shortly after. In moments a third man, whose name Simon never learned, clattered across the cobblestone gateway on a bay, leading a chestnut for Calkin and a Barbary Arab for the captain. With practiced ease Bellows swung himself onto the gray and reached a hand toward Simon. The boy stood for a moment uncomprehending, then realized he was to ride with the captain. He had never been near such a spirited horse before, much less ridden one, but he gulped and gamely offered his right hand. Bellows pulled him up behind the saddle as easily as if he'd been a feather.

Simon was amazed at the feeling of being up so high. He'd ridden in carts and on ponies, of course, but had never sat on a horse's back. He almost forgot the seriousness of their mission in enjoyment of his new viewpoint.

The captain led his party northeast, following Simon's directions. As they rode, he cautioned, "I have informed one that the king trusts of what this boy told me. Until His Majesty gives us further instructions, we will speak nothing of what we see today. Is that understood?"

The two soldiers nodded solemnly, and Bellows turned to see that Simon signaled agreement as well. He wondered at the secrecy. Surely they would ask everyone nearby if they knew anything of the murder. Being not yet a man, much less a soldier, however, Simon did not speak his questions.

Hampstead Castle was visible from a long way off, its stark outline rising above the surrounding homes and shops. As they approached, Simon told them about the two gates and the custom of leaving the side one unlatched during the day. Bellows led them around to the front, rightly assuming that Blakewell had bolted the smaller gate to prevent further coming and going without notice. Sir George met them as they clopped through the entry, speaking briefly in private with Hugh. Calkin and the other used the time to secure the horses near a shady wall before they all headed to the garden.

Captain Bellows took in their surroundings almost casually as he went, and Simon saw them anew through the soldier's eyes. The castle faced south while the main part of London was to the southwest. The gate opened onto a large courtyard edged by stables, run down and almost empty, and several outbuildings, most in disuse. The front of the castle itself was imposing, being of the old Norman style and built of stone. Around the west side, to the left of the inner bailey, was the garden, separated from the courtyard by a high wall of hedge. Over the entrance to the garden pathway arched a trellis of ivy, now tipped with green as leaves made their timid appearance. On either side of the path, myrtle and phlox sent out new shoots, and here and there tiny pink or blue flowers peeped from among the green leaves.

Blakewell led the way to the spot where the body lay. A young manservant left on guard had a greenish look that hinted at uselessness had action been required. Simon was struck again by the horror of the scene: a headless corpse, its blood spilled like an overturned pitcher, and nun's habiliments where no nuns had existed for ten years, were in fact forbidden by law. All was calmly arranged among silent, nodding daffodils that symbolized new life as much as the congealing blood demonstrated new death.

Jacob Maldon squatted beside the corpse, examining the throat, or what was left of it. He calmly felt inside the gory wound then wiped his fingers on a small, often-stained cloth kept in his belt for that purpose. Turning as they approached, he stood and greeted Bellows.

"Captain, you came with good speed.

How is the arm?"

"Well, thanks to you, Master Maldon," was the reply.

"Good, good. Now here we have a terrible crime." Jacob indicated the corpse as if anyone there had been looking at anything else. It was like a magnet, drawing the eye despite the revulsion it caused. Still, Simon became aware of two things. First, he did not feel the tightening in his chest that occurred with living patients. The fact that the woman was beyond help released him from his crippling pity, allowing him to think clearly. Second, he felt a strong desire to know who had killed her and why. He bent to examine the corpse as his father spoke to Captain Bellows.

The woman's robe was black with a white collar. Beside the left shoulder lay the wimple that should have covered the head. Folded hands held a rosary of green stones linked with gold chain, the crucifix looped over the thumb and forefinger of the right hand.

Simon dimly heard Sir George's gravelly voice explaining that he had told the princess of a death in the household but had not elaborated. He had asked her to stay with Mary Ward and her women, but they had found that one of them, Alice LaFont, was missing. Blakewell's voice shook when he said it.

"Then this may be she?"

"This woman is the correct age and has the same coloring."

Simon spoke without realizing it or he might have had the sense to keep quiet. "She was strangled, beheaded, and then dressed this way."

There was a silence, and then his father asked calmly, "How do you know this?"

He looked up, embarrassed. "The marks on the throat, here. And the bloodstains are smeared where the collar was put on."

"I agree." Jacob sounded surprised, even pleased, at his son's display of logic.

"I believe this is Alice, who attended the princess. When we first met I noticed that she had wide, flat thumbs, like tiny spades." Simon picked up the hand nearest him and displayed what he had described.

"It is Alice," said a voice behind them, and they turned to see Elizabeth standing frozen ten paces back. Her voice sounded as if it came from far away, tremulous and weak. "I recognize her slippers." The girl's face was white and her eyes wide with the distress she experienced. Simon knew that her shock was not only for poor Alice. Surely her mother's headless image rose in her mind's eye.

"Highness, you should not be here." George Blakewell stood and imposed his wide shoulders between Elizabeth and the sight of the once-familiar Alice. "Let me take you inside while we remove her to a place of dignity."

She let herself be led away, but not without looking back once, her eyes fixed on the body. Simon doubted she even knew he was there, though he longed to comfort her. Blakewell's wife Bess hurried down the path and took the girl into her arms. On either side, the couple accompanied her into the castle, heads bent toward her in sympathy and concern. Those about the princess did indeed care for her.

Hugh Bellows watched them go, then shifted his feet and faced Jacob again. "Master Maldon, I asked your son to speak nothing of this, and I must ask the same of you."

"What do you mean? It is a murder, and the killer must be found, I would think."

"We will do everything possible, but His Majesty orders it kept quiet."

Jacob's intelligent eyes showed understanding. "Ah. There have been others killed in this way?"

Simon's eyes widened at the captain's nod

of assent. "You have promised your silence. Can the boy be trusted?"

"My son will say nothing."

"She is the fourth." Bellows puffed out his breath in a heavy sigh. "The first two were common sluts, found in different sections of London about a month apart. The mutilation was horrible, but no one thought much of it. That type of woman takes her chances, and there is seldom a way to discover which man she last met. Still, the investigators found the deaths unusual, the women being dressed as nuns, and so reported it to those above them.

"A month ago, a third headless woman was found. This time it was the daughter of Thomas Brandon, uncle to the Duke of Suffolk. He'd had a devil of a time with the girl, who was rebellious and defiant. She disappeared one night and later was found in the same state that you see here. His Majesty ordered silence on the matter to avoid panic."

Privately Jacob added additional reasons. Beheaded women might be associated with Henry, since he had disposed of two of his wives so. In addition, a connection with Catholicism seemed implicit in the costumed corpses. If this was a message for the king, what did it signify?

Nuns, priests, and friars had been outlawed in 1536. Existing members of the Catholic clergy had been pensioned off, the few who resisted executed. On the surface, dissolution of the monasteries had rid England of the pope's influence, but both crown and nobility had profited hugely in the process. Selling church properties filled Henry's coffers, and the noble buyers got bargain prices on some of the best holdings in England. Now a headless "nun" lay in Henry's backyard, at least in his daughter's.

The body was wrapped in a blanket and taken inside. The head was gone, as had been the case with the others. "She was used after her death, Hugh." Jacob said in low tones after the others had moved off. Simon, overhearing the exchange, recoiled in shock.

The captain said grimly, "As the other three were."

As they walked home together, Jacob voiced his thoughts. "They say as the king approaches death, he ponders things he has done. I do not know if this is true, since I have not seen him of late. My suggestions for curtailing his diet earned me glowering looks and a cold, 'You may take your leave.' It was probably too late anyway. Nothing can be done for him now. The queen can ease his suffering as well as anyone." Jacob sighed. "Still, Henry is king. If he says the murders will be investigated quietly, then it must be so. He will watch closely now that the matter has touched Elizabeth."

"Who would do such a thing to poor Alice? She was frivolous but quite harmless."

"We do not know what goes wrong inside such a man's head. Praise God, folk as twisted as that are rarely seen." He walked on a few paces. "If she was feather-headed, the girl was probably persuaded to a bit of fun."

"What do you mean?"

"I would guess that this Alice was with a man all night and meant to come creeping back at first light, before someone found the gate unlocked. It is unlikely that the killer came through a locked gate, went into the castle, dragged her out unseen, and murdered her."

"Could it have been this morning?"

"Few assignations take place before breakfast. I'd say she slipped out when the house quieted last night."

"How can you be sure the man was her lover?"

"I cannot, but Alice was no virgin. I simply conclude that a lover would easily draw her out at night."

Simon frowned. "Her heels were scuffed, dragged over the pathway. It appears he brought her to the gate as if to say goodbye, strangled her, then dragged her inside, finished the business, and left shortly before I arrived."

"You would not usually have been there so early in the day," the elder Maldon agreed. "If he knew the routines of the household, he would not expect to be disturbed."

Simon had a chilling vision of what he might have encountered had he come a few minutes earlier: a man bloodied by the awful task just completed and carrying a woman's head.

Jacob had the same thought. "There was nothing you could have done, lad."

After a moment Simon said, "He must have carried some sort of satchel in which to conceal Alice's clothing and the head."

"If he had a cape to wrap himself in afterward, any blood spilled would be hidden by it."

"But why does he take their heads?"

"Only God knows the answer to that."

They fell silent, considering the planning and cruelty needed to prepare for and enact such a vicious crime. The fact that it had happened three times before ruled out a spontaneous murder of passion. Someone had plotted the brutal death of Alice LaFont in some detail. Simon found that more than anything he'd ever desired, he wanted that person brought to justice.

Elizabeth sat in a chair, outwardly composed but deeply shaken. The sight of the headless corpse had brought to reality the images of her mother's death, even more horrible than those her mind had conjured. How could anyone do that to silly, childish Alice who'd cried when Sir George drowned a litter of kittens no one wanted to take care of? To take a life was bad enough, but to separate the head from the body? Was it a warning to her? The work of a madman? Someone who hated her father? Mary Ward hobbled in, the crutch's tap announcing her approach, and put an unsteady arm around her. "Poor lamb, to see such a thing! You must put it from your mind completely."

Elizabeth nodded compliance, used to outward agreement even when her inner self screamed defiance. It was the part she played in life: the compliant child, the last in line, the disgraced princess. But the image of Alice's headless body stayed in her traumatized consciousness: the smell of gore, the unnatural corpse, the end of a life.

She had badgered the story out of anyone who might tell it: Anne, her mother, comes dressed in a loose gray gown of damask, an ermine mantle over it and, with a bit of defiance, a red petticoat. Her hair is bound in a coif to keep it out of the headsman's way. She steps to the block, gives a short speech in which she blames the king for nothing. She is blindfolded, she kneels . . . the head separates from the body. Oh, God, the blood!

Returned to the present, Elizabeth made a silent vow that someone would pay for killing Alice. She would see to it, and she suspected that from his expression at the scene of the crime, Simon Maldon would be willing to help.

CHAPTER SIX

His Majesty Henry VIII was not in good humor, but that was not unusual of late. Jaw jutting and red-rimmed eyes hard as glass, the king sat wrapped in an embroidered robe as the day's events began with a hum of hushed voices around him. Henry had a vicious temper when his leg was hurting, and it hurt most of the time. The queen did what she could to comfort him, her patience and gentle touch never failing. Prince Edward enquired politely as to his health. Even the girls were paragons of tact on the infrequent occasions when he was forced to see them, Mary throwing no baleful glances his way and Elizabeth remaining demurely quiet. Since he was not long for the world, he thought grumpily, they allowed him some peace for once.

The babble in the room continued, but Henry's eyes, which had almost disappeared into the folds of his face these last years, narrowed further as he glared at the man before him. "You know nothing after two full days?"

Hugh Bellows stood rigidly at attention, his face flushed. It was uncomfortable to be in the king's presence these days, so unbalanced were his humors. Taking in the sovereign's bloated body, Hugh felt pity despite his nervousness. Henry was a travesty of the man he had been in his youth. The throne had had to be replaced with a larger one, his chest swelled before him like a toad's, and he had no neck at all, merely folds of skin stacked under his chin. The diseased leg smelled, and the color of the stain on the bandage was disgusting. His physical state would make a man miserable enough, but Henry had the French, bickering courtiers, and the precarious health of his son and heir to worry about as well. Now headless women haunted his days as well as his nights.

The king surveyed Hugh with similar thoughts: how simple to be a soldier, how complicated to be Henry Eight. He liked Bellows, in fact, had great respect for the man. One of several captains of the Yeomen of the Guard of the body of our Lord the King, Hugh was intelligent and efficient. Still, it did not do to let any man think himself favored. Hugh's task was to find the killer who had entered the castle of a Princess Royal and committed murder. Such a one could not be allowed to escape the king's justice.

Henry shifted impatiently and the room quieted, every occupant ready to respond if his name was spoken. Henry waved a careless hand and the tiny crowd relaxed, returning to its gossip. He regarded his captain again speculatively, perhaps enviously. He had chosen Hugh to see to this matter discreetly, since investigation of crimes could become a complicated matter. London had its own government, and even the king was careful of the city fathers' dignity. Bailiffs, marshals, and constables were in varying degrees responsible for protecting the citizenry from each other's excesses. The Crown had officials who enforced royal law, and since Henry VII, a Palace Guard created solely to protect the king and his family.

Originally formed of Welshmen fiercely loyal to the Tudors, the Guard was only grudgingly accepted by the populace as a permanent force. Henry found the sight of the colorful troops and the sounds of their masculine presence in the palace reassuring. He'd expanded the guard from fifty members to over six hundred, using them both to impress other monarchs and to perform tasks he required, from the imperative to the customary. For example, only a Yeoman of the Guard, under strict supervision of an officer, could make the king's bed or even touch it. Each piece was laid on with great ceremony, each portion of the bed examined separately. His Majesty never retired to rest until this task was reported well and completely done.

Simple obedience to procedure was required for such things, but investigation of four murders required wit and diplomacy. Hugh's military background demonstrated courage, and years of acquaintance made Henry trust Captain Bellows as much as he trusted anyone.

"Sire, we spoke to everyone nearby. No one revealed anything helpful to our cause. If you like, I can question more closely . . ." Hugh's tone betrayed his aversion to torturing people for information.

Henry agreed, at least in this instance. "And have them say what they think you want to hear?" People often kept to themselves what they knew in fear of retribution. Who could predict the repercussions from saying too much?

"Without giving details, it is difficult to

ask the important questions —" Henry glanced around the room cautiously. They were not alone, but was he ever?

"Come, Bellows, attend me. The rest of you may go." The bedchamber, filled with men awaiting the king's pleasure, cleared quickly, although a few looked miffed to have missed their turn at dressing the king. It was an honor for courtiers to hand Henry his garments each morning, and minor nobles enjoyed describing to their families the rich texture and vibrant color of each one.

"Bellows, I grow weary of the world," Henry said candidly as he watched them shuffle out the stone archway.

"Yes, sire."

"Shall I send word that I am ill and cannot go to dinner this evening? Play king for a moment: what say you?"

"His Grace of Sweden is here, sire. Can it be done?"

"Oh, it can be. I am the king here, not he."

"And as king, you know your duty."

Henry sighed. "I do, but this cursed leg pains me, and I walk like an old sow. He will go home and report how lame Henry of England is."

"Might you seat yourself first, before the

others enter? You have every right to sit at your own table."

Henry brightened somewhat. How like Hugh to think outside protocol. Could the monarch not decide as it pleased him to break the unwritten rules that governed such things? Had he not shocked the world by facing down the Holy Father all those years ago? Rather than limping in at the last, he could be seated in grand style, apparently at his ease, when the Swedish delegation entered the banquet hall. He imagined the scene: the clink of the table settings, the hum of the hall, and most inviting of all, the smell of the joint placed before him.

"Capital idea, Hugh. You make sense when others around me prate gibberish." He reverted to the reason for Hugh's presence. "Now, how are we to find this slayer of women? Four dead, and the last in my own daughter's garden." Henry seemed truly distressed by this. Despite himself, Hugh guessed, he recognized in Elizabeth a kindred spirit more like him than the other two put together. He would not see her harmed, although the sight of her was painful to him.

"The princess is now well protected. Still, we must discover how the man got inside Hampstead and how this relates to the other deaths."

Henry snorted, an unfortunate habit in one so porcine. "He got in by an age-old method: sweet words to a woman whose virtue was equal in worth to her intellect."

Hugh smiled grim agreement. "But someone there knew she was seeing a man, maybe even knows who he is."

"What do you propose?"

Hugh looked embarrassed, his face reddening again. "It is not my idea, Your Majesty, but it has some merit."

"Then speak up, man!" Henry used both hands to gently pick up his swollen, heavily bandaged leg, grunting in pain as he did so. Hugh moved clumsily to adjust the pillow under it, not knowing exactly what was needed. They got the leg settled more comfortably and Henry leaned back, strain showing on his face. "What is this idea and who has hatched it?"

"Sire, the princess —"

"I might have known. That minx has ideas on all subjects. She writes me letters giving advice on running the country, always very subtly, but telling all the same." Hugh said nothing. Henry's voice revealed both pride and exasperation with his daughter. *Why couldn't she have been the son?* each man thought to himself.

"Her Highness has an acquaintance, a young man whose physician father treated one of her ladies-in-waiting —"

"I am aware of Mary Ward's accident," Henry broke in. Hugh was not surprised. He might not see his daughters often, but any king worth his crown kept close watch on his offspring, careful of any trouble they might cause.

"This Simon studies languages with the princess."

"His father is a learned man," Henry interrupted again. "Pompous, though. Tried to tell me what I could eat. Sent him packing."

Hugh avoided the urge to glance at the ulcerous and decaying leg. Could a person's diet cause that? Silently he agreed with the king that it could not. How could a doctor blame the patient for poor health, when everyone knew the heavens controlled such things?

He began again. "This Simon has become a sort of pet around the castle. He is in a position to ask questions, observe, and learn things an officer of the Crown cannot."

"But surely he is just a boy."

"As the princess is just a girl." Henry responded with a wheezy chuckle and Hugh went on. "Both are extraordinary, I assure

73

you." Seeing Simon's interest in the crime, Hugh had decided Elizabeth's plan was worth mentioning to the king.

She had calmly proposed it to him the day before, the thirteen-year-old voice contrasting with the imperious manner. "Captain Bellows, you must tell my father the king that Simon should be your eyes and ears in this matter. He is unlikely to be suspected of being your agent."

Hugh continued to make his case. "The lad has the run of the place. He knows everyone and can ask questions when people are at their ease. Of course, I will continue my efforts to discover the killer." Elizabeth too had vowed she would discover Alice's secrets, but he omitted that part of her message to Henry. If His Majesty knew that his daughter was dabbling in murder, there was no doubt what his response would be.

Still, to stop these grisly deaths, Alice was their best starting point. Other investigations had led nowhere, and those in authority were at a loss as to where to turn next. Simon might learn things about the woman's private life that Hugh could not. As for Elizabeth, no one could stop her once she had her mind set on a thing. In that she and her royal father were like two peas in a pod.

Henry considered the matter, his leg for the moment only a dull ache. He knew all about Simon Maldon. George Blakewell was well paid to keep him informed of the princess' activities. The guardian had been suspicious of the physician's motives in sending the boy at first, but Henry knew enough about the Maldons to be unworried on that score. He also had little fear for his daughter's virtue. In all likelihood Elizabeth would someday be wed to cement an alliance, and Henry saw no reason to prevent her practicing feminine wiles on this crippled boy. Not that the girl needed practice, having her mother's ways. At times, when Elizabeth's voice sounded unexpectedly, he looked up to see if Anne had come into the room. He missed her then, the great passion of his life, and found it impossible to forgive their only child for being a girl, for forcing him to set Anne aside.

He had to agree with her now, though. It was possible that the boy might uncover something to identify the man who had butchered four women.

"Bring him in the morning." Henry stood, his face grimacing with pain. "I will see this paragon for myself."

CHAPTER SEVEN

Simon and Elizabeth sat in the afternoon sunlight on opposite sides of a window seat. The south side of the castle was almost welcoming on a bright day, overlooking the garden and warmed by rays streaming through the open window. With a map spread between them on the broad seat, they traced with their fingers the routes to foreign lands.

"If I could, I would go everywhere," Elizabeth declared. "Monsters and mermaids, I want to see them both."

Simon looked sideways at this remarkable girl. How unfortunate that her position and her sex would decree that she be closed in by walls and courtiers throughout her life! It was unlikely that Elizabeth would travel at all. If the occasion did arise, she would be surrounded by watchful attendants and jealous gossips anxious to report to her father or brother every mistake, every unguarded utterance.

Before meeting the princess Simon had seldom had thoughts about the plight of females of his day. His mother and sisters hummed and sang at their work, content to practice the homely arts of sewing a fine, straight seam or cooking hearty, inviting meals. Men made decisions for them on life's larger matters. Elizabeth knew something about everything, even though her knowledge came vicariously from books and study. Simon could picture her standing in the rigging of one of her father's stout little ships, shouting orders and fighting wind and water, a striking privateer.

"Perhaps someday they will send you to marry the Emperor of the Chins, and you will see foreign places after all."

Entering into it, Elizabeth made a low bow with hands pressed together in front of her. "Your Majesty, I am wife number sixty-three, the one who arrived yesterday on an elephant." They both chuckled, but Simon reflected on the waste if such a female as Elizabeth were relegated to a trading piece on the chessboard of politics. Sobering then, she said, almost to herself, "No, that's wrong. I shall never marry. Never." Simon made no comment, reflecting that he had never been so often at a loss for words until meeting Elizabeth Tudor.

Mary Ward, still using the crutch but on the mend, sat tatting in a heavy chair nearby. She smiled indulgently, ignoring the princess' prediction and thinking how nice it was for her to have a companion, and a clever one, too. She herself had no idea where China was or what an elephant must be. Some kind of litter, she imagined, such as one could be carried around in by slaves in foreign lands.

Margot appeared in the doorway and barely had time to announce, "The captain of the king's guard, Your Highness," before Hugh strode in, his long legs bringing him across the room in only a few steps. Stopping close to the window seat, he spoke so that only the two of them heard.

"Your Highness, I have spoken with the king. He desires to see this young man tomorrow morning."

Elizabeth tried to hide her smile, but Simon caught it. "What have you done?"

"We —" she included Hugh in her glance — "thought you might discover the identity of Alice's lover."

Simon didn't know whether to be pleased at her trust or distressed at the scope of the task. "How am I to do this?"

"By being yourself, shaping your ques-

tions a bit, then conveying what you learn
to me or to Captain Bellows."

Hugh seemed uneasy at her inclusion of
herself in the plan, shifting his lank body
slightly, but he made no objection. Elizabeth had made up her mind to be part of
this, and there was no stopping her. His task
would be to restrict her input to ideas rather
than actual deeds. Glancing at Mary, snor-
ing lightly in her chair, the unfinished lace
in her lap, Elizabeth went quietly on.

"You shall meet the king, who will satisfy
himself that you are no half-wit. Speak
bravely but respectfully."

"Highness, I can't promise the king that I
will solve these murders. Who am I, and why
should I be trusted?" Simon stopped, not
even able to voice his objections.

Elizabeth said to Hugh, "I will have to
come along."

Hugh looked even more uneasy, and the
pitch of his voice rose slightly. "His Majesty
may not react well," he began diplomatically. Henry's reaction to his daughter was
never predictable. One time he might pinch
her cheek or stroke her hair, so much like
his own in younger days, but other times he
glowered at her or ignored her completely.
"He is in much pain of late and dislikes
surprises."

79

Elizabeth remained calm. "He will have to accept this one. Simon is likely to be tongue-tied and overawed, and my father is, as you say, short-tempered in his pain. I will be there to inspire Simon's confidence."

So it was that the next morning after matins, Hugh escorted Elizabeth and Simon to the palace, with the bewildered Bess Blakewell acting as chaperone. Simon rode in a litter for the first time in his life, feeling both important and a little foolish. The babble of London seemed different from inside, removed and somehow less welcoming.

At Whitehall, a clerk led them to Henry's private chamber. Bess and Hugh were told to wait in the vestibule. When Elizabeth fell in behind him, the clerk did not know what to do. Not expecting the princess, he had been given no authority to permit or deny her entry.

The king's private office was smaller than Simon had expected, but it was warmly decorated and filled with books that made his fingers itch to touch them. As a young king, Henry had impressed the civilized world with his lively intellect. Now he sat behind a beautifully carved table on which lay documents, the paraphernalia of writing, and a few personal items: a globe, a silver box, and a jeweled knife that Simon guessed was used for sharpening pen nibs and opening wax seals. Under the table was a stool on which he had propped one heavily bandaged leg.

Beside him, Queen Catherine sat in a U-shaped chair, embroidering. She was dressed in a gown of deep red hue becoming to her coloring and frame. Long, full sleeves rustled as her needle moved in and out of the fabric. Alone with her husband she wore no farthingale, which made kneeling to care for his legs too difficult.

Henry wore his favorite color, yellow, but because of his size and the odd tint that his illness lent to his skin, that hue no longer flattered him. Both wore elegantly decorated stomachers matched in design, although the king's was more elaborate. A basket of bandages and salves sitting on the floor revealed that Catherine had dressed Henry's leg already this morning, and he looked to Elizabeth to be in good spirits at the moment. Two sticks lay beside him on the floor. Lately he found it impossible to walk without them or his servants to lean on.

The queen flashed a look of momentary anxiety when she saw who accompanied Simon Maldon, but with her customary courage, she rose and approached them, greeting her stepdaughter in a warm, low voice, "Why, my dear Elizabeth, how wonderful to see you."

Henry saw that his wife had defeated him, as she often did, with her natural kindness. Now that Catherine had greeted the princess so warmly, he would appear churlish if he ordered her from the room. This quality in his sixth wife both amused and irritated him: her ability to put him on the defensive as none of the others had done. Today, because his mood was good and because he was truly fond of Catherine, he made no comment on his daughter's uninvited appearance, but merely grunted at her. Briefly, however, he wondered if other men felt so manipulated by their women.

The Maldon boy hardly knew where to look, so nervous was he. Having no patience for delay, Henry began immediately, asking several questions about his background in order to gauge the young man's character. The boy answered honestly and without unnecessary embellishment. Finally, the crucial question came. "Has Bellows told you of the plan he and the princess have hatched for you, boy?"

Simon felt Elizabeth's presence beside him, heard the nervous shifting of her feet as she willed him to be impressive. She had faith in him, as did Hugh. "Yes, Your Majesty. I am willing to do what I can to discover information on the matter, although I fear it will be little enough. People have been questioned already."

"True. But I flatter myself that in fifty and more years I have learned a few things. Folk may fail to tell Hugh's men something because it seems unimportant, or they don't want to become involved with the affair, or even because they have something of their own to hide. But later they may speak to one such as you, who appears to have no motive aside from curiosity. Once the hue and cry dies down, they will speak more freely to each other as well. You, boy, must be there to listen when they do."

"Your Majesty, I will do my best to earn your confidence."

The queen, who listened with interest, asked, "Is Elizabeth in danger, Henry? Should we —"

"She is safe if she minds her own matters and stays where she belongs," he answered roughly. Elizabeth stiffened beside him and Simon felt for her, discussed as if she were not there. Catherine, too, felt the sting and gave the girl an oblique glance of sympathy.

Elizabeth, though she loved her father, had a sense of herself that could not be shaken. "Your Grace's concern for me is most gratifying," she said in her sweetest tone. "Captain Bellows has provided loyal men to guard me day and night." Her choice of words implied that Henry had nothing to do with the matter. "Master Maldon and I will go now, unless there is further service we can provide." Her tone and facial expression were perfectly correct, as only an adolescent daughter can be when defying her father to complain of her sauciness. Without waiting for an answer, she curtseyed perfectly and turned to go, her exit marred only by the need to pull on Simon's sleeve as he stood, unsure of whether he was dismissed or not. He stumbled against a table, causing a clatter of shifting objects. Horrified, he caught a glimpse of a quickly repressed smile from the queen and saw Henry set his heavy jaw. Deeming it best to get out as quickly as possible, he bowed and beat a hasty retreat from the room.

CHAPTER EIGHT

After supper that evening, Simon delighted his mother with an account of his visit to the king. They finished the meal, which by some small miracle was uninterrupted with calls for the doctor's attention. The home the Maldons occupied in Hampstead village was modest but comfortable, consisting of a large, open space with one corner partitioned off for the parents' use and a half-loft with blankets hung between two sections, one for the three boys and the other for the two girls, Annie and Ella. Mary Maldon had been lucky, having lost only two infants so far to the illnesses that so often carried away the young.

Little Ella, only four, was excused to play with her rag dolls on the floor in a far corner of the main room. The younger boys, twins of ten years, had eaten as hurriedly as their mother's glare would allow and asked to be allowed to go outside for an hour before doing their evening chores. The spring nights, longer and gentler now, made them long to savor every minute. Twelve-year-old Annie carried in buckets of water for household tasks.

Mary Maldon, unable to be still for long, cleared away the evening meal: rabbit given in payment for the doctor's services, cheese, and pickled cabbage with fresh brown bread to dip into the juice. As she bustled back and forth to the table, Simon told the events of the day. "To think you've been noticed by His Majesty himself and you not fifteen," his mother crowed, setting work-reddened hands on ample hips.

"You must tell no one," Jacob cautioned her. "Simon's value to Henry is that none will suspect one so young of being . . ." He groped for the right word.

"A spy," Simon finished. "It sounds sinister, but one who seeks a killer is not like other spies."

Jacob nodded agreement, but his wife frowned, taking in the term. "What if the king wants Simon to continue this spying in the future?"

"Let us not borrow trouble, Mary. We will deal with that if it arises. Now, Simon, what will you do with this charge you have?"

Simon had discussed that with Elizabeth.

"Her Highness says I must continue as I have been, only visit at various times of day so as to meet the different people who go about the castle. She will at times arrange on some pretext to be busy when I arrive and bid me wait. I will then wander about, speaking to people randomly, it seems, but in truth trying to discern what they know."

"It sounds feasible."

"Where should I begin?" He respected his father's judgment, and Jacob had seen the corpse.

"Since a man is sought, I would start with the man who was nearest: Blakewell. Liaisons occur through proximity more than anything else. A man in a castle full of women may find the temptation too much despite his wife's presence, and I remember that Alice was far from plain."

"You took some notice of this woman, Husband?" Mother's voice took on the tone that Simon knew signaled trouble for Father. He thanked his father and excused himself to do his own chores. Behind him his mother's questioning tone rose as she sought more information about Jacob's notice of Alice's beauty, forgetting that the girl was dead these three days.

The next day Simon arrived at Hampstead

around his usual time, but Margot informed him that the princess was at work on a difficult piece of music and requested that he wait until she satisfied herself that she had mastered it. Simon tried to appear disappointed and saw a hint of satisfaction on Margot's stony face. *She doesn't like my coming here,* he thought. Turning as if to leave the room, Simon pretended to change his mind.

"What's to be done to fill Alice's place?" The dead woman had been laid to rest quietly, with only the residents of Hampstead and her grieving parents in attendance. Simon had gone to the service but kept apart in deference to the mourners present.

Margot considered his question, her black eyes flat and unfriendly. "The king will send someone: a woman of no other use to him, like us." Anger vibrated in her voice. Margot was not as emotionless as she liked to appear.

"Surely it is an honor to attend the Princess Royal."

"It must be so, if the physician's boy says it is."

Simon felt unfairly attacked by the sneering tone. "I am sorry if I offend you."

Suddenly venom poured out of the

woman, and her white face, oddly shaped at any time, contorted further with spite. "Villain!" The insult was chosen to remind him that he was a commoner. "You entertain the princess while we wait, expecting nothing, doing nothing, looking forward to nothing. You dream that she will someday be queen and remember the clever boy who spoke Greek with her. Forget your hopes, as Elizabeth would forget you were she queen, which she will never be!"

Margot swept from the room, leaving Simon in shock. Was she so resentful of companions Elizabeth might have? The thought led to one even more sinister. Had Margot hated Alice, too, and wanted her out of the way?

Simon gave Elizabeth only a hint of the incident, making her promise she would not let on to Margot that she knew. They made their way outside, and Simon carried two trowels and a bucket of water while the princess brought a bag of spring bulbs. "I doubt it is more than spite," she declared. "Alice was no threat to anyone's position here. She had embarrassed herself somehow at Court and so was sent to my household just after Christmas as a sort of punishment." Elizabeth's expression indicated that she understood the irony involved. "Alice, barely able to put a sentence together, was no real companion to me. Not that Margot is either, being a spy for the Catholics."

Simon gaped at this new revelation and her calm acceptance of it. "The Catholics spy on you?"

Elizabeth looked up from the spot prepared for planting and grinned at Simon's disbelief. "Think on this. There are three of us who might one day rule England, and the day of choosing is not far off. They cannot stop the rot that affects my father's limbs, and it will one day kill him. Edward will take the throne, and he will keep to the Church of England. But Edward is not well and has stayed alive this long only with constant care by the best physicians. If he, too, dies, then it will be between Mary and me. Mary is first, and likely to return to Papist worship. There are those who would rejoice at that, but I could be a rallying point for the Protestants. Although Father has named her first, when he is dead things may not fall out as he wishes. I am watched to see if I lean one way or the other."

Simon bent to help, digging six-inch holes with the trowel as Elizabeth sorted out the corms and dropped them into the hole, point upward. Elizabeth's tendency must be to support the Church of England, and those who approved of it would press her right to be queen rather than return to Catholicism. Did Elizabeth want the throne? He didn't know, and she herself might not. The safest course would be to abdicate any claim to power when Henry died, but would they leave her alone even then? Doubtful. Simon thought how glad he was to be born outside the politics of royal blood. How did she manage? And Margot was a spy.

Covering the last bulb with earth, he picked up the bucket and splashed each spot with water. "You let her stay with you, knowing why she is here?"

"If I dismissed Margot, they would simply send someone else. At first I found her interesting. She has some education and more wit than poor Alice or even Mary. Still, her constant hints that the True Church should return to England became tiresome, and her learning is by rote, with no thought to accompany it. She tells her Catholic friends who my visitors are and what I say that pertains to politics, so I say nothing. George Blakewell tells my father everything I do, and I suspect that Mary Ward may be in the pay of some leaders in Parliament."

"Mary Ward? But she loves you, I would swear to it."

"She simply passes on information. She no doubt believes the one does not preclude the other."

"At least I don't feel so guilty now about spying on them."

Elizabeth chuckled, surveying her neat row critically and wiping her muddy hands on her apron. "We'll make a courtier of you yet, Master Maldon. You must learn that the first loyalty is to whoever can do you the most good."

Simon faced her solemnly. "I would not contradict you, Highness, but a man's first loyalty should always be to what he knows is right."

Elizabeth gazed at him with fond amusement, her expression far older than thirteen years should warrant. "I thought you would say that." She led the way to a dilapidated shed where they replaced the tools. The place smelled of old potatoes and rusty metal, and the light came through loose boards in slits, revealing the dust motes between them as she faced Simon in the dimness.

"When first you came to visit me, I wondered in whose pay you might be, and what you thought to gain. I supposed that you dreamed I would give you an emerald ring or the like, since people usually want something from me. Most can't fathom that despite my royal name, I have nothing to give. No present," she said, chuckling at the pun, "and no future either. I have since concluded that you are, unlike most people I know, exactly what you seem."

Simon was embarrassed but had to ask: "And what am I?"

Elizabeth stepped back into the sunshine before she answered. It would not do to stay too long out of sight of her ladies, no matter Simon's innocence. "A talented man who desires to make the world right according to his standards. Because of that, you are unlikely to be suborned by me or anyone else. If ever I were queen, I would put men like you in the highest positions of my government."

Simon lightened the mood as he took his leave. "I would not want that, Highness. Now that I know what you must abide, I would rather row a boat on the Thames, even with this —" here he held up his weak arm with a smile — "than try to sort my way through the maze of riddles that is government."

A maze, certainly. He felt Elizabeth's gray eyes on him as he departed her moldering castle. Her maze, far more complex than the one at Hampton Court, began at the unmarked grave in the Chapel of St. Peter ad Vincula where her mother's body lay. Her father's marriage to her mother was dissolved, supposedly because she had been promised to another man, Harry Percy. Yet she was later executed for adultery, impossible in a marriage that did not exist. Anne Boleyn had been unable to exit the maze that she'd entered so happily, and it was the death of her.

Now her daughter, born a princess, wandered through her own maze. For years she had lived in limbo, known only as the Lady Elizabeth. Now she was again a princess, but with no clear path before her. In a way, Elizabeth had killed her mother; had she been male, Anne would have lived. Now Her Highness could trust no one, had to find her way alone, choosing carefully, and considering none but herself. Even Simon, unused to the ways of the court, understood that much.

CHAPTER NINE

The more Simon considered Alice's murder, the more he wanted to know about the other murdered women. There had to be a connection between them, something that drew the killer to them and not others. Hugh's inquiries had found the whole affair piecemeal in approach. Two prostitutes had been killed in separate sections of London, and the local burgers had paid only minimal attention. The third young woman, of noble birth, had caused more concern, but the shamed family had given as little information as was required about their wayward daughter and no more.

Simon and Hugh were ordered by Elizabeth to a planning session in her garden the next morning. As they sat on mossy stone benches still cold from the night's chill, Mary Ward served as chaperone from above, looking out the window, able to see but not hear what was said. Hugh had considered refusing to attend, had pondered telling His Majesty that the girl interfered with his work, but he did not for two reasons: he liked the princess, and she was a valuable resource. If only she would remain on the intellectual side of the matter.

"The name of the murdered noblewoman was Joanna Brandon, daughter of Thomas Brandon."

Elizabeth gasped when he said it. "The Brandons are kin to me." At Simon's frown, she explained. "Many years ago, Father sent his sister Mary to wed old Louis XII, thirty-four years her senior, and keep peace with France." She stroked the rough stone bench absently for a moment, her thoughts no doubt on the fate of royal sisters.

"Is she still there?"

"No." Elizabeth's solemn countenance broke for a moment into a smile. "When Louis died after only a few months, she wed Father's best friend, Charles Brandon, whom she'd always loved. They told Father about it afterward."

"Was he very angry?"

"For a time, but eventually he forgave them both. Sir Thomas is Charles' brother, not the star at court that his brother was, but a respected and loyal man."

Hugh returned to the subject at hand.

"His daughter was not respected. She was rebellious and disobedient, chasing men, slipping out of the house at night, and defying her parents no matter how they punished her. They might almost be relieved to end the scandal, although the manner of her death was a terrible shock."

"How sad to face such a ghastly loss," Elizabeth said. "I will visit them and see what I can learn."

"Thomas Brandon is not closely related to you, Highness," Hugh protested, grasping at straws to keep her from interfering.

"Close enough. I will devise some pretext and then convey my condolences when I learn, quite accidentally, of their daughter's death." She clearly enjoyed the prospect of play-acting.

"As for the prostitutes, I could play the curious boy where they lived, as I do here," Simon picked idly at the rough threads of his sleeve. "It is not unusual for someone my age to be interested in a grisly murder, and enough time has passed that people may be more at ease and tell what they know."

"Be careful in those neighborhoods," Hugh cautioned. "They are a rough lot that live there."

"I will," Simon promised in the exasperated tone of voice that all young people use when an older one warns them of danger.

"One of the dead prostitutes lived in Winchester Close," Hugh said, his face reflecting doubt about Simon's understanding of the danger. "The other lived in the Shambles, Calkin says."

"The soldier with the freckles?"

"The man isn't as simple as he appears. Behind those freckles is a memory for all sorts of detail. Calkin makes pictures in his mind and can recall the placement of objects and the contents of a scene with remarkable accuracy."

"Then we have our tasks set," Elizabeth said in conclusion. "We will meet again tomorrow."

Hugh rose and Simon followed suit, pulling up his hood in anticipation of the breezy conditions outside the sheltered garden. As they parted Hugh said, "I will speak to the constables involved with the first two murders. Mayhap they will remember something more if pressed." He clapped Simon's shoulder with a hand as big as a bear's paw. "I hope your endeavors bring new information, as Her Highness has confidence they will."

That could be more daunting than encouraging, Simon thought as he made his way home through a freshening wind that resisted his forward progress and promised rain that night. Why did Elizabeth have faith in him? She seemed to have her own methods of gauging people, and they had little to do with who they were or what they appeared to be. Maybe she thought his crippled arm led people to feel sorry for him, making them more approachable. Simon hoped it wasn't that. He preferred to think she found him perceptive. Despite poking gentle fun at his stolid belief that right would triumph over wrong, she claimed to see in him an ability to relate to people. Maybe he'd learned it from his father; often he had watched Jacob calm a hysterical patient with soothing tones or ask probing questions to diagnose an illness without further upsetting those involved. Wherever it came from, the princess said it was a useful gift. Now he would see if it could be employed to stop monstrous crimes.

It stormed that night, but the morning was clear and bright, everything washed new with the gift of hard rain. Colors looked more vibrant, and it was worth stepping around the many puddles that collected in the streets to smell less of London's refuse and more of plain fresh air.

Simon's mother would have been furious if she'd known where he was heading that day. He had heard her rail about the Bishop's "Winchester geese," and she was right. It was hypocritical of the clergy to preach against prostitutes when a large area around the Bishop's residence was provided for just such women. Apologists said that it was the church's civic duty to ameliorate the evils of prostitution by licensing and regulating brothels. The more cynical pointed out that it was a very profitable business, and the church took full advantage of its exclusion from city government by allowing prostitutes to live on its property. At any rate Mary Maldon would have whipped Simon, old as he was, had she known his intention.

The various communities of London had their own personalities. This one, at least the part where Therese Blanc had lived, was not welcoming. Garbage on the streets had rotted to a black-green slime that lay like grease underfoot and produced a variety of odors, none pleasant. People in the poorest areas seldom had pigs, chickens, or dogs to clear their streets, so whatever was thrown out windows and doors merely lay there. If it was this bad in spring, Simon wondered, how much worse would it become in the heat of summer? Outside each door sat some sort of container for water, required by law in case of fire. Every household was expected to join in fighting a nearby blaze or face a stiff fine.

Simon for once made no effort to hide his infirmity, intending to signal that he was no threat. The alley where the corpse had been found showed him little, but he looked at it all the same. It was blank and dark, probably deserted at night. The street was like dozens of others, a narrow, bumpy passageway between two old "party walls" erected centuries before to prevent the spread of fire.

Later Simon realized that he should have been more casual, less openly curious. His demeanor revealed that he was unfamiliar with the area, out of his element. In fact, he was so engrossed in his thoughts that he didn't see the group of boys until they had surrounded him. Silence reigned as they observed him critically. It was broken only by the nervous click of something in someone's pockets, stones by the sound. A large boy, clearly the leader of a group bent on belligerent fun, stepped close, his face close to Simon's.

"You there. Where yer gettin' to?"

In a trice Simon was faced with not one

but two versions of the aggressive lad, for another stepped up beside the first as like him as could be. Both had over-large heads and long bodies that towered over him. Scrawny, his mother would have said, but the muscles that tensed in the bare forearms promised strength.

The twins had the same face: round as the moon with pale skin, small blue eyes that had a curious flatness as if there were stone behind them, and large jaws that protruded as if the teeth inside did not fit well. The second one's features seemed slightly less defined than the first. His eyes were paler, the jaw and cheekbones a shade less prominent. He aped his brother, taking cues from him as to stance, angle of head, and expression. Both grinned menacingly. Peripherally Simon saw the others close around him, watching to see what the twins did. Sensing rather than knowing how to respond, he did not look away from the leader. With neither fear nor aggression, he kept both voice and expression blank.

"I'm looking for a woman."

"What would the likes of yer do with a woman, boy?" Although no older than Simon, the spokesman was years ahead of him in experience, his tone said.

"I seek my aunt, Therese Blanc, since we

have had no word from her. Someone told me she lives in Winchester."

The expressions on the two identical faces registered familiarity with the name, and the larger boy spoke again for the group, in fact for the whole community, it seemed.

"She don't want no bother from the likes o' yer. We don't like strangers 'round here." The click of the stones grew louder as adrenalin invaded the possessor's eager fingers.

Again carefully keeping his tone even, Simon pointed out, "I am a stranger, but my aunt is not." Speaking of Therese as if she were alive, he hoped to convince the group that he was indeed a relative come to visit, unaware of her fate and therefore harmless.

A voice behind him said timidly, "Jack, she's —"

"Shut it!" the one called Jack growled without looking away from Simon, and the other lapsed into silence. "So yer lookin' for yer aunt, ey? Did yer bring her anything, any presents, mebbe some money from her careful family?"

Simon looked rueful and stuck to the story he'd concocted. "Not likely. I came to see if she'd help me out. I mean to leave home and need to get a start."

Jack sniffed derisively. His only interest in

speaking to Simon had been the possibility of robbery, and now that was negated. If he couldn't rob this visitor, other options would please him as well or better.

"I told yer, we don't want yer here. I'll give yer somethin' to remember us by, so's yer don't come 'round again." He raised a fist, sticking his jaw out even more belligerently, and his twin took a similar stance half a second behind him. There was a general rustle of anticipation through the circle of boys that surrounded them. One boy, braver than the rest, poked Simon sharply in the ribs and laughed inanely at his own boldness.

Simon looked desperately around, sure he would be beaten soundly and just as sure that there was neither appeal to this group nor any assistance nearby. Irrelevantly, he began to plan how he would explain the bruises and scrapes to his mother. He had never fought anyone in his life; other boys had left him alone out of respect for his father and because of his withered arm. He wondered how much it would hurt and how far they would go to teach him a lesson.

A voice came from his left, moderate but commanding. "Leave him alone, Jack."

The tormentor was as surprised as Simon at the appearance of a defender. His blunt face screwed up for a moment, absorbing the fact that someone might interfere with his fun. Looking past Simon at the new-comer, he rolled his eyes. "Hello, Peto."

The voice that Jack had shushed before spoke again. "This fellow is askin' after your Therese, Peto."

"Luke." A word from Jack silenced the loquacious Luke. "There's naught here that concerns yer, Peto."

"True," the voice replied, coming nearer. Simon glanced to his left and saw a man a few years older and slightly taller than he. There was nothing about him to inspire fear. His build was slight, his expression mild. Straight, blondish hair fell around his face, which was largely unremarkable with high cheekbones, straight brows, and a shapely mouth. As he glanced once his way, Simon realized where Jack's nervousness came from. The icy blue eyes held assur-ance that this person would get what he wanted, no matter what it might be. Oddly, he sensed no evil in that confidence, only acceptance that if this Peto said he should be left alone, he would be.

The circle of boys had gone still. Even the one with a pocket full of stones seemed frozen, for the clicks stopped as everyone awaited the outcome. Peto stepped between

Simon and the twins. "True," he repeated. "Still, this man comes here with a purpose. How can he find out about his aunt if he does not look for her? Beside that, he is a cripple. Would it not be the worst sort of varlets who harmed a man with only one good arm, who has enough misery in his life as it is —" here Peto looked briefly at Simon again — "and may soon have more?"

Jack did not give in easily. "He's not one of us."

"Nor am I . . . one of you," Peto's voice betrayed the first sign of emotion: contempt for Jack. "I simply do what I must, as this young man does. Shall we be left alone, or shall we be molested by witless churls?"

He included the group in his gaze at the last, and the tone said something to them all, something they did not challenge further. To Simon's surprise and relief there was a general foot-shuffling, and the tight circle around him opened as all except Jack and his twin stepped back. The twin looked uncertain, wanting to step away but fearing his brother's wrath. Finally, Jack spoke grudgingly.

"Some day, Peto, yer will push in where yer not wanted once too often, and it will not go well then."

"I suppose," said Peto offhandedly. "There

must always be a day of reckoning, but it is not today." He stood relaxed and at ease before Jack's towering, tense form. Abruptly he changed tone, addressing the other twin. "Hal, will you take my greeting to your mother?"

Hal, the uncertain one, now made his decision, and took up Peto's friendly thread of conversation. "Of course, Peto, and she will flay me if I fail to ask yer to supper of an evening." He did not look at his brother, who glared at this betrayal. For his part, Simon's amazement deepened at Hal's polite display of manners toward a man who evidently struck fear in the hearts of each one present. Supper indeed!

The band of boys had moved a short way off, not daring to desert Jack but clearly not willing to offend Peto. Suddenly Jack spun away without further speech and strode off with Hal behind. He disdained to sidestep puddles on the street, stomping through them with no regard for his clothes or his brother's. The others followed tentatively, staying a few paces back.

Simon turned to face Peto, who stood watching Jack disappear with no malice in his expression. "Thank you," he said. "I was sure I would be bloody by now."

Peto looked at him directly for the first

time, his blue eyes still assured but less threatening. He wore better clothes, Simon noticed, than had any of the boys in the group just departed. Not fine clothes, certainly, but well cut and fitted. His entire ensemble was black: leggings, tunic, undershirt, hat, and boots. It might have looked sinister, but not to one who saw the man as his savior.

"It is foolish for one such as you to wander around these parts." Peto's tone was languid. "Your looks give you away. Not rich, certainly, but as an outsider who may be toyed with. I might not be nearby to save you another time."

"Why did you intercede?"

Peto considered, running his tongue over even white teeth. "I don't know," he answered finally. "It did not seem fair of them to attack a cripple."

Simon's face flushed; how he hated that term. Peto saw it and made a small ironic smile. "Do not be offended. We must each use what we are given to make our ways in this world. You have a weak arm and dread the pity that people might feel for you because of it. But remember, Jack and the others would have beaten you despite it, so your arm is no amulet. I suggest you take up a defense suited to your ability, like knife-throwing. You cannot count on the pity of others, cripple or no."

"Why did they obey you? There were eight of them."

"That's hard to say. I suppose it is reputation, although I try to maintain a certain standard of behavior." That seemed all he was willing to reveal, for he changed the subject. "You will be safe enough today, I'll wager, but you must be careful wandering areas such as this."

"Do you live near here?"

"I? No, I live here and there," Peto responded vaguely. Simon remembered the man's comment that Therese's "nephew" would soon meet with more misery. Peto knew, then, that Therese was dead. He did not seem willing to volunteer the information, and Simon dared not let on that he knew it as well. "I will leave you now, um . . ." Peto stopped, head tilted in question.

"Simon."

"Simon. You might ask down that street." He pointed to an offshoot a few steps onward. "I think you'll find what you need to know there."

"Thank you. And I am most grateful for your help with . . . the other."

"Throwing knives," Peto said with a slight

109

nod, as if he had just decided it. "I'm sure that would be best."

"I will remember." Simon went off, wondering what sort of world he found himself in. Friendly advice from his mysteriously powerful rescuer was to learn to throw knives. Simon shuddered; even if he learned the skill, could he ever harm another person? His life so far had been dedicated to saving lives, not taking them.

CHAPTER TEN

As the smaller street turned away from the main one it narrowed, closing out the light even further. Simon began his quest for the correct door by speaking to some boys of about seven or eight who played a game with bits of wood and stones. Tough and uncommunicative, they were not easily befriended until Simon got the idea of dividing a bit of cheese he'd brought along as his lunch. They were more than willing to share that.

As he put chunks of the soft white treat into warm, grubby hands, Simon again told the story that he had an aunt in the area that his family had lost touch with. Conspiratorially, Simon whispered, "She's taken up the Life, and my parents will have nothing to do with her." The boys savored their cheese without reaction to this supposed family tragedy. Lots of girls were abandoned by their families for this reason, but in this part of the city, any paying job was acceptable.

"My aunt is Therese Blanc. She's quite pretty, with very light hair."

Glances were exchanged, and each boy finished his cheese lest it be taken back once they told what they knew. "Her is dead," the tallest boy finally said. "Got herself killed by a madman last winter."

"Dead?" Simon affected surprise. "Murdered?"

"By a madman." This was the part that interested them.

"Is there anyone here who knew her well?"

There was silent discussion that involved looks, eyebrow raising, and shoulder shrugging. Finally the tall one spoke again. "Her lived with Daisy. Down there." He pointed to a building a few doors onward.

Thanking the boys, Simon went on, arriving at a door that hung crooked, not serving its intended purpose well. As he raised a hand to knock, it opened and a plump young woman stepped out, a rush of stale odors accompanying her. She was probably less than twenty, but her face had the look of one who knows too much of the ugly side of life. Pleasantly proportioned but well padded with flesh, Daisy was not beautiful, only attractive in an earthy way. Her greasy brown hair had been dressed high on her head at some recent time but strands of it now fell in lank strips onto her neck. The dress, cut to reveal the shape of her figure, had worn spots at the elbows and was faded under the arms. A ring of brown showed at the hem where it had dragged in the mud.

"Oh," the woman said in surprise as she saw Simon. Immediately her manner became professionally welcoming. "I was going out, but there's no hurry. Come in."

Simon, naively surprised to be welcomed into a woman's home just by showing up, followed Daisy into a small room that held everything it possibly could. The room smelled of sweat and various other human secretions. He had the impression of a wild jumble of clothes, household items, bric-a-brac and feminine accoutrements with no order or theme to it. Various bottles, several small boxes, and ribbons of many colors covered any available surface. Simon wondered where she found room to eat her meals.

The woman sized Simon up, making no comment on the room's confusion. "You an't very old, are you?"

"I was sent by some boys down the street. They said you could help me."

"Oh, dearie, I can help you, truly."

With a start Simon realized the woman thought him a customer. "Please, Mistress Daisy, I'm sorry to — I mean I don't want . . ." Her eyes, which had been wide with false cheer and professional invitation, turned flat and hard.

"What are you about, then?" Even her voice changed.

"I've come to ask about my aunt, Therese. The boys said she lived here. I didn't know she was dead."

Daisy's lips protruded as she took in Simon's story. "You an't Therese's family. She didn't have anyone."

Simon decided to brazen it through. "She may have lied about that. My mother is her sister but my parents washed their hands of her when they learned how she earned her living. Therese was always good to me, and when I came to London, I thought I would try to find her. A man named Peto told me to ask about her here."

Daisy's eyes showed interest and she moved closer. Simon resisted the urge to back away as her breath assailed his senses. "You spoke to Peto?"

Simon seized the advantage the name seemed to bring him. "Yes, he said I would find what I needed to know here, but he told me nothing of how she died."

"Took it hard, I heard," Daisy mused. "Therese was his luck, y'see."

"His luck? You mean Peto?"

"Yeah. A man like Peto, he's got to have luck with 'im, or it's the Clink and Tyburn afterward. Peto was told by a witch-woman that luck would come from over the water. Then he meets Therese: French and pretty to boot. Peto was sure he'd found his luck, but soon enough she was dead."

Many depended on such beliefs to re-assure themselves: the stars, amulets, and the like were believed to increase chances of good, and who was to say they were wrong? Science had discovered that the heavenly bodies controlled the movements of the sea. Why could they not also control events in men's lives?

"So Peto believed Therese to be his good luck charm, but she was murdered. What did he do when he heard?"

Daisy turned reticent. It didn't do to speak too much of the affairs of one such as Peto. "I couldn't say. There are plenty of other girls willing to ease his misery, though. Peto never lacks for friends." Her manner turned wistful. "He favors blondes, though."

Looking about the room, Simon had a thought. "Had Therese received any presents from men she knew?"

"She didn't leave nothing. This were all mine," the woman averred.

"I want nothing of hers," Simon assured, "and I'm sure she'd want you to keep her things." He surveyed the room, committing the contents to memory. Surely some of it had been Therese's.

Daisy relaxed a little but was still suspicious. She moved to a bureau protectively, leaning against it as if to block his view of what was there. Tapping a nervous finger on its surface, she challenged, "You don't talk Frenchified like she did."

Simon flinched at the new inquiry but forged ahead, trying to look sincere. "My real mother died. My stepmother is the only one I have known, and Therese was her only sister. Now I'm told that she is dead." He did his best to look grief-stricken as he finished.

Daisy's doubts seemed to collapse at this, and she turned breathless and confidential, savoring the story. "Not only dead, but murdered most awfully!"

"Murdered!" Simon tried to match her tone. "But who would murder Therese?"

"I could never tell you that," Daisy said with a shiver that made her once-elegant coif slant precariously to one side. "A better roommate no one ever had. Her was always generous when money was to be had and cheerful even when there were nothing. Therese didn't get drunk and threaten to do away with herself like the girl that lived here before her, neither. I miss her, I do." Daisy talked herself into shedding a tear, although Simon doubted she cared for anyone beside herself. The life she led simply didn't permit it.

"Where was Peto when Therese died?"

Daisy looked at him with disdain. "He accounts to no one for his whereabouts, just comes and goes. A businessman, he is, and nothing interferes with that." She thumped a palm on the bureau for emphasis, placing the dead Therese outside Peto's care.

Simon tried to picture the relationship between Peto and Therese: a loose connection, nothing like the bond between his mother and father or other couples he knew. Their respective professions would have made such a bond unlikely.

"And Therese, you have no idea who might have wanted her dead?"

"The constables said it were a madman because of —" Daisy stopped as it occurred to her that one so young might be shocked at the manner of Therese's death. "You're best off knowing nothing more," she finished dramatically.

"Did she say who she would be with that night?"

"Who-oo," Daisy got a chuckle from that. "What do y' think we are, ladies of quality? Therese probably never knew his real name herself. We often don't in our trade."

"Besides Peto there was no one she was special to?"

Daisy's eyes hardened again. "Women like us are special to none," she spat. "The Bishop's Winchester geese, allowed to live here only to make His Eminence money, never spared a thought once our usefulness is over. Therese was hardly cold before they stopped looking for who killed her, and if he was to come back for me, I'd get the same consideration from the likes o' them." Daisy leaned toward Simon, taking his arm in a firm squeeze. "After what happened, I went out and got myself an upright man." Simon looked at her quizzically. "He's a man watches out for a girl. 'Course he takes a good share of the money, but he deals with anybody who might come after me. My Adam's a ruffler, and a big 'un."

Simon knew that term: a ruffler was an ex-soldier who made his living by crime rather than look for honest work. They were common enough, men who had no other skills than those the military had taught them.

Daisy had turned thoughtful. "If Therese had been some man's mort, she might still be alive. At the very least, her man might go after who killed her."

"Would Peto not do that?"

Daisy considered. "Naw, I don't think so. Peto must look to himself, y'see. He can't be pining for what's past. He were sad that Therese died, and we didn't see him in these parts for a month or two after. Then he appears, same as always, and the old Peto too. Forgot her, he did, and took up with another." She put her hand on Simon's shoulder in sympathy. "Now you 'n me are the only ones sorry Therese is gone. I suppose that's all she could expect since the first time she took money from a man."

Simon felt a surge of pity for Daisy. Unlike most people, this woman knew her worth to the world in exact coin, which didn't make for a happy accounting. Thanking her, he left the crowded room, somewhat sorry that he'd lied to her. At least she believed now that someone cared about her friend Therese. In reality no one mourned the girl's death, unless the faint regret of a man who'd lost his lucky whore could be counted as mourning.

■ ■ ■ ■

Hugh made his way to the home of Frobish, the constable who had handled investigation of the first murder. They had spoken before, and Hugh had found Frobish an able enough man for the job he held, which was not to say he was clever or insightful, simply thorough.

Frobish greeted Hugh cheerfully, inviting him to take a seat on a rickety stool beside him in front of the small house he and his wife occupied with their four small children. Three of the four played noisily around their feet, so close in age that it was difficult to tell who was oldest and who youngest. Frobish seated himself on a stool even worse off than Hugh's and again they went over the details of the murder that had occurred in February. Balanced carefully lest the stool give way under his weight, Hugh asked questions designed to bring out details that Frobish had seen but forgotten or deemed unimportant.

"Therese Blanc was dressed as a nun?"

The man took up an old rope and begun pulling the fibers apart, dropping them into a basket at his feet. He would later re-twist them into a new, stronger rope. "Yes, sir. It

— she — wore a gray robe with a rosary at the waist, like the Franciscans I knew as a boy. Where her head should have been was the wimple and veil."

"Do you know what happened to the rosary?"

Frobish frowned, toying noisily with a section of gum where several teeth had gone missing. "I suppose it were buried with her. Someone might a' took it, but a thing like that can only bring trouble these days. Stop that now or I'll get your mother out here," he threatened as one child slapped the other, setting her to howling. Neither paid him any mind at all, but Frobish seemed to think he'd solved the problem, returning his attention to Hugh.

"Can you describe it for me?"

The frown deepened with thought. "It were black beads o' some kind on a silver chain. The work on the rood and the clasp was very fancy, as I recall. It was too fine by half for a girl o' the streets to own, now that I think of it. Do ye think she stole it?"

"Or someone else put it on her."

"You mean the killer dressed her like a nun afterward? Why would 'e do that?"

"I wish I knew."

"We thought it some man's fancy to have his doxy wear such as that," Frobish admitted, his grin exposing even more toothless gum.

"Not an impossible explanation," Hugh agreed, unwilling to reveal how he knew differently, "but he may have done it to some purpose, if we can perceive it."

The frown disappeared as the man voiced the only reason he saw. "Why, to make her a Catholic. He must be one o' them Papists that wants the pope back in England."

"It would seem so. Did those you spoke with report seeing anyone unusual in the area that night?"

"An't nothin' around there but unusual types. The unusual be usual." Frobish chuckled at his own joke, air hissing through his oral spaces.

Hugh smiled patiently. "Anyone different from the usual unusual characters, then?"

"No." Frobish shook his head. "Nobody admitted to nothing. Daisy, the girl Therese shared rooms with, was afraid she might be next, but nothing's happened since."

Hugh could have countered that statement, but he simply rose to go. "Try to find the rosary. I would like to see it."

"As you will." The man's tone said what he did not: the crime happened months ago, the woman was a prostitute, and the rosary was long gone. Still, it did not do to disagree

with the king's man, so Hugh was certain
he would make an attempt.

CHAPTER ELEVEN

While Hugh questioned the constable, Simon prepared to again brave London's seamier side and learn what he could about Mathilda Harrison from those who had known her. This time he wanted even older clothing than before. The freckled soldier, Calkin, gave him some malodorous things. He would not say where he got them, which Simon guessed meant they had once belonged to a condemned prisoner. He tried not to think about it but put them on, making himself as unlikely a robbery victim as possible. Offering one of the figs he'd brought along, he asked Calkin where he might get the best instruction in the throwing of a knife.

Calkin grinned and tapped his own chest with a finger. "I hate to boast, but I am said to be the best hereabouts. That's not something your father would approve of, is it?"

"No," Simon admitted. He told Calkin

briefly of his narrow escape from Jack and his cronies. "The one who warned them off, called Peto, said I should take up the knife, having only the one good arm, you see."

Calkin gripped Simon's shoulder and shook it once in surprise. "You met Peto the Pope?"

"They called him Peto. He was not a big man, but they all seemed to fear him."

"And no wonder. Peto can kill a man twenty different ways, or a woman, too, I hear. He's an odd sort of criminal: very mild-mannered and treats folk kindly enough unless they cross him. If they do, they're very likely to turn up dead or disappear entirely."

Simon shuddered. Was his rescuer such a cold-blooded killer as all that? Remembering how people treated Peto and spoke of him, how he had advised using what was given and taking up knives, Simon admitted it might be true.

"Every officer in London has hunted that one, for he has his hand into every kind of crime. The common folk look up to him. They fear Peto, but they protect him, consider him one of their own."

"Yes. Even after he stopped their fun, one boy asked him to supper, saying his mother would demand it."

"Peto rewards well those who do a service for him." Calkin took a bite of the fig and chewed thoughtfully. "That sort has nothing. He is generous with them, knowing that in return they will keep his affairs secret. We don't even know what he looks like."

Simon gave a brief description but found in the attempt that there was nothing memorable in Peto's appearance. The man was ordinary-looking except for the air of confidence, the expression of will, which was not in his physical makeup but within the man himself.

Calkin listened carefully. "Not much, but it's a start. Someday we will corner him and he will hang for sure."

Simon found the prospect unsettling. Despite what Peto was, he had found him likeable. It was repellant to think of the spectacle his death would be at Tyburn.

The second prostitute had operated in the Shambles, according to Hugh's information. The constable involved had discovered no permanent dwelling for her. Mathilda, or Tildy as she was known, had been a newcomer to London, probably from the north. The girl had worked at an inn in exchange for her keep while she earned extra on the side from willing customers.

Simon found the area around the Ox with Flowers Inn every bit as depressing as Daisy's neighborhood had been, although the streets were drier today and therefore a little less treacherous. The inn itself had been neglected until it was probably past repair, the landlord ostensibly planning to wring every last dollar from it and leave just before the roof fell in on his head. Inside, two customers sat at separate tables, one asleep with tankard in hand, the other gazing into space with the glazed look of one whose days run together from lack of activity and stimulation.

The landlord looked up from stirring a cabbage-laden stew and glared as Simon came through the door. The bright sunlight that knifed in caused the man to squint even more than his unfriendly disposition did. Simon closed the door with some difficulty, it being swollen from the damp. He had to put a shoulder to it, but it finally grated shut with a loud protest. Guessing from Simon's appearance that he had no money, the host chose his course at once, growling, "What would you want here?"

Simon again told the story of a misplaced aunt who had been disowned by her family, claiming he'd followed her from Lincoln and was now living nearby. "I hoped that we could share lodgings and save money," he finished.

"I never heard Mathilda mention a nephew."

Simon had learned that a bold lie was best. "I don't suppose she talks of her past much to you, does she?"

The innkeeper frowned again. "No point in discussing it. She won't be found by you or anyone. She's dead."

"Dead?" Simon used his innocent face again. "How?"

"Murdered in an alley not a stone's throw from here." The landlord turned back to the stew, spilling a little into the fire with a hiss as he turned it. Simon saw burned cabbage float to the top, smelled its bitterness.

"Was she here the night she was killed?"

"Aye, but she left when supper was done. Terrible cold it was, too. I remember saying that she might freeze, but Tildy laughed and said she would go out. That's all I know." His set face indicated he was through with conversation. "Will you be having a drink now?" His tone said it was time to produce money or leave. Simon chose the latter from necessity.

For lack of anything better to do, he located the alley where Mathilda had been found headless. It told him the same thing that the first one had: nothing. Gray even in broad daylight due to the buildings that shaded it, the place felt cold and uninviting. If a man had pulled the poor woman to the back of the dead end, blank-walled lane, no passerby would have seen them even if he'd stopped and peered into the blackness. Who would do that anyway in an area such as this? Strange noises were best left uninvestigated by those who wished to remain alive and unharmed.

Coming out of the alley, Simon bumped into someone, which sent both of them tottering backward. Looking up, he was surprised to be face-to-face with a man who had been in the inn, the one who'd stared out the window apparently unaware of him. Seen in the daylight, he looked to be about thirty years old, with a pleasant, simple face. His clothes were tattered and none too clean, and his hair lay however it would with no attempt made to tame it. Simon guessed that the man was slightly lacking in wit, one who could work only at the simplest tasks, his movements almost comically slow. Though he had made no indication of listening to the discussion with the landlord, he now seemed well aware of it.

"That's where they found her," he said with a knowing nod. "I went in and saw the body myself, before the constable arrived." The man's speech was difficult to understand, garbled and mushy. "Poor Mathilda! We didn't even know it was her that morning, because she'd been dressed up in old nun's garb, and because she had no head." If he waited a moment after the fellow spoke, Simon found that his mind grasped the whole and the words made sense. "That's right, no head at all." The simple face demonstrated residual shock; the head bobbed in emphasis. "We only found that it was Tildy when she turned up missing. Someone said she'd had a mark on her back, here." He indicated the left shoulder blade. "Once they knew where to look, they saw it was her, right enough."

"Poor girl," Simon said, sad for Mathilda's final terror. How had it felt when hands tightened around her throat, when she realized that someone intended to choke away her life, someone she may have known and trusted?

"I saw the fellow," the man bragged.

"How could you have seen him?"

"I was passing here on the way to the inn, y'see, like I do every night, and there he was, standing right about where you are now. All covered up with his cape, he was, but I thought then that he waited for somebody, and I thought, too, that he didn't belong in this place. Something about him said quality, maybe his boots, maybe that fine cape, maybe the way he stood there, but I said to myself, 'There's a gentleman that wants himself a doxy.' I could never know what he wanted her for, though." He seemed genuinely sorry for that.

"I appreciate your telling me," Simon said, warming to the odd fellow. "Is there anything else you can remember about M — my aunt?"

The man's eyes rolled upward as he searched his memory. "She were good to me," he finally said. "Not like a bawd is, of course. I mean she were kind and treated me like a friend, not like a cur dog t' kick."

"Yes, she was kind," Simon seized on the statement. "Did she ever bring a man to the inn when you were there?"

"For certes," the fellow said, chuckling. "It were her livin', wa'nt it?"

"Can you remember any one man, what he looked like?"

The fellow thought carefully, small patches of wet appearing at the sides of his mouth as the jaw hung slack. Finally, he nodded vigorously. "One I remember had eyebrows like two big caterpillars crawlin' across his forehead."

"How old?"

"Forty, I'd say, more or less. Big shoulders on 'im."

"Gentleman?"

"Oh, yes. He held his nose up in the air and frowned hard, like we was going to infect 'im with something. But he was not too good to chase Mathilda's skirts. Fair nice 'e was with her, like Puss in catnip. She called him Georgie."

Simon recognized one possibility in the description: Sir George Blakewell had such brows and such a manner when he chose. "Anything else? Can you think of anything about the man in the cape? Could it have been the same man?"

"I cannot say for sure. But somebody had give her a pin: pretty thing, it was. Pearls 'round the edge, y'know. She showed it me the night before, said there was more to come if she pleased a certain gentleman. But I never knew which man it was gave it to her. The one at the inn I would know again, but the other I paid no mind, until they found poor Mathilda. I didn't even tell the bailiff's men, 'cause I never thought of it until later." He rolled his eyes in thought again. "I would say he were taller than the one with the big eyebrows, and not so broad, either."

"You've been most helpful," Simon began, and then remembered the character he was supposed to be. "I shall tell my parents that my aunt had one true friend who will miss her, and that may temper their grief. May I tell them your name?"

"I am Penitence Brook, mostly called Pen." His slurred speech made it difficult to hear the consonants, and Simon frowned. Pen repeated his name obligingly until Simon had it.

"I thank you, Pen." Simon turned to go, leaving Pen Brook smiling after him, already trying to fit what he'd learned into some sort of pattern.

CHAPTER TWELVE

The arrival of the Princess Elizabeth caused a quiet but definite wave of nervousness in the Brandon household. Sir Thomas and his wife were clearly puzzled at what the reason for a visit might be, but they received the princess and Bess Blakewell politely.

Elizabeth, whom Bess later said could have been a play-actor if women were allowed to do such things, made up a story out of whole cloth about dedicating a chapel in Westminster to her aunt, Mary Tudor. She wondered, since she had not known her aunt, if the Brandons could advise her on what Mary would have liked as to décor. Listening to these outright lies, Bess admitted to her husband that she should have stopped it but did not know how to deal with this new, determined side of Elizabeth. The girl had been an easy charge until recently, with only her studies and her little crippled friend. Now she was quite different, and Bess was at a loss as to how to handle her.

Sir Thomas had been too long a courtier to say aloud that the king would never fund such an undertaking, his dead sister and disgraced daughter's desires notwithstanding. Apparently deciding that this was a dream the girl had concocted to brighten her humdrum life, he politely shared his memories of Mary and the things she had enjoyed.

"Your aunt was the most beautiful princess in Europe," he declared, then added, "It is England's good fortune to ever have the loveliest royal daughters."

Elizabeth smiled brightly. "I'm sure your daughter Joanna has become a beauty, but I haven't seen her for years. How is she?"

The silence that greeted her question made Elizabeth sorry to cause these kind people renewed pain, but she reflected that it was worth the price to bring the girl's murderer to justice.

"Our daughter is dead," Sir Thomas said finally. His square face, which in old age had flattened much like her father's, took on a haunted look.

"Oh, my dear sir, I am so sorry to have brought up a painful memory. Living as I do, I often miss news of important matters.

It is distressing that I did not send condolences at the very least."

Lady Brandon spoke for the first time, a sound like paper fluttering in the breeze. A wraithlike woman who had never had much spirit, she seemed to be fading away before Elizabeth's eyes. "Please, Your Highness, think no more of it. We have not gone to Court for some years now, and we too hear of things long afterward. We have accepted Joanna's death, hard as it was."

"She was our youngest, and the last child is often spoilt. Still, she was dear to us." Sir Thomas looked into the distance, away from harsh reality.

Elizabeth felt a second qualm of conscience, but she asked anyway, "Was it some illness?"

The old lady's nostrils quivered and her lips compressed. "She was murdered by some sort of monster."

It was clear they did not want to discuss the matter further, for there was a long silence after that. Elizabeth could not let it lie.

"But word of such a crime must have gone out, if only for the safety of other women. I heard nothing."

Sir Thomas' handsome face showed his quandary. "The king your father, because of our old family friendship, has respected our grief and kept the matter private. Joanna was . . . unwise, and her death was the result." He seemed to have finished, but then more words burst from him as if pent up to the point of explosion. "I would cry 'Murder!' from the rooftops if I thought it would bring justice or prevent another such death."

Lady Brandon stepped in to ensure that Elizabeth did not return to Henry with tales of their discontent with his actions. "Of course the king sent men to find the killer, but they had no success. We have accepted that the crime will never be solved. Now I have an idea that might appeal to you for the chapel." And with that she changed the subject with a determination one would not have expected.

That would have been the end of it had Elizabeth not had the good fortune to meet Enid Brandon, Lady Monteagle, on her way out of the Brandon home. Enid, Sir Thomas' older daughter, had come to visit her parents, and as luck would have it, insisted Elizabeth stay and dine with them. They dined simply, and the conversation often lagged. Enid chattered like a bright bird, trying to keep her parents' interest, but they were clearly beyond caring about earthly matters. After the meal, Bess and Elizabeth departed. Enid left at the same time, kissing her father's wrinkled cheek and hugging her mother's thin frame with the same determined cheerfulness before saying goodbye.

Enid Brandon was not beautiful, but within five minutes of meeting her, one was convinced that she was. She radiated a sense of caring for those around her, and while not blind to human faults, was in sympathy with mankind in general. As they waited in the entry for their respective conveyances, she spoke to Elizabeth warmly.

"Thank you, Your Highness, for visiting Mother and Father. They have not recovered in the slightest from my sister's death, and although I spend a few hours each day trying to lift their mood, I fear they are destroyed."

"Your mother told me Joanna was murdered. I am so sorry," Elizabeth said in response. "They did not find the one who did this terrible thing?"

"No." Enid's greenish eyes reflected sadness and anger too as she pulled on soft gloves of calfskin. "My sister was the youngest child of aging parents. She led them a merry chase — at least she found it so. There were incidents that embarrassed all

of us, but they took the brunt of her wasp-
ish tongue and her sneering at them."

Bess, who had said little the whole day,
spoke up. "As well not to have children as
to have an ungrateful child. As the Bible
says, a regular serpent's tooth."

Enid smiled thinly, pulling her wrap closer
in the evening chill. "So it is said, but I love
my two and would never give them up."

Bess pursed her lips and was silent.

"Did Joanna give you any indication of a
man in her life? Surely such a one would be
suspect."

"She revealed nothing to us." Enid took a
deep breath and said plainly what was on
her mind. "My sister was a flirt, and not
always with propriety."

Elizabeth was reminded of the girl's uncle,
Charles Brandon, famous for his affairs.
Handsome Charles had often promised
marriage in order to get his way with
women. It seemed Joanna followed in her
uncle's footsteps, but men were allowed
much more license in such things.

Enid went on thoughtfully, "She screamed
at Mother dreadfully sometimes. Once
when they tried to speak sense to her,
Joanna claimed that she could marry a man
from an old, distinguished family, one with
a fine education who spoke Latin and

Greek. Whether she had a particular man in mind or was simply trying to hurt them, I don't know." She paused. "Grandfather came from common stock, of course. It was your grandfather who knighted him."

Elizabeth thought to herself how fragile this thing called nobility was for people like the Brandons. Those with older bloodlines often despised newcomers, calling them upstarts, which made a scandal such as Joanna's death even worse for her parents. Established families looked down their noses and made comments such as "blood will tell." Yet Henry's own ancestor, her great-grandfather Owen Tudor, had been low-born, and his issue sat on the throne of England. Only a few generations, and the Tudors were so mighty that they even defied the Pope. She pitied the Brandons: a wayward child, a scandalous murder, and their own lowly beginnings combined to make them feel mortified indeed. Elizabeth herself felt that blood was not so important as talent, wit, and courage.

"I was aware of it, yes," she replied warmly, "but my dear Lady Monteagle, your nobility shines in your character, and no one would deny it who has met you."

Enid bent her head for a moment. "I don't mind for myself, but Father feels both her loss and the scandal of it deeply."

"Is there no other clue to the identity of the man your sister may have set her cap for?" Elizabeth asked, turning the conversation back to her purpose.

The lady thought for a moment. "Joanna had a small silver box that she cherished, so it could have been a gift from a man she considered special. Father believes it to be of foreign design: a filigreed pentagon, rather curious shape, and very finely crafted."

"Interesting." Something struck Elizabeth about the description, and she filed it away in her mind. She had gone as far as politeness would allow in asking about the girl's death. She must either change the subject or confess that she was investigating four murders. "Will you be spending time in the country this summer?" The litters arrived, and after a few minutes more she and Enid embraced warmly and took their separate ways home.

Simon reported what he had learned to Hugh, and they discussed it as Calkin, repairing a piece of worn harness, added a comment from time to time.

In the courtyard a condemned prigger, a horse thief, was being prepared for execution. The man's hands were strapped to a horse's saddle so that he would have to run along beside the galloping animal all the way to Tyburn. Crowds of people along the road would shout jeers and satiric encouragement as the wild-eyed man struggled to keep up, sometimes being dragged, sometimes getting his feet under him and running until he fell again. Simon felt the familiar pressing in his chest as his lungs compressed in sympathy with the pain of another. Guilty or not, he pitied the prisoner. Hugh and Calkin seemed unaware of both the man's terror and Simon's discomfort.

"So this Penitence has given us two men to look for." Hugh was thoughtful. "And you think Sir George might have consorted with Mathilda Harrison?"

"That's something you must deal with, I'm afraid. I can't see him confessing his adulterous ways to me for any reason."

"The other man, the one in the shadows, could someone else have gotten a better look?" Calkin suggested.

"The landlord at the inn was no help. I don't think the man would have gone inside if he planned to kill Mathilda that night. I can go back tomorrow and try places nearby. It was cold, and he may have gone inside somewhere to warm up."

"Right. And I'll speak to the local constable." Hugh stood up just as the prisoner and horse were started off at a dead run. A cheer went up from those nearby, and Simon looked away.

The constable from the Shambles, Brook, was less savory both in manner and in personal habit than Frobish. He lived alone, that was obvious. The small house that he invited Hugh to enter was in terrible disorder, with food-encrusted dishes and smelly clothing strewn about haphazardly. A pallet bed in the corner looked most unwelcoming, with rumpled and dirty blankets in a heap at the bottom. Brooks himself was slight and disheveled, almost defiantly so. He was the type of petty tyrant Hugh most disliked, disdainful of the people he was paid to protect and almost admiring of the criminals who preyed upon them.

"I've come about the events surrounding the death of Mathilda Harrison."

"What's all the fuss about a dead whore?" Brook asked suspiciously. "Is there more to tell? Was the slut some criminal's skainsmate?" His face, never handsome, took on an unattractive leer. "Or some nobleman's private property?"

"It is important that we find out everything we can about her," Hugh answered noncommittally. "There may have been a gentleman in the area that night wearing a long, dark cloak with tassels for decoration."

"So she was slain by a noble. That's why she matters, eh? Old Henry will want to forget the whole thing if one of the high-and-mighty is in on it." Brook spat, barely missing his visitor's boots, and Hugh felt his face redden with the effort of keeping his temper.

"I did not say that, nor do I know any more than what I've said. The man was in the area, and I would like to question him." His tone was a reprimand.

Brook knew when to pull back. "Nobody said anything to me about no gentleman in a fancy cloak being nigh. Who saw this ghostly nobleman?"

Hugh hoped he wasn't getting the man into trouble, but he wanted to know if Penitence was a reliable sort. "His name is Pen something." Hugh's brow furrowed as he recalled Simon's story. "Penitence Brook."

The constable's face registered disbelief, and then crumpled into a mask of merriment as he laughed heartily. "Pen! Pen!" he managed before he fell back into throes of amusement. Hugh waited stoically until the man got control of himself. "My good captain: Pen, that wonder of laziness, is my cousin, and less than half-wit, more like a quarter, I'd say. He does not remember the night Mathilda died, because all of his nights are exactly the same. He might have seen your man in the cloak a month before or a month after, to him it's all the same." Brook chuckled a few more times, trying to pull himself together. "Put no faith in what Pen says."

Grimly, Hugh gathered his dignity as best he could and took a different approach. "The Catholic clothing and jewelry the woman was wearing, you tell me about them in as much detail as you can." It was not a request.

Brook sobered and tried to be helpful. "She were dressed in a brown robe, like the barefoot Carmelites wore. There was a rosary, pink beads of stone on a gold chain, with a cross studded with the same stones, a nice piece." Hugh could almost see the thought flit across the man's face that he'd wanted to keep it for himself.

"What happened to it?"

"I turned it over to the authorities, as was proper."

Hugh formed his own explanation of the

man's virtuous statement. Someone had been watching. Still, there was little chance of finding the rosary now, months after the fact. There had been many opportunities for someone to pocket a piece from an unsolved and unimportant murder.

CHAPTER THIRTEEN

Hugh Bellows appeared at Hampstead Castle early the next morning, before the princess had stirred from her room. He found George Blakewell in a chilly anteroom off the hall that he used as his office, going over accounts with a man Hugh had seen before but did not know. Blakewell seemed inordinately glad to see him, and he deduced that it was the interruption rather than Hugh's charming personality that Sir George appreciated.

"Ah, Bellows. No, no, don't go. I believe we are finished here. Do you know Master Ninian?"

"I don't recall our meeting before, though I have seen the gentleman at court."

"Ninian is a clerk in the king's exchequer who oversees the funds spent for the expenses of the princess' household. We were completing the monthly accounting. Of course, Captain Bellows is of the king's

Guard."

Blakewell's manner implied that accounting for expenses was not his favorite thing. Did he have something to hide, Hugh wondered, or was it only that the king was notoriously stingy with his daughters' upkeep?

The clerk collected several sheets covered with neat figures and notations into a pile, making sure each one was where he wanted it and perfectly aligned with the others. Opening a capacious leather bag, he set the stack inside, closed it with great deliberation, then stood and leaned toward Hugh. "Dreadful, this murder. Can you tell me, sir, was the woman, uh, violated, as one hears?"

Hugh ignored the question but deduced that spending time with this man would be distasteful. Maybe Sir George just wanted Ninian out of his sight.

Tall with large bones, the clerk had no substance, like a skeleton draped with white and dressed in clothing by children for sport. A huge forehead and an almost equally large chin dominated his face, leaving little room between for eyes, nose, and mouth. The mouth was a slash in the pale skin, and the eyes not much more. The voice that emanated from somewhere in the long neck echoed as from a well. The man was a perfect picture of the worst in some who deal in numbers: humorless, pasty, and fixated on his work, except for an apparent ghoulish interest in the death of Alice LaFont. Hugh had a moment of pity for Sir George, who must justify every penny he spent to men like this one.

The clerk made no immediate move to leave but fixed his gaze on Hugh. "His Majesty has set you to finding this foul murderer?"

"Yes." Hugh gave no details, hoping the man would go.

"I suppose it is most distressing to him that a woman was murdered in the princess' very garden."

"Most distressing, I'm sure."

"There was another murder recently, I believe: Brandon's daughter."

"Really." Hugh kept his face still. People were bound to put those two together, especially if a whisper got out of the state of the corpses.

"A sure sign of the wrath of God, when young women are not safe in this land. We must look to our ways."

Hugh sighed. Another prophet of doom. England had more than its share of people willing to predict the end of the Age due to either Henry's rejection of the Catholic Church or his keeping of too many Catholic ways in the Church of England. Hugh guessed this one would lean toward the latter but encouraged no further comment. Something about the man didn't ring true, but then clerks were seldom allowed to have their own opinions, their positions being dependent upon their betters.

Apparently unfazed by the fact that he had received no information, Ninian started for the door. He gave Hugh an encouraging clap on the shoulder, revealing a surprisingly strong hand, well muscled with long fingers that gripped like a clamp. The smell of old dust enveloped him as if his clothes were permeated with it. "Be vigilant, sir," he urged. "Our king depends on men like you."

"And on you," Hugh responded politely, and Ninian was gone, the satchel of papers folded under his arm.

Sir George looked after him with distaste. "At least that's over for another month. What brings you here so early, Captain?"

Hugh swallowed, for a moment feeling guilty about piling more trouble on the older man's head, but then went forward determinedly. "I have a witness who says that you consorted with the woman Mathilda Harrison, recently murdered in the Shambles."

Blakewell's face turned ashy. He opened his mouth. Hugh thought he might deny it, but his face closed and he merely nodded. "I have known the girl," he said slowly, looking at Hugh directly. "She is murdered, you say?"

"Last winter."

"I wouldn't have known that. I stopped seeing her in January, just after Twelfth Night. I remember because . . ." He didn't finish, though Hugh waited to hear the reason. "Is this related to Alice's death?"

"We believe so."

"Then the head was missing?"

"Yes."

Sir George realized his situation. "You must believe me, Bellows. I had nothing to do with it. I knew the woman, yes, but only as her . . . profession allowed. I would never hurt her. Mathilda was a kind girl, fun-loving and gentle with an old man." Blakewell's face showed shame and guilt, but was it only for his fornication, or for something else?

"Why did you stop seeing Mathilda?"

Sir George licked dry lips, and his eyes darted around the room as if looking for something. "My wife . . . does not enjoy the marital bed." Hugh must have looked doubtful, for he went on, "Being a single man, you will not understand. I love Bess, and she loves me. But years ago, when we first were wed, she conceived a child born a monster: deformed, convulsive, and," he shuddered at the memory, "without eyes. It lived five days, and we did not know whether to pray for its life or its death. When it died, Bess changed. She is loving and careful of me in every way except in that one wifely duty. She cries if I approach her and shakes most pitifully."

Hugh was embarrassed to be the confidant of so painful a secret. "So you find companions elsewhere?"

"Yes." Sir George was both defensive and ashamed. "I believe Bess knows, but she says nothing. I could divorce her, of course, take another wife, but in truth, I love her. We get on well together except in that one thing."

Hugh struggled to find his way through a maze of emotions: pity, surprise, and, he was embarrassed to discover, curiosity. As a bachelor he had seldom looked beneath the obvious aspects of marriage, but here was a complicated couple. Did Bess know of Sir George's philandering? Could he have murdered Mathilda to keep her from going to his wife with stories of his unfaithfulness?

A sudden thought occurred to him. "Did you know Alice well?" No response was needed; the reddening of the man's face said it all. "So you left off seeing Mathilda because you had formed a liaison with Alice LaFont."

Sir George bowed his head. "I am a stupid old man," he said, his voice nearly breaking. "She was so lovely, and she liked me right off, I thought." He cleared his throat and continued more strongly. "Now I realize that I was the only man about. The girl was simply passing the time, relieving the tedium of life away from the Court."

He stood and moved stiffly to the window, unwilling to face Hugh with his folly. "She was sent here, you see, because she could not behave with men. There was some outcry and she was 'banished,' she called it, to where it was believed she could make no more trouble. Who'd have thought she'd take up with me," he asked bitterly, "and who'd have thought I'd be fool enough to chase a witless child like that?" He turned to face Hugh finally, relieved to have it said. "It wasn't long before she wanted nothing more to do with me. I had come to my senses by then, and we ended it peacefully."

Hearing voices in the corridor, Hugh

waited until they had passed before asking his next question. "Had she found someone else?"

"I don't know who it could have been. There are few visitors here, and even fewer men. I doubt even Alice would take up with a villain." Sir George spoke of the males employed at the castle as servants. "There is the princess' mathematics tutor, Greengage, but he's older than I. It seems unlikely that —"

"I'll speak with him," Hugh interrupted. "Do you have proof that there was someone else?"

Blakewell looked even gloomier than before. "No. Only a feeling that Alice had found greener pastures. She said that we must stop meeting because my wife's presence made her feel sinful. It hadn't done for two months, but suddenly her shame was unbearable. I felt the lie in it."

"And when was this?"

Sir George pondered for a few moments. "Around Eastertide. Alice had avoided me for several days. At service on Maundy Thursday, she stayed in the chapel after the rest had gone, and I approached her there. The verger was putting the chapel to rights, so we had to be discreet. That's when she told me of her guilty conscience and made a great show of penitence, kneeling at the altar so that I had to either leave her alone or stand there disturbing her pious devotions." The man's voice took on an edge. "Piety was not one of her usual virtues, I can tell you."

Hugh wondered how angry Sir George had really been at the rejection. Easy enough now to say he'd come to his senses, but who was to know? "I must assume there have been others, besides Alice and Mathilda?"

Shame reappeared on the man's face, but he set his jaw and answered calmly. "It has been eighteen years since our son was laid in his grave. Such a tiny casket, it was." Straightening his shoulders, Sir George sat down at the table again and began clearing it with an angry clatter. "You may think me a sinner. That I am and I know it. I am a man, though, and I have done right by Bess in every other way. I serve my king as best I can, in spite of his sniveling clerks and their insinuations, and I harm none of the females I befriend. Other than Alice, they were all women of the streets. I would never have soiled my own nest had not Alice herself been more than willing. When it was over I was in some way glad, for I had more guilt those last few months than ever before. Still, I did not wish Alice harm, nor Mathilda, either. I do not understand the crime, the evil of it."

"You are a connection between them. You cannot deny that."

Blakewell stuck out his chin stubbornly. "I cannot deny I knew them both, but I do deny that I harmed them."

"Do you know a woman named Therese Blanc?"

Sir George considered. "No. Is she also a victim?"

"Yes, the first to die, at least that we know of."

Sir George shook his heavy head with disbelief. "I tell you again, Captain, I would never harm a woman. You must look elsewhere for your killer."

Hugh had his own opinions in that quarter, but he thanked Blakewell for his help and left him, thoughtfully descending the spiral stone stairs that retained their chill even though spring had now arrived in full.

CHAPTER FOURTEEN

Sally Meadows could not resist sharing her secret with Addie, a fellow servant in the Derwent household, as they lay in their tiny chamber after the household was quiet. Although the space under the stairs was so cold at night that they huddled together for warmth, the girls considered themselves lucky to have the privacy that it afforded. Addie was anxious to hear the details her friend was willing to divulge.

"He's very handsome and so charming. He treats me as if I was a duchess," Sally claimed. "He talks foreign, calls me 'little love' in Latin, like he were born speakin' it."

"Go on," Addie chided. "To a serving girl?"

Sally pulled open a cloth sack kept under the bed. "He give me this." In the dimness Addie saw the glint of a small brooch. "It's real silver."

"Who is he?"

"I've made a vow not to tell," the girl answered, her perfect face dimly illuminated in a shaft of moonlight, "but he says some-day everyone will know what I am to him."

"Likely he'll ruin you and leave you with child. Lady Agnes would not like that. You'd be out on the streets."

"Oh, fie on Lady Agnes!" Sally spoke with fire, and Addie gasped at her audacity. "I'll be gone from here any day, soon as he gets things ready for us."

Addie shook her head in the dark. How could Sally believe that a man of rank would have anything to do with her other than what men did to women? Later, when Sally squeezed her hand and crept from the room, she said nothing. Sally was her friend, after all. Only the next morning, when Sally did not reappear, did Addie feel a shiver of dread. The lovestruck girl would lose her place when Lady Derwent found her missing, and the mysterious lover would tire of her soon enough. Then where would she be? Addie claimed she knew nothing, wanting no part of her mistress' wrath over Sally's disappearance.

Hugh waited outside the garden gate when Simon arrived for his daily visit with the princess. His long frame leaned casually against the rough stone wall as he idly watched two squirrels chase each other around a huge oak tree, chattering noisily. In a few words he told what he'd learned from Sir George.

"I cannot think that we should tell Her Highness this," he finished. "Not only is it improper for a young lady to hear, it may prejudice her against her guardian."

"If he is guilty, she should be prejudiced against him."

"Still, consorting with sluts, dallying with Alice. The princess is but thirteen."

Simon considered. "True, but she is wise beyond her years, she is involved in this affair, and —" here the boy's eyes twinkled — "she will be most perturbed if she finds we have kept anything from her. I for one do not want to face her wrath if that should ever happen."

Hugh chewed his lip, considering Simon's argument, then let out a long sigh. "Nor do I. I hear she has a vicious temper when upset —" here his voice dropped to a whisper — "like her sire."

Simon, Elizabeth, and Hugh each told a story that afternoon that contributed to their general knowledge of the four murders. As Mary Ward sat in a warm nook some way off, the princess told her story first, summarizing what she'd learned from the Brandon visit.

"So it may be that the man we seek speaks Latin."

"Most educated men do," Simon observed.

"Most educated men studied Latin," Elizabeth corrected. "That does not mean they speak it."

"It could also have been exaggeration, either on the man's part, boasting to impress a pretty girl, or on her part, to make her relatives feel inferior," Hugh put in.

"The man in the cloak may be a useless bit as well," Simon admitted, "if Pen is unreliable, as Hugh's friend says."

Hugh waved a hand in denial. "The constable is no friend of mine. But he does know Pen well and says the man has little sense of time, being half-wit."

"Even half-wits might remember murder," Elizabeth commented. "You must speak to Pen again, Simon."

"I will try. Now what other things have we seen in common in these crimes?"

"Lady Monteagle described a box her sister had, a gift from a man. It struck a chord in my memory, and now I have remembered that Alice too had such a box.

She once found a robin's egg on the ground. She put it in a silver box on a bed of perfumed cloth, hoping it might hatch in such an attractive nest. The box was five-sided and filigreed, very unique."

"I would like to see it," Hugh said.

Simon frowned. "What you describe seems familiar."

"Alice's things were sent to her parents, but I will ask to see the box again."

They proceeded to Simon's story, which he told as Hugh watched the princess' face for signs of shock. She seemed unfazed by prostitutes and their men, upright and otherwise, which gave Hugh the courage to tell his story. He glossed over the nature of the relationship between Sir George and the two women, calling them "friendships." Elizabeth merely smiled gravely. Simon had no doubt, having observed her natural curiosity, that she listened at keyholes while the servants gossiped and therefore knew more about the affairs of men and women than might be imagined by those around her. Surely as she was growing up she had heard stories about her own father and his six wives and come to understand the need a man felt for a woman's soft body.

When Hugh had finished they took their accustomed places on the two stone benches, Simon and Hugh on one facing Elizabeth on the other. They had to decide what came next. Elizabeth's pale brows joined in a firm line.

"It is clear to me that I must visit Alice's mother. We should know what happened at Court to cause the girl to be banished to my household." Her ironic smile made Simon's heart ache for her. Royal and at the same time despised. "And I might retrieve the box as well."

"That would be helpful." Hugh was relieved, both that she had not proposed Sir George's dismissal and that she had chosen a task he deemed safe.

"This Peto seems an intriguing rogue. Should he be added to our list of suspects?"

"I'd say he must be, Your Highness," Hugh said firmly. "We know he has killed before."

"But how would someone like Peto gain access to Alice LaFont or Joanna Brandon?" Simon objected. "Calkin claims he's a common criminal."

"One successful enough that he could pass himself off as wealthy if he chose," Elizabeth argued. "A fine suit of clothes and he slips into a gathering, choosing a likely girl to approach. It would have been easy, since neither Joanna nor Alice seems to have been discerning in her choice of companions."

"And the man in the cloak? Peto is not tall."

Hugh stepped in. "I'm not convinced that it wasn't Sir George. He may not want to admit that he was in the vicinity when Mathilda was killed, even if he is innocent of the crime itself and Peto is the culprit."

"So we add Peto to the list and try to find what we can about him," Elizabeth said with brisk efficiency. "I hope we can eliminate some of them with our efforts."

"Hugh, you must speak with the princess' tutor, Master Greengage," Simon suggested. "It doesn't seem likely that he and Alice were . . . friends, but we must be sure, and he is most likely to respond to your authority with the truth. I shall go back to Daisy's and see if she recognizes Sir George's description as someone Therese knew."

"This Daisy, is she pretty?" Elizabeth's thin lips pursed and one eyebrow rose humorously.

"Not so beautiful as you, Highness, but she does speak Greek very well, I'm told," Simon answered, and Elizabeth laughed aloud. Simon liked the sound of her laughter but reflected that he had not heard it often enough. He resolved to cause her to laugh more often, as soon as they caught the man who had killed Alice LaFont.

Hugh found Elizabeth's interim tutor at his home in Cheapside. The house was modest but well built, and in the usual style, narrow and long. Officially retired from public life, Greengage was an unlikely candidate for a murderer. Elderly and frail, the old man could barely keep himself upright, much less murder a healthy lass. He nevertheless delayed Hugh for some time describing his brilliant pupil, praising in nasal tones Elizabeth's skill in mathematics, language, and oratory. "She will move the hearts of men, if given the chance," the old man insisted.

Hugh could not help but reply with irony. "She certainly has her way with me."

Greengage looked shocked for a moment then saw the humorous intent. "Yes, I fancy that protecting so strong-willed a personality is difficult. We have great need of discipline in our nation, sir. Discipline will make a better life for all. Why, to look at the young men of today sickens me. Brandon, Pemberton, Collins: what are they but women with beards? A man can hardly tell the difference with their coats of goose-turd green and their hose of popinjay blue." The old man minced in stiff-jointed mimicry of the courtiers' movements. "And do you note the codpieces, sir? Embroidery and baubles on their privates, sir! Noble birth or not, God never intended man to look so."

Hugh waited through the diatribe with patience. He had not much use for the foppery of the young nobles either, but the older generation had been decrying the dress of the younger for centuries with no result but the encouragement of its own apoplexy.

"Speaking of clothing, a man seen at the castle several times before the murder wore a dark cloak with gold tassels as decoration. Do you know of such a cloak?"

"I pay little attention to a man's outer trappings, sir. The true man is within." Hugh groaned inwardly at the old man's inability to focus on the matter at hand, but the tutor did glean the purpose of the question. "But surely this murderer was a madman who has since moved on?"

"Of course we hope that is so, but we must be watchful of the princess."

"Of course, of course," the old man croaked. "I shall arm myself when next I come to Hampstead."

The picture of Greengage with skinny arms raised in fierce defense of Elizabeth was both hilarious and heartwarming. The old man was obviously fond of his pupil. "I thank you, sir," Hugh said politely. "We must be vigilant, and another pair of eyes will be helpful."

Elizabeth's trip to the LaFont home brought little in the way of information. After being led through room after silent room empty of activity, she was ushered into a comfortable study where sat Sir Lionel LaFont and his wife. The knight looked up from a table, setting aside a book he had been reading. His lady sat in a chair in one corner, feeding sweetmeats to a lapdog with ribbons on its ears and tail. She rose to meet the princess, welcoming her to their home and pushing the dog forward in introduction as well. The mother was Alice grown old: doll-like and childish. She had lost most of her teeth, which ruined the lines of her face, but it was possible to discern that she had been a beauty in her day. Her voice, however, was unnaturally high-pitched and whining, even when she said the most pleasant phrases.

Sir Lionel, Alice's father, was clearly bored with his wife and probably had been for years. She deferred in everything to him, gazing at him with a look that said he was too far above her to contemplate. An intelligent man who read and studied widely, judging from the trappings of the room, he must have found his wife's ways as grating as Elizabeth herself did. He was not the first man who had married a face and found nothing behind it. Watching her coddle the spoiled dog, Elizabeth wondered if Lady LaFont understood how lucky she was to have captured such a handsome and accomplished man.

That the couple were shocked and saddened by their daughter's death was obvious. Although not told the grisly details, they must have guessed, when not allowed to see their daughter's remains, that her death had been horrible. They knew little of Alice's life, having seen almost nothing of her since she went to Court. They claimed they seldom went anymore, Sir Lionel's tone implying he was sick of the intrigue and upheaval though his words did not. No rumor had reached them that Alice had caused trouble for the queen. She had told them only that she would be living "for a while" in Elizabeth's household.

Seeing that she would learn nothing more from the LaFonts, Elizabeth stood to take her leave, the faithful Bess following suit. With a searching look Sir Lionel asked, "Is there some reason that you ask about my daughter?" Elizabeth had to admit that the man was no coward, and she scrambled to appear innocent and girlish.

"Please don't be disturbed by my questions. I wanted to express my sympathy in person, but it seems now that she is gone that I hardly knew Alice at all."

"I see." LaFont was not convinced, but he said no more. He led them out through the hollow hallways and offered them his boat for the trip home, since it had begun to rain. Left with Alice's mother while he arranged it, Elizabeth seized her chance. Patting the dog's silky head she asked, "Lady, I wonder if I might borrow a small box that belonged to Alice. I was taken with its design and thought to ask one of the smiths to copy it for me."

The tiny woman responded as she had hoped. "Your Highness must have it if you find it pleasing. I have not touched my daughter's things yet," here her shriveled face pulled in even more as she steadied her tone, "but I will have it sent to you as soon as possible."

"Thank you. I will return it in a few days."

"No, really, my dear, you must keep it. It will remind you of my Alice." Her eyes misted but she blinked back her tears. Like Alice, she was tender-hearted for all her childishness.

"That it will, Lady, and I am honored that you would give it to me. However briefly I knew her, Alice brightened my household with her smiles and her warmth."

On the way home Elizabeth ignored Bess' comments on women who waved goodbye by use of a dog's paw. She had an idea of how to learn more about Alice's troubles at Court. Within an hour she had written a message and sent it off, begging a word with Queen Catherine Parr.

CHAPTER FIFTEEN

Simon returned to Hampstead Castle, passing by the Guardsmen now permanently posted outside the main gate. He wended idly, chatting with this servant and that, careful not to be too direct with his inquiries. Since he had been there almost daily for some time, and since he was known as a curious sort, his queries were answered readily enough. Cook, a woman almost as large and round as the oven she was taking bread from when he approached, cut off a slice of the hot, grainy stuff and smeared it with grease before handing it to him. It burned his fingers, but it tasted wonderful.

"Is Her Highness too busy to meet wi' you today, then, Master Simon?"

"She'll be back later, I believe," he told her, and saw a flash of sympathy in her eyes. The staff had concluded that Elizabeth was tired of his company because he was so often left apparently waiting for her. Simon hated being the object of their pity, even in the cause that they had agreed to. It brought on the old feelings of inadequacy so familiar because of his infirmity. He explained, "She went to visit Lord and Lady LaFont, to give her condolences."

"Ah," Cook nodded. "Very kind of her."

"I don't suppose you knew Alice very well, since she wasn't here that long."

Cook gave a look that spoke volumes. "It doesn't take long acquaintance to get the measure of one such as that."

"She was unkind to you, then?" Simon played innocent.

"Oh, she was always good enough to me." The woman cut herself a slice of bread and munched as she spoke. "But it was her own behavior got her killed, sure enough."

"And what do you know of her behavior?"

"I shouldn't speak ill of the dead," Cook reminded herself. "But that one fell backward a time or two or I'm mistaken." She wheezed out a chuckle. "And I'm not mistaken."

"How would you know something like that?" Simon had learned that a slight challenge often caused people to tell more to justify their information.

"Didn't she come right through my kitchen from time to time? Late at night, when she thought I'd be asleep, I suppose. The princess stays up all hours, so I often make her a light supper around midnight. She's too thin, that girl. It isn't healthy. But here Alice came, and when she sees me, she smiles and does so—" she put a finger to her lips "—and hands me a penny."

"Did you see her meet someone?"

"I did. Twict, for certes. It were a tall man, all wrapped up in a cape, so I couldn't see him well. When she slipped out the back, I saw 'im waiting for her." The round face smiled slyly. "And didn't she always have a new present the next morning. I can put two and two together as well as anyone. Once she mentioned him outright, said he was wondrous wise and book-learned. She admired them that could read, Alice did."

Simon recalled Alice's face as she told him that she would learn to read someday. "Not today," she had said, and now it was too late, forever.

"I should have told Sir George on her," Cook said, breaking into his thoughts, "but she was young, and shut up here with no society. I understood her wanting a bit of fun."

"And when she was killed, did you tell anyone then?"

Cook's plain face took on a look of shame.

172

"One who sees such things and doesn't tell can't very well own up to it later, now, can she? What would Sir George do if I admit now I let the girl carry on so and said nothing?"

The king had been correct. With familiarity and time, people revealed things that they'd hidden earlier. Henry, and Elizabeth as well, seemed to understand the workings of the human mind, to know when to press and when to wait.

Simon led the conversation into other areas so as not to create suspicion of his purpose, encouraging Cook to tell him of Elizabeth's likes and dislikes at table. After a time he wandered off, seemingly aimlessly, down to the lower floor. There he came upon Hannah, a maidservant, drawing water from the well and hurried to help her. Hannah was a beauty of about Simon's age, with brown waves of hair that defied taming and green eyes that left him speechless when she looked at him directly.

"Thank you, Master Maldon," the girl said as he took one of the filled buckets from her. Easily embarrassed in her presence, Simon was keenly aware that he could not take the second bucket because his crippled arm would not hold its weight. She made no comment but smiled to show she was grateful for his help.

"What are you about today?"

"I'm waiting for Her Highness to return."

"I believe she has returned," Hannah said. "She was writing a letter when I came past the solar a minute ago."

"Then I'll let her finish before I go up." Simon followed Hannah to the scullery, each leaning to one side to counter the weight of the buckets. "I was talking to Cook, and she mentioned that Alice had been meeting a man at night. Do you know anything of that?"

Hannah's pretty face clouded. At first it seemed she'd say nothing, but some decision was made. Setting her bucket down with such force that water sloshed unnoticed on her slipper, she faced Simon. "I do not, and if I did, sir, I don't care to gossip. It's hurtful and mean."

Simon was taken aback. Caught up in the process of gaining information, he'd offended this sweet girl whom he liked enormously. Hannah picked up her bucket, ashamed of her outburst, and they walked together toward the steps, she silent from indignation and he from the need to make a decision. Finally, he stopped at the foot of the staircase and set his own bucket down, facing Hannah.

"If I tell you something, will you keep it a secret?"

The girl was cautious, not sure where he was headed. "I suppose so."

He told her then of the investigation that he was making into Alice's death, explaining that his gathering of information was necessary to put together a picture of the killer. He didn't mention the other deaths, feeling that the king would not include Hannah in those who needed to know about them. He saw her face clear as she understood, and finally she smiled with relief. "I am glad to hear that you are not such a Prying Peter as you have seemed these last few days."

"And has everyone the same opinion of me?" Simon said, disgruntled.

"To be truthful, yes, but most don't mind it. It was only me who thought — well, and spending so much time with Her Highness and all." It was her turn to be embarrassed. She had judged him a hanger-on and a sensationalist, and now had discovered he was neither. At least Simon hoped that was the case.

Hannah now frowned with decision. "What you say puts another face on it," she mused. "I did wonder at a man who visited perhaps four times in the last few months.

He came when the princess was at Court once, another time around Easter, I believe, and yet again when she was gone to visit her sister. A fourth time he came early in the morning, and Her Highness was not yet awake. I only spoke to him once, when I happened to answer the door. Saying he knew the way, he brushed past me and went up the stairs. I never saw him leave, so I can't say how long the visit was. I had the feeling, though, that Her Highness never knew he was here."

"What did he look like?"

Hannah put a finger to her pretty lips as she brought the image to mind. "Tall, very good-looking, and quite charming. He dressed well, and seemed taken with his own appearance. He was fashionably dressed, with all the ribbons and velvets that are so popular with courtiers. Oh, and over it all he always wore the same cloak, dark in color and hung around the edge with tassels of gold."

CHAPTER SIXTEEN

Despite her request, Elizabeth was surprised when a litter arrived at Hampstead Castle the next day and Queen Catherine herself stepped out. Bess Blakewell nearly went into hysterics, poor Mary stumped around on her crutch trying to put the solar into better order, but Elizabeth simply went down to meet her stepmother.

Catherine Parr's matronly appearance belied her intelligence and moral character. With the chaos that Henry's marital, religious, and personal decisions had created in England, the climate for a staunchly Protestant sixth wife was perilous. Henry was disillusioned, spoiled, and wracked with pain when they married. Catherine had weathered storms over her religious views, her family, and Henry's children, creating for the king a calm center that he had needed his whole life long. In addition, she had taken all three children into her heart, seeing to their care as no one had done before her. It was typical that if Elizabeth asked to see her, she would come with dispatch.

"When your note arrived I was about to leave for Whitehall. I thought it not too much trouble to come by here, since you seemed anxious to talk." Catherine kissed her stepdaughter's cheek and stood back to take inventory. "You have grown an inch since Christmas, I declare. I told Henry so when you came the last time, and now I am sure of it."

Elizabeth kept her face a polite mask. It seemed adults always began conversations with comments on one's height. Taking her stepmother's hand she urged, "Please, come up to my sitting room. It's more comfortable there."

Catherine looked around with some distaste. "This place is little better than a barn. I must hurry the masons along so you may return to Hatfield."

"That would be most kind. Hatfield is my favorite of them all." Elizabeth had been shuffled pillar to post all her life without much care for her wishes. It was comforting that the queen took note of her situation, and she had no doubt that Catherine would do as she said. It would be nice to return to

Hatfield, still close to London, which Elizabeth loved, but more like a house than the fortress Hampstead had been during the time of William the Conqueror.

"Now, my dear, I am guessing that your request to see me has something to do with the death of Alice LaFont. I came here to help, but also to reassure myself that you are safe from whoever killed Alice. I do not doubt your confidence, nor do I believe your father would misjudge the situation. It will simply make me feel better to see for myself this place and its security."

Elizabeth felt the humorous disdain of an adolescent girl for the worried mother figure. "Surely the man would not come to this place a second time. The other murders were all in different locations."

"The other murders?"

Too late, Elizabeth realized that her stepmother did not know the whole of the affair. Briefly, she told her, after asking for her promise not to reveal to the king what she knew. Catherine seemed to sense immediately why the matter was so upsetting to Henry. No one knew better than she how he suffered: what man could recall without a qualm two women he had known intimately, one the mother of his child, being dragged to the block and beheaded? Surely they had cried out his name in fear, in pleading, and possibly in a curse at the last.

"Has your friend Simon learned something of the man?"

"Yes, as has Hugh Bellows of Father's Welsh Guard. Putting the information together, we hope to find a common thread. The killer may speak fluent Latin, and possibly gave both Alice and Joanna Brandon silver boxes as gifts. In one matter you can be of help. Alice was at Court, and something happened that caused her to be sent here. Do you know what it was?"

"I'm afraid I do. Alice's behavior with men was scandalous." Catherine's face took on a look of regret. "Truthfully, I don't think one can blame the girl. She had only her looks, no wit to speak of, and I remember her mother being much the same before marriage. For some women, there is only the capture of men as a goal in life." Her eyes twinkled as she settled herself more comfortably on the lumpy padding of the widow seat. "Having 'captured' three husbands, I would recommend something more to achieve true contentment. You, for instance, have too good a mind to be merely a decorative wife."

"I will never be that if I can help it." Elizabeth's tone must have revealed without her awareness how strongly she felt about the matter. Her stepmother's eyes widened in surprise, but how could one not resent marriage when it had led to her mother's death and her father's loss of reputation? Despite his strengths as a monarch, Henry would be forever remembered as the king with six wives. Elizabeth thought with a moment's dread that there could even be a seventh, if her father's councilors had their way. However, Henry seemed blind these days to anything but his own pain, physical and emotional.

"Alice flirted with any man who came in sight," Catherine said, unaware of her hostess' concern for her future. "Her detractors claimed she was willing to do more than that. Angry wives and sweethearts buzzed round my head until I had to dismiss the girl. The father came and asked very humbly, without excusing her behavior, that I find her another post until he could marry her off. Knowing your Kat's situation I sent her here, thinking she would be harmless in a household of so few men."

So LaFont had known more than he admitted. Elizabeth realized that she would not always get the truth just by asking. People would protect family secrets if they could.

"I gather she was not entirely so, madam," she responded, offering her stepmother a bowl of nuts that sat nearby. She also took a handful, and they munched as they continued. "Recently she seemed to have found a new interest. I wonder if it was an old one that resurfaced."

"Possible, I suppose," the queen answered. If it struck her as odd to be having this conversation with a princess of England barely in her teens, she kept it to herself. "I shall try to remember who complained about Alice, but I cannot say whether their concerns were real or not."

"That would be helpful, Your Majesty." She knew the queen would have preferred to be called Catherine, or even Mother, but she preserved the formalities, distancing herself from any ties the other terms might create.

"Let me see, there was the Countess of Hereford, Blanche. There was Lady Agnes Derwent. I believe Mary Blount complained about her son's being enthralled. And the most vehement was Patience, Lady Burford, raised in Oxfordshire and only recently come to Court. The woman's voice still jangles in my head."

"She feared that Alice would steal her husband?"

"Yes. When she first came to me, I judged her inexperienced in the ways of courtiers. There is, of course, much flirting and overblown praise." Catherine smiled ruefully. "At first I enjoyed being told how charming and lovely I am, but that wears off when one's heard the same phrases over and over."

Elizabeth thought privately that she would never tire of being told she was lovely and charming, but men seldom said such things to her, and, she chided herself, probably never would. Her friend Robin Dudley sometimes did, but only to practice on her so he could learn to lure older girls.

The queen rose briskly from the window seat. "Now I shall inspect the wall, the guards, and any other protection this Hugh Bellows has provided for you. I must satisfy myself that you are well cared for." Still cataloging the names in her head, Elizabeth rose to escort her stepmother around the castle.

After Catherine had approved of Hugh's methods and left in her litter, Simon appeared, his eyes wide. "Was that Her Majesty?"

Elizabeth enjoyed his awe. "I asked to see her, and she came straightaway. My latest stepmother is kind to all of us, and today she was informative as well." Briefly she told Simon what she'd learned.

"So now we must make our way through a list of possibilities." Simon took out the knife he had taken to carrying and sharpened a pen nib so Elizabeth could write down the names for him.

"It isn't as bad as it might seem. At this time of year many with estates have gone into the countryside to oversee the seeding. I'll wager some of those mentioned have been away since mid-April."

"And how do we find this out?"

"Hugh can find out from the clerks at Court. You will take this list and give him instructions."

Simon smiled to himself. He'd give orders to a captain of the king's guard? It was an odd trio they formed.

As Elizabeth wrote, he told her what he had heard from the cook. She looked pensively out the window. "If the man she met is tall, that would eliminate Hereford and Christopher Blount, who are under middle height. Derwent is quite tall, but I don't know this Burford. The queen said he has only recently come from the country. Oh, I wish I could go to Court and see them! How can we investigate if we cannot speak

184

to those who might know something? I dare not go uninvited again, though. My father would not abide another visit so soon."

Simon realized that Elizabeth was as taken with the quest as he was.

"Would the queen help by asking questions?"

Elizabeth sighed. "She would, but we have the same problem there that Hugh has. Anyone official makes the truth less likely rather than more. Who would admit to the queen that he was having an affair with a murdered woman?"

Simon was thoughtful. "And we must remember that just because a man had an . . . attachment to Joanna or Alice does not make him the murderer."

"You needn't tiptoe," Elizabeth interrupted crossly, tossing a cushion at him. "I am not the child everyone seems to take me for."

Simon understood her frustration, knew that she snapped at him because she could not speak so to her father. "All right then, a lover isn't necessarily a murderer. It's complicated, but we shall have to be undertakers. Is it possible that you might visit this Lady Derwent?"

"If I can think of an excuse. Sir George has no objection to my visits as long as Bess goes along."

The man had no choice, Simon reflected, what with the king's desires and his own guilty conscience influencing him. Bess, too, had made no objection to the princess' uninvited visits. She might know more about her husband's activities than she admitted. Should Sir George be their focus? Hugh didn't think so, though he could not dismiss the possibility of his guilt.

"I might have a way inside their households," Simon said, "as long as Mother never discovers what I am up to."

Elizabeth's eyes lit immediately. "It sounds like something I can't wait to hear." Simon told her his idea.

Patience Burford was passably pretty, with reddish brown hair and large brown eyes. Her soft, pouty lips contrasted with the paleness of her face in bright fullness, and she was used to being the prettiest girl, now wife, in the area. London had been a shock to her. Pretty, even beautiful, women abounded, and her first weeks at Court had been a nightmare of self-doubt. Lately she had calmed somewhat and begun to accept her new life.

Patience liked to work in her garden in the early morning, when the narrow street outside her rented home was fairly quiet and the air was cool. If they both liked London, her husband planned to buy the house, but that decision was yet to be made.

As she inspected the tiny plants one by one, Patience hummed a song she and Will were practicing to present at Court, a humorous ballad she thought very clever. Things had been better between them lately, and she was much relieved. When first they had come to Court, she had been shocked at the goings-on, and had feared for a while that she had lost her husband's affection. Lately, however, he had been more like himself, attentive and loving.

"Good morrow, madam," said a voice, and Patience looked up to see a young man standing outside the low wall. He was of middle height, dressed simply, with a plain face rescued from homeliness only by intelligent eyes that missed nothing and yet judged nothing. She should not be friendly to strangers, her husband admonished many times. But Patience was a country girl at heart and as such was used to speaking to everyone she met. She returned the greeting before she thought, and the answering smile assured her that the boy was no rogue. He set down a bag that clattered slightly with the sound of bottles and jars wrapped to protect them from breaking.

"I am Mark, son of the physician Biddle, with medicines in my bag for whatever might ail you or your household. I'd be glad to give free samples if you like."

"That's very kind, but I am seldom ill," she told him.

"Might your husband have need of something?"

"My husband has gone home to Oxford to oversee the planting. When he returns he may want something, for his muscles will ache from days in the saddle and hours spent bending over accounts."

"Has he been gone long?"

"Three weeks." Too late the young wife realized she had told a stranger that there was no man here to protect her. Fear flashed in her eyes: one heard such stories of London. "He will return any day, mayhap this very one."

The boy bowed and smiled sweetly, his long upper lip covering most of his teeth. "Then I shall return when he is present to see if I may be of help to him. Good day to you, milady. I hope your garden prospers."

That answered one question, Simon thought as he moved on.

CHAPTER SEVENTEEN

Flower Wilteby was not aptly named. There was no floral quality about her at all: no beauty, no frailty, and truth be told, no aroma that was at all pleasant. Whether for this reason or another, she was generally called Florrie. The old woman was tolerated in the Derwent household, despite her ugliness and her terrible breath, because of a skill that showed her employers in an excellent light: Florrie was a master brewer. Her beer was golden and full-bodied, her perry and cider flavorful and tart, and her mead far above what often passed for mead these days. Despite her lack of care for her own appearance, she was relentless in overseeing the malting, pressing, and squeezing required to make fine drink.

Florrie was a country woman who had developed her skills over years of trial and error, her long nose seeking out the smell of perfectly ripe pears, her strong fingers probing for weevils through the drying barley, and her bulging eyes watching critically as her assistants mixed the malt and the wheat meal. Florrie was indispensable to Lord and Lady Derwent, since it was their provision for the king's household that brought them to His Majesty's attention. First they had tempted Henry with Florrie's beer. Later they had sent along, with their compliments, several barrels of cider and perry, a cider-like drink made from pears, and finally, they had, at Easter, sent mead for celebrating of the end of Lent. The king, much impressed, had invited them to be presented at Court. It had cost her husband dearly, but Lady Derwent had her heart's desire.

Although she brought Florrie to London, Lady Derwent allowed His Majesty to believe that she herself was the genius behind these glorious libations. Florrie didn't mind that. What she did mind was being away from all that was familiar to her. The London house was squeezed in among others, no land around it at all. There were no drying sheds or presses or fields to oversee. Florrie had nothing to do all day but taste her own concoctions.

It was with some enthusiasm, then, that Florrie answered a knock at the kitchen door one day and found a young man with a bag over his shoulder.

"Good morrow. Would you be the lady of this house?"

Florrie smiled at his innocence and scratched absently at an insect bite on her neck. "No, young sir, I would not, but she won't see the likes of you no-how. Best be on your way with your bag."

"I heard the lady was in need of a physic and thought I might help. My father is an apothecary, and I sell his medicines door-to-door so that folk need not come to the shop for relief." He waited a beat and then added, "The first dose is free, of course, in order to assure that the medicine is effective."

Florrie thoughtfully rubbed a shoulder that had pained her of late. Seeing the gesture, the youth cleverly tailored his pitch. "Here I have a most helpful salve for aches. When rubbed onto a sore spot, it eases the sufferer's pain within minutes, and the joint moves more easily. Made with the finest ingredients, and my mother adds a bit of mint to make the salve smell pleasant." He waved a small, fragrant jar under Florrie's nose.

"There's no charge?"

"We are sure that you will buy our medicines once you have tried them."

"Then I shall try it myself and tell the lady of the house about it when she returns." Florrie thought herself clever, tricking the lad into a free dose of physic, but he seemed not to mind at all.

"Please, do try it."

Florrie fingered some salve out of the jar and applied it to her shoulder, pushing aside the loose-sleeved blouse she wore. The boy had not lied; her skin felt warm and, as she rubbed, the pain seemed to melt away. She kneaded the spot, rolling the shoulder and feeling its extended movement, and a smile came to her homely face. "I daresay it is a miracle!" she cried. "The arm has hurt for weeks."

"I am glad to have been of help. You will commend me to your lord and lady?"

"I will," Florrie replied. "Lady has trouble with a rheumy chest, and London's air has made it worse. She may want to see your wares, although she is still abed."

He replaced the cover on the jar of salve and returned it to the bag with a soft clink. "Shall I call tomorrow?"

Florrie considered. "Come just after midday, before she begins her visits. That's when she'll see you if she will at all." Bowing humbly, Simon thanked the old woman and went on his way, satisfied with the day's revelations.

The next day just before the time Florrie had mentioned, Simon again went round to the Derwents' back door, where the brewer let him in. To his slight dismay, she had two other servants with her who wanted free samples of medicine: one for a stye and the other for an infected toe. Ignoring the familiar tightness in his chest, Simon managed to calmly treat the afflictions. The toe, he suggested, should be seen by a physician, but the man refused with fearful eyes. Simon gave him some drawing salve and hoped it was enough.

When he had finished, the brewer coached him in slushy tones before taking him to see her mistress. "She is a proud one," Florrie said, "and sometimes she can be difficult. You must not speak unless she asks a question, and then only as much as you need to answer."

Simon understood, having met this type of petty noble before. At the bottom of the pecking order in their own circle, they maximized their power over those below them in rank. Pressing his lips together, he followed Florrie to a small dressing room. Servants came and went behind a screen in great agitation, but it was almost an hour before the lady herself entered, wrapped in an embroidered robe. Evidently he was to be interviewed as she dressed for the day.

Agnes Derwent was tiny and well proportioned, but there was little else to recommend her. Her face called to mind an axe, and the eyes looked in two different directions. Simon found it impossible to decide which one was looking at him. After surveying him appraisingly, Lady Agnes stepped behind the screen's panels without a word. Thereafter Simon tried to look elsewhere and ignore what was happening, but he heard the occasional slap as a maid displeased somehow and sensed that from time to time the lady peeped out at him around the edge.

"You must speak up, for I am preparing for Court." This process, requiring several hours, Simon perceived only minimally. Two maidservants had begun early that morning achieving fashion's look of the season for their mistress. Agnes stepped behind the screen and removed her robe. As she stood in only a muslin shift, the maids went to work putting together all they had prepared. "It is my third visit since coming to London," she told the unseen Simon in a smug, strident voice. "His Majesty is much impressed with our Derwent brews."

"I am pleased that London agrees with you, Lady."

"There are things I could criticize," Agnes Derwent said petulantly as stockings of silk were pulled on and tied below her knees with garters. "One of the maids has run off, and I can find no suitable replacement." A soft voice mumbled an apology after a sharp slap.

"Florrie tells me you sell medicines?" This came as the maid tied on a "pair of bodies," a corset shaped to the desired figure.

"Yes, m'ady. Of all kinds."

"Quality?"

"Yes, ma'am. My father is a prosperous apothecary."

Around the nipped waist was tied a verdingal, also known as a farthingale, a cone-shaped hoop that fastened to the corset and flared several petticoats that fell over it. Today Lady Derwent had chosen to add a bumroll, a padded crescent that flared her skirts even more at the back.

"Then why hawk your physic like a bawdy-basket to my servants?" The tone was sneering, the insult implied.

Simon flushed. A bawdy-basket was a thief who gained entrance to a home by bringing trinkets that would attract the servants, chatting them up until they were at ease. Eventually he returned and robbed the house. "Father finds that some people of quality —" Simon emphasized that word — "do not want their business known to unfamiliar servants and shop customers. They prefer a private meeting, where they can be honest about their needs."

As Agnes Derwent considered Simon's argument, she was helped into a kirtle, a fitted, decorative underskirt. Sleeves that laced into her gown matched this kirtle. "It is vexing to be away from home, where one does not know where to find needful things," she pouted. "And the miasmas of London are most upsetting to my health." Peering around the screen, she eyed Simon critically. "How would I know you are not a rogue?"

The maids waited until she was still again, then added a portlet, a garment like a shirt with a ruffled neckline that would show over the low-cut top of her outer gown. This last was Paris-made and elegant, laced up the front and with stiff rolls at the shoulder.

"You might try our medicines with no charge, my lady. If you are satisfied, I will return with more."

A trained and especially talented maidservant now readied neck and wrist ruffs, starched and ironed into shape and kept in a bandbox until the last moment. When they were in place, jewels were added to decorate the whole costume: a choker of pearls, a pendant of gold and garnet, and ruby and pearl earrings. The maid held up a small mirror and the lady craned her neck to consider herself from different angles.

Ready for the final stages of her preparation, Lady Agnes swept out from behind the screen. It was difficult now to tell what her natural shape was. The blue brocade dress looked more like armor than fabric. Everything about her was overstated, giving the effect of a woman's head set atop some otherworldly manikin's body.

The lady's hair had earlier been arranged into large curls by yet another maidservant. False hair was braided into her own and then "sewn" in and out with a ribbon that held the whole mass in place. Now the harassed maid thrust several small bodkins, tiny swords tipped with pearl, in among the curls. A tall hat of brocade that matched the dress was added, held in place with an enameled hatpin. Two feathers sprouted from it like the horns of a goat.

She returned her attention to Simon. "You could poison me. How would I prevent that?"

Sudden inspiration worked to his purpose. "There are those who will speak for my honesty. For example, I have given physic to Alice LaFont."

"Alice LaFont?" Agnes stepped toward Simon indignantly and gave him an angry push. "You do not choose well, young man, for I would sooner speak to the devil himself than that woman."

Simon tried to appear apologetic. "I only meant that she is of quality and knows my reputation."

"Reputation! The woman has no idea of reputation. She is more interested in —" But she recovered herself, not about to air her grievances before a street peddler.

"I am sorry to have offended you," Simon said, bowing his head. "It is just that I met the Lady Alice at the Princess Elizabeth's, and I thought —"

"You deal with the princess?" Her sharp nose came up smartly.

"Not with the princess herself, who is in very good health and requires no medicines, but those in her household have used them to good effect." It wasn't really a lie, considering Mary Ward's treatment and recovery.

The lady considered. "I must admit you are an honest young man. You may leave me something for my cough, but mind, nothing that will put me to sleep." Everyone in London had a cough: smoky, damp homes and streets choked with dozens of irritants played havoc with the lungs.

"Very well, my lady." She was countrified indeed to accept only his word that he knew Elizabeth. He might still be a rogue, as she had feared until he mentioned a royal name. Handing a small phial to the nearest maidservant, he turned to go.

"Wait." Lady Agnes snapped her fingers and all four maids scurried out of the room, trailing unused ribbons and rejected jewelry. There was silence until they were well away, and the lady once again studied Simon, although with which eye he could not discern. Agnes stood perfectly still, apparently working up her courage. She did not sit in order to give the least possible damage to her costume. Beside her on a stool a servant had left her safeguard, a long, protective overskirt and cap to shield her ensemble from damage on the way to St. James. Fingering the dark fabric, she finally made her decision.

"Boy, do you have in your bag a philtre?" Her face turned red as she said it, but she kept her eccentric gaze on him, chin held high.

Simon knew his father's opinion of those

who sold such things: the lowest sort of tricksters. Still, there was something desperate in the woman's mien. Her gaze held his, pleading, although all her pride fought against asking. "I have nothing with me today," he responded, "but I will see what I can do." She gave him a tight-lipped grimace that might have been a smile, and he left the room, wondering what Lady Derwent wanted with a love potion.

CHAPTER EIGHTEEN

Elizabeth found Blakewell in his cramped office, studying a page of figures. "Are we overspending again, Sir George?" she asked lightly, knowing that no amount of money was considered well spent on her care.

"We shall manage," the old knight replied, attempting a smile. His eyes would not meet Elizabeth's, and she felt a pang of guilt for the man's pain. He could lose his post and his reputation if word of his affairs reached the king. Still, he was not a bad man, merely weak, and she had seen the folly of men chasing after the favors of women often enough. He pushed the paper away and set down his pen with a heavy sigh. "Every time Ninian visits, things seem worse. My humors are much unbalanced."

"Master Maldon could bleed you. He seems a competent doctor."

"My wife prepares a physic for me, which I drink with my beer in the evening,"

Blakewell answered, "but I thank you for the thought."

"I would like to visit an old friend this afternoon: Lady Derwent. Would you arrange it?"

Blakewell's remarkable eyebrows met in a frown. "Twice in one week to go visiting, Highness? Is there something I should know?"

Elizabeth said smoothly, "I believe it is the spring weather finally chasing the chill from the air that makes me long for company."

Sir George looked closely at the girl, well aware that she could prevaricate when it suited her ends. Still, she was of teen years, and he knew that marked changes came when children reached that age. She was not saucy or sulky, although Bess confided that her temper, when roused, was terrible to witness. He missed Kat, who took complete responsibility both for the princess' safety and her social life.

"Very well, if my wife will accompany you, I will see to the transport."

When they arrived before a fine example of a town house located in the fashionable area close to St. James, Bess sent a litter bearer to inquire if Lady Derwent might be at home. Elizabeth had been quiet as the litter jounced along, trying to form a convincing reason for her visit. She tapped a finger absently on her teeth as they waited. Knowing anything at all about these people might have given her a better idea for an approach. All Hugh had learned was that the Derwent lands were in the north, and that the inhabitants were an ancient, though not particularly distinguished, family.

The servant returned to report that Lady Derwent was not at home. As he explained, Elizabeth's face broke into a smile. The lady was visiting Princess Mary, who was at the home of a friend, Rosalind de Marcia. "Well, then," Elizabeth told Bess as the litter swayed upward, "we may accomplish our visit and another at the same time."

It was not difficult to find the de Marcia home. Rosalind Beaumont had married a Spanish count, Phillip de Marcia, sent to England originally to dissuade Henry from divorcing the Spanish princess Catharina d'Aragon. Because de Marcia failed, and because he had fallen in love with the beautiful Rosalind, he stayed in England. Wisely he kept quiet about his Catholicism, and his wealth combined with Rosalind's allowed them entry into homes of all but the most vehemently Protestant families.

Elizabeth had met Rosalind a few times and was sure she would welcome Mary's younger sister, being as famous for warmth as for beauty.

In a matter of half an hour, Elizabeth and Bess were shepherded into a small room designed for comfort. The walls were paneled in dark wood, and heavy velvet curtains that framed the windows had been thrown back to let in the delicate spring sunlight. Carpets of fine wool covered the floor, and the arras on the north wall depicted scenes in the history of the Beaumont family. Some of the decorations showed a Spanish flair: heavy sconces with fat candles lined the walls, and a portrait on the east wall showed a gentleman garbed in the somber black clothing and stern expression that it seemed all Spaniards insisted upon. The artist had dutifully painted each vein in the man's pale hand, clearly displaying the "blue blood" that separated the nobility from the rest of the world, at least in their own minds.

Like the figure in the portrait, Princess Mary wore black. Her eyes widened in surprise when Elizabeth was announced, but she did not rise, as the others did. Taking in her sister's appearance, Elizabeth reflected that Mary fared no better than she herself. Her dress was of another time, probably her mother's, and had been taken in to fit her thin frame. Many years Elizabeth's senior, Mary was a woman of cold passion. Her eyes seemed to burn, and her pale face had the look of the martyrs portrayed in stained-glass windows. There was about the elder princess an air of repressed hysteria that Elizabeth always found unnerving. She had never seen Mary lose her composure, but the possibility always seemed imminent.

Years of living in poverty and being ignored had told on them both, but Mary's mother had insisted until her death that she was the only queen of England, that Mary should be the heir, and that England must be returned to the True Church as soon as the opportunity arose. Catherine had made her daughter into a fanatic, a type Elizabeth secretly despised. Still, Mary was her sister and kind in her odd way. They shared the triple shame of the king's rejected children: they were unwanted, born of unmourned past queens, and female besides.

The other women in the room looked up curiously as Elizabeth and Bess entered. Rosalind de Marcia rose and came to greet them with a friendly smile. She grasped Elizabeth's hands in hers warmly. "Why, Your Highness, what a pleasant surprise."

Mary's lips bent in what for her passed as a smile. "Good day, Elizabeth. It is wonderful to see you." Elizabeth thought that if ever words and facial expression said two opposite things, it was now.

"Sister," she murmured. "When I heard you were in the city, I had to come. It is so seldom that circumstances permit us to be together. How go things with you?"

As Mary murmured something appropriate, Bess, at her right, took breath to say something, but Elizabeth shot her a glance and she did not. Turning to the other three ladies in the room, Elizabeth said to Mary's companion, "Lucretia I know of course. How are you, my dear? I have not, I think, met these ladies."

Lady de Marcia introduced her daughter Isabella, a girl of about Elizabeth's age who had her father's dark eyes and hair. She eyed her guests as they were introduced, curtseyed briefly, then grinned at Elizabeth, who sensed mischief in the girl and liked her immediately.

"And this is Lady Agnes Derwent, a friend from Lancashire who has come to visit before London becomes too hot for all of us."

Elizabeth took in the overdressed, self-consciously dignified Lady Agnes, formed her own opinion, and kept it carefully hidden. "Lady, it is a pleasure to meet you." At her side, Bess made a sound distinctly like "Humph!" but Elizabeth ignored her. "I believe we have an acquaintance in common: Alice LaFont."

There was a silence as the lady considered what she might possibly say. Mary made a tense movement as if to alert Elizabeth to her gaffe, and her frown deepened even more. Finally, Agnes squeaked, "I have heard of the lady you mention, Your Highness."

"Sadly, Alice is dead," Elizabeth went on innocently. "She was murdered in my garden last week."

Mary gasped, although how she did it without opening her lips was hard to tell. "Elizabeth! You should not speak of such things."

"It is true. Poor Alice. There might have been a lover, you see."

"Elizabeth!" Now Mary was shocked beyond words. "You may not come into the home of my friend and make such inappropriate conversation. I must ask you to leave the subject. Murder, indeed!"

"I am sorry to have caused you distress, sister." Elizabeth could tell that at least two others in the room were dying to hear the details, but she meekly changed the subject to plans for the king's birthday celebration in June. They chatted amiably of trivial things for the next hour, Elizabeth enjoying the others' ill-disguised curiosity as to the purpose of her visit. Finally, Lady Derwent rose stiffly, her extravagant costume almost creaking with the movement, and excused herself, saying that she must return to oversee the dinner she was giving that evening for her husband's aunt and uncle. Bess walked out with her, claiming she needed to speak to their escort.

As soon as they had gone, Isabella de Marcia said, "Mother, may I show the Princess Elizabeth our garden? It is beautiful at this hour of the day." Rosalind correctly surmised that her daughter wanted to be removed from the restricting presence of adults.

"We shall play cards later, so you must not be long if you want to be included."

Isabella led the way out a small side door onto a terraced garden that made the most of the small space it occupied. Elizabeth was relieved to be gone from the room. Mary always cheated at cards, and it was embarrassing to watch, especially when strangers were present. Her usual companions were resigned to it.

An added benefit was the beauty of the de Marcia gardens. Cleverly placed hedges served as dividers so that each section was all but invisible until one was in it. Often the fragrance of the next preceded the sight of it, and Elizabeth was reminded of the scents of Hampton Court. The luscious gardens of the wealthy, tended by servants, often imitated the king's in miniature. Here each section was laid out differently and planted with interesting specimens, which the girls ignored as they became acquainted. Now that they were outside and away from her mother and the forbidding Mary, the bubbling good humor that Elizabeth had suspected in Isabella showed itself, and the girl asked more questions than she could find time to answer. What was it like being a princess, did she have any offers of marriage, could she eat whenever she liked, did she have to go to bed when told to, did they really have servants who dressed them each day, and so on. Elizabeth disillusioned her gently, explaining that she was not a typical princess.

"Oh, I know, your mother being the —" she stopped, but Elizabeth knew the rest: the Great Whore. "— being dead," she finished lamely. Anne was especially hated by England's secret Catholics, which Elizabeth suspected Isabella's family was. She said nothing, as she usually did when her mother was mentioned.

The girl stopped briefly to clear a pebble from her slipper, leaning without conscious thought on Elizabeth's shoulder as she did. "A woman was murdered at your home?"

"Yes, Alice LaFont."

"Alice, yes. They spoke of her before you came."

"Really?"

"Yes. I was not in the room, but sometimes I, um, overhear what the grown-ups are saying."

"Yes, it is interesting to, um, overhear." Elizabeth grinned in admission that she had done the same thing.

"Mother was saying that she thought this Alice was harmless, but Lady Derwent was not so sure. She wouldn't say why, but she insisted that Alice was a slut. That was the word she used." Isabella seemed to enjoy reporting the lady's calling Alice low-born.

"Hmm. I wonder what her husband is like."

"I've seen him. He's always smiling, and he's handsome for an older man." The girl considered for a moment. "I don't like him, though. He always calls me the little Spaniard and pats my head as if I were a lap dog."

"A lap dog, eh?" Elizabeth teased. "Are you certain he doesn't call you the little spaniel?"

"I wager you are right. When next you see me I'll be wearing a jeweled collar and yipping at you." They laughed together.

This is what it is like to have friends. She and Simon laughed and teased each other, and Robin too, but she had never had a female companion who was lively and friendly, as this girl was. Such friendship was intriguing, better even at her present age than Kat's loving care. Neither Simon nor Isabella was paid or obligated to spend time with her. It was pleasant to be with a person one's own age, to compare thoughts and dreams, to laugh in the sun-warmed garden without a reason, to feel like a thirteen-year-old and nothing else.

When the girls returned to the adults, they were absorbed with gossip and card-playing, their voices and faces low around the table. Mary was just finishing a story that had the others *tsk*-ing and bemoaning the ways of modern society. "There were several good pieces of jewelry and some silver ornaments in a set of nesting boxes that my mother cherished. It has been several months, so I have given up any hope of its being located."

Rosalind remarked, picking up a trey and

rejecting it without pause, "Imagine an entire casket going missing. The occasional servant has filched an item here and there, but the nerve it must take to walk away with a box the size of a loaf of bread."

Isabella glanced at Elizabeth, who shrugged. They knew enough not to ask for an explanation, but both wished they had heard the entire account. It seemed the Princess Mary had discovered the theft of a box of jewelry that had belonged to her mother. Elizabeth resolved to ask her sister more about it when she could find a private moment.

CHAPTER NINETEEN

On the way home a fitful rain began. The wind picked up, and Elizabeth and Bess pulled their hoods about their faces, for the waxed cover of the litter did not provide total protection. They passed through noisy crowds of people who ignored the rain almost completely, the babble only occasionally breaking into recognizable words. After a while Bess looked at Elizabeth smugly. "I've something to tell you, Highness." Her round eyes sparkled slyly. "I'm not so blind I can't see what you're up to."

"I don't know what you mean." Elizabeth felt her face flushing.

"I mean, we didn't go to that house to visit your sister. You said we were going to visit your friend Lady Derwent, but it turns out you've never met the woman before. What were you thinking? We could have been turned away, and what an embarrassment that would have been."

"Well, I do know Lady de Marcia, and I knew she wouldn't refuse me entry," Elizabeth admitted. "I wanted to meet Lady Derwent because she knew Alice."

"To discover why Alice was killed, am I right?"

"Yes."

"My dear, we all are interested, but one cannot go about inventing reasons to visit people just to pry into their affairs. With the LaFonts, it was acceptable to visit and pay condolences for a lady of your household, but this Lady Derwent, why should she tell you anything of her private affairs?"

"It's true I hoped to learn more about Alice from her. It was silly, I suppose."

Bess still wore that smug smile, and she touched Elizabeth's hand conspiratorially. "What it really takes is a bit of woman-to-woman confidence."

Elizabeth's eyes widened. "You mean, when you left the room with her . . . ?"

Nodding, Bess let the words tumble out. "I walked down with her, pretending I had to speak to Peter. On the stairs I apologized for your behavior — oh, hush, now, it worked, didn't it?" She forestalled Elizabeth's objection.

"I said I could see that the mention of Alice's name had upset her, and that I understood, since the girl had thrown herself at my husband's head from her first day at Hampstead. That's God's own truth, I can tell you. She told me everything then, standing at the foot of the stairs. Once she began, she couldn't seem to stop.

"Her husband is a mouse-hunt and she's always known it, but with Alice, she's sure it was worse. The girl was not discreet but hinted broadly at who her lover was when Lady Derwent was nearby, which was an embarrassment. Not that men do not have their little affairs, but it is not wise to treat with such discourtesy a lady of the Court. When another woman, Lady Burford, complained to the queen of Alice's behavior, Lady Derwent and others added their urgings, and Alice was sent away."

"To us, where she was murdered."

"Now, Your Highness, you may pass on this information to that captain when he next visits, but then I think you must put an end to this questioning. It is not seemly for a Princess Royal to delve into the sordid affairs of faithless men and women of easy virtue."

Elizabeth sat back in the chair, watching her escort sidestep a deep puddle as they turned north onto the road to Hampstead. She wondered if Bess knew of her own husband's dealings with Alice. Was she trying to stop them from discovering what they already knew? Or was she merely making judgments based on her rather limited view of societal do's and don'ts? Either way, Elizabeth had no intention of stopping. She had never felt so worthwhile. Putting on an imperious expression, she sat upright in the seat. "Lady Blakewell, my father the king has given permission for this investigation. In fact, he ordered it. I shall ask questions where I like."

Bess made no answer, although her eyebrows raised and her nostrils pinched. Elizabeth sat back, admitting only to herself that Henry had made no inclusion of her in his orders to Hugh and Simon, in fact had pointedly stated that she should keep out of the matter completely.

Simon returned to Winchester to speak to Daisy that afternoon. She was less friendly this time, demanding, "What are you doing back here?" upon opening the door.

"I want to discover who killed my aunt, so I spoke to a few people." The woman's face showed understanding. Revenge was often the responsibility of family members among her kind, and a boy might take on a man's role to achieve it. She opened the door and admitted him. The room was no less cluttered than before, and today it smelled strongly of leek soup.

"What do you want of me?"

"A boy on the street described two men he'd seen with Therese in the days just before she died." Watching Daisy carefully, Simon described Sir George, but Daisy did not remember him. Nor had she noticed a man in a tasseled cape.

" 'Course, I didn't see most men Therese went with." Daisy twirled a finger in her hair absently. "We often accompanied gentlemen to places of their choosing, but I won't do that no more. Adam keeps nearby, and I don't leave Winchester."

As Simon glanced around the room, his eye lighted on a small silver box. He had noticed it almost unconsciously before, but Elizabeth's description had stayed in the back of his mind. Like Alice's gift from her admirer, this one was an odd shape and was finely filigreed.

He pointed to the item. "Is it real silver?"

"It belonged to my grandmother."

The answer came so quickly that Simon knew it was a lie. The box had belonged to Therese. Daisy still clearly feared that this "nephew" might claim the dead woman's things.

Simon tried to reassure her. "I only want to help the constables catch the man who killed my aunt if I can."

"Oh, he's long gone, Adam says, 'cause no one's bothered us other girls." Not here, Simon thought. How small was her world. Anything that happened outside Winchester was foreign to Daisy. If she knew of Mathilda Harrison's death, would it frighten her or would she be relieved that it happened across the river, which to her was far away?

Leaving Daisy's house, he stopped at places likely to notice or cater to strangers in the area: a tiny grog shop, a nearly deaf woman selling flowers on the corner, and a man with a half-starved horse hitched to a wagon. No one remembered anything particular about the night of the murder. The woman said she once sold chestnuts, her winter trade, to a gentleman in a tasseled cape, but she had no idea when. What she remembered was the cape itself.

" 'Twas a cold day, y'see," she shouted at Simon, apparently assuming that he was as deaf as she. "The cape was beautifully made and looked warm enow for such an outing. Someone spent a deal o' time on it, I'd say."

"Can you describe it?"

"Let's see. Dark blue, almost black. Lots

of tassels down the front of each side and around the bottom. Two more hung from cords that tied at the neck. I remember thinking that the bottom ones would suffer from being dragged through the slush."

"Thank you." Simon moved off. The garment was distinctive; it shouldn't be impossible to find its owner. It would prove nothing, but it was a start. He would ask at Hampstead if anyone knew of such a cape.

Elizabeth was at that moment being reprimanded, ever so carefully, by one of her least favorite people, Ninian. The king's agent found her in the garden, and in his oily way gave a greeting completely correct and yet vaguely annoying. She noted the odor of incense about him, as if he had come directly from chapel. Ninian had been sent, he said, to caution the princess about recent visits to families of the Court.

"They are odd visits," Ninian said, folding his large hands in a parody of meekness. "Those you visited are puzzled by your interest and wonder if the king sent you. In view of the recent tragedy, your royal father prefers that you remain at home."

Elizabeth listened patiently as the man danced around the point in his attempt to give orders without offending. She was not surprised that her father knew her every move, but it was galling to be lectured by this petty civil servant about the requirements of her position. Why couldn't Father have worried about her safety, as the queen did? No, it was all duty and appearances with him. Knowing that Henry had a sense for what the people expected from royalty, she had to respect his judgment if not his choice of messenger. Swallowing her anger, Elizabeth promised she would make no further "odd visits."

"I shall tell His Highness that he need not concern himself further with the matter," Ninian intoned. "Your Grace is most wise, both in filial duty and in royal understanding."

He would have kissed her hand had she offered it, but Elizabeth did not. The man fairly oozed flattery, which is how he had achieved the post in the first place. One of Cranmer's lesser clergymen, he had risen, as others had, by proving to be both an able man with figures and one willing to toady to those above him. That did not make him likeable, thought the Princess Royal as she turned her back and renewed her efforts at pulling the weeds from a bed of dianthus.

Simon returned to the castle tired from the

long walk but anxious to ask about the tasseled cloak. He began with Mary Ward, she being the friendliest member of the household and talkative as well. Her leg was healing well, and she had begun moving about the place more freely, although the stairs were still a trial for her. She was mending in the hall, and had a stocking pulled over a darning egg, a wooden ball that stretched it tight so that holes could be repaired with needle and thread. Two piles lay on either side of her chair, those finished and those yet to be repaired. She looked up and smiled at Simon.

"Look at you, all warm and damp. Come, sit and cool off here away from the window." It was true the sun had warmed the room, but the stone inner wall was refreshingly cool. Hampstead had its moments. He sat and watched Mary's deft movements, which brought a relaxed feeling that he often felt as homely tasks were performed. Something about them signaled peace and contentment, despite recent events that spoke otherwise.

"I spoke to someone who saw a man outside the wall on the night Alice was murdered," he lied.

"Now, Master Simon, you mustn't dwell on it so. It was an awful thing, but there's naught we can do about it."

"This person wore an unusual cloak. It was deep blue and had gold tassels hung around the edges. Do you know such a cloak?"

"Well, there, you see, there's no sense fussing about that. The cloak belongs to our own Sir George, and he was out checking the doors, I'll be bound. After all, it's his job to see that the place is secure."

"But it wasn't secure that night. The garden gate was left open."

Mary frowned and put her darning in her lap for a moment. "I don't believe it was left open. I'd say it was closed as usual, and Alice herself opened it for her lover." So she knew Alice had had a male caller. "Poor thing, how could she know that a madman would sneak in and kill her because of it? I suppose the lover is afraid to speak out for fear of being blamed."

"And why is he himself not the murderer?"

"My boy, he came here several times, according to gossip I heard. Why would he wait all that time and then kill her?" She touched his arm in assurance. "It was some lunatic, who saw poor Alice as she returned from her tryst and took his chance."

Simon said nothing. Mary didn't know all the facts, didn't know about the other deaths, and had made up her mind anyway. It was not his intention to argue. He had learned what he needed to know.

Chapter Twenty

The next stop Simon made was at the Blakewells' quarters, taking some time in between to come up with a plausible story. Hampstead castle, begun as a fortress in the days of the Conqueror, had expanded, as most castles had over time. The need for the security of thick walls had lessened as London sprawled beyond its old fortifications, absorbing neighboring areas that maintained some of their rural aspects but were for all practical purposes part of the city. Defensibility had given way slightly to comfort in later additions to Hampstead.

Off the east side a wing extended that was modern in style, with less stone and more timber. Real windows stood open to the sunlight, cheering the grim atmosphere somewhat. The second floor of this wing provided private quarters for the princess and her ladies as well as an apartment for the Blakewells. When Bess ushered Simon into her tiny sitting room, he was struck by its hominess. The furnishings were well made and hand-rubbed with lemon oil. The room was arrayed in every possible space with handmade dolls, Bess' creations. Many of them were infants, each perfect, each smiling peacefully.

Time had made Bess less distrustful of Simon, and she looked at him now with affection. "What is it you're about today, Master Maldon?"

Simon had his story prepared. "I spoke with Mary Ward, who tells me that Sir George has a blue cloak that is very finely made."

Bess glowed with pride. "She is very kind to say so. Though I made it myself, I still say it is good work." She added modestly, "Sometimes a garment goes together almost of its own accord."

"May I see it? My mother has promised to make me one for my birthday, and I'm to choose the trimming. Mary says Sir George's is unique."

It seemed for a moment that Bess would say something, comment that a physician's son should not be aping his betters. But innate kindness squelched whatever it was, and she led Simon down the hallway. "He leaves it on a peg by the entry and wears his old brown one for every day."

They reached the door and the small alcove beside it where several outer garments hung, some over others. The smell of wet wool predominated, with lesser odors of sweat and faint perfume under it. Bess rummaged through until she found the blue cloak and pulled it out. "There we are, but look. He's got it dirty and never said a word about it. Men! Such carelessness!"

She brushed at the bottom of the cloak, where the tassels had obviously been wet and now hung disarrayed and caked with mud. "I shall speak with him about this," she murmured, but there was no real anger, just irritation at her husband's thoughtlessness.

"When do you think he wore it last?"

"As I said, he does not wear it for every day. When he goes to Court, of course. I couldn't say when I saw it most recently." She looked rueful. "Truly, I believe it is too heavy and restricts his movement. Tell your mother to choose her goods carefully."

Simon had to pause a moment to remember his lie. This spy business did not come naturally to him yet. "Oh. Certainly I will. And I give you thanks for your pains, my lady. It is indeed a fine cloak."

"Perhaps she might come herself and see

it before she begins."

"It is most kind of you to suggest it."

Simon was standing close to the castle's large wooden door, which at that moment flew open with great force, almost whacking him in the back. He felt the rush of its passage behind him, quickly followed by the door's slamming against the wall with a crash. In the doorway stood Sir George, red-faced and panting with exertion. He held a sword in one beefy hand, its entire hilt covered by sausage-like fingers. His other arm was stretched outright, where he grasped the collar of a sullen-looking man.

"Boy, for once you are a welcome sight. Run and fetch Hugh Bellows. Tell him I have captured his murderer for him. I shall keep the fellow here until you return." With that he shoved his captive across the threshold. The man looked for a moment as if he might turn and fight, but the sword raised to his chest stopped him. "Down those stairs and into the larder with you. Bess, have you the key?"

"Y-yes," her response was full of unasked questions.

"Follow and lock this fellow in. If he eats some of our provisions, we must accept it, for we have no other stout room with a lock to keep him in. Boy, are you still here? Go!

Tell Bellows to bring soldiers. I want this man gone from my charge as soon as possible."

Despite his questions and his earlier weariness, Simon took off at a run. The sooner he found Hugh, the sooner he would learn why Blakewell believed he had found the killer.

Two hours later Simon sat quietly in a corner, hoping Sir George would not notice and send him out. Hugh had returned with him, bringing Calkin and the same soldier as before, who Simon learned was named Gooderich. The two stood guard at the larder while Hugh spoke with Sir George.

The old knight was anxious to tell his story. Not a man of pretty speeches, he nevertheless made himself clear in a slightly pompous style. Rubbing the hilt of his sword absently he told Hugh, "It is my duty to be vigilant, and I noticed the fellow some time ago, always surly and ill kept."

That was an understatement. The glimpse Simon had gotten revealed a figure positively filthy. Over medium height, the man had brown hair that showed no sign of comb or cutting, clothing that actually revealed layers of stains and dirt, and tattered boots cut open to accommodate feet too big for them. The look of him conveyed repressed anger that signaled violence.

"The varlet seemed to appear every few days and hang about the gate," Blakewell continued. "At first I thought he was looking for alms, which is not likely from anyone here. After Alice's murder, though, I paid him more attention. With a bit of investigation I found where he has made himself a home, so to speak, in the graveyard." He paused to show he thought that significant, but when Hugh said nothing, he went on. "The fellow rants to anyone who will listen that a witch lives in Hampstead Castle."

"A witch?"

Sir George lowered his voice. "Some say that the late Anne Boleyn practiced the black arts."

Hugh shot a glance at Simon but returned quickly to Blakewell. "Why do you believe this man killed Alice?"

"Found him on the grounds this very day," the knight stated positively. He stood, scraping his stool backward, and pantomimed his story as he told it. "I came out of the gatehouse and saw a glimmer of movement in the garden, someone trying to stay out of sight. I went on and then doubled back, surprising the knave so that he almost fainted. After that, the fellow gave me little trouble." The old knight was proud that he could still prevail in a physical confrontation.

Hugh put a hand on the other's shoulder in congratulation. "Sir George, you may well have prevented harm to the Princess Elizabeth. The king will hear of this, and His Majesty is unfailingly grateful to those who perform such services to the Crown."

"I do my job, sir. It is no more than I owe my sovereign."

"I will transport the prisoner to a secure holding, with your permission." Hugh rose to his feet.

"By all means, Captain." Blakewell handed Hugh a ring on which the key to the storeroom hung.

Within minutes, the bedraggled prisoner was shackled and brought into the courtyard. Hugh spoke briefly to Simon as Blakewell assured that Calkin and Gooderich had done their job well. "Meet me at Newgate Prison if you want to hear the man's story."

Simon was filled with curiosity about the unknown man, and Hugh evidently understood. Weariness gone, he started for Newgate immediately, stopping to tell his mother he would miss supper. The corners of her mouth turned down in disapproval, and she tried tempting her son in a wheedling tone.

"But I've baked a nice joint and made a pudding."

"I will eat when I return, Mother."

The bane of Mary Maldon's existence was disorder. She liked things to happen at a particular time and with predictable results. Her husband's occupation, though a source of pride, was also the primary disrupter of her carefully laid schedule of domestic events. Now Simon was, willfully it seemed to her, making things worse, running off after his precious Captain Bellows.

"Difficult enough to keep a reasonable time for meals with your father rushing off to this house and that caring for folk. Do they not realize you are a growing lad who needs food?"

Simon played his trump card. "It is the king's business."

"King or not, he has no right interfering in the running of my house," Mary complained. "You'll have cold mutton and bread-heels, young man, and eat it gladly."

"Yes, Mother." He was relieved to hear the tone of resignation in her voice. He left the house quickly before she could find something else to chastise him for.

Simon reached Newgate shortly after the soldiers had locked their captive in a cell.

The prison sprawled over a large area with no planning apparent in its design, and Simon lost some minutes wandering through several unpleasant, stinking corridors, asking this person and that where Captain Bellows might be. Finally, he spotted Hugh, who might even have been waiting for him, though he made no indication of it. They went on together, Hugh again warning Simon to stay quietly in the background.

The prisoner hunched in a corner of a foul-smelling cell, which was empty except for a bench built into the wall that served as chair, bed, and table. The corners were dark. Most of the stench emanated from the one opposite the man's chosen spot. Calkin closed the door after the two of them and locked it, a sound that made Simon's shoulders twitch. What would it be like to be locked away, forgotten by those who held the keys?

Hugh motioned Simon to the corner closest to the door. He himself stayed back from the man, squatting on his haunches to bring his eyes level with the prisoner's.

"I am Captain Bellows, of the king's Welsh Guard. It is my job to protect His Majesty from harm." Simon noticed with interest that he did not include Elizabeth in his statement. After a few moments of silence,

Hugh asked, "What is your name?"

There was silence for a long while as the man gazed past Hugh at the wall. He was very still, almost wooden, but finally he spoke, his voice rough, as if he often shouted. He spoke softly now, barely audibly. "I am Wat."

"Have you another name, Wat?"

Another pause. "No."

"Wat, then. Let me tell you my duty. I see to it that no harm comes to our king, Henry Eight. I protect him from enemies seen and unseen."

Wat's head turned a fraction toward Hugh, not looking at him directly, but closer. "I also," he whispered. Simon heard Hugh let out his breath. He had guessed correctly, at what Simon was not certain.

"Is His Majesty in danger, Wat?"

Very faintly: "Yes."

"What must we do?"

"Witches must be handled with care. They are not easily revealed." The man's voice sounded more confident now, and his eyes narrowed in concentration.

"When they are revealed, what happens to them, Wat?"

Wat frowned. "I suppose they must be killed."

Hugh tensed again, Simon saw the

233

muscles in his shoulders bulge. "Are they sometimes beheaded?"

"Yes, that will kill a witch." This time the answer came swiftly, eagerly. Wat was warming to his subject.

"Is there another way that I don't know about? Can you help me learn about witches, Wat?"

Wat now looked for the first time directly at Hugh. His face lit with secret knowledge, and he grimaced almost comically. The look confirmed Sir George's claim that the man was mad. "You must burn a witch."

"Was Alice LaFont a witch, Wat?"

"No!" The low brow furrowed with disgust. "Not that one. Nan Bullen's spawn. It is she who will destroy the king." Those who had hated Anne Boleyn refused to pronounce her name properly, in the French way, but changed the emphasis to the first syllable.

"You believe Elizabeth would kill her own father?"

Wat struck his fist against his open palm with a smack. "Not her father. Nan the Witch beguiled many, many men. Nan and her minstrel conceived that child and tried to foist it off as the heir to the throne." Wat grimaced again. "They didn't count on it being female, o'course. Now the girl grows to be a witch, like her mother. She is no daughter to Henry, yet he calls her princess. He is enthralled by her power, as he was by her mother's."

"You went to Hampstead today to kill Elizabeth?"

Wat's manner changed. His head drew back and his brow cleared. "It is not for me to be executioner. I am no man of God. I only point them out, because I know them, you see. Most can't see it, but I can."

"See what?"

"The witch mark, of course. It will be on her neck, here." The man indicated a place on his own neck. It was the belief of many that witches had a vulnerable spot, usually a wart or a mole, by which their true nature could be determined. Some made their living identifying supposed witches by puncturing the skin at the "witch mark" and interpreting the results, usually favorably to whoever offered the larger reward, the accused or her accusers. If the mark bled, the accused was human, but lack of bleeding was evidence of a tainted soul. Anne Boleyn had had a small strawberry mark on the back of her neck, it was said.

Simon's father had little belief in witches, pointing out to his son that those accused were usually mad, quarrelsome, or feeble-minded. Simon had no idea how Hugh felt about the subject. The captain listened gravely, his face never changing.

"How did you get over the castle wall, Wat?"

The dirty face smiled cunningly. "I climbed it."

"The walls are very high and smooth, are they not?"

"No worse than a mast. And I had a rope."

Hugh pictured it. An agile man could scale Hampstead's wall easily enough if he had a stout rope. "One more thing. Have you come into the castle before today? To observe the witch more closely?"

Wat shook his head vehemently, his loose lips vibrating with the motion. "Can't get too close. She will know that I am not in her power. They have the sense, y'see, they feel it. Once they know, it's hard to catch them. Best to stay back until just the right moment, when the witch is at her ease. When you get close enough to see the mark, you must take hold and keep her fast, or she will disappear." He made the motion of snatching at something. Simon shivered at how close the lunatic had come to Elizabeth. Would Wat have only descried her as he claimed, or would he have tried to hurt her?

Wat lost focus then, watching his own hand as it repeated the gesture over and over. "Fast, fast," he repeated softly, his breath sounding around the word. He sank into a kind of trance, hand grabbing at the air, lips still moving, but no sound came. Hugh stared at him for a moment, then gestured to Simon and turned to the door, where Calkin waited to let them out.

CHAPTER
TWENTY-ONE

"You don't think he's the one?" They were seated in an outer room in Old Bailey, the hall of justice that sat next to Newgate Prison. Men came and went, but no one paid the boy and three soldiers much attention as they discussed what they'd learned.

"No, I think he meant to reach the princess and cry out that she is a witch. She would have been embarrassed and frightened, but I see no intent in Wat to kill her." He puffed his breath out in a long sigh. "What she's going to say when she learns about his claim is not pleasant to contemplate."

"Nor is what His Majesty will say," Gooderich put in. Kings were notoriously unhappy with harbingers of bad news, even if the danger had been averted. "I fear he'll find some way to blame us."

"I doubt that," Hugh reassured the young man. "His Majesty recognizes facts, and the fact is that royalty will always be in danger from crazed, violent men. We could have done nothing differently. Still, if Henry has heard that we have the killer . . ."

"You won't be popular when you tell him it's not true," Calkin finished.

"Right."

"Captain, the man's certainly mad enough to kill. Don't four corpses say he could have done so already?" Calkin's freckled face showed hope that the case would be solved.

"I see several reasons to doubt that Wat is our man." Hugh counted his arguments on the fingers of his extended hand. "In the first place, there was no reason for Wat to murder the other women. He is focused on the princess, Anne Boleyn's daughter. Second, he wouldn't have gotten within a stone's throw of any of them: the first two because it's obvious he has no money to pay their fee, and the last two because he is so far below them. Third, I saw no indication that the man knows or cares about the Catholic symbols left behind. Finally, I believe him when he said he'd never been inside the castle grounds before. His reason was that the witch might sense his presence, which seems to me oddly logical, at least in the way a man like Wat might think."

The two soldiers nodded reluctantly. "I

wish we had 'im," Calkin muttered, "but I agree we must keep looking."

That afternoon at Hampstead, Elizabeth was surprisingly calm when told the story of Wat's attempt to reach her. Hugh had taken to assigning himself guard duty at the castle most afternoons, so that it was normal for him to be seen there, and he explained the day's events as soon as he arrived. Elizabeth had obtained a hautboy somewhere and was making determined attempts to play it. Simon found her attempts interesting, but Hugh found them irritating and was glad for the slight loss of hearing he suffered from years in noisy service.

"I've dealt with madmen before," she told Hugh and Simon as she adjusted the reeds for the third time. "Mary tells me that after my mother was arrested, one of my attendants made a thorough search of my skin, looking for a mark that might signify the dark powers. Evidently I am unremarkable, at least on the outside." Her eyes glinted mischievously as she said this.

"Do you agree that the man is not likely to be our quarry?" Simon asked.

"I do. Crimes of this sort are carried out by madmen, but not Alice's murder. It is a clever man we seek, one every bit as mad as your Wat but who hides his evil center with an acceptable outer skin."

Hugh broached a subject he had been mulling over. "There is a possibility we have not discussed. Simon, when you went to see this Daisy, Calkin tells me you met a criminal named Peto."

Peto's face appeared in Simon's mind's eye, the mild look of the man so oddly different from the chilling effect of his gaze. "Yes. I've heard something of his history, and I saw for myself that people who know the man fear crossing him, even in a group."

"Peto is a sort of legend in London," Hugh explained. "The man can't be more than twenty-two, yet he strikes fear in the heart of anyone who'll even speak his name."

"Calkin called him Peto the Pope. Why?"

Hugh frowned. "I always thought it simply meant that he ruled the way the pope does: devotion tinged with fear."

Catching the drift of Simon's thought, Elizabeth asked, "Could the man be a Catholic punishing fornicators?"

"I suppose Peto might be Catholic, but I don't see him as the hand of God," Hugh replied. "More like the hand of Satan. The man is involved in every crime in London, I'm told, yet he is never betrayed, never implicated, never even seen by those of us in authority. Simon is the only person I know who could identify Peto and would."

Simon's mind rebelled at the statement, though he could not really say why. If Peto was as bad as they said, he was honor bound to help Hugh end his crimes. Still, a part of Simon understood why Peto had not been betrayed. There was a tacit communication from the man that formed a bond somewhat like friendship, in part an appeal to a person's integrity. Peto's code of behavior had required that he rescue an unknown boy from harm, and Simon's own code required that he repay that act.

When he spoke, none of this inexplicable conflict showed in Simon's manner. "I don't think Peto is the type for public crimes such as headless corpses laid out as nuns. If he is as you say, uncatchable, it is because he has learned to be discreet in his actions, not calling attention to what he does against society's rules."

Hugh was not easily convinced. "A man so twisted as Peto may go deeper and deeper into madness, as Wat has. What Peto might not have done once may become a need in his soul, if he has one."

Elizabeth served as arbitrator. "I believe we must consider him with all of the others.

Our personal feelings, such as my belief that Sir George is no murderer, must be set aside, no matter how difficult it might be, and each possibility carefully examined."

"All right then. I will set Calkin to work on finding more about Peto's relationship with Therese," said Hugh.

Simon silently vowed to set his debt to the outlaw aside, at least for now. Leaving Elizabeth to her unmusical squawks and squeaks, Hugh walked Simon to the back gate, kept locked and guarded at all times now. Dusk was falling, and they could hear the frogs beginning to call from a nearby pond as Hugh continued the conversation.

"Peto is the most likely killer if it isn't Wat, which I'm almost sure it is not."

"Sir George was so certain."

"Blakewell has his own reasons for wanting this mess declared finished, and he'd be credited with saving Elizabeth from the lunatic as well. But I can't be sure that we have found the killer."

The mention of Sir George in that context brought to Simon's mind the cloak, and he quickly filled Hugh in. "So he has a cloak like the one the tall man wore, but I would not think him tall."

"No," Hugh agreed. "And if he left it beside the door, anyone could have worn it and put it back."

"Bess was upset that the bottom was soiled. She felt he would have told her so it could be cleaned."

"Would he not have noticed it missing?"

Simon frowned. "It's doubtful. I saw several cloaks hung there, and she said he wears an old brown one for every day, which I have seen him do. It might have been missing for several days before anyone looked for it."

"One who has been in the castle then, but who? Old Greengage is no killer of young, strong women."

"Ninian?" Hugh opened the gate for Simon. The wood was warm to his touch, baked dry by the afternoon sunlight.

"Comes only by day, and he doesn't seem the type to me to chase women." Hugh's tone said far more than his words. Ninian a lover of men? Simon knew they existed, but he'd never met one before. It made him curious to meet this clerk that no one spoke well of. Hugh went on: "I doubt that Sir George's cloak is tied to the murders. It is muddy, you say, but there would be blood in such a case."

"Odd, though, that someone wearing it has been seen in two places that are suspicious. And what of the mysterious visitor

Hannah described?"

"Your goal must be to find the lover," Hugh said with decision. "He may be the man the Brandon girl spoke of."

"I will speak to Hannah again tomorrow."

"A pleasant task, eh, lad?"

Simon blushed, grinning. "She's a wonderful girl." His face changed, and Hugh saw doubt on it.

"Has this Hannah got a good mind?"

"Why, yes. She's most interested in learning."

"Well, then. Any girl with a brain would count herself lucky to have the admiration of so fine a young man as you."

Simon blushed even deeper; Hugh had seen into his mind too well. His withered arm made him tentative around girls, and despite his attraction to Hannah, he avoided her company because of it. "I don't even know how I'll earn a living," he mumbled.

"You'll earn your living with your intellect, not with your hands. The world has need of clever men." Hugh clapped him on the shoulder in a manner meant to be friendly, but Simon was jarred a step forward nevertheless. "Talk to Hannah and to anyone else you can, until we get something helpful to our cause. I have to convince several people, including Henry Eight, that we cannot simply hang a madman and forget these crimes."

Following the advice of Peto the Pope, Simon requested Guardsman Calkin's help in learning the art of the throwing knife. He was often frustrated with his own clumsiness. Because of his affliction, Simon had all his life been allowed to do what he excelled at and excused from things that he did not. Most challenges of physical dexterity he avoided. Now he strove to develop his eye, achieve muscular control, concentrate on the feel of the knife in his hand, gaze at the target, and "think the blade to its mark," as Calkin demanded. At first the knife might go far left or right of the target, might even clatter off it as the handle rather than the blade met the soft wood. Gradually Simon learned how to heft the knife's weight correctly, to anticipate how it should feel when it left his hand, to move exactly the same way each time and to follow the movement through with a snap of his wrist.

Calkin was patient but insistent. "You must practice a skill every day, Master Simon," the soldier told him. "Once you have the basics, it takes repetition to make it feel right, so that you do not think at all, only react."

Simon doubted that he could react by throwing a knife at a human being, but he did become fairly good at striking the wooden target. Calkin nodded with satisfaction when he hit the circle three times in a row. "Do that every day fifty times, and you'll have naught to fear from any foe you can see."

Simon obediently moved forward, retrieved the knife, and continued his practice as Calkin watched, munching a stalk of rhubarb and puckering accordingly. "What news of the lunatic?" Simon once more took aim at the board.

"We learned his last name. A man in the area befriended him briefly, tried to tame him, so to speak. He finally gave up, but Wat did tell him his last name, Rogers. Common enough name in London. This Good Samaritan says Wat was once a sailor."

At that moment they were summoned by a soldier who looked young enough to be one of Simon's little brothers. "Calkin," the man called. "Captain wants to see the young man. He believes they've caught Peto the Pope."

Simon followed Calkin into the guardhouse with some misgiving. If the call was to identify Peto for Hugh, he must do it, for the man was a known criminal. He passed

247

with little interest through the guards' room, neatly arranged with accoutrements of the trade. Pegs on the walls were festooned with caps, sashes, and sword-belts, the floor below lined with shoes in a colorful array. Men worked at various tasks while a noisy dice game proceeded in one corner and a heedless man snored loudly in another.

They descended a stairway that took them to the lower level, where two small rooms for the use of the guard officers were found. In the first one sat Hugh, and opposite him, Peto, wearing the same mild expression that Simon remembered.

"Is this the man called Peto, Simon?" Hugh asked. Simon found his demeanor totally different than the quiet, almost amiable approach he had used with Wat Rogers.

"It is."

"There, you see?" Hugh told the man. "We know who you are and what you are. You might as well tell us about the murder of Therese Blanc."

"I can tell you very little," Peto replied amicably. "I was not in London when Therese died. I had gone north on some business." His face turned a shade colder for a moment as he added, "If I had been here, things might have gone worse for the one who killed her."

"And do you know who might have done it?"

He shrugged. "Therese's trade required that she go with any man who had her price, Captain. I had no argument with that."

"We hear that the girl was your luck. Mayhap you disliked sharing her with others."

"Why would I kill her if she was lucky for me? Would that not be killing the goose that lays golden eggs?"

Hugh stood suddenly. "I must see to some other business, but I will speak with you further. Simon, stay if you will. I will be but a few minutes." With that he was gone, closing the wooden door with a firmness that proclaimed its solidity.

There was silence in the room for a few moments. Simon, embarrassed by the revelation that he was what Peto would term a nark, said nothing. When the prisoner finally spoke, however, there was mostly curiosity in his voice.

"Do I understand, then, that you are no relative of Therese's at all?"

"No. I have good reasons for my behavior, which I cannot explain, but —"

"Other women have died so." It was a statement.

"Yes." Simon was both surprised and relieved.

"I have heard it. I travel here and there, and such crimes are spoken of long afterward. How many?"

There was no point in lying. "Four are known."

"Four of them!" The words burst from him in a cry of disgust. "Why do they not cry it from the rooftops and find the man responsible?"

"His Majesty wishes the matter investigated quietly. However," Simon said, voicing what he had just concluded, "it cannot be kept secret much longer."

Peto reflected. "Was Therese the first, then?"

"Yes. February second, Candlemas, was the first murder we are aware of. The next was some weeks later, in March."

Peto smiled with a rueful shake of his head. "By then I knew my luck was truly gone," he muttered, rising and moving around the tiny cell as if measuring its possibilities. "The first time ever I was jailed, and now here is the second. When I can, I must go to my witch-woman and find a new amulet."

"You were imprisoned on March first?"

"Well, Peto the Pope was not, but there

was a fellow in York who ran afoul of the authorities and spent several days on the king's hospitality." He leaned toward Simon. "If they'd known who I was, I would not have been able to bribe my way out eventually. They had, as far as they knew, one Thomas Master in custody. The man disappeared on the third night, which is a lesson to jailers everywhere to be more vigilant, I'll be bound."

"Then you could not have murdered Mathilda Harrison!"

For the first time Peto looked offended. "I could not have murdered any of them. It is not the sort of man I am."

Simon nodded involuntarily, sensing that it was true. "How did you come to be arrested today?"

"Ill luck." Peto's eyebrows bounced ironically. "I was walking with a certain lady who, although charming, has both the wit and the voice of a peacock. She said my name loudly enough to be heard just as a certain constable happened by, and for once a constable was sharp enough to react and honest enough to refuse a bribe." He sounded surprised at the latter.

Before Simon could comment, Hugh returned. "Lad, come with me," he ordered. Outside the cell, he moved far enough away to not be overheard by the prisoner. At a twist in the passageway, already bent low to avoid hitting his head on the ceiling, he squatted on his haunches, back against the wall, and offered a handful of currants. "Did he tell you anything useful?" he asked, taking one for himself and popping it into his mouth.

"You meant for me to speak with him."

Hugh chuckled. "It's an old ploy. One man plays the role of the stern upholder of the law, using his position to intimidate the prisoner. Then he leaves the prisoner with one he might see as more sympathetic. He is likely to talk to the second person, to explain himself, and valuable information often results, leading to his conviction."

"But I found just the opposite," Simon protested. "Peto was locked up at York on the date of Mathilda's murder. He cannot be the one."

Hugh considered the information. "The man is a killer many times over. He is lying."

Simon explained the circumstances surrounding Peto's incarceration. "You'll have to send to York for someone to come down and identify him. If he was there, then he could not have been here, so he must be innocent."

"Innocent is not a word that applies to Peto." He finished the last morsel and, seeing the earnest appeal on Simon's face, sighed. "I will send to York, which will take several days. But even if he is not the murderer we seek, Peto will hang for other crimes. Now that we have him he will not see the light of day until he is taken to Tyburn."

CHAPTER
TWENTY-TWO

Elizabeth was pleased to receive, a few days later, an invitation to go with her sister Mary to visit Rosalind de Marcia. There was to be a small gathering of friends, and Elizabeth thought she saw the influence of Isabella in the matter. Since most of the de Marcias' friends were Catholics, she would not ordinarily be invited, but Sir George, Ninian, and even her father could not object to her accepting an invitation to play cards. It was especially appealing to escape Hampstead today, for the rat-catchers were coming with their dogs and their sticks. Much nicer to visit the kind Rosalind and the friendly Isabella and enjoy their hospitality.

Elizabeth hoped that the invitation and the chance to see Isabella again was not her sister's doing. Mary might do such things with thoughts of converting her or convincing her to relinquish her claim to the throne. Edward had been ill this spring, and her ascension to the throne seemed more and more likely. *What will she do with me then?* It was hard to tell with Mary, not overtly unkind but not warm, either.

The greatest obstacle to a peaceful reign for Mary was her younger sister, a rallying point for Protestants and for those who hated and feared Spain's influence in England. Elizabeth might find herself banished, beheaded, or simply imprisoned and forgotten, none of which was an attractive prospect. Safest for her if her brother lived to rule despite his frailty. After that, her best hope was that her sister would marry her to some foreign prince to get rid of her rather than using more drastic means. Elizabeth was careful never to let anyone think she wanted the throne, and truthfully, she didn't know if she did. It was such an awesome responsibility, and she saw how hard her father worked to balance his enemies, both internal and external. Then there were the problems of finance, keeping the good will of the people, controlling crime: the list was endless.

For a moment Elizabeth forgot her dull surroundings and imagined herself as queen. As she'd once told Simon, she would begin by seeking out men of intelligence and integrity to run her government. Not that she always believed in integrity herself, it must be admitted, but it would be essential to trust and have confidence in her ministers. She shook herself back to reality: silly to dream of such things when the likelihood of her taking the throne was so slim. Better to plan for her outing with Isabella; that was something definite.

Simon found Hannah in the laundry, her hands and arms invisible in a deep tub of dingy water. Damp with exertion, Hannah's hair curled even more tightly, and a strand fell over her left eye as she smiled in greeting. "Master Simon, good day." Wiping the stray lock away with a forearm, she returned to her scrubbing.

"Hello, Hannah. I wonder if we could speak again of the man you saw in the castle."

"Certainly, but I've told you what I remember of him."

"You mentioned he wore a cloak with gold tassels."

"Yes, all round it."

"Are you aware that Sir George has such a cloak?"

Hannah's pretty face crinkled in thought. "Sir George? I've only seen him wear a brown one, quite plain. This was made of better stuff and decorated, as I said."

"As is Sir George's better one. It seems he left it on a peg by the door where someone may have borrowed it."

Hannah's eyes widened and she stopped dousing the clothes, again pushing the stubborn tress back. Simon would have liked to touch it, to feel its springy softness, but he did not. "The man I saw?" she asked. "Why would he borrow Sir George's cloak?"

"I don't know. I'm trying to discover who he is so we can ask him. Do you remember anything else about the man?"

"I'm afraid not. My work is mainly in the kitchen and laundry. You should ask Susan Porter."

Thanking Hannah and receiving her brilliant smile in response, Simon hurried to find Susan, Bess Blakewell's trusted assistant. He found the woman ironing in the pressroom, also warm from exertion but not nearly so attractive in that state as Hannah had been. Susan was a heavy woman with a jaw like some lap dogs Simon had seen, the lower teeth jutting over the upper. Whether her looks helped form her personality or not, she evinced the same attitude the dogs did: share nothing. Every word uttered came with great reluctance, and the jaw closed almost before the sound was out.

Simon had thought quickly on his way up the stairs. "Good morning. I am sent to see if Sir George's cloak has been cleaned."

"There." Susan pointed with a beefy arm to a number of garments hung on pegs behind her. The cloak's gold tassels showed below a freshly pressed dress hung over it.

"Good. Lady Blakewell was upset that the cloak was muddied and left all this time." Simon tried for a confidential tone, although Susan's demeanor did not invite such things. She continued her work, setting one iron down to heat while she plied the other, raising the smells of warm fabric and hot starch. "The lady believes someone else wore it and got it dirty, and she's determined to find out who did such a thing. Now I heard . . .," he paused for dramatic effect and went on, "that a man visited wearing such a cloak. You might have seen him, since he came several times."

Susan looked at Simon as if he were a bug. Watching her face, he could almost see the thoughts crossing it. Here was a favorite of the princess, who could get her into trouble if he reported disrespect. She hated it, but she was going to answer just the same. "Mayhap."

Simon wasn't going to get much from her, but Hugh would get a description. "He must have worn the cloak to impress Alice, but why would he take such a chance when the owner was nearby?"

"Not Alice." The jaw snapped shut. Simon looked at Susan with surprise. Her small, black eyes showed no desire to cooperate, but her reluctance to speak was less than her ability to abide an error. The jaw opened again, a mere inch. "Came to see Margot, not Alice."

Hugh, Simon, and Elizabeth walked in the garden that afternoon, discussing Peto's arrest. To one side a manservant cut mulberry branches to put under the beds as a deterrent to fleas, and the grate of his saw in the new leaves came and went through their conversation. Mary Ward sat in the warm sunlight, alternately embroidering and dozing, while Elizabeth's own embroidery lay forgotten on the stone bench, precisely done but proceeding very slowly. "Even if Peto isn't the murderer in this case," Hugh told the others, "we have captured a dangerous criminal who will no longer threaten honest folk."

"It was happenstance that he knew Therese," Simon argued his point. "There is nothing to connect him to any of the others. We must question everyone again and listen even more carefully."

The household was suspicious of his presence and the meetings of the three unlikely associates, but it couldn't be helped. Hugh, it was decided, must speak with Margot, since she resented Simon. Hugh could use his position to impress, if not intimidate, the recalcitrant woman.

Simon and Elizabeth took seats on the stone benches among the myrtle and awaited Hugh's return. Planning to use all the authority he could muster, Hugh called Hannah aside and asked her to fetch Margot to the hall with some hint of demand.

"Try to seem just a trifle afraid, if you can." Hannah's eyebrow rose in understanding, and he saw why Simon's face lit up when he mentioned her. She was a rare girl, blessed with both beauty and lively intelligence despite her humble background. Hugh hoped she saw that Simon himself was unusual.

As he waited Hugh paced the empty hall, the rushes beneath his feet softened by the crunching of countless feet. He thought of Simon's determination and mature outlook, like that of the princess herself. But Simon had an inborn need for justice that drove him while Elizabeth had, understandably, more inclination to self-preservation. Not that she was a bad sort, but Hugh leaned more to Simon's type of person, with whom a man knew where he stood. He had to admit, though, there was danger for those who sought truth above all else. One Thomas More, once Henry's friend, had put honor above obedience, and it had cost him his head.

Margot entered the room as if by an effort of will, fighting an invisible cord that pulled her backward. Her eyes, green as a cat's, met Hugh's directly but effectively screened all emotion. She might have been an attractive woman, but there was a coldness to her that made her white, flawless skin conjure to his mind adamant stone. Her too-slender frame as well seemed to proclaim a refusal to enjoy whatever edible delights the world offered. In her hands she carried a book of prayers, a nice prop, he decided.

"You asked to see me, Captain?" her voice was higher than he'd expected, and he grimaced to himself at the irony of her words. She well knew that he had not asked.

"I must ask you some questions concerning the death of Alice LaFont."

"We were interviewed by Sir George after it happened. I told him what I knew at that time." Her face was calm, but he thought the high tone of voice indicated nerves.

"Did you discuss at that time a man who came to visit several times when Her Grace was away?" he asked casually. The woman's face paled and her spine stiffened even more than her usual posture required.

"There was no cause to mention it," she said through thin lips. Opening the book, Margot began paging through, apparently looking for a specific page.

"When we learned of the man's secret visits, we thought he was Alice's lover."

Margot said nothing, playing a game of waiting. Finally, Hugh continued. "Now we have learned that he came to visit you, not Alice."

Still nothing. She turned the pages slowly, letting him feel her contempt. Hugh waited for some time, and then said, more gently, "It is better if you tell the truth now. If your lover turned to Alice —"

The book closed with a snap and dark eyes rose to meet Hugh's light ones. "Don't be vulgar, Captain. Of course the visitor was not my lover." Margot actually shook with anger at the suggestion. "May not a man come to see his sister without evil conclusions being drawn all round?"

"Your brother?" Hugh's surprise threw him off his planned course.

"My brother."

"I am sorry, madam. My information was that you were alone in the world."

"Except for Guy, I am." Margot's eyes softened at the mention of her brother. "He lived abroad from the age of twelve but returned home last Christmastide. His visits bring me joy." Her tone said she found little else in her life that did.

"But why the secrecy? Surely no one would object to your receiving family."

Margot's face tightened. "There was no secrecy involved, Captain, merely discretion. You must understand; we are true Christians." *Catholics*, Hugh amended silently. "My brother was sent to the Continent to receive a proper education." Again, Catholic. "My father was a loyal subject of the king and took the oath." Like many others who swore Henry's required oath of loyalty while continuing in secret their old ways. So Margot's father had kept his property by going through the charade of acceptance, had kept quiet the fact that his son was being "properly" trained in the True Faith. How Margot must hate waiting on the Whore's Bastard, as many Catholics called Elizabeth!

Recovering somewhat, Hugh asked, "I know of no one at Court named Beaumond other than yourself. Is your brother not welcome there?"

Margot, having turned the tables on Hugh, smiled, but there was no warmth in it. "Of course he is welcome. Guy is my half-brother."

"And what was his father's name?"

"Pemberton."

"Guy Pemberton?" Hugh's eyebrows rose as a familiar face flashed into his mind. Pemberton was handsome, striking, and totally dissolute, one of the young bloods who caused the authorities trouble both at Court and in the town. Although his name was old and respected, the drinking and whoring of Guy, his crony Robin Brandon, and their ilk caused both humorous and outraged gossip.

In his head, Hugh quickly ran through what he knew of the family. Guy's father had been an elderly duke who married the much younger daughter of a wealthy farmer, a union that had unexpectedly produced Guy. After his death, the duke's adult children had managed to take the lion's share of the old man's wealth, leaving the widow with only a small income. She had subsequently married Beaumond, a knight with even less than she, and had thereafter lived a life of dignified penury. They must have sent the boy away hoping he could make his fortune on the Continent. It appeared he had not.

So Margot was the daughter of Lady Beaumond's second marriage, half-sister to the son born in Pemberton's old age. The family had no fortune to give either child much of a place in the world. From what he knew of Guy, Hugh guessed that his reasons for visiting his sister would have been self-serving. A gallant, Hugh thought, in the worse sense of the word.

Seeing recognition in his face, Margot became as human as Hugh had seen her. "You know my brother?"

He forced an even tone. "I am familiar with his face, though we have seldom spoken." *He's usually too drunk to speak by the time I'm forced to deal with him.* "He and his friends are a merry group."

"Oh, yes, my brother is full of good humor," Margot said primly.

Hugh reflected that Guy must have gotten her share, since she showed no trace of it.

Chapter Twenty-Three

"Where do we find this Guy Pemberton?" Elizabeth asked, swatting at an insect droning near her ear.

"He is great friends with young Brandon." Hugh's tone implied that his opinion of Robin Brandon was as low as the one he had just expressed concerning Guy Pemberton.

"The brother of Joanna Brandon who was murdered?" Simon was using his knife to cut and peel twigs for tooth cleaners, and the smell of juniper scented the air.

"A cousin. This Brandon, Robert but called Robin, brought Guy home with him from Italy or some such place, and they have been a thorn in my side ever since."

"So because of different names, the servants mistook him for a lover when he slipped in to visit his sister Margot." Simon tried to get it straight in his own mind.

"When I was absent," Elizabeth snapped.

She had taken up her embroidery, and now punched the needle through haphazardly and had to pull the stitch back out.

"Don't be too hard on Margot, Your Grace. Imagine the humiliation she suffers, given the gulf between her outlook on life and her brother's."

Hugh was inclined to agree. "All Lady Margot has is her pride, and her brother was a part of that. The family no doubt expected great things from him, and it must have cost them dearly to keep him all those years on the Continent. Now he returns to England and consorts with wastrels and peacocks." Hugh did not mention the stories he'd heard of the young bloods that surrounded Robin Brandon. Brandon himself was rumored to have once had two men hold his father's gamekeeper while he raped the man's wife. And Margot's brother traveled with these men.

"She could have told me."

Finished, Simon replaced the knife in its sheath with a soft click. "Tell His Majesty's daughter that she is proud of her Catholic roots, that her brother has gone bad, that he visited here to beg money and ended up flirting with Alice? Which of those things should she have told you?" Simon's smile took the sting from his words. "Highness,

267

people will never want to tell you things that will displease you."

Elizabeth ran a hand over her hair. "You're right, of course, with three exceptions: my sister Mary, who loves to tell me what I don't want to hear, and you two, who I insist must always speak your minds, even when I rail at you for it."

It was indicative of their respective ages and outlooks that, though both nodded agreement, only Simon believed that he might safely comply with that directive.

Simon returned to their purpose. "I had a thought on a different matter. Where does the killer get the robes in which he dresses his victims?"

Hugh's eyebrows rose. "A good question. He can't very well ask someone to make him such costumes, and one does not find Carmelite, Franciscan, and Cistercian robes just lying about."

"I'd wager they are stored somewhere. My family is not prone to wastefulness." Elizabeth's face showed a twitch of humor. Her grandfather had been known for his careful, almost miserly spending habits. "Can we find out where they might be kept?"

Hugh rose to go. "I'll set Calkin to the task. He knows a bit about everything, that one."

■ ■ ■ ■

The next day Simon went to the Old Bailey to see Peto, aware that the man would not go free even if the jailer from York identified him as the prisoner jailed on March first. Still, it would ease Simon's mind to prove that Peto was not the killer, feeling as he did that he owed a debt to the man.

The prison, unwelcoming at the best of times, was today downright threatening. Dark clouds hung low over London, seeming to scrape their bottoms flat on its very walls. Thunder rumbled low and far away, promising nature's rage to come. He asked at the gate and was allowed in, being known by now as Hugh Bellows' trusted messenger. A guard led him through the maze of passages until they came to a corridor with cells on either side designed to hold a single man.

"We keeps 'im by hisself," the guard told Simon. "Don't want this one gettin' away."

The guard opened the door to a dark, earthy cell and stood back to let Simon enter. A man peered out, wincing at the light. He was of the correct height, weight, and coloring, but he lacked that expression of assurance. Nor was there any sign of recognition for Simon.

"I'm afraid he has already got away," Simon told the guardsman, "for that is not Peto the Pope."

Footsteps in the corridor alerted them to the approach of a second guard, also leading someone to this cell. "I am from York," said a dust-caked fellow. "Where is the man I am to identify?" Leaning around Simon, he stared into the cell. "That is very like the man we lost, but it is not he. That one were saucy-looking, like he would do as he pleased and pay others no mind. This one is too timid, though he is very like otherwise."

In less than twenty minutes Hugh arrived, angry beyond anything Simon had ever seen in him. "How is it that you let the man escape!" he shouted at two guards who, although not responsible, were close at hand.

Eventually the story came out. A man had arrived that morning, claiming he had come from York to identify the prisoner. He spent some time with Peto in the cell, ostensibly to find out how the outlaw had escaped custody.

"And as soon as they were alone, the two changed clothing and Peto left as the jailer from York," Hugh concluded. "I warrant His

Majesty will be pleased with this bit of news."

"But Peto is not the killer," Simon argued. "The jailer described him accurately. Peto was, as he claimed, detained in York."

"A double." Hugh peered at the substitute prisoner. "This fellow knew that he would be punished, yet he came willingly and took Peto's place."

"Why would he do that?"

"I'd wager that his family will want for nothing, whatever happens to him. He claims he was knocked unconscious, of course. At worst he'll be branded."

Simon shuddered at the thought of a hot iron burning a man's flesh, but among those of Peto's kind, it was considered a light punishment.

Since Hugh was not approachable at this moment, Simon decided to go his own way. His sense would return when his anger cooled, and he would see that Peto was innocent of the women's murders. Peto operated under his own odd set of morals and Simon sensed that a man like him had no need to arrange elaborate, public murder tableaux. If he killed it would be from necessity, and by stealth.

Later that day, shouldering a bag of his

father's medicines, Simon returned to his role as apothecary's assistant. He approached the back door of the Derwent home the second hour after noon, hoping to catch Lady Agnes in. Florrie answered the door, slack-jawed and loose-limbed from sampling her concoctions all morning. Tripping over a chair and cursing it for being where it belonged, she at last sent a maid to see if the mistress wanted anything from the bag. Hoping the lady would remember the promised philter, Simon had brought something that would suffice. After twenty minutes or so, not long for a tradesman to wait, he was ushered into Lady Derwent's presence.

"Thank you, Annie, you may go." Lady Derwent did not look the least interested in Simon's presence, but he sensed her attitude was pretense. As soon as the maid closed the door behind her, she turned to him. "Did you bring it?"

"Yes, my lady, but I warn you, it is not magic. The medicine is merely an aid."

"Let me see it."

Jacob had made clear his unhappiness with this part of his son's investigations, having no respect for potions and amulets. "But Father," Simon argued, "you say that the patient's belief is a large part of treatment. Could not a woman who believes her husband is under a spell be more enticing and bold, capturing his interest despite the potion's uselessness?"

After a moment, Father had had to grin. "Your understanding of the human mind is beyond your years, my son." With that he had suggested a harmless mixture of mead and sweet-smelling oils.

Now Lady Derwent looked greedily at the small bottle. "How much?" Simon had no desire to cheat the woman, but he knew that paying a fairly high price would convince her of the power of the mixture. He named a figure he had heard his father quote to a whining merchant's wife who nagged at him constantly about imaginary complaints. The lady's eyes narrowed as she considered. Finally, she snapped, "Wait here," and left the room. When she returned she stood for a moment holding the money, finally asking the question Simon hoped she would ask. "Are you certain this works?"

"I have never tried it, but a certain gentleman claims that it always works for him."

"Really." The hard eyes considered him thoughtfully, although not both at once. "A man buys this love philtre from you? A gentleman?"

"He is very popular with women, his sister

says, and he told Margot that he was happy with . . ." He stopped, as if embarrassed to have said the name.

"Margot Beaumond's brother? You sell this potion to Guy Pemberton?"

"I beg you, lady, don't mention it to anyone. The name slipped out, and he would be angry with me if he knew." Simon slapped his forehead with the heel of his hand as if furious with himself.

Suddenly, it was as if Lady Agnes were his best friend. "Don't worry, lad. I would never tell a soul what you've told me." She gazed over his shoulder for a moment. "I ascribed his popularity to good looks and charming ways."

"He is a gentleman of great charm, of course. We merely provide what one might call insurance."

"And as a result he is irresistible to women, able to do as he will." How silly of her to imagine that magic was involved when sex itself was such a powerful force.

"He recently bought yet another philtre, my lady, so be watchful."

She laughed. "Oh, la, lad, I am not Guy's type. And I am of course happily married."

"So all of Guy Pemberton's ladies are unmarried?"

She giggled. "Not all, if what I've heard is

correct. But they are discreet about it. The queen likes not fornication."

"Do you know where Guy lived before coming to England?"

"Italy, I heard. That's where he met Robin Brandon." Suddenly, Agnes' left eye found Simon's accusingly. "What do you care where he comes from?"

"I'm sorry, madam. My curiosity got the better of me, and I apologize."

"As well you should. It is no place of yours to be sticking your nose into the affairs of your betters." Having forgotten the moment of shared gossip, she was back to the grand lady role. Thrusting the coins into Simon's hand, she took the bottle and dismissed him tersely. "And mind, boy, no more yapping about who buys your wares."

CHAPTER TWENTY-FOUR

Hugh let his tall frame slouch against a trellis as Simon related his findings. Elizabeth sat on a stool, cooling herself with a paper fan that Simon's sister Ella had made and shyly bade him take to the princess. The day was warm enough to make it a timely gift, and Elizabeth seemed pleased with its hand-painted though childish design. It was a measure of their ease with one another of late that Hugh would reveal his fatigue and Elizabeth her discomfort with the heat while the other was present.

"Do you have an impression of this Guy Pemberton's character? Could he seduce girls and leave them dead?"

Hugh made a grimace. "More likely to seduce them and leave them weeping. His older partners know the games he plays, but the young ones may be different."

"Like Joanna Brandon?"

"Yes. Such as she might suffer when he

moved on to the next woman. To him they are mere conquests, but they may imagine that they can capture his heart."

"Captain, you have the soul of a romantic," Elizabeth teased.

Hugh blushed. "I merely surmise, Your Grace."

"But we don't know that Guy was the man Joanna Brandon mentioned, nor can we link him to any of the others. Only Alice, and even that's not certain."

"One of us must meet the man and take his measure," Elizabeth announced. "You, Captain, would immediately put him on his guard if he is the one we seek."

Simon saw the direction her mind was going and headed her off abruptly. "It is my task. He will not suspect that I am investigating for the Crown."

Elizabeth's thin nose twitched. She had considered arranging a meeting but had no cause to acquaint herself with any particular courtier and many reasons not to, her father's displeasure foremost. The fact that she made no argument now was enough to make Hugh suspicious that she had her own plan in mind. He sighed. It was not easy keeping rein on a determined princess.

"I think I will change my approach somewhat, play the part of a boy from the

Shambles. This boy saw a man the night of Therese's murder. He might speak to some of the men we suspect, hinting that he saw them nearby."

Hugh frowned. "Blackmail is a dangerous game, Simon. If he is the killer, he could twist your neck and throw your body in a midden somewhere."

"I'll go disguised and accost them in a public place, where they dare not attack me. When I've found what we need to know, they'll never recognize me again."

"Where will you get a disguise?"

"I have heard," Simon said with a grin, "that a certain princess likes to arrange theatricals and as a result has collected a trunk of such things as might make a fine costume." He saw the smile spread across Elizabeth's face as she pulled an old tunic in two with a quick rip. "Is that true, Highness?"

Her answering nod made Hugh hope that helping with Simon's disguise might satisfy her need to be involved, and she would give up any ideas of her own about questioning possible murderers.

Hugh changed the subject. "Now as to nun's robes, Calkin found that indeed there is a storehouse of such things. There was nothing to be done with them when the monasteries were dissolved." Although Henry had sold the property of the Catholic Church to fill his own treasury, there was little market for the trappings of monks and nuns. "Most of the items from the south of England are stored at Croydon, near the Archbishop Cranmer's estate."

"Who would know where to look?" Elizabeth asked, now engaged in pulling the buttons off an old vest. She sent each one into her skirt pocket with a click.

"Clerks who keep Crown records," Simon suggested.

"Ninian." Hugh's mouth turned down as he said it. "Did you not say that he ordered you to stop asking questions about the murders, Your Highness?"

"But the order came from my father."

"Who's to say it did? You'd not be likely to bring it up to the king, believing he disapproved of your actions."

"Still, I say Ninian is unlikely," Simon argued, reaching out to touch a velvet ribbon Elizabeth had removed from a quilted jacket. "He isn't the type of man to charm the likes of Alice, and if he followed her and her lovers, they'd have noticed. The man looks like a walking corpse."

Hugh countered, "But he visits Princess Mary's home, and being a clerk, he would know where to look to find records of nun's robes and the like."

"Others might know, too," the princess mused, straightening her three stacks of finished work. "For example, those who bought the lands that were once monasteries and convents. Were they not responsible for converting them?" Each buyer had received the lands at bargain prices, but the renovations and removal of church property had been left to them.

"Derwent!" Hugh exclaimed. "I know the family bought a large property that had been Franciscan. The crops alone reversed their fortunes and made them wealthy."

"I don't know if the same is true for the others," Elizabeth put in. "Not Sir George, certainly."

"No, I've asked some discreet questions. Sir George's income derives from his stewardship of Hampstead Castle for the king. It is modest, but he seems satisfied with what he has. A soldier first, Sir George won his spurs fighting in France and has no ambition to be a star at Court."

"We know that Guy Pemberton received no lands from the monks, since he has not a penny to his name."

"No, it is wealthy women and Robin Brandon who keep Guy in fine estate:

partners in debauchery."

"Did the Brandons buy church lands?" Elizabeth asked, bundling the rags and tying them with a coarse rope.

Hugh frowned. "I will find out. In the end, though, it means little. Anyone might have discovered where such things are kept just by asking a few questions, and I'm sure a storehouse of such items is not heavily guarded. It would be a matter of creeping in at night, taking what will never be missed, and hiding the clothing somewhere until he is ready to use it."

"I wonder if it is chance or planning that there are different sects," Simon muttered.

Elizabeth answered, "I would say planning. Logic indicates the robes would be stored in like bundles. It would be quicker to take half a dozen of one type, but this man chose to take one of each."

"And what is the message there?" Hugh asked. "Is it merely the man's whim that each woman be of a different sect, or something else?"

"Who can solve a madman's riddle?" Elizabeth bundled the clothes to be given away and handed them to Simon, who would take them to his mother for dispersal to the needy.

"We must try," he said fiercely. "It is up to

281

us to see that this madman is caught."

Elizabeth nodded and Hugh echoed the sentiment. "You are right, lad. We must try."

Anthony Derwent stepped out of the inn where he had spent the night with a certain lady. Although somewhat the worse for wear and smelling of sour wine, his clothing was fashionable and expensive: fawn leggings with soft calf shoes dyed to match, a padded doublet that fell below the waist, a short cloak thrown over one shoulder despite the warmth of the morning, and framing his startlingly handsome face a stiff white ruff, now somewhat crushed from the night's revels. His fair hair curled tightly around his face, completing the picture of a lover most becomingly. Approaching the man, an unrecognizable Simon spoke in a guttural tone. "A word with ye, fine sir?"

Derwent turned to see beside him a street boy of the worst sort. Dirty and disheveled, of course — they all were — but he seemed to have lost most of his teeth, and his skin was covered with lesions of some disgusting disease. Simon and Elizabeth had had great fun with the disguise, and she had urged the "sores" as a way of making people look not at his features, but at them, further hiding his identity. His shape was veiled by layers of rags, and he had a pronounced limp as he scuttled at Sir Anthony's side. He smelled like rotting vegetables.

"Begone, wretch!" Derwent growled, making flapping motions with his hands. It was time to return home to his cross-eyed, demanding wife, which put him in a foul mood.

"I have something to tell ye which is to yer benefit." Derwent walked on until Simon hissed, "It concerns the interest of the king's guard in your activities."

The man stopped and turned. "The king's guard has no concern with me whatever," he replied. "And how would the likes of you know if they did?"

The boy grinned, his mouth showing black where teeth should be. "I were out one night last winter when a certain girl got 'er 'ead cut clean off. The king's man, 'e come by the other day and asked me all abou' it. 'Course, I never said nuffink, cuz I an't one to talk to the likes o' him. But I got to thinkin'. I did see a man that night that didn't belong in the Shambles. He looked a lot like you."

"Lots of men look like me," Derwent averred, "and lots of men go to the Shambles to find a willing doxy."

"True, sir. But I recognized yer face, and

I probably should tell the captain what I saw that night. It's me duty." He grinned, again showing what appeared to be toothless spaces but were actually bits of pitch folded over his teeth.

Derwent regarded the boy for a moment, and then he giggled, a sound Simon never expected in response to his ploy. "Then do your duty as you see it. I cannot stop you. If you think I'm some sort of criminal, you must think as you will, for I can't stop you. I bid you good day, although —" he surveyed Simon with distaste — "I cannot see it in your future." With that he causally tossed a coin at the boy's hand and went off, not bothering to look back.

Later that same day, another man heard his name called, this one less richly dressed but even more handsome than Derwent. Guy Pemberton turned to see the same ragged figure that Derwent had. "Good sir, a word wi' ye concerning the king's guard."

"I've met a few from time to time, lad," Guy answered lazily. "What would you tell me of them?"

"They seek a man guilty of killing a certain woman in the Shambles in March. I was there that night, and I saw a man looked a lot like you, waiting, in a fancy cape."

Guy considered for a moment, leaning back slightly to avoid the boy's stink. "If I was in the Shambles, I was probably drunk. If I was standing still, I was probably unable to walk. If I was unable to walk, then I probably could not have killed anyone, so I must conclude I have nothing to fear from the king's guard. If it's money you seek, I have nothing to give you. I will admit to it if you say I was there. In March I hardly knew where my nights were spent. Today, however, I am a different man altogether. Now I must leave you, for I have an appointment with the girl I am to marry." So saying, he went off leaving the distinct impression he had not a care in the world.

CHAPTER
TWENTY-FIVE

"Derwent and Pemberton both seemed unconcerned." Simon finished his telling of the day's events. He had cleaned himself and changed his clothes, leaving the rotten potato in the folds of the costume in case he needed to play that role again. "For what that's worth, since our murderer must be a man of some daring."

"I've asked about Margot's brother Guy," Hugh said. "The man is of light mind by all accounts. His concerns are drink, fashion, and bedding women, in which order is hard to say."

"Might he be the lover of Alice or Joanna or both?"

"Probably Alice, perhaps both, although to seduce the cousin of your benefactor is both base and ungrateful."

"But convenient," Elizabeth put in. "He would speak Latin if his education is as good as Margot believes."

"And he's only been back in England for a year. I have heard of no crimes such as this before last winter."

"Derwent bought a house in London last fall, so we must consider him a possibility," Elizabeth said. "Sir Anthony frequently comes to London without his wife. I've heard some comment upon it."

"But he was unconcerned at my accusation," Simon protested. "He giggled like a girl at it."

"I don't giggle," the princess contradicted him. "Still, it doesn't sound like the reaction of a killer. Could it be bravado, to convince you that he is unworried?"

"I suppose. Since I don't know him, I can't gauge his reaction truly. We must try another tack."

"I already thought of that." Hugh paced between the two of them. "Calkin and Gooderich have been trying to discover where each of the men we've been considering was on the nights of the murders. Easiest to check is the most recent death, Alice. Sir George was in his bed, that's confirmed by his wife."

"Who might lie or may not have known if he left it," Simon argued. "The more so since they have separate sleeping quarters."

"Others who claim to have been at home

are Greengage and Ninian. Burford's wife spoke true when she said he was working at his estate. I sent a man who confirmed that he has not left since the planting began. Of course, no one knows where mad Wat might have wandered that night." At a calming gesture from Elizabeth, Hugh sat, adjusting his belt more comfortably and stretching his long legs out before him. "There was a masque at the home of the Earl of Northumberland, which Guy Pemberton and Anthony Derwent both attended. Derwent arrived and left with his wife. Pemberton came alone, and no one we spoke with remembers how or when he left."

"Where was this masque?"

"His Lordship's home is near the Old Priory, St. John's. It has been confirmed by others there that both men were in attendance."

"All evening?" Elizabeth wanted to know.

"That is hard to say, but several people thought so. Derwent at least was there at the end of the affair, to escort his wife home."

"I would say that leaves him out, for no one could have done what was done and remained spotless." Simon was tactful, but they all realized the killer must have been covered in gore, must have reeked of it.

"He could have taken his wife home and gone out again," Hugh countered. "She remembers they were at home by two, which gave him plenty of time to slip out again and meet Alice. As for Guy, no one could say when he left, but several ladies danced with him, and he escorted one Isabella de Marcia in to supper." Here Elizabeth's eyebrows rose with interest, and Hugh smiled grimly. "She told Calkin that he was 'most kind' and 'very gallant.' Do they never learn?"

"Does anyone?" Elizabeth replied, and Henry's six tries at finding happiness flashed through the mind of each. Hugh and Simon dropped their eyes, and the princess continued. "Are they suspect, or no?"

"We have eliminated no suspect yet," Simon answered.

"While I don't believe mad Wat is the killer, I would not rule any of the others out at this point," Hugh stated.

"I had hoped we could absolve Sir George by now." Elizabeth glanced up at the window of Blakewell's office. "To me he does not appear a murderer."

"I believe, Highness, that murderers look like everyone else," Simon teased and was promptly thwacked with the fan his sister had so patiently painted, decorated, and folded for the princess' use.

When they left Hampstead, Hugh and Simon traveled together for a way before their paths separated. Hugh brought up a topic he hadn't wanted to discuss in the princess' presence. "I understand from Calkin that he is giving you lessons."

There was a pause as Simon decided how to respond. Would Hugh be angry or derisive concerning his attempts to learn self-defense?

"It was suggested by an acquaintance," he said blandly. "He advised that I learn to throw a knife, since I have but one hand for combat."

Hugh looked straight ahead and matched the bland tone. "It is not my intention that you engage in combat. If you feel threatened, I will consult His Majesty. He will understand and release —"

"No!" Simon stopped and faced Hugh pleadingly. "I will not look for a fight, but I must be a man, despite this." He glanced at the weak arm angrily. "Don't you see? It is not so that I can fight, it is for the knowledge that I could if I had to." The boy stopped, unable to explain further, but Hugh's face changed as he recognized what Peto had seen earlier, Simon's need to prove himself.

"Well, then," he said gruffly. "I will add to

your friend's advice and Calkin's teaching. I once had a terrible wound in my left arm, which your father ably saw to. The arm is not what it once was, but I find that regular exercise helps to make the most of what power is there. When you practice with Calkin, do not neglect your weak side. Balance is important in any combat, and any gain you make will stand you well when you need it." With that, having reached their separate ways, he bade Simon good day with a friendly cuff to his good arm and went off to the south.

As he walked homeward, Simon dwelt briefly on Elizabeth's enjoyment of the chase they had undertaken. Her young life had been one of duty and scholarship, and she excelled at both. But there was no goal for her to aspire to. Since it was unlikely she would ever rule England, she served no purpose worthy of her talents. In this matter, her quick mind and her probing curiosity were actually useful, and while hampered by her position, she found ways to contribute to their body of knowledge.

Traveling in the opposite direction, Hugh also considered the princess, but in a more critical way. The girl seemed determined to cause trouble, for herself and for him, by meddling in the investigation. Hugh found

Simon inventive but on the whole cautious. Elizabeth was unpredictable, and he disliked his lack of control over the girl. She would not answer to him, but Hugh knew that ultimately, he would answer to her father if trouble arose.

Upon arriving at the gatehouse, Hugh met Gooderich, whose expression was grave. "Another dead woman, Captain."

"God's blood!" Hugh's anger rose. Could they not stop this? A man of action who could kill when the occasion called for it, this petty pace of asking questions and weaving answers together made Hugh half mad. "Tell me."

"We can't say for certain whether she is a victim of the same killer or not. It is only because we know of the others that Calkin and I found this one odd."

"Why can't you say? Is the head missing?"

Gooderich looked sick. "Only pieces of her are left, sir. Beasts have been at the body, both dogs and pigs, judging from tracks around the area. Much of it is, um, gone." Hugh felt his stomach turn over as the man continued. "There was scraps of clothing strewn 'round, such as might have been nun's robes. And Calkin found this." He pulled from his pouch a four-inch strand of beads, ivory possibly, threaded on a gold chain.

"This could well have been a rosary." Hugh took the segment, touching each bead in turn to feel its hardness, then put it in his own pouch. "But there was no head to be found, am I right?"

"None, sir. Animals might have carried it away."

"But more likely it was never there to begin with."

"Yes. The other bits are rent apart, but the neck might have been cut through."

"Thank you, Gooderich. Who else knows of this?"

"Many saw the body, but with its condition, no one marked the head being gone. Some say the girl was attacked and killed by the beasts. I think that unlikely."

"Where was she found?"

"Across the river, near the baiting grounds."

"Any idea how long she had been there?"

"A week at most. Few cross the area except when there's a show, and the last one was on Saturday last. Old Sackerson fought off six dogs, they tell me." Sackerson was the most popular bear in years, being both wily and strong. Hugh, however, had no time for talk of sport.

"Six days."

"Yes, sir." Gooderich passed a hand over his eyes, trying to forget what he had seen. "We must find him, Captain. We must work harder."

"Exactly what His Majesty says, Gooderich. But how do we put it all together?"

"Can't we arrest them all and put them to the question?"

Hugh considered the suggestion with reluctance. If he made enemies of these men, he might pay for the rest of his life, and there was no evidence that clearly pointed to any of them. "For now we'll keep asking questions, hoping at some point to find something that gives us a clear direction. Find out who the woman was. If she's been missing for days, there should have been a hue and cry for her."

"Yes, sir."

An hour later, as Hugh finished the duty roster for the coming week, Gooderich returned with news, his breath short from hurrying to tell it. "Lady Derwent asked about a servant girl who'd apparently run away. Another of her maids confessed that the missing girl boasted she had a rich lover before she disappeared. Now, this Sally may be off with her light o'love, certainly."

"But the story sounds familiar."

"Yes. Calkin has gone for a description of the girl." He looked doubtful. "If it helps. With a few bones and no head, certain identification is not likely."

"Sooner or later, something will turn up." Hugh started for the stables, wishing he believed the prediction.

Chapter
Twenty-Six

Simon found that he enjoyed his disguises. Walking the streets of London as someone else, someone other than a respected physician's son, was an eye-opening experience. He was growled at, glared at, and even threatened if he stopped too near a peddler's cart or an open shop door. Still, he found it exciting and decided to try a different disguise on his next outing.

Unwilling to confess his enjoyment of playacting to the princess a third time, he borrowed an old coat from his father's brother and took to the streets as a sailor. He hoped to learn more about Wat, now held in Newgate. Investigation had revealed that he'd made his living on British merchantmen until he became too distracted even for that life. It being the busy shipping season, Simon hoped to find sailors who remembered Wat. The loan of the coat had included a warning from his uncle, however, to watch his back: a strong young lad might be knocked unconscious and wake to find himself aboard a ship bound for distant shores. For this reason Simon hung the coat over his good shoulder and openly displayed his withered arm, exposing his uselessness as a sailor.

The London docks were a busy place, and movement seemed almost frenzied as men moved on and off ships and piers and even rigging. The day was warm, and most had shed their outer garments, working in the sun and letting it warm their backs. An olio of smells assailed the visitor, fish, tar, and wet hemp predominating. A hum of voices blended with the creak of vessels shifting on the water and the squawk of birds hovering overhead, their bright eyes alert for any chance at a morsel of food.

It was easy enough for a youth of fifteen to show curiosity about the ships and cargo found at the docks. Simon's short frame for once was an asset. He looked young, and most of his queries were answered patiently. Approaching a sailor or a small group, he would ask a few questions, comment on the weather, then bring up the subject of Wat.

Most of the morning he got no response, but as the bells chimed noon, Simon greeted two sailors loading barrels onto a trim little carrack, a Flemish ship of bluff design with high stern and bow. It was 160 feet in length, its width the traditional one-fourth of that. Rigging ran everywhere in complicated patterns, but Simon's uncle often bragged that these ships were superior both in maneuvering for battle against pirates and for fitting into rivers and narrow harbors. He'd had the presence of mind to bring along a jug of cool water, and the men were only too willing to rest a while and refresh themselves from it. Knowing just enough of shipping to ask questions that would get sailors talking, he drew them out by letting them boast about the vessel they worked for a while. Once they had warmed to the conversation, he worked it toward his real purpose.

"My uncle makes short runs: to Calais, usually, or Scotland. He once knew a sailor named Wat, who raved about witches. What stories he tells of him!"

"He means Wat Rogers, I'd wager." The older sailor, whose beard was going gray in streaks, grinned, revealing blackened teeth. "I sailed with him a few times. An odd one." For a sailor to call another odd was unusual, for in general they were a strange lot. It took a certain type of man to brave the seas in small boats, in close quarters and often in danger, away from home most of his active life.

The other man had his hair pulled back into a pigtail and tarred at the ends, not a bad idea for one required to climb through rigging dense as grass. Not to be outdone, he added his own comment. "Wat was nigh thrown overboard by the crew of the *Fair Wind*. Drove us all half mad with his ravings." Hefting the jug expertly on one shoulder, he drank without touching his lips to its mouth.

"Witches, I suppose. He's ever after witches, my uncle says."

"True enough. Wat has a great dread of them and suspects most women in the world of the craft." The sailor's cheeks, burned almost black by the sun, crinkled as he grinned at the memory.

The older man spoke again, showing black stumps of teeth as he grimaced in pity. "When first I sailed with Wat, he were just odd, but he grew worse and worse. To Wat's mind, if a queen of England could be a witch then they must be everywhere."

The younger sailor spat disgustedly. "Who believes that? Henry wanted his Jane, and Nan were in the way."

The other was not convinced. "She were a witch, Nan were. Now I'm no Wat, and I don't see witches everywhere I look, but Nan bewitched Henry for certes. Six year he courted her. What man would do that for a woman natural?"

"Aye, a woman is a woman when the lights are out, I'll give ye that," the pigtailed sailor agreed. "Not that Wat didn't bed a few himself." He slapped the older sailor's arm playfully and they both chuckled in remembrance.

Simon's curiosity was piqued. "Wat was a man for the ladies?" The information didn't fit with the disheveled, filthy creature that he'd seen at Newgate.

"He were, by God's hooks, he were. When first we sailed together, Wat were different, as I said. Odd, but a handsome devil who could turn a pretty phrase. The women flocked to him, and he loved 'em all." The two laughed again. Simon couldn't believe it. Wat, the staring hulk he'd seen babbling in a cell? Could his lunacy be an act? Was he at times more lucid, more human, than they had seen?

"What happened to his wits, then?"

The gray-beard pondered that for a moment. "The life at sea is not for everyone, as your uncle will tell ye. A man's alone a lot, and he thinks on things. Wat's mind centered on women, but it twisted. He decided they was all witches like Nan, and he could speak of nothing else. A man was safe only at sea, with no women for miles. A female aboard ship drove him to a wild state, and he would rave against her the whole voyage until finally there was no captain who would take him on."

"And what happened to him then?"

"Haven't seen him in a year or more. I hear he's a pitiful wrack now, beggin' his living and mumbling holy verses to scare off the evil ones." Simon could have told them that Wat was worse off than that, but he turned the conversation to shipping again briefly before moving off. The two sailors returned to loading barrels onto the ship, rolling them up the gangplank with energetic thumps.

If Wat hadn't been on the docks for a year, where had he been? Simon worked his way through taverns on a line between Hampstead and the docks, asking if anyone had seen Wat Rogers. It took the rest of the day, but finally he found a tavern keeper who recognized the name. The man was sweeping the floor as Simon entered, and the dust in the air made him sneeze before he could ask about Wat Rogers. "Threw him out," was the response. "Wouldn't leave the patrons alone with his raving on about witches."

"Do you know where he is now?" When the tavern-keeper's face showed curiosity, he added, "Wat was a sailor, and my mother thinks he knows the whereabouts of my father, who shipped with him."

That seemed to satisfy him. "Haven't seen him for months, but Wat had a brother north of here."

"Where?"

"Up in Holborn, I think." His eyes rolled upward as he accessed the memory. "Yes, Wat used to say there were no witches on Holborn Street because his brother kept them away. I believe the brother is a church-man."

It didn't take long to find a clergyman on Holborn Street named Rogers, but it was late afternoon by the time Simon reached the man's home. Rogers, he discovered, was in charge of a small local church but was not well liked by his neighbors. The woman who finally pointed out Rogers' house informed him with a sniff that its owner was "too proud by half" and had a way of "judgin' others by a different staff than himself."

The man who answered Simon's knock was easily recognizable as kin to Wat, although like his brother, any attractiveness he might once have had was hard to discern.

They shared the same overhanging brow that brooded even in repose, the same strong nose and chin. Even their eyes were similar, although where Wat's burned with madness, this man's were cold and measuring. "What is it?" he demanded in a manner unexpected from a good Christian.

"I am come about your brother, Wat."

The face hardened. "What about him?"

"He is in Newgate, sir, accused of trying to assassinate a Royal Princess."

The information startled the man, and he faltered, but only briefly. Folding his hands in a self-righteous gesture he declared, "I have washed my hands of Wat this three month. He is beyond my help, though God in heaven is witness that I tried to save him. The wicked world overcame my efforts, and now Wat must face its wrath."

Simon wondered how to proceed with this tense, pompous man who seemed small despite being a head taller than he. "There are those who would help Wat if we knew how. Can you tell me where he has lived of late, and how?"

"Who are you?"

The truth would not do. "I work for a certain pious lady who would not see a lunatic put to death if he can be helped."

Peter Rogers' face tightened. "It is my

belief that he cannot. I did everything possible, as I told you." He considered ending the communication there, Simon could tell, but something compelled him to explain himself. "Wat is ten years my junior. I looked to God's guidance and gave him a good home when our parents died, but he insisted on going to sea. For years I cautioned him concerning that life, which is naught but whoring and drinking. Wat refused to heed my warnings and became increasingly troubled. I believe that in the end, he recognized his wasted youth and brooded on his sins."

"So you have not seen him since he returned to London?"

Rogers straightened his brown worsted tunic fussily and continued, "Wat returned to my home when he could no longer find work on the docks. I took him in and, seeing his condition, tried to show him the path of righteousness. He needed strict guidance, but he would have none of it."

"He is most afraid of witches, believes they are everywhere."

"As they are, sir, as they are. I warned him of such things many times, for it is when man is drunk or debauched that a witch may creep in and steal his soul."

Simon began to understand Wat's unstable

state. Raised by the overly religious Peter, he had rebelled, but the diatribes he endured must have made him fear for his soul until his mind could not cope. He had come to focus on women as witches, seducers of men into sinfulness, a common enough teaching from Sunday pulpits.

"Wat has been sleeping out these last weeks. Do you know where he stayed the winter?"

"Here," was the reply. "It was my last attempt to save him. When I saw that he was losing the battle with the Evil One, that his wits were addled, in desperation I locked him in for three month, even though the devil inside him begged to be set free. I prayed over him night and noon, encouraging him to fast, to pray, to scourge himself, to drive the demons from his body. If anything, he became worse."

As would anyone shut in a room for months by his own brother.

"When was this?"

Rogers thought for a moment. "It began just after Christ's mass. I remember telling him that the birth of the Christ was the perfect time to open his heart and receive God's blessings. It must have been around the feast of St. David that I admitted defeat."

Early March, then. Wat could not have killed the two prostitutes or Joanna Brandon.

Rogers went on self-righteously, "I found my brother's cause hopeless, and God's instructions are clear. One who is of the world must be shunned by those who know God. I have left him to the justice of others."

"He is in a pitiful state now."

Closing his eyes, Rogers recited, " 'We serve in a tavern where the devil is master and the world is mistress. The world is a stable full of wicked rascals; therefore one must have laws and authority, judges, executioners, the sword, the gallows, and all such things, to keep down the wicked rascals.' " Rogers set his narrow mouth with decision. "The law must now take its course."

Although he did not recognize the words of Martin Luther, Simon deduced that Peter Rogers was a reformer. Like many faced with confusion in the church, he had taken the most extreme route to salvation. The sad result was that he contributed to the destruction of his own brother's sanity with his fanaticism, and now Wat would die for it.

CHAPTER
TWENTY-SEVEN

The next morning, in his disguise of ragged street boy, Simon stepped up to a heavily veiled woman he had followed all the way from Haymarket. He had, with the help of the princess, determined that Derwent's current lady love was one Constance Maillot, wife of a wealthy but elderly gentleman who served in the courts of equity, responsible directly to Henry himself for dispensing justice. Simon wondered what justice the old man would dole out to his pretty wife if he knew she had had many lovers.

"My lady." Simon had planned his approach. "This pomander fell from your litter."

"As you see, I have mine." She waved a perfumed silk ball that hung from a band on her wrist.

Simon leaned in closer so that only she could hear. "A word, lady. You may be in danger from a certain man."

Her dark brows rose in amazement. "What? Mind your manners, boy, and don't speak to your betters so."

"A certain man spends his nights at the King's Nose Inn. That man may be one who does violence to women. I speak only in warning."

"Away!" she ordered. "I know nothing of any such inn, but I'll have you whipped if you speak to me again."

Simon moved off. He had done what he could to warn Constance. If Derwent was the killer, she was in danger, but there was no other way to help her if she chose to return to his bed at the King's Nose.

Elizabeth was surprised the next day to receive a summons to Court: her father wanted to see his children. She chose with great care a velvet dress in blue, trimmed with gold along the sleeves and bodice. In her hair she placed a band studded with seed pearls the queen had given her, all the time wondering what the reason could be for this call. It was no holiday, and she hoped war with France was not brewing. The last one had occasioned a great stir as they were all packed off to safe areas until the threat passed. Whatever the cause of the summons, at least she could speak again with her sister Mary and try to discover something of help to Hugh and Simon.

When she arrived at Whitehall, an unusual hush made her heart sink. She had felt it before, the pall that hung over the household when her father was in a certain state of mind. Who had displeased him now? She hoped it was not she. What if he had received further word of her involvement in the murder investigations? Still, he would not call all his children together to berate one, would he? Elizabeth dreaded the coming hours. Henry's wrath was awesome, and no one could soothe it except sometimes the queen.

Looking around she saw no one. It seemed everyone in the place was in hiding. Finally, a servant appeared who informed Elizabeth in hushed tones that her father, brother Edward, and the queen were in the garden. Hurrying there lest she be late (although no time had been set), she found them seated among sweet-scented lilacs, but the impression gained from the tableau did nothing to ease her nerves. Henry sat on a bench, his sticks leaning against one end. He was reading something and did not look up when she approached. Catherine and Edward sat on low, backless chairs. The prince was clearly distressed, his thin body moving in twitches and his pale cheeks colored with the familiar red splotches that trumpeted his delicate condition. Catherine's glance strayed to him, as if wanting to comfort him but not daring to speak. Behind her stood a man Elizabeth had not seen before, but his clothing and the bag on the ground beside him suggested a physician.

Henry's case was hopeless these days. Although several new doctors had been in, none could ease his pain or stop the festering of his legs. The usual dressing of fat, ground pearl and scorched lead did nothing to relieve the infection. As Elizabeth came close she could see that the morning's fresh dressings had already begun to discolor as an ugly substance seeped from the rotten flesh they covered. Her father's breath wheezed in and out, each breath an effort.

The last figure in the tableau was Wil Somers, Henry's fool, who had become his close friend over the years. The only man permitted to call His Majesty Hal, Wil was a loyal supporter of Henry, whatever he did. Somers too grew old, Elizabeth noticed, and concern for his sovereign, and perhaps his own position, showed on his face.

"Henry, here is Elizabeth, come to visit." Catherine's voice sounded forced, affecting pleasantry in an unpleasant situation. Henry looked up, said nothing. His face was impassive, taking in his daughter's carefully chosen costume and neatly plaited hair. Elizabeth sensed she was not the source of his anger. Who, then?

"You should not lecture me, Madame, you should not." The king's gaze never left Elizabeth's face, but the reference was clearly to his wife. Elizabeth felt a shiver of dread. Rumors had flown for months that Catherine was a secret heretic, a reader of forbidden Protestant tracts and a believer in reforming the Church of England.

Henry had refused to listen at first, but the urgings of some of his councilors had been insistent. What if they had convinced the king that his wife worked against the church he had himself established? What if Catherine were caught in some act that proved her reformist leanings? Despite the care that she had given Henry, despite her kindness to his children, Catherine Parr could burn at the stake if Henry believed she dabbled in these matters.

Henry had left the Catholic Church but, to pacify England's Catholics, had changed little in the ceremonies performed at worship. Reformers wanted more changes, but he had gone as far as his conscience would permit. The king was a man who needed to feel that he was in the right according to his own beliefs, and although he often twisted ideas to fit his desired goals, he could not go beyond what his eccentric conscience would bear. The present Lord Chancellor, Wriothesley, was only too eager to search out those who might think wrongly concerning the New Religion and put them on the rack until they confessed their heretic beliefs. And the queen might be one.

Elizabeth truly did not know how far Catherine's belief in reform went but suspected she was sympathetic to the cause. Once people began reading the scriptures for themselves, different views evolved about what it meant to be a Christian. These divergent ideas were hotly debated throughout Europe.

Now Henry had accused his wife of "lecturing" him. Had she been so foolish as to try to change his mind, to urge him to accept further reforms of the church, as rulers of other states had? Elizabeth recalled Mary's account of her own mother's appeal to the king's mercy. Dressed in yellow, Henry's favorite color, Anne had come to the courtyard below his window, for he would not consent to see her once he had decided she must die. Raising Elizabeth above her head, Anne had asked Henry to have mercy on the mother of his child. There had been no response.

Now would poor Catherine meet a similar fate, death by the king's command? If Henry could harden his heart against the mother of his child, had already beheaded two wives and divorced two, such a thing was possible. Elizabeth prayed that the third of her father's Catherines had not pushed him too far, argued her points of religious freedom too energetically.

She did not blame her father. Elizabeth despised the councilors who gave Henry such bad advice, and he sick almost to death. Men like Wriothesley wanted to rid themselves of a strong queen to pave the way for their own power when Henry died, and he was too sick to see it. Elizabeth would help the queen if she could, but she dared not speak openly to her father on the matter.

Calmly taking a seat, she began to tell her father and his wife about a tapestry she was making. Wil, taking his cue, kept the conversation going with a brightness that, like the queen's, was false but successful in preventing further outbursts. Henry sat staring at the ground, and Catherine could not decide where to look. Doctor Wendy was eventually dismissed and left with unseemly speed.

After a half-hour Mary arrived, which did nothing to cheer the little party. After inquiring in her stilted manner after her father's health, Mary greeted Catherine with her usual tight-lipped politeness and dutifully kissed Elizabeth and Edward. The boy was well taught and did not squirm, despite the fact that he thought himself too old — and too important — to be kissed by his sisters. At eight the Prince Royal, sickly and weak, was well aware that his destiny was to be king of England.

The visit wound down with agonizing slowness, everyone except Henry striving to achieve a sense of normality. Elizabeth wondered if her father's sanity was affected by his illness. Surely pain wracked his entire body at this point. What if he had lost his mind? What if he died?

It was dangerous when a monarch left a child to rule after him, and in this case it would be a very sick child, with religious controversy swirling around him. If Edward died and Mary took the throne, she would return England to Catholicism. If she did not rule there was of course Elizabeth herself, but there were others as well. Lady Jane Gray, their cousin, was believed by some to have a better claim to the throne than either Mary or Elizabeth, and there was the child in Scotland, another Mary, descendant of Henry's sister Margaret. There was even Henry's illegitimate son, Henry Fitzroy. Too many possibilities to make a smooth transition. *Please, God,* Elizabeth prayed, *let Father keep his life and his wits. It is the best chance our poor country has.*

Finally, Henry's gaze moved to the fool. "Inside." Understanding at once, Wil called for attendants to carry him into the palace. Without so much as a glance, Henry left them. Edward's tutor, waiting at a respectful distance, came and escorted him away, leaving the three women. Catherine tried to smile. "His Majesty is much pained today. I'm sure he will call for you again soon." They never discovered why they had been sent for.

Elizabeth longed to speak to Catherine, but Mary's presence was a danger to both of them. It was well known that she reported every scrap of information that might discredit the queen to Wriothesley. The safest thing was for the sisters to leave together so that Mary could hold no suspicion that Elizabeth had spoken to their stepmother alone.

As they navigated the passages of Whitehall, Elizabeth remembered what she had heard Mary relate at the de Marcia home. "Did you find the missing casket, Sister?"

Mary's brow knitted. "No. It is most vexing."

"Was there someone unusual in your home around the time you found it gone, someone who might have stolen it?"

"None of my friends is a thief, Elizabeth." Mary was so prickly!

"I certainly did not mean to imply that. I meant extra servants or anyone not usually given entrance."

Mary considered it. "No. I have few around me, as you know. Father's clerk came to check my accounts, I remember." She suppressed a flicker of distaste a moment too late. "Other than Ninian, in my home are only loyal servants and friends." Something flashed in her eyes, and there was a hesitation before the word *friends*. Some who had been there were not supposed to be, but Mary automatically protected them. Catholics, of course, but who?

"I hope the box is found," Elizabeth said, and they parted, each to her conveyance.

CHAPTER
TWENTY-EIGHT

Simon found Elizabeth distracted and distant that afternoon. She reported that the Princess Mary had not found the casket of jewels mentioned at the de Marcias. Simon related his findings on Wat's background, but Elizabeth had never put much stock in the idea that Wat was the murderer.

"A lunatic!" She had dismissed the man when told of his capture on her grounds. "One such as that could not convince four women to let him approach them." Now she half-listened as Simon finished, glossing over references to Anne Boleyn's supposed witchery. When he finished, her gaze was far away, as if she had not heard.

"Highness, is something wrong?"

"Do you think it matters how one worships God, Simon?"

Simon hesitated a moment, bending to sample the sweet, heady fragrance of the lilacs Elizabeth had cut to brighten her dining table that evening. He was aware of danger, but in the end trusted that Elizabeth really wanted to know what he thought. "I have met those who like to tell others how to think. It seems to me they enjoy the power it gives to them more than the help it might give to others."

"But if a good person really believes she is right, should the mistakes of others be pointed out?" Simon picked up on the word *she*. He doubted Elizabeth meant herself, since he had observed that her faith, although earnest enough, did not require proselytizing. She must mean the Princess Mary, much more likely to press her religion on those around her.

"I suppose one might feel compelled to," Simon responded. "But people who can think for themselves generally do not like to be told what to think by others."

Elizabeth's gaze focused on him with a thin smile. "That, Master Maldon, could be the greatest understatement in history, and the cause of revolutions the world over."

Elizabeth went the next day to the de Marcias as planned. She found a much larger gathering than before, and several tables of card players had already begun games of gleek. The room hummed with conversation, the whirr of shuffled cards, and muted laughter. Among several men present was Anthony Derwent, whose name had come up in connection with Alice LaFont. Within half an hour Elizabeth had managed to maneuver herself to a table with Sir Anthony, a man as tall as she'd remembered, as handsome as his wife was homely, and very eager to be charming. Complimenting everything a woman did was automatic to him, and the other females at the table simpered each time he spoke.

As they chatted, the game being secondary to gossip and favorable impressions, Elizabeth decided she felt sorry for Agnes Derwent. Her husband was an insufferable lecher who smelled so strongly of scent that it made her nose tingle to be near him. He commented on how clever the princess was at cards until she was irritated almost beyond bearing the obsequious and condescending tone. Finally he exclaimed, "Bold play, Highness!" when she trumped a hand that only an imbecile would have missed.

Seizing a sudden inspiration, she murmured, "Fortes fortune adiuvat."

Sir Anthony's face went blank for a second, but then he smiled broadly. "Well said, Your Grace." The falseness in his tone revealed what she wanted to know. He had no idea what she'd said. Whether his lack of Latin meant he was or was not the lover of Joanna Brandon, she could not say.

After a few more hands, Elizabeth excused herself and went to find Isabella. Escaping again to the garden, now aromatic with spring blooms, the two girls idled along, enjoying each other's company. Shy pansies peeped out from low spots while the taller peonies formed walnut-sized buds, ready to open in their glory with a few more days of sunlight. It was relaxing to be out of the crowded room, and she was pleased with herself at having managed to meet Derwent. As they surveyed the newest flowers, touching the velvet petals and sniffing gently at their centers, Isabella shyly offered sympathy for the king's illness. It was obvious to everyone that Henry was failing badly. Elizabeth thanked her and changed the subject, hoping the girl would not try to determine her views concerning succession.

Soon they were exchanging impressions of people they both knew with the thoughtless cruelty of the young. Lady Dinsmore, a beautiful but disagreeable woman, had been stricken with pox the year before and now would not show her ruined face. The girls decided it was punishment for haughtiness. Edward Seymour and his wife, the Count and Countess of Hertford, were ridiculed for their faults: his vanity and her shrewishness. Finally, Elizabeth brought in the name that most interested her: "I'm told there is a man at Court nowadays who thinks himself indispensable to women there. Pembrook, Pemberton, something like that?"

Isabella's face clouded. "Guy Pemberton? Why, Your Highness, Guy is very charming."

So Isabella was stricken. Elizabeth dismissed her statement with a wave. " 'Twas probably evil gossip I heard. What is he really like?"

"You might have noticed for yourself." Isabella's cheeks dimpled in a smile. "He sat at the table behind you."

Suddenly Elizabeth was anxious to return to the stuffy card room for a chance at a second of her suspects in one afternoon. "You must introduce me when we return. How did you meet him?"

"At your sister's. Guy has lived in Spain, and Her Grace longs to hear of it. Since her mother's death she is lonely, and news of Aragon makes her feel close to the queen."

Elizabeth didn't bother to correct Isabella's mistaken reference to Catharine of Aragon as queen. "Guy lived in Spain?"

"Oh, yes. Not near my father's home, but

he stayed some months outside Seville. He has traveled widely and is most interesting to listen to." Something in Isabella's voice told Elizabeth that not only stories of faraway places attracted the girl to this man.

Like a good hostess, Isabella searched Guy Pemberton out when they returned inside and brought him to meet Elizabeth. Luckily, Rosalind called Isabella away at that moment and the two were left alone for a time. He was tall but not as tall as Derwent, with dark hair like his sister Margot. His eyes were deep brown, and where Margot wore a stern, even dour expression, Guy's face was pleasant and he smiled often, showing white, even teeth. Altogether he was startlingly handsome, and Elizabeth found that she liked his direct gaze. Collecting feminine hearts would be easy for this man, blessed with both looks and charm.

After a few minutes of polite conversation, Elizabeth decided to be direct. "I was interested to hear, Master Pemberton, that you have visited my home."

Guy was taken aback momentarily, but then his smile broadened. His voice, round and deep as any actor's, turned playful. "You've spoken to Margot." Elizabeth was surprised to have won so easily what she thought he would deny. "I wanted to see my sister, and I knew she was of your household, so I appeared on your doorstep. I'm afraid it was without your permission." His brown eyes looked sideways at her: amused, not at all contrite.

What was she to say? For a moment anger threatened. She had not been treated with the respect due a princess. Then Guy's smile melted her anger and she laughed aloud. "The next time you must let me invite you so that you do not have to use the back door."

"I'm afraid Margot is ashamed of me," he confided. "I am not what she hoped I would be." *Who could live up to Margot's standards?* "My sister's greatest fear is that I will embarrass her."

Guy drew away from those about them, taking Elizabeth's arm and speaking earnestly. "I am certain you have noticed Margot's devout piety. I, on the other hand, find religion deadly boring after the first two or three hours. Margot has stronger knees than I, but I have a stronger stomach." He waved his glass of wine in explanation and almost spilled the contents. His eyes widened as he righted the glass, and Elizabeth wondered if he'd had too much of the stuff already.

She reminded herself that Guy had a rakish reputation, and here she was, encouraging him as he belittled his sister's rectitude. Still, she liked a man who knew and candidly admitted his faults. It was for his women to decide how much they mattered, she supposed.

"Did you meet Alice LaFont when you visited Margot?"

Guy's eyebrows rose. "You are direct, Highness. Actually, I met Alice at Court when I first came home to England. She . . . left shortly after, but I was pleased to see her again at Hampstead."

"You know that she was murdered?"

His brow furrowed. "I heard it, yes. We met a few times in the spring, around Eastertide, I think. Alice missed the excitement of Court life, and I found her an engaging companion. Then we quarreled, oh, I would say a week or ten days before. I'm afraid I had found interest elsewhere and therefore avoided her company." Guy's handsome face took on a serious expression and he turned away, setting the wineglass down with a decisive clink as if reminded of an earlier resolution. "I am sorry now, for I fear she may have come to harm because of me." He didn't elaborate, but Elizabeth thought she understood. If they had an assignation, Alice might have waited there for her lover and met instead a killer.

Isabella returned, taking Guy's arm in a proprietary way. "Have you two been talking about me?"

"Of course we have," he answered immediately. "I can speak of nothing else."

Elizabeth controlled her shocked reaction. So Isabella's quick defense of Guy was explained. As she wondered what their exact relationship was, Rosalind de Marcia approached and put her arms around the two of them, revealing the truth of the matter. Guy's "interest elsewhere" was Isabella. Did she know he was practically penniless, living on the generosity of Robin Brandon?

Of course she did. Money hardly mattered to the de Marcias, and marriages were arranged for many reasons. For Guy, the money would be important, but for Isabella's parents, a Catholic background might be the main consideration. Even if Guy was not devout, his sister was firmly Catholic. If he and Isabella made a match, both families would get what they wanted, and that was the way it was done. Since further speculation was none of her business, Elizabeth spoke of other things.

Thunk! The knife hit the wooden target soundly, handle quivering from the impact, point deep in the center of the circle Simon had drawn for himself with chalk. Once he had become passably good at hitting the target straight on, he'd begun practicing more difficult feats such as turning his back to the wood, then spinning and throwing all in one movement. His body had responded to training in a gratifying way, and Calkin said his eye was excellent. In addition to working with the knife, Simon had begun lifting a bag of sand with his weak arm, starting small and adding more each day until the bag was half full. The arm responded better than he had hoped, and although it would never attain normal ability, he saw improvement in terms of balance. If the need ever arose, he hoped that he would be ready to defend himself.

CHAPTER
TWENTY-NINE

Sir George could give no explanation for the mud on the hem of his cloak. They found him in the stable, overseeing the shoeing of his favorite horse. He seemed more at home here, among the smells and murmurings of animals, than he ever did indoors. Bess questioned him about it, fussed at him was more to the point, but he could not remember wearing the thing in foul weather. In truth, he told Hugh after she had gone, he wore the garment only to please his wife, feeling silly about the "frippery" attached.

"One of the servants remembers a man coming into the house wearing a tasseled cloak," Hugh told him. "Do you know Guy Pemberton?"

"I do. He came to visit Margot. Pleasant fellow." The old knight squinted at Hugh. "My wife saw that there was no tomfoolery between them. They sat in the hall and behaved with decorum."

"He is Margot's half-brother."

The bushy eyebrows rose from their customary line, separating for once into two distinct pieces. "Now there's a surprise. Thought he was sweet on her. I did wonder how a man would warm up a woman like that, but there's no accounting for tastes, you know."

"Why would he come wearing your cloak?"

Sir George shook his head like a horse with flies. "You'd have to ask Guy himself. Unless Margot knows."

"Margot might have lent him your cloak?"

"I admit it doesn't seem probable."

"Let's ask her." Hugh stood quickly and strode from Blakewell's office, Sir George following. They found Margot reading from her book of prayers in the hall. The room was empty and as cheerless as usual, and she sat straight backed on a wooden bench, no part of her relaxed. As her fingers traced the line she read, her lips moved, reciting the prayer to herself. She looked up as they entered, eyes turning hostile as she recognized Hugh.

"Margot, there is a question," Sir George began, but then stopped, unsure how to proceed.

"We want to know if for any reason you lent your brother Guy a cloak that hangs beside the door, a tasseled cloak of blue wool," Hugh finished for him.

"No."

"He was seen wearing it when he came here to visit. Would he have borrowed it without telling anyone?"

Margot's lips tightened. "Sir, you seem determined to think the worst of my brother and me. Guy had no reason to borrow" — her voice dripped sarcasm — "Sir George's cloak. The one he wears is his own, which I made for him myself. Bess liked it so much she made a copy as a Christmas gift for her husband. The two are almost identical." She glared at them for a moment then pointedly returned to reading her book, plainly ending the conversation.

"I could have told you if you'd asked," Bess clucked after Hugh and Sir George found her in the kitchen and confirmed Margot's information. She was in the midst of meal preparation, and two maids bent over pie crusts as a third chopped meat for the filling. Hugh found himself wondering if they would turn out as well as his mother's always had. He could almost smell the pies baking as Bess explained. "It's a fine cloak, and Margot helped me with the pattron, which she devised herself. Why, even the boy wanted one like it." She stopped, her brown eyes widening. "He said false, did he not? Wanted to see the cloak to tell you all about it?"

Hugh blushed. Bess Blakewell seemed a good-hearted woman, and it galled him to be a snoop, checking up on her husband because of his association with two murdered women. He didn't want to hurt her but feared that events might demand it. "Simon helps with the investigation, ma'am. You must think of what he does as working to catch a killer. He meant you no harm."

Her eyes showed some doubt, but she nodded once, lips in a tight line.

A girl appeared in the doorway, broom in hand. "Sir George, Master Ninian is here, waiting in your closet. He has some bills to go over with you."

Sir George sighed but said nothing. As he rose to leave, Ninian himself appeared behind the girl. "Ah, Sir George, forgive me, but I wanted to greet your charming wife. Good day, Lady Blakewell." The servant ducked past him and moved on, but Ninian stayed in the doorway, surveying them all from the stone steps that curved down the passageway.

"Good day to you, Master Ninian," Bess

was carefully polite and no more. She bent to pick up a pail of leeks that sat waiting beside her and began cleaning them with quick chops of a sharp knife.

Ninian seemed unaware of Bess' cool response. Today he carried with him a cloth sack filled with the paraphernalia of his profession, smaller than the bag Hugh had seen before. The clerk had to hold it closed with one hand to keep the papers from spilling out. "Did you lose your leather satchel, Master Clerk?"

Ninian's lips pursed disapprovingly. "Lose it? No, Captain, I did not lose it. It was stolen while I was at my work, by some rogue within the Princess Mary's household. She says I am mistaken, that I did not bring it thither, but I know, sir. I know where my things are."

They all made sympathetic noises over Ninian's loss, but Hugh wondered if the man's emotional outburst wasn't overdone. Had he lost the bag somewhere and now refused to take responsibility for his carelessness?

Ninian settled himself like a rooster soothing ruffled feathers. The look of prurience came on his face again, and he put a hand on the captain's arm. Hugh fought the urge to recoil from the cold fingers, the insistent grip. "Captain Bellows, you seem much involved with business at Hampstead. Have you learned any more about the death of that poor woman?" The cadaverous face split in a smile that was wide but not deep, the teeth hardly showing beneath it, and the man's head teetered as he spoke. Hugh had a vision of a pale snake, weaving and testing the air.

"Nothing worthy of mention. But as you say, I must be about my work." He rose and moved toward the back of the room, where a door led outside. Ninian watched him go, the reptilian smile seemingly stuck on his face. Once again Hugh felt sorry for Sir George, who of the three could not escape Ninian's company. He decided he would find out more about the clerk, how often he visited, and if he might have known Joanna Brandon. Would any of the four women have considered Ninian as a lover? Doubtful.

The evening was pleasant, and Simon walked to Hampstead Castle after supper knowing that Hugh planned to take the evening guard shift. The air was moist and noises magnified in the clear air: a cough, a kettle being scraped at the back entrance, and the ever-present frogs. They met in a small anteroom, since the hall was not yet cleared of the evening meal. Hugh first brought up the subject of the clerk, describing their meeting. "But I can't see Ninian close to Alice or Joanna. He has neither charm nor wealth to attract them."

"True, but we can't assume the killer was close to any of the women. He may follow them when they meet a lover and slay them to punish their sin."

"Yes," Elizabeth put in. "Guy Pemberton was Alice's lover, but he claims he'd finished with her."

"He has a tasseled cloak," Hugh mused. "He could be the man who waited for Mathilda Harrison."

"Yes, and Sir George has one as well, which was beside the door where anyone could have taken it, even Ninian."

"And Ninian claims he lost his leather satchel," Elizabeth said. "Could it have been employed for other, more wicked purposes, and now is ruined for its proper use?"

"Nothing we know is certain," Simon rose and paced the small space. "The man may speak Latin, but he may not. Ninian probably speaks the language, being an educated man. Our quarry may have been lover to these girls, but he may not. He may be the man in the tasseled cloak: Sir George, or

Guy, or someone else, but again, he may not be. It is maddening."

"We need something that ties the crimes together," Hugh said. "It is two different things to arrange an assignation with a woman like Alice or a woman like Mathilda. We must think of what makes them similar."

Elizabeth said thoughtfully, "Someone gave both Alice and Joanna similar silver boxes."

Simon brightened. "Can you show me the box, Highness? The one Alice had?"

Elizabeth obligingly went to find it, her slippers scuffing lightly as she ascended the stairs. As they waited, Hugh and Simon argued the case for Anthony Derwent. "He's certainly one with the ladies," Simon said. "I met him coming out of an inn. When I inquired of the keeper, she told me he'd spent the night with a lady whose name she did not know. She had been there with him once before."

"She may be in danger. If Derwent is the madman, it would follow that he will entice her out and kill her some night."

"A certain boy of the streets told her that very thing," Simon said with a grin. "It was all I could think of to protect the lady, if she chooses to heed the warning."

Hugh grinned in response. "You're starting to enjoy these roles you take on, are you not? Next you'll be treading the boards at the Globe or some such. I'll be able to spend a penny to watch, elbow the man next to me, and say, 'I knew him when he was only an everyday sort of lad.' "

Elizabeth returned with a five-sided box filigreed at the edges. The inside was lined with velvet, the catch heart-shaped. "Excellent metalwork," Hugh commented.

"I saw one like it at Daisy's," Simon said excitedly, running a finger over the delicate silver lace. "Smaller than this but with the same design and catch. You said Joanna Brandon received such a box?"

"Her sister said so, but I never saw it."

"You need to get a look at it, or show her this one, to see if they are similar."

"What are you thinking, Simon?" Hugh asked.

"The one I saw was small enough to fit inside this one, I think." If the other is larger, I'd guess they were nesting boxes. They were made as a set, but someone has given them separately as gifts to his lady loves. Tell us again, Highness, of your sister's loss of a casket of her mother's belongings."

"It disappeared in January. She said the value was mostly sentimental."

335

Gold chains, pearls, silver ornaments: neither man disagreed with the princess openly, but Mary's assessment of such things might be different than a servant's or even a tradesman who came to Kimbolton regularly. Such items would be worth stealing if the box might not be missed.

"If someone took a set of nesting boxes and was using its contents as gifts to please women, that someone is the link to all the deaths."

Hugh stood. "I'll send a man right away to get the other box from Daisy."

Simon had little expectation of success there. "I'd guess she sold it right after I showed interest. Daisy wouldn't miss a chance."

"I'll send this one to Enid Monteagle with a note asking if it matches the one her sister had," Elizabeth offered.

"How will you explain your curiosity?"

She considered the question, pacing a few steps and then turning to them with a soft clap of her hands. "I'll say I remembered her description and want to purchase the box if it is similar to this one, to make a set."

"She may feel obligated to offer it to you as a gift," Simon protested.

"If she does, she does." Elizabeth smiled,

and he realized that was her intent in the first place. "Either way we shall know if the boxes match, as we believe."

"When will you see the Princess Mary again?"

Elizabeth smiled once more. "I believe I am even now feeling very lonely for my dear sister's company, and I probably will not be able to stay away another day."

"Good." Hugh settled into a Dante chair that squeaked at the movement and counted his thoughts out on his fingers. "Find out what you can about the nesting boxes, and learn what else is missing as precisely as you can. Also, find out who visited around the time of its disappearance. Question her about the men we suspect: Derwent, Pemberton, and — oh, see if she knows Sir George at all." He seemed unaware that he was giving orders to a Princess Royal.

Simon observed that the princess did not mind a bit. She obviously had never felt so useful. No one had ever needed her help, nor could she have had any impact if anyone had. Elizabeth had always been someone to be seen to, grudgingly on her father's part, respectfully on everyone else's. Now she had two matters in which her help was essential: the queen's precarious position and the murders of four young women. Simon was glad for her, but a tickle of dread accompanied the thought. Both matters could become dangerous if the princess was not very, very careful.

By the time he left Hampstead, the night had changed totally and a heavy rain fell, soaking everything. Simon plodded home slowly, going over things in his mind. How were the crimes connected with the Catholic faith? Did the killer hate Catholics and kill the women as symbols of the faith? None of the victims had been a secret Catholic as far as they could discern. Why dress them up so? They had all been women of loose morals, which had probably caused their deaths. Did this man set himself above them, fornicate with them, but still believe they were to blame? That sounded like Wat, for whom women's "enchantment" was his excuse for debauchery. Wat, however, had been imprisoned by his brother at the time of the earliest murders.

This killer was twisted as well as violent, taking the heads and dressing the corpses as nuns. If it was the man in the cloak, they might eliminate Derwent, who had never been inside Hampstead Castle. That left Ninian, Sir George, and Guy Pemberton. Hugh thought Ninian too effeminate, and

Elizabeth didn't like to think Sir George could be a killer. Guy was probably a secret Catholic. Did it make sense for him to dress women as nuns and then kill them? Simon couldn't see how.

They must find out more about the religious feeling of the men involved. Derwent might also have Catholic sympathies, being close to Princess Mary. Ninian and Sir George should be proponents of the Anglican Church, since their positions came from the king. They could be secret Catholics, or they might hate Catholics. Simon's head spun with the possibilities. The killer was mad. What was the point of trying to find reason in senseless acts?

No, he told himself as he navigated the muddy road, sinking in mud up to his ankles. The act might be beyond the reason of sane men, but within the madness, there was something that made sense to the killer. He thought there was purpose in both the killings and in making each one the same. It was up to the three of them to follow his line of thought somehow, twisted as it was.

CHAPTER
THIRTY

Mary rose to greet Elizabeth and the two leaned toward each other for the customary kiss. Her sister's cheek was cold, as usual, but it did not do to show hesitation. Sitting in a room almost empty of furnishing except for two stools, Elizabeth admired the piece Mary worked on, a needlepoint book cover. They caught each other up on news, which wasn't much: a planned present for their father's upcoming birthday, a kitten rescued from Sir George and sent to Edward, progress in embroidery. They seldom discussed lessons, a cause for unwanted comparison. Mary's years in the schoolroom were long behind her, and Elizabeth was superior in every subject. Finally, enough time passed to bring up the casket.

"It was never found," Mary replied to her question.

"Do you remember exactly what was lost?"

The theft was something Mary did not want to discuss, but unable to avoid her sister's question, she gave a reluctant answer. "Some jewelry: bracelets, brooches . . . other jewelry items, some made of silver. Only one was gold, if I remember. Most were seldom-used gifts from admirers. The queen always saved things rather than putting them to use. For what, I don't know."

"Kat is like that. We save this dress or these shoes for good. I never know when an occasion is good enough."

Mary almost smiled naturally as she snipped a thread with small silver scissors. Elizabeth wondered what went on in her sister's head. Did she love their father, or did she blame him for her drab existence? Another king might have remained married to his first wife no matter how many other women he bedded. Of course there had been the matter of a male heir, the disappointment of Catherine's only child being a girl.

Elizabeth knew how great had been the anticipation of her own birth. A boy would have validated everything Henry had done to possess Anne Boleyn. Great feasts and joyous celebrations were planned. When the disappointing news that the child was female reached him, Henry was so unhappy that he had not bothered to attend her christening. How sad her mother must have been, and how frightened.

That was the beginning of the end for Anne, and nothing went well thereafter. She miscarried, she was plotted against, and she made mistakes in her handling of Henry. Elizabeth's thoughts turned to Catherine Parr, the current queen. Had she also made one mistake too many?

But her sister had gone on, and now she heard what she had come to hear. "— kept in a set of nesting silver boxes made by Jewish craftsmen in Spain. They do such work most expertly, and these were beautiful. They fitted within each other, three of them, with little heart-shaped latches." The description matched the boxes they sought.

"I wish I could have seen them."

Mary looked up from her stitches, running a finger over the smoothness of the design. "Why?"

"We have no Jews in England, so I have not seen much of their work."

"No Jews who openly practice their religion," Mary corrected.

Of course there were Jews, just as there were Catholics, biding their time, quietly worshipping as they preferred. Elizabeth wondered for the hundredth time what the correct approach to national worship was for a sovereign: choose a religion and insist upon it, or allow the people to express their faith as they wished? Either method seemed to breed trouble. She knew what Mary's method would be. Where would she fit when her sister demanded that everyone return to the Catholic Church? Saying a silent prayer for her brother's health, the younger princess turned the conversation to the cultivation of flowers and vegetables.

At the end of the visit, Elizabeth and Bess started for their boat. They had come upstream on one of the bright little ferries that carried passengers up and down the river several times a day, allowing a much more pleasant trip than any overland route. The rivers of London were more the highways of choice than roads, which were primitive and inadequate for the most part. Boats were quicker and more comfortable, and the carefree boatmen likely to entertain with songs, teasing, and even flirting if encouraged.

As they left the house, Elizabeth stopped short. "I was to ask Mary's cook for her recipe for mince pie. Do wait for me at the bank. I won't be long."

She turned back into the house to look for the person in Mary's household who was truly friendly to her. Elsie, a red-cheeked Welsh girl who worked in the kitchen. About Elizabeth's own age, she had often shyly said a few words to the younger princess, once giving her a special tart from a batch the cook had just taken from the oven. If anyone in the house would tell her the truth, it was Elsie.

The girl was cleaning the kitchen floor on hands and knees, a large brush and a bucket of gray water beside her. Hurriedly she got to her feet and Elizabeth, seeing no one nearby, spoke quickly. "Elsie, you have ever been kind to me, and I hope you can help me now. My sister is missing a casket of valuables."

The girl's eyes widened in fear and she dropped her brush into the bucket with a splash. "Oh, Your Highness, I would never —"

"Of course not." Elizabeth touched the girl's arm. "I did not mean to imply that you might know something of it. I only want to know who might have been to visit the princess in the day or two before the casket was lost."

It did not occur to Elsie to ask why she should tell Elizabeth about the goings-on in her sister's house. Rank has its privileges. "They discovered it gone after Twelfth

Night, I remember clearly. The house was full of people for once. What a coil we were in when the theft was discovered! The princess was . . ." Elsie thought better of what she'd been about to say. "We were all questioned and our rooms searched, of course. But it was never found nowhere."

"Had anyone been to see Lady Mary more than once around that time?" Elizabeth theorized that the theft could not have been accomplished in one visit.

Again Elsie considered. "A few." It wasn't good for one's career at Court to be a frequent visitor at Mary's. "The Spanish ambassador, of course, and the lady that married the Spaniard."

"Rosalind de Marcia?"

"A good lady, for all she married a foreigner. There was a man from up north, a gallant, always kissing her hand, and the princess' hand, too."

"Derwent?"

"Yes, that's him. Thinks he's . . ." She stopped again from letting her mouth run away with her common sense. Of nobility she had no right to an opinion except among her own kind. She pushed back a sleeve that had unrolled and was now soaked from her scrubbing. "Your Margot came once."

Margot? She was bolder about her religion than Elizabeth would have credited. "Was there a man with her? A handsome man with a tasseled cape?"

"I don't think so. 'Course he might have taken it off before I saw him. If you'll wait, I'll ask." She was gone in a trice, and Elizabeth was left to wonder if she'd done the right thing. If the girl asked someone else, that person might tell Mary that she'd been nosing into her household's affairs, or Mary might come along herself at any moment and see for herself that her sister was still there.

Thankfully, Elsie came back quickly, face flushed with success. With her was a young man who blushed deeply when introduced. "This is my friend Nathaniel, who took the cloaks, so he remembers the man you asked of."

Nathaniel smelled to high heaven and his hands were grimy with dirt. The spring task of digging out the midden was his for today, she guessed. Elsie nudged him and he spoke haltingly, looking at Elizabeth's shoes the whole time. "There was such a man, who came twice, once to play cards and a second time to Twelfth Night supper."

"But he didn't come with Margot," Elsie put in. "He came with Father, um, Reverend

Francis the first time, and Robin Brandon the other."

A secret priest, one who claimed to have transferred loyalty to Henry but remained true to his original calling. That was probably the "friend" Mary had mentioned with hesitation.

Elizabeth was sure that the first Catherine had held secret masses, and Mary probably still did. Henry had not concerned himself much with the thousands of priests, monks, and nuns left in England once he outlawed their livelihoods. Policy had been to allow the old clergy to simply transfer their loyalty to him. A few who refused had been put to death as examples, and others unwilling to serve Henry's new church had been pensioned off. Catherine and now Mary would find men willing to keep the old ways alive in hopes that someday the nation would return to what they deemed the true faith.

And Robin Brandon? What reason had he to visit Mary's home? Or had he simply come along with Guy, out of curiosity or looking for adventure?

"Has Brandon been here often?"

"Only once." Elsie's eyes widened. "He is not the sort of person Her Highness finds sociable, and she firmly recommended that Pemberton not bring him again." Her thin

347

face showed agreement with Mary's edict, and even Nathaniel made a small sound of agreement.

"And the missing box, what do you remember of it?"

"It were three boxes, each smaller than the other so that it fit inside. The smallest one were so big," here she made a circle with her fingers about ten inches in diameter. "We heard some of the late queen's baubles were inside, though I never saw them."

"And you noticed nothing unusual at Twelfth Night supper? No one where he should not be?"

They both considered, and finally Nathaniel said, "I met Lord Derwent in a corridor. He said he were looking for the water closet —" he blushed to say it before the princess — "and I showed him the way. He give me a penny."

As they traveled back to Hampstead, Elizabeth answered Bess' comments with minimal replies. The little boat slipped downstream with barely a wobble, and the banks that slid by were riotously colored with rhododendron in full bloom, but she failed to notice.

Guy Pemberton was a secret Catholic, in all probability. His sister's ardor, his presence at Kimbolton with a Catholic priest, and his attention to Isabella de Marcia added up to that. Derwent and Pemberton had both visited about the time the casket was stolen, as had Robin Brandon. Pemberton was penniless and therefore suspect, but Derwent's wife might be one who kept watch over finances. Brandon certainly had no need of money, since the family had prospered under Henry's friendship. Any visitor at Twelfth Night Supper could have taken the casket, hoping no one would notice in the confusion of a celebration. Whoever did so used its contents to win the trust of four women who died as a result. She was almost certain of that.

Chapter
Thirty-One

Hugh's thoughts had turned in another direction entirely. He wondered if he was wise to concentrate on the lover — or lovers — to the exclusion of other possibilities. It was possible that another man had killed the women as they returned from a rendezvous. The boxes could have been separated and sold by a thief long ago, even if the three boxes were matched, which was not certain. He thought of Wat. It was doubtful he was the murderer, but what if he had seen something, someone, on the night of Alice's death? He decided it was worth a second trip inside Newgate.

The day had become warm, although it had rained in the early hours. This was good because rain kept down the smells of too many people in too little space. He rode through the noisy streets, noting in the crowds of everyday people clad mostly in dull shades and the petty criminals who tried their best to appear something they were not. On a corner sat an Abram man, growling and muttering, his face bloody where he had apparently scratched himself. He seemed a pitiful lunatic, but the scratches had no depth to them, in fact were trails of some berry concoction rather than blood. Abram men, beggars who pretended madness, succeeded because people often gave money in fear of them. Coins in a bowl beside this one showed that his act was convincing to those less aware than Captain Bellows.

As he approached the Old Bailey and Newgate, Hugh passed the pillories, where sat two unfortunate souls, probably man and wife. Their heads and arms were fastened into wooden frames that forced them to stand bent at an awkward angle. Their faces showed shame and discomfort. On one side, a boy of about thirteen knelt with a bucket of water and a cloth, wetting the woman's lips and washing some mud from her face as well. "Leave her be, lad," a nearby man warned. " 'Tis right to punish shopkeepers that make folk sick with bad food. They must learn to be more careful." The boy did not answer or even look up; he simply moved to his father and repeated his ministrations. The bystander said no more, and the boy sat down between the two pillory frames in the midday sun, mitigating his parents' shame in the only way he knew.

A stable boy took Hugh's horse outside Newgate, and he entered the relative coolness of the old building. The shade was welcome but the place smelled ten times worse than the London street. Locating the officer in charge, he asked to have Wat Rogers brought to him.

"I'm sorry, Captain. The man is dead."

"Dead? How?"

"Killed himself, sir. He had rope concealed about his waist, apparently, and managed to fasten it to the grate of the window and hang himself. Saved us the trouble, he did. Still, the people would have enjoyed it."

"Wat was searched at his arrest. He had no rope."

The officer looked confused for a moment. "He had a visitor. Yesterday, I think it was."

"Was the visitor a tall, self-righteous prig with a beetle brow?"

"That would describe him well enough."

"His brother Peter." No doubt he'd had a suggestion for poor, mad Wat. To save Wat's soul, he would say, but truly to save himself disgrace. Or was there more than that to

352

Wat's death? Had the lunatic known something that Peter didn't want anyone else to know? He would ask Simon where to locate this brother, and then he would find out.

As Elizabeth had hoped, Enid Monteagle provided her with the box as requested, with a note insisting that she keep it. The two were exactly matched except for size; Alice's fit neatly inside the one that had belonged to Joanna Brandon. Hugh's man was unsuccessful in finding the third box: Daisy had indeed sold it. She did, however, describe the peddler who had bought it, and inquiries were being made as to his whereabouts.

The three met in the garden, shaded now with leaves almost full grown. Although she and her ladies had done what they could to soften the harsh aspect of the old castle, making it less stark, Elizabeth complained that the place still smelled of mold, so outside was preferable on a fine day.

"What do we know?" Simon said rhetorically. "Five women have died in the same horrible manner." He avoided mentioning beheading. "Each had a mysterious lover that no one else knew. Each was given a trinket, probably by this man."

"Was Mathilda?" Elizabeth interrupted.

"According to Pen, yes. She had a pin with

what looked like small pearls on it. Nothing like that was found with the body or among her things."

"I see. So each woman had a recent gift unexplained by other means."

"Yes, and the Princess Mary lost nesting boxes containing just such items a few weeks before the murders began. She said there were brooches?"

"Yes." Suddenly Elizabeth's eyes widened and she tapped a finger on her own forehead in frustration. "'And other jewelry!' At the time I did not mark it, but Mary hesitated as she said the last."

Simon leaned in eagerly. "Could that other jewelry have been rosaries?"

"Of course. She would not mention them specifically, but of course they had them. Such items once were popular gifts." Although not officially banned, rosaries smacked of papist leanings and were not as popular in England as they had once been. They had discovered something important in the matter of the box of trinkets.

"If whoever took the princess' property is the lover of these women, he is also the one who killed them and laid them out with rosaries from the nesting boxes."

"We know that Pemberton, Brandon, and Derwent were at Mary's home near the time of the theft."

"As was Ninian."

"Ninian?" Simon echoed.

"The man keeps your sister's accounts as well as yours, Your Highness, and has done so for nigh on two years. He would know his way around by now, I'm thinking."

"Just when we thought we'd narrowed the number down," Simon moaned, slapping a spirea bush and releasing a flurry of tiny white petals.

"We don't know enough yet. We must keep looking."

"But he will kill again. He killed Therese in February, Mathilda and Joanna Brandon in March, and Alice in April, and almost certainly this unknown woman in May." Grimly, the others nodded. If they did not succeed soon, there would be another death. The problem was they had no idea who was in danger, too many possibilities for who was danger, and there was the rub.

Leaving the house where it was supposed she would spend the evening, a woman made her way down the street, her face hidden by the hood of her cloak. If it had been visible, passers-by might have marveled at it, for the lady was renowned in the highest circles for her beauty.

The night was clear, and her footsteps echoed on the cobblestone until she turned down a street of hard-packed dirt. Ahead she saw the inn that was her destination and quickened her step slightly, although it was not her wont to appear eager for anything. She generally let things come to her, but this new affair was the best in years. Young, handsome, and aware of just the right things to say and do to make lovemaking sweet, he was different from the others somehow. There was a quality of . . . danger to him.

Her thought stopped there, for he stepped from behind a doorpost, blocking her path. His eyes were illuminated briefly in the moon's light before his face passed again into shadow. There was something there, something hungry that sent a shiver of anticipation through her. He was hers, she knew it. As she exulted in her conquest, his arms went around and pulled her into the shadows with him.

She went willingly, but dream turned to nightmare as strong hands curled around her throat and tightened their grip until she could not breathe. The beautiful face contorted as she tried to scream, tried to beg, but at last there was quiet except for sounds best undescribed.

■ ■ ■ ■

Elizabeth decided to do something she rarely did, invite a relative stranger to Hampstead. Isabella de Marcia, she reasoned, was not the type to take tales back to others about the mean estate in which the princess lived. The half-Spanish, half-English girl was one of those rare creatures who took everyone as she met them and thought little about appearances. Obligated to ask Rosalind de Marcia, too, Elizabeth was pleased when the mother declined politely, begging a headache. It was an excuse she too had used to get out of unwanted invitations, but Elizabeth was glad to have Isabella to herself.

Of course, Isabella came with a companion, a duenna in fact, from Spain. The woman was outgoing for a Spaniard, though, and in no time she and Mary Ward were comparing notes on tapestries, with Mary demonstrating her own style while the other nodded enthusiastically, the language barrier overcome by common interest. The girls were free to wander and speak of what they liked.

What Isabella liked was Guy Pemberton. She could not remain sedate, but gripped

Elizabeth's hand as she asked, "Your Highness, did you find him handsome?"

Elizabeth assured her new friend that she had. Something in her voice must have alerted Isabella to her reservations about the man, for she launched into a defense. "He is penniless, but that does not matter. Between my father and mother there is wealth a-plenty, and I am an only child."

Looking at the girl, Elizabeth reflected that this might have been she had Henry Tudor not been her father. Isabella was a year or so older, probably fifteen, so it was time her future was decided. Her parents had looked for a man whose name and social position were good, of course. But in this case they had also taken note of their daughter's interest in Guy Pemberton.

Not all parents were so caring. Elizabeth knew of more than one girl forced by her parents to marry the man of their choice despite stubborn refusals. In fact, daughters were sometimes beaten or starved into submission. It was, after all, the parents' right to bestow a child where they pleased. Her own mother Anne had planned to marry elsewhere until she caught the eye of the king. When that happened, Harry Percy had been whisked away, possibly by royal order but certainly by consent of both her own family and his. Would she have been the same person if Harry had been her father, if the two young lovers had been allowed to marry? Her life would certainly have been different.

She returned to listening to praise of Guy Pemberton. "I met him through Robin Brandon, when they came to your sister's home for Twelfth Night. Robin was not well behaved and is excluded from the princess' company in the future." She made a pretty grimace of regret. "As a pair they have not endeared themselves to some at Court, but young men are often so. Guy will settle down once he is married."

Isabella parroted what were obviously her mother's words, and Elizabeth could imagine Rosalind's hopeful tone as she said them. Preparations must be well underway for the uniting of the two families. Remembering Guy's charm and good looks, she could understand her friend's excitement at the prospect. She hoped that he did settle down after marriage, but the picture of Lord Derwent lingered in her mind. He had not, according to Simon's reports.

At a sudden impulse, she asked, "My castellan, Sir George, has a most remarkable cloak copied from one Guy's sister made for him. Have you seen it?"

"I have. It was most finely wrought, but he does not have it anymore."

Interest quickened. "What became of it?"

The girl's face turned serious and she thought a moment before replying. "I have said that Guy is without resources." She twisted the ribbons of her dress absently until they were a mass of wrinkles. "It does not matter in the least to me, but it goads him. He feels the shame of depending on his friends for support, imagines comments made about our relationship and why he sought me out. Whenever it is possible, therefore, he bestows gifts on his friends. If he wins at cards, he immediately spends the money on those present. If he receives some fine gift, he gives it in return to another. His sister made him the cloak, which was finely done. Sir Robin admired it, and without hesitation Guy gave it to him."

Elizabeth could almost understand. She would dearly love to give extravagant gifts to Kat, or to Robert Dudley, even to Simon and Isabella, her newest friends. So Guy had given away his cloak, as the scriptures advise. She approved, although it was certain Margot would not.

Isabella's thought had run on, and she added now, "Robin, of course, has not the care for fine things that he should. The cloak was ruined the next time Guy saw it, great stains all over it and a long tear where one of the tassels had been torn away."

"How ungentle of him." Elizabeth filed that information away for her report to Simon and Hugh.

CHAPTER
THIRTY-TWO

Simon wandered the Shambles, asking whether anyone remembered Mathilda Harrison and the night of her death. He had no luck for the better part of the morning. As the day became warmer, his frustration rose at his lack of progress. They had learned things, but nothing led to a definite result. Where to go next? He decided to try the Ox with Flowers again.

As he moved toward the inn, he was hailed from across the street. After a moment he recognized Penitence Brook shuffling over to meet him. Moving into the shade of a building, Simon waited, but with some exasperation.

"Is it you? Mathilda's nephew?" The man's mumble seemed even worse than before. Simon almost made his excuses and moved on. Hugh had reported the constable's opinion that Pen was "less than half-wit," and he had no inclination to listen to tales of mysterious men today. Because it was not in him to be rude, he asked, "Pen, how goes the day?"

"When the sun shines, naught can be ill, am I right?"

"I was on my way to an appointment so —"

"Concerning Mathilda's murder?" Pen's face showed much more understanding than Simon remembered. In fact, he looked positively knowing.

"What do you mean?"

"They think I'm daft," Pen said quite clearly, "but I know a thing or two. Now you are asking everywhere in the Shambles about Mathilda and how she died. You an't her nephew, 'cause she didn't have one. As I told you, her and me talked sometimes. She didn't treat me like I was an idiot." The man's point was evident in his tone, and he tapped his forehead meaningfully. "So if you an't kin and you're makin' inquiries, I wonder who you are."

It was time for honesty, at least in part. "Pen, my name is Simon. I work for those who want to find Mathilda's murderer. I was sent because folk may speak more freely to me than to a constable or an official of the court. I'm sorry I didn't tell you before, but . . ."

"You took me for a half-wit." He didn't seem at all insulted. "I don't mind. People that thinks of me that way leaves me alone. I like watching the world go by, and I pay no mind to what others say. Still, I were fond of Mathilda, and I would like to see him hanged that hurt her so. I have something that may help if you'll come with me."

Simon followed without another word, unable to believe both his luck and Pen's change in demeanor. A perfect disguise was the appearance of lack-wit. He must remember that for future reference.

Pen led the way down an alley and at the far end squatted before a rough plank wall that blocked it from the houses beyond. Before the planks was a pile of discarded items: a staved-in barrel, a two-legged stool, and various pieces of broken crockery. Digging beneath it all, Pen came up with a bag made from bits of cloth pieced together. From the bag he took several items, almost reverently.

"These were her things," he told Simon. "She left them at the Ox, but I took 'em away before John could sell them, as he would have for sure. I heard him tell the constable she had nothing there, but I knew better. I took the bag when he wasn't looking and hid it here."

In its three-month stay mice had chewed holes in the bag and the simple dress inside it. Other than that the items were dirty but intact: a comb, a pair of woolen stockings, some rags Simon guessed were for a woman's monthly bleeding, and a brooch with pearls set into its edge. Rubbing it on his shirt, he examined it and decided it was silver.

"Pen, may I take these things away? I promise that I will return them to you."

"No need, lad. I want none of it. Although —" He touched the stockings. "Do you think Mathilda would mind if I had those? My feet gets so cold in winter, y'know."

A silver brooch, and Pen chose the stockings. "I'm sure she would want you to have them. The rest I will dispose of once they have served my purpose." They turned to leave the alley. "I thank you for your help. I need one thing more. Information, if you can give it."

"O' course."

"Did Mathilda ever say anything about who gave her the brooch, the man she was meeting?"

He thought carefully. "He said that he might set her up somewhere. She told me if she had a place, that I might come and visit, 'stead of sitting at the Ox." His voice was wistful, but Simon clung to his purpose.

"Could it have been the man you saw on the street?"

"I got the feeling he were waiting, as I said."

"Would you know him again?"

Pen looked disappointed. "No, lad. I never saw his face. He had that fancy cloak o' his pulled tight and the hood over his face, but it were cold that night, so I did not mark it."

"A fancy cloak, you say?"

"Yes, it were made of good stuff, which is why I noticed him. No one 'round here has one like it. It was decorated all 'round with those threads that are fastened together at the top and hang loose below."

"Tassels?"

"Them's the things."

"Did he carry anything with him? A bag?"

Pen frowned thoughtfully. "I did not see such. It might have been in the alley, o'course."

"And you're sure it was the night Mathilda died."

"Yes, poor thing. She were chipper that day, now that I think back. Like she thought her fortune made." His pale face brightened. "That's why her things were all in the bag, 'stead of set out in her room. Do ye think

366

he was taking her away that night?"

"I'm afraid she thought so. I think the man woos women and tells them that on a certain night he will take them with him. Instead he kills them and leaves them dressed as nuns."

"Them? Then there have been others."

Simon groaned. He'd been careful up to now to refer only to Mathilda's death, and now his thinking out loud had betrayed him.

"Don't worry, lad. I'll tell no one." Pen laid a finger beside his nose in the gesture of complicity. "They wouldn't likely believe me if I did, but I can keep my own counsel. If it has happened to others, that's more reason I should help you stop him. I will keep my ears open. You'd be surprised what folk will say around one who never pays attention to anything." A grin belied his last statement.

"You are content to let the world think of you that way?"

Pen looked slyly at him in a sidewise glance. "Master Simon, I noticed something at a very young age. If a lad is clever and learns to do something, then he must learn more. If he learns that, well, he is given more again. But, if a lad drifts away and cannot seem to keep his mind on things, folk begin to leave him alone. They call him lack-wit and idiot, but he is asked to do nothing very difficult. I am an odd 'un, I suppose, but that fits what I want from life. I don't mind what folk say if they leave me alone."

Simon left with respect for Penitence Brook on two levels. The man was a staunch ally in his search for a killer and, he admitted wryly, able to convince those around him that he was not worth bothering with, which left him free to live precisely the life he chose.

Pondering Pen's information, Simon moved down the street and out of the Shambles. A quick movement beside him caught his eye, and there was Peto the Pope, looking at him with those grave blue eyes. He stopped short, unsure of what to expect. The outlaw regarded him mildly. "I thought we might talk."

"I . . . of course."

"Things have changed for me lately, and I have come to believe that you know something of it."

Simon was at a loss for words. Was Peto determined to harm him, thinking he had set the guard on him?

It seemed unlikely when he gestured toward a nearby public house. "Come, lad. I'll stand us both to some ale, and we will discuss the state of the world." He clapped an arm about Simon's shoulders and steered him along. Peto could not attack him in such a public place. *Maybe later,* fear whispered.

The pub was a better one than the Ox with Flowers. The girl who brought them mugs of brown ale was cheerful and neat, the floor was swept clean, and even the walls were fairly straight. They sat at a rough wooden table in the corner and Peto ordered, calling the girl by name and getting a giggle in return. It seemed that his habits were known, for the girl moved away quickly after serving their drinks. For his part, the host greeted them almost reverently then left them to their business.

Peto took a drink of ale absently and wiped his lips. "Your friend Captain Bellows has made my life difficult of late," he remarked, looking at the door and not at Simon. "He seems convinced that I killed Therese."

Simon fingered the tankard before him, not trusting his stomach to hold down the liquid it held. It was best to hear the whole thing before he chose how much he would tell.

"I have spoken to Daisy. After your last visit, the guard became interested in a certain box, and she believes you are responsible. If you set them onto Daisy, I ask myself, could you not have set them onto me as well?" Again Peto lifted his mug of ale, took a longer drink this time, and set it carefully down in the same spot as before, aligning the bottom with the ring of moisture on the table.

He suddenly felt unafraid of Peto's reaction to the truth. "I am commissioned by His Majesty the king to investigate the death of Therese Blanc and the other women who met the same fate." If they did not trust someone, did not admit that this monster existed, more women would die. Peto had vast knowledge of a world that Simon did not know, and he could help if he chose to. "I do not think you had anything to do with these deaths. However, I did not know of your reputation when we met the first time. It is only natural that some might think . . ." Words failed him, but the outlaw's eyes widened in understanding.

"Ah, I see. I am a criminal, yet you do not think me capable of the murder of helpless women?"

"As I said, it does not seem likely to me."

"Here is what you need to know about me. I am a man who treats his friends well and his enemies as they deserve. I do not murder women, and certainly not for sport, as Therese was killed." He fiddled with the ale mug again, setting it so the handle turned first this way, then another. "I don't know why I care to explain myself to you, lad, but I will tell you a story, since you stood for me at the prison and convinced the captain to send to York. It showed that you have a fair mind —" here Peto allowed himself a smile — "and it gave me the opportunity to arrange my escape."

"That was cleverly done," Simon said with a grin.

"I have many friends, or at least many who will befriend me should I need them." Settling himself more comfortably in his chair, he began the promised explanation, staring off most of the time, but catching Simon's gaze intermittently, as if judging how much the youth believed him.

"Once I was as you are. I had parents, a home of sorts, and a fairly respectable life. My best friend was a boy called Thomas — Tom, to me. One night on his way home from some innocent boyish entertainment that he and I had shared, Tom saw something he should not have seen, some doings in an alley that were best ignored. The men responsible decided that Tom could not live on with the knowledge he had, so they put a knife between his ribs."

He paused for a moment, remembering. "They did not do their work well enough. After they left him, poor Tom managed to stumble out into the street. Someone saw him fall and ran to him, but he was barely alive. He whispered the names of those who had done for him. Then my friend died in the street, with no friend or family to touch his hand in farewell or whisper their affection. I heard the names he spoke repeated through the dark streets of London. Everyone knew who the killers were, but no one would do anything about it. They were bad men, feared by all."

Peto's eyes lit with the first real fire Simon had seen in them. "I decided that I would do something, for Tom. I was not full grown, but I took on a man's vengeance." He rubbed his smooth, boyish face with a hand that was almost delicate. "First I learned everything I could about how to kill. I spoke with old soldiers, branded criminals, anyone who could enlarge my knowledge of murder. When I was satisfied as to my method, I followed the men who killed Tom for weeks, learning their habits, their favorite places, their weaknesses. When I was ready I took them, one at a time. They died quickly. I gave them that since it was to me an extermination, necessary to prevent harm to other innocents."

As he spoke, Peto's voice was calm, almost toneless. He seemed to have finished, but again Simon waited and at last he went on, more normally now. "Surprisingly, the deed made my reputation. I became known as a ruthless killer, a fact I could not deny. I had given those men no mercy, and the result was that I took their place: I am one who is feared by all." He took a quick drink, saluting himself ironically with the mug before he did.

"How old were you when this happened?"

The man's lips tightened. "Thirteen." After a pause he added, "Tom was only twelve. He never saw thirteen." His gaze met Simon's directly. "I capitalize on the dread people have for me. Those who are outside the law cluster about me, willing to do my bidding." He gestured vaguely with the tankard in his hand. "If I suggest that I be included in someone's schemes, it is done. If I advise someone to make himself unknown in London, it happens." An innocent smile flashed for a moment. "I have been credited with murders that never happened. The supposed victim simply leaves the city rather than face me. In short, I have become a legend, yet all I am is a man who dares to do what others only think on."

Although not convinced that everything Peto said was true, Simon sensed that rumor might do as much for a man's reputation as action after a certain point. Once a man had hunted down and killed two of London's worst, that might well have been enough to make him legendary. Somewhere between this version and Calkin's was the real Peto: not the cold-blooded killer of rumor, but ruthless enough. None of it convinced Simon that he would have killed women such as Mathilda, however, or that a girl like Alice LaFont would have dallied with him, either.

"As I said, I do not believe you had anything to do with Therese's death or any of the others," Simon told the outlaw. "But the killer must be stopped."

"I will see what I can do," Peto promised, his languid manner once again in place. "If you will do what you can to get this Bellows to leave me in peace." He lifted a cord that hung around his neck and pulled it over his head. On it hung a curiously fashioned amulet of base metal cleverly formed into the shape of a fleur-de-lis.

"Therese gave me this, and now I give it to you."

"Why give me your amulet?"

Peto seemed a little sad. "Such things protect the wearer only while the giver lives. It may work for you, coming from one whose life you helped to save." With that he placed a coin on the table to pay for the drinks, gave Simon a solemn nod, and disappeared onto the busy street.

CHAPTER
THIRTY-THREE

A Princess Royal would never skulk, but Elizabeth was decidedly furtive as she crept through the palace, searching for some sign of her father or stepmother. Her footsteps were careful on the rush-strewn floors, her progress stopped at each crossing as she listened for signs of occupants ahead. She had come uninvited, having learned that Catherine was to be arrested for heresy. Despite the strong chance that she would incur her father's anger and possibly be banished forever, she had come to plead for the queen. What good it would do, she did not know. Her influence over her father was negligible, but she had to try. This woman who had been so good to Henry and all of his poor, disjointed family must not suffer the same fate as two other wives.

Turning a corner, she almost ran into Doctor Wendy, hurrying from the palace. "Oh, Your Highness, forgive me," he apologized. "I did not hear your steps."

"I have come to see Her Majesty. Is she . . . well?"

The man gave a deep sigh of relief. "Oh, Highness, I believe she is. It was most distressing, I must tell you, but I believe the crisis has passed."

"Please, tell me." At his hesitation, she assured, "I only wish her safety and peace of mind."

The doctor's doubts vanished at her earnestness, and the story came out in a whispered rush. "We heard this morning that she was to be arrested. As you know, others of the Court have already been charged for their Protestant views. A few days ago when the king ordered the queen's accounts examined, it was not a good sign."

"I had heard as much."

"Today the king sat alone in the garden." *Separating himself from a woman he rejects,* Elizabeth thought, *as he has done before.* "The queen, however, had been warned of the matter and came rushing out to his side, where she fell on her knees and quoted scripture to him. She had found passages that indicate women must be obedient to their husbands, and she begged to 'be taught by His Majesty, who is a prince of such excellent learning and wisdom.' "

"Did she indeed?" The way to Henry's mercy: submit totally to his will. Elizabeth leaned against the paneled wall for a moment, needing its strength to support her.

"I was there, having just changed the dressings on His Majesty's legs." His face flickered with something, perhaps dismay at not being able to stop the decay. "At any rate, he looked at her for a long time, and I trembled for her. But he said, 'Then, Kate, we are friends again.' He embraced the queen, who was by this time weeping, as I was myself, I am not ashamed to say."

Elizabeth felt like weeping herself but would not, of course. Oh, that her own mother could have moved the king so, but not even concern for his own child had saved Anne Boleyn from the block.

"Very shortly there came a crowd of guards, led by Lord Wriothesley, to arrest the queen." The doctor's dignified face betrayed enjoyment of this part. "The king fairly growled at them to be gone and stop invading his privacy. The soldiers left quickly, and His Lordship did not know what to say. He tried several times to excuse himself with dignity, but in the end backed into a hedge and disappeared into it."

Elizabeth's whole body relaxed, and she was able to smile at the image. It would not do to say anything that could be repeated to her detriment, so she merely thanked the doctor for the information and bade him good day.

She found the queen in her apartments, near collapse. Poor Catherine! She had not asked to be queen but had done her best for all concerned. How unfortunate that the times were so dangerous. In her heart, Elizabeth knew that her father had made mistakes, but she told herself over and over that it was the times, the advice he received, the pressures of his role as king that brought about those mistakes. Henry would never hurt anyone willingly, she was sure of it.

It was a testimony to her nervous state that Catherine relived the last few days with her stepdaughter, admitting her fear and distress. "I received a warning that my arrest was imminent through a friend whom I believe you know. I will not say his name, but I was . . . most grateful for the message."

"And I am glad the information was used to best advantage." It was as close as either could come to admitting that the girl had, through browbeating Hugh Bellows, ferreted out details of Henry's intent and sent Master Greengage to warn the queen. Open discussion would be dangerous; it was treason to plot against the king's wishes. Still, if a monarch was manipulated by evil counsel, Elizabeth reasoned, a word of warning was not actually working against her father, only against the evil counsel itself. For the first time ever, she initiated a hug as she took leave of her stepmother.

Elizabeth avoided her father and sought instead her sister. Mary was with Wriothesley, who flattered her shamelessly in hopes that she would one day be queen. Elizabeth stood in the corridor, listening to the hum of voices. One, high and petulant, assured the Lord Chamberlain that his honest intent was evident. Wriothesley's cold and nasal tones repeated the words as if memorizing them, and he took his leave. Stepping out of sight until he was gone, Elizabeth then entered and kissed her sister's cheek. Ignoring the recent crisis, which could only divide them, she came immediately to the point of her visit. "Is this piece part of the missing jewelry we spoke of?" She held out the brooch that Pen had given to Simon.

"Why, yes. Where did you get it?" Mary's thin nose pinched suspiciously.

"An official of the Court found it in connection with the investigation of a crime. He believes it was given as a gift to a young woman by the man who stole it from you."

She rushed on before Mary could comment. "We suspect a man of your acquaintance who is fairly tall and speaks Latin."

Mary sniffed dismissively. "What is this to you?"

Elizabeth looked directly at her sister. "It may have to do with murder, Mary. Not only that of Alice LaFont, but several others. You must tell me so that I can pass on what you know to the officer." She'd taken a perilous step. If she was wrong, Mary could run to Henry and tell on her. If she revealed to the king that Elizabeth was helping Hugh, both of them would face his royal anger. To her relief, Mary's face showed real concern.

"Do you mean someone uses my stolen trinkets to get close to women and then kills them?" She twitched her skirts in agitation.

"Yes. He dresses the girls in the robes of nuns and places rosaries on the bodies."

"Rosaries!"

"There were also rosaries in the nesting caskets, is that not so?"

After the briefest of pauses, Mary answered, "Yes."

"Do you remember what any of them looked like?"

"One was pink stones, I remember. When I was a child Mother let me look at it sometimes, such soft color for a stone. Another was black, obsidian, I think."

The description tallied with Hugh's descriptions, although neither rosary had been found. "Alice's body was found with a rosary of green, the only one I actually saw. The stones were striated and the chain was gold."

"Oh, yes, I had forgotten. That piece was given to my mother by His Majesty of Spain. The green stones come from Russia and are called malachite. They ward off illness."

"These are the items found at the scenes of recent murders." Elizabeth put a hand on Mary's arm in earnest supplication. "A killer is sought, sister, of most cruel nature. Will you help?"

"What affair is this of yours?"

What should she admit to? Swallowing, Elizabeth made her decision. "Our father has commissioned a certain captain to look into the murders. I volunteered to help him since I may speak freely with people that he may not. I offered to come to you, since our relationship makes us more likely to trust each other." How hard that was to say. "It would help if you gave me your impressions of certain gentlemen."

"Father believes a gentleman does these

awful things?"

"We think it is so."

Mary obviously did not want to believe that a nobleman could be so base. Her values and her self-worth were built on a belief in the superiority of her bloodline, the joining of two royal families. Neither Elizabeth nor Edward could claim such fine breeding. It was little enough, the younger girl supposed, considering what Mary had suffered in her life.

"Which gentlemen?"

Elizabeth relaxed a little, one hurdle overcome. Now she must tread carefully. It would not do to list only Catholics, or Mary would take offense. She also did not relish sharing information with her sister, who was not always discreet. "What do you think of the Earl of Hereton?" He didn't even live in London, but it was a good place to start, to gauge her sister's cooperation.

"A silly man," Mary said with a sniff of disapproval. "He tells disgusting jokes and then laughs louder than anyone else."

"I've noticed. What about Guy Pemberton?"

"Guy?" Mary's tongue clucked. "A charming wastrel. When he first came to visit me, I expected great things, because of his background." *Catholic.* "He is a great disap-

pointment." *No religious convictions.* "However, he dances well and is a diverting companion."

"I see. Do you recall Anthony Derwent?"

"Dear Anthony, surely you don't suspect
him? These men are all quite harmless.
Anthony is the soul of piety, a godly man
and deep." She certainly had that one
wrong.

"Alistair Brown?"

"Now I don't like him. He could easily be
a murderer. A greedy little man!" Elizabeth
smiled inwardly, since Alistair was outspo-
ken in his criticism of Rome.

"Ninian, the clerk who sees to your finances?"

"I cannot say that I've actually spoken
with him. I see him coming and going like a
ghost, so tall and intense, but I usually manage to be busy when he visits. John meets
with him." John Allen managed Mary's
household.

Elizabeth was running out of names. It
would not do to mention Sir George, since
she should know him far better than Mary
could. "Lord Burford?" He had been proven
incapable of Alice's murder since he was
away at his estates, but it couldn't hurt to
ask.

"A hard man to judge. There is a fire

384

within him, but I know not from whence it comes."

"Robin Brandon?" The name came to her at the last, almost without thinking.

Mary's nose lifted. "Not fit for the company of decent folk," she said in clipped tones. "He is a swine."

"Yet he is Guy's friend."

"A man may do things that are necessary but not palatable. Since Guy has no fortune, he is forced to suffer Brandon's company. I do not approve, but I understand."

Money and power are what it comes down to. Mary understands because, like me, she has neither and must smile and accept what she would rather not.

Elizabeth had a moment of admiration for her sister. At least Mary had beliefs and stood strongly for them. Elizabeth had no such commitment to religion. To what was she committed? She believed in her father, she believed in England, and she was beginning to believe in herself, not as the unseen princess, but as a person of intellect, one who could attack problems and solve them. Could intellect be put to better use than finding a fiend such as the one they sought?

Impulsively she hugged her sister's bony shoulders. "You are a help, Mary. I thank you."

To her amazement, pure happiness shone in Mary's face, a look seldom associated with her. Elizabeth took leave, reflecting that she was not the only one of Henry's daughters who longed to be of some use to the world.

CHAPTER
THIRTY-FOUR

Hugh spent the day learning all he could about Wat and Peter Rogers. He soon concluded that the latter was no true cleric, but one of a number of self-ordained preachers who held informal "meetings" at which they railed against sin and decadence. Such men were outside the established Church of England, but if careful to observe the letter of the law, they were left to their eccentric doctrines.

The area known as Holborn was a simple gathering of dwellings, most occupied by tradesmen. The metallic sound of many hammers on tin proclaimed the area's main trade, metalware. At the front of each house was the workplace, and the families lived at the back. Hugh guessed that the items made, usually with the help of all family members under the guidance of the father, were taken to the streets of London, since there was scant opportunity for commerce in the tiny hamlet.

Beginning with the woman who had helped Simon locate Rogers' house, he tried to get a sense of the man. Middle-aged and arthritic, the woman nevertheless knitted a steady stream as she talked, never pausing and never looking at the piece, either. It quickly became clear that she did not like Peter Rogers. She repeated her claim that the Parson Peter was prone to judge others more harshly than himself.

"Do you mean his brother?"

"Poor Wat was his favorite target." She scratched at a sore on her elbow. "Not that Peter doesn't find witches and fiends among the rest of us, but he browbeat his brother from the time Wat was a boy. The lad ran away to sea, but he couldn't break away from Peter's influence. He went mad and was finally shunned by the sailing masters. That's when he showed up here again.

"Peter took him in, playing the part of a good brother, but Wat suffered for his sins. We never saw him for months, but then one day I met him on the street and saw for myself what he'd turned into." The expressive face turned sad, and she pinched her lips at the memory. "Talked to the air, he did, and pointed at things no one else could see. Then Peter came out and drove the poor thing away with a stick, told him never to return. That is the last time I saw Wat. Have they locked him away?"

"He's dead. Hanged himself in Newgate."

She shook her head and clucked her tongue. "He were odd, scared of things, you know? But that one —" she tossed her head at Peter's house — "played on his fears, made him worse. He's every bit as mad as Wat, but he's taken up a profession to cover it."

Other neighbors confirmed the woman's opinion. None felt kindly toward Peter Rogers, although there were those who attended his meetings, either from curiosity or from fear of perdition. Some felt sorry for Wat, but most wanted no part of either brother. Hugh tried to learn whether Peter had gone out on the night of Alice's death, but no one could say. He was known to shut up his house after dark and remain indoors, ostensibly for fear of the evil forces thought to operate more freely at night.

"Witches, y'see," one old man told Hugh in a voice coarsened from hours over a bellows fire. "Rogers fears witches, and it was he who put that fear into Wat. Preaches most convincing when he's on that subject, but at other times, he is less noteworthy."

Hugh had to hold back a smile. Like many

others, this man enjoyed services enlivened by talk of the supernatural. People were drawn to the unexplained, and talk of magical occurrences held more allure than polemics against drink and bear-baiting. Maybe clergymen like Rogers chose their topics accordingly.

If, however, Peter Rogers shared his brother's dread of witches, might he have put Wat up to his attempt on the princess? It was time to meet this man in person.

Rogers' face showed fear when he answered Hugh's knock. "I've come to inform you of your brother Wat's death." Hugh stepped forward without an invitation, and Rogers backed up, allowing him inside.

The interior of the small house was almost empty, the man's poverty plain to see. Rogers wore a plain brown tunic and trews. His hair was pulled back and tied with a strip of leather and his feet were shod in loose shoes that caused him to shuffle to keep them on.

"Dead? Walter is dead?" The man tried for a shocked tone, but his eyes showed cunning, not surprise.

"You know it, I'm thinking."

The man had the nerve to feign ignorance. "I, sir? I broke ties with my brother weeks ago. He was beyond my help, and I judged there was no more to be done for him."

"You brought him the rope. Did you have to suggest it, too, or was the poor fool miserable enough to do himself in without urging?" Hugh's anger lashed out at this hypocrite who spouted righteous blather while at the same time driving his own brother to madness with his fanaticism. "Wat, drooling and blank when I met him, was once a lad with dreams. Was that not why he became a sailor, to find a different life?" His voice was loud in the tiny room, but he didn't care. "Your teaching had already twisted his mind, and the long nights at sea played upon his fears. He became so unstable that the captains rejected him. Wat returned to you, his brother, and you locked him up like an animal."

Rogers had backed away until he stood against the wall, but he found the courage to defend himself. "For the good of his soul, sir." His thin nose lifted with the strength of his argument. "I did my best to bring my brother back to God."

"Then you threw him out." Hugh's face was grim.

Rogers explained his self-righteousness patiently. "He did not respond to teaching. He cursed and railed at me most abominably."

"Why did no one hear him and come to

see to his condition in all those months?"

The man actually smiled. "My cell is most carefully made, having been constructed for private devotions."

From the superior smirk Hugh concluded that Rogers was probably a flagellant, the sort who found pleasure in punishing himself and in this case another, in the name of God. Anger turned to disgust.

"When the boy came to tell you Wat had been arrested, you decided he must die?"

Rogers leaned forward knowingly. "Better he take his own life than be hanged in a cage until the flesh fell from his bones. I did for Wat the last service I could. I saved him the shame of a traitor's death."

Hugh swallowed his wrath, admitting that the man spoke truth. Wat was better off dead, and quickly. He was unable to believe, however, that when he smuggled a rope into Newgate prison, Peter Rogers was thinking of anyone other than himself. Before he forgot that he represented the Crown and justice, the captain left Rogers standing in the doorway, staring after him with hands folded and lips firmly pressed together, a picture of righteousness.

"It is not possible that Rogers killed Alice," Hugh told the others later that day. "He left town with two other men on the day before her death, and they did not return until the following Friday, May first. Some meeting for their enlightenment up at Oxford." His tone revealed contempt for Rogers and his ilk.

"If he and Wat worked together, they might have done all five between them," Simon suggested uncertainly.

"No, that doesn't fit," Elizabeth argued. "It's one man. He lures these women on with gifts and promises, then for some reason we don't understand murders and leaves them as he does, forming a message that only he understands."

"It is one man," Hugh agreed, "but is it the lover? The fiend may follow him and kill those he seduces."

Elizabeth, who practiced with a pen handwriting that was already near to perfection, brought up the subject they had all avoided. "Why does he take their heads, do you think?" Surely it cost her to speak so calmly of beheadings. "Is there a message meant for my father?" For a few seconds there was only the sound of the pen scratching its way across the thick parchment.

Hugh spoke first. "It could be, Your Highness."

"I believe the killings are religious in one

way, Hugh," Simon stepped in to save Hugh mentioning the two queens who had gone to the block. "But I can't help but think that the crimes are personal. The victims mean something to the man. As for the king, the murderer began with prostitutes. Why would His Majesty hear of such crimes when he has the nation's business to attend to?"

"It sounds more like perverted lust than political disagreement to me," Elizabeth agreed. "But why does he take the heads? Why not leave them with the corpse?"

Hugh was disgruntled that they'd joined together to oppose his theory. "He's a lunatic, is he not? Since when did a madman make sense?"

"But it must make sense to his way of thinking. He always does the same things, so they mean something to him." Elizabeth set aside the pen and paper and led the way outside. Rain had washed the garden earlier, but a bright sun was fast drying the pathway for their passage.

"If the killer follows the lovers and intercepts the women on their way home —" Simon took up the subject again.

"That opens up the suspects again. We would have to include Ninian and the delightful Rogers brothers, who can't very well have been the girls' lovers."

"I never forgot them," Hugh said with conviction.

"Have we eliminated Sir George?"

"No," came two answers, Elizabeth's with reluctance and Hugh's with assurance.

"So we've eliminated no one. We have five men at the very least: Derwent, Pemberton, Blakewell, Ninian plus the remote chance that the brothers Rogers worked together. And we can't discount the possibility of someone we have yet to discover."

"Then there's your knight in black fustian, Peto the Pope," Hugh added. "You believe him guiltless, but the man is a cold-blooded killer for all that he says nay."

The three stopped walking and stood silent, each with his own thoughts. It was thus that they heard horses' hooves in the courtyard and turned to see Yeoman Calkin dismount and hurry toward them. The look on his face was ominous, but he said nothing until Hugh indicated they all would hear the message.

"There's been another murder."

"Oh, Lord," Simon breathed.

"Where?"

"On the west side, off St. Giles. The body was found this morning in a churchyard."

"Like the others?"

"Yes, sir.

"I must go. Highness, I'll return —" Hugh stopped when he glanced at Elizabeth, who reeled, eyelids fluttering. As she fell he caught her, scooping her light frame up in strong arms. *A woman in a child's body* passed through his head, but he hurried toward the doorway, shouting to Simon to fetch his father.

Elizabeth woke to Jacob Maldon's touch on her forehead. Vague memories floated through her mind of fearful faces peering down at her: Hugh, Mary Ward, even Margot. For an instant she wondered why, then recollection returned. Another murder, the one they'd feared but could not prevent. They must work harder to stop this terror. Her mind conjured another woman lying headless, in a churchyard this time. *At least my mother's head was retrieved by her ladies and buried with her.*

"Where is Simon?"

"He's outside, Your Highness. He would not leave, although the captain went off as soon as it was determined that you had simply fainted from shock and were in no danger. This business is too much for you. They will continue by themselves."

"No!" The word was out before she had

time to temper it with her usual tact. "Master Maldon, I want to help." She looked at the kind face, like Simon's but older, more aware of forces working within his patients. "I need to help."

"I understand, but the king would not. It is easy to imagine what he might do to those he thought had placed his daughter in even the slightest danger."

"But in this business I have some purpose. Everywhere else I am useless, counted only as a threat or a duty. This once in my life I feel part of something important. It may never happen again."

Jacob gravely took her small hand in his. "I advise that you keep to your bed for today and tomorrow. You may have visitors, and you will decide who they may be. I shall come tomorrow, and in the meantime advise the palace that all is well. The princess indulged in too much exercise in the hot sun and had a mild fainting spell. Will that do?"

"Oh, yes, that will do nicely. And thank you." Her eyes fastened on him, and he knew a question waited there. She thought about it for a while before verbalizing. "Was my mother very beautiful?"

Jacob Maldon was an honest man with none of the courtier's skill at invention.

"No," he answered honestly. "Not beautiful. I don't know what to call what Anne had: a liveliness, an attraction. It did not work on all men, but when it did . . ."

Nine years. Father waited nine years to consummate the relationship because she vowed she would not be mistress, only wife. The gossips speak of it with amazement, that a king was so besotted with a mere lady-in-waiting. The next question is do I have any of her charm? Will a man ever give up everything he has for me? That was no question to ask an old man like the physician, so she thanked Maldon, saying she would rest.

Jacob told his son as they returned to their home, "I understand why you are steadfastly loyal to this girl. Elizabeth will always have men around her who would move heaven and earth to do her bidding." He walked in silence for a while before adding, "Not that her ability to inspire such devotion is good. Given her circumstances, it means only trouble for a daughter of royal blood with an uncertain place in the royal hierarchy."

CHAPTER
THIRTY-FIVE

The woman lay posed as Alice had been. This time the robes were brown, the crucifix silver, another beautifully worked piece. She lay in a small hollow, invisible from only a few feet away, but the ground framed her as if it were created for her resting place. There was no hiding the facts this time. People had gathered in small groups, curious or horrified. The local constable spoke quietly with Gooderich, who had sped to the scene while Calkin came for Hugh. Gooderich left the man beside the corpse and moved to meet his fellow Guardsmen.

"Constable Huxley says she was found by some boys who cut through the churchyard on their way to do some fishing on the Strand. They saw no one, and it appears she had been here since early morning."

"Do we know who she is?"

"No, sir. There's a burn scar on one leg, though." Calkin moved the robe aside enough to show the scar, and he noted stockings of finely woven silk.

With a feeling of dread, Hugh told Calkin, "Ride to the Marquess' home and see if his wife is there. If her location is not known, ask if she has such a scar." Calkin's eyes widened, but he nodded and mounted his horse again.

Gooderich watched Calkin ride off. "If it is she, we will work in secret no more."

"Aye, with hell to pay if we don't catch him soon." Carefully, he knelt beside the corpse, memorizing everything about its position. When that was finished, he took the rosary from the dead hand and placed it in a small pouch hanging from his belt. Next he walked slowly around the area, looking carefully at the ground and moving in widening circles. Nothing. Aside from the horror behind him the area was green and peaceful. An apple tree in blossom stood nearby, its scent almost overcoming the metallic smell of spilled blood. "The woman was carried, probably dead, to this spot, and beheaded. Then he dressed her like this and took her clothing and her head away, leaving no trace of his going."

"Grass is difficult for tracking."

"He must carry a thick bag that seals in the blood. He brings the nun's robes and the knife in it, then puts the woman's clothes and the head inside when he's done with her. A fiend, Gooderich."

"Aye, Captain, and worse. Making religious things into a travesty."

"See if anyone saw a man in the area in a long cloak, with such a bag." Everyone had a cloak and lots of people carried bags, but the night had not been cold, so a cloak might have been notable. "Tell the constable he may remove the remains." Hugh strode toward his horse and his next task: telling the king that there was yet another headless woman in London.

His Majesty Henry VIII was almost out of his mind with pain. Every movement was agony, and he could take no more of the concoctions his physicians made to ease it, for they made him sluggish and woolyheaded. Catherine, bless her, did what she could, and he was grateful. Had he really considered her arrest? He couldn't remember why, but he felt a vague anger at Wriothesley; sure it was his fault. He glanced around the room for him, but the man was absent.

"Where is the Lord Chancellor?" he grunted to the nearest person, a man of the Privy Chamber. Through his pain Henry could not recall the man's name, but it did not matter. To Henry they were all alike after so many years.

The fellow's face sank to a blandness that signaled dishonesty. "His Grace is ill, Your Majesty. He begs to be excused."

Illness: the excuse for avoiding duty. Henry had encountered it many times, but he would have his way sooner or later. The man continued, "Captain Bellows is without, sire, and begs a word with you."

"Send him, and clear these jays out of here. The noise jars me." In thirty seconds the room was empty except for Hugh and the king, most only too happy to leave their grumpy monarch's presence. One look at his captain's face told Henry that his day was not going to improve.

"Another one?"

"Yes, sire." Briefly but completely, Hugh outlined the facts of the newest murder, ending with the worst. "The woman is Constance Maillot, the Marquess' wife."

"Old Seyton? God's eyes! Could you not prevent it?"

Hugh flushed deep red, and his clothes felt too heavy, constricting at the neck and the armpits. "Sire, I have worked to discover the man's identity, but he is clever. All clues are carefully removed from the scene, probably in a bag of some sort. He leaves nothing of himself." He went on to relate their theory that Mary's lost casket had provided the man with bait to lure the women in and rosaries to leave on the corpses.

Henry's mind followed then leapt ahead. "So the man has been a guest in my elder daughter's home?"

"Possibly. We showed the rosary to the Princess Mary and she confirms it was in the nesting boxes. Of course, a servant may have taken the casket and sold it. Or an unknown person who is the killer may have crept in and stolen it without anyone's knowledge. Even a hooker may have taken it, if it were left in the wrong place." Hookers were deft criminals who used a long pole with a hook on one end to reach into open windows and "hook" valuables. "Still, when all is seen together, it is my belief that the killer is a man with an outward face so charming that he is welcome in the best houses. Beneath is a monster, well hidden thus far."

"Do you have names?"

"Half a dozen possibilities, sire." Hugh hesitated. Did the king want to know? Did he dare name men of the Court? Name Derwent, possibly the woman's lover?

Henry waved a hand. "I leave it to you.

Here is all you will need." He scrawled a few words across a sheet that lay beside him on a small table then signed his name with a flourish. As he handed it over, his face tightened with pain and he tried to seat his bulk more carefully in the huge chair. He waved a hand, which Hugh took for dismissal, but as he turned, Henry's raspy voice stopped him. "The boy, has he been of help?"

"Yes, sire. He is adept at finding things out with an innocent question, an offhand remark. I believe he has a talent for this sort of thing."

A wheezy chuckle. "So my daughter was right. Her judgment of men is sound for one so young. She may yet do well." He seemed to be finished. After a long pause, Hugh bowed and turned away. "It is a pity." Henry mumbled.

"Sire?"

"Nothing, Bellows. You may go." Hugh was almost to the door when Henry gasped a last order. "Find him, Bellows! No more dead women, do y' hear? No more news of headless corpses to shake my dreams nightly."

Hugh bowed a last time as he backed out of the room. "Your servant, sire."

When next the three met, Elizabeth noticed the amulet under Simon's tunic when he bent to pick up a kitten rolling playfully in the garden.

"Have you gone over to the French, then?"

Simon blushed, unwilling to explain in front of Hugh. "It was a gift, Highness, and I dared not refuse to wear it for fear of rudeness."

"It's nicely wrought but don't let my father see it. He's particularly angry with Francis at the moment."

Hugh was impatient to share his burden. "I have the king's authorization to make an arrest." The king's captain observed the two who, he reminded himself, were children, nothing more. It was he who would bear the weight of Henry's wrath if the wrong man were arrested. Calkin and Gooderich had made their case earlier. They favored arresting Derwent with all speed. "Search his house, question his servants, and he'll be ours," Gooderich had asserted, slapping a fist into his opposite hand. "Once we arrest him, we can make him talk."

Hugh had shaken his head in answer. "Tortured men say what you want them to say. We may get a confession, but would it stop the killing if he is not the one?" Calkin was less sure than Gooderich but argued the need to do something or appear lax in their duties.

Now Elizabeth's pale brows knitted in uncertainty. "It could be Derwent. He was at Mary's during Twelfth Night. He slips out nights without his wife's knowledge, and there is no doubt he has an eye for a pretty female."

"None of that makes him a murderer," Hugh growled.

"Highness, a gentleman to see you." Hannah appeared in the doorway, looking charming in her plain gray dress and white apron, Simon thought.

Elizabeth's brows rose in surprise. "A gentleman?"

"It's Margot's brother, Guy Pemberton," Hannah informed them in a low voice.

"Bring him to my sitting room in ten minutes, Hannah."

"We will go, Highness," Simon said. "He should not find us here, and he may speak more freely to you alone."

"About what?" Elizabeth asked.

Hugh chuckled. "We'll never know if he finds you here with the two of us." He rose from the bench. "I've things to be about, anyway. Simon can wait in the kitchen and come to find me if there is aught I should know of."

"Very well," she murmured, turning to the castle, "but I've only met the man once. He isn't likely to confide in me that he is the murderer we seek."

In the small room used for private meetings Elizabeth composed herself, picking up a sketch she had begun earlier and adding a few lines to it with charcoal. The task filled the few minutes until Hannah guided Guy Pemberton in, and she looked up and greeted him with a nod.

"Master Pemberton, Your Highness." Hannah took an unobtrusive position by the door, both servant and chaperone.

Guy moved into the room with a slight bow and a smile. He had carefully prepared for this meeting, she was sure. His clothing was elegant but more dignified than fashion-able, unlike their earlier meeting. His hair, too, was less flamboyant, although it smelled of perfume and glistened with oil. "Your Highness, forgive my unannounced visit. I realize it is unusual."

"Unusual, but not undesirable, sir. I am glad for visitors in this chilly old place."

He looked around the room curiously.

"You have done wonders warming it, Your Highness. The touch of a woman here and there can do much to cheer a cold room, or a cold heart." His eyes twinkled, seeking understanding. He was leading up to something, a comment on his relationship with Isabella, she guessed.

"I've heard it said that a man may succumb to the love of a woman and become a new creature."

Guy raised an admonishing hand. "So you have heard stories about me. I feared as much." He approached as close as protocol permitted, leaning toward Elizabeth in a tacit plea for understanding. "I admit, Your Highness, that I have not been circumspect in my behavior since my return to England. I make no excuses, but I am truly sorry for those who may have been hurt." His expression grew pained. "It was not easy growing up away from my homeland and my family. My parents thought it best that I be educated in Rome, but it was hard for me. I was a lonely youth and became resentful. Upon my return to England I had nothing, no prospects, no friends except Robin, who is full of fun but sometimes does not think beyond the moment. I'm afraid we have made poor reputations for ourselves this past year."

Elizabeth remained silent. Why was he telling her all this?

Drawing a deep breath, Guy went on. "Then I met Isabella, through the Princess Mary, actually. Within an evening's time I knew that she was a girl I could truly love all my life. Incredibly, she has come to love me in return, and her family is accepting." He stopped again, and Elizabeth felt that she had to say something.

"It is good when all parties are happy with a match."

"It is. Only . . ." He smiled sheepishly. "Your Highness, Isabella is so sweet, so innocent of the ways of the world. I could not bear it if she turned from me." He paused. "She thinks highly of you."

"Of me? What have I to do with you and Isabella?"

Again he looked embarrassed. "My sister tells me that you and a certain soldier talk for hours about the death of Alice LaFont. I fear you do not see me in a good light in that matter, although I swear that I did no harm to Alice. If you would, say nothing to Isabella or her mother of that." The brown eyes were pleading.

"I would never say anything to either of them that was not proven," Elizabeth assured him stiffly. "I do not act on rumor."

Guy's face cleared. "I am glad to hear it, Your Highness."

"Now I have a question for you," the princess said, seeing an opportunity for information. "Alice had a filigreed box with a heart-shaped latch, given to her by a lover. Do you know anything of it?"

It was some seconds before he spoke. "Robin had a cunningly made set of boxes with filigreed sides. They nest within each other, for ease of transport, I suppose. I have not seen them of late, but I could ask."

"That will not be necessary." It came out too abruptly. She must practice making her requests less commanding. Gentling her tone, Elizabeth forced an innocent smile. "In fact, it is nothing of importance."

He didn't understand, but he didn't question her motive. "Of course. Now, I must take no more of your time. This conversation has relieved my mind, Highness, and I hope to see you again at cards in the de Marcia home."

"You should not, sir," Elizabeth replied. "If you recall, I won the last time."

Guy bowed over her hand and kissed it lightly. "You are a true princess, kind as well as clever."

"It is gallant of you to say so." As he left the room Hannah gave an impish smile, wiggled her eyebrows in recognition of Guy's good looks, then followed him out. Elizabeth stared after him, pondering what she had learned.

CHAPTER
THIRTY-SIX

Simon slipped into the room after assuring that Pemberton had left the castle. Expensive scent, probably Robin Brandon's to begin with, lingered in the room, and he sniffed dismissively. "So, Highness, did he confess?"

"Not to murder, only to love."

"Isabella de Marcia?"

"Yes. He feared I might squash his hopes with a word about his liaison with Alice. I assured him there was nothing to tell."

Simon's face turned serious. "Sadly, there's nothing to tell about any of them. We have proven nothing."

"But it was the lover who killed the women. The casket of jewels warrants that conclusion. He gave them gifts from my sister's missing cache of jewelry and left pieces on the corpses as well."

"Then Ninian is guiltless?"

The princess thought about that. "I admit

it is unlikely he is the killer, given his cadaverous look and his position, but it is possible that he convinced these women that he is more than he appears. He would not be the first clerk to plan a rise in wealth and status for himself."

He surmised that the reference was to Thomas Cromwell, a lowly servant who rose to great heights as a supporter of Henry's divorce from Catherine of Aragon. Those who rise quickly sometimes fall with equal speed. Cromwell had advised the king to take as his fourth wife Anne of Cleves, a German princess, but Henry found this second Anne homely and distasteful. She was promptly divorced and adopted as Henry's sister so that her generous dowry remained in England. Cromwell, less lucky and more disposable than Princess Anne, was executed. Still there was no shortage of men waiting to take their chance at power, and Ninian was probably one of them.

"So we eliminate no one?" Simon asked.

"I eliminate Sir George in my own mind," Elizabeth answered, returning her attention to the charcoal and making several quick additions. "There is no reason behind it, but my sense tells me he is not capable of these acts. The others I do not know so well, so I cannot judge."

Simon was inclined to agree. He had seen Blakewell's face when Alice's corpse was discovered, and the man had been sickened and horrified. It was unlikely, too, that Sir George would have left a body in his own back garden, risking exactly what had happened: the discovery of his connection with Alice.

The next day Hugh questioned the servants at the Derwent home, especially Annie, who had shared an attic room with Sally Knowles. "She was afraid to say it but finally admitted to me that she saw Sally creep out on the night of her disappearance," he told Simon and Elizabeth later. "The girl said her lover, a rich and well-educated man, was taking her away so they could be together."

"A speaker of Latin?" Simon asked from his place on the floor where he teased a kitten unmercifully with a length of twine and a small bundle of fabric. The kitten pounced at the thing with fierce growls as he pulled it out of reach with quick jerks.

Hugh shook his head at their antics. "Sally said he called her pretty names in that tongue."

"And are we certain this Sally is the dead woman?"

"We cannot say. She had no identifying marks, so it is impossible to be sure."

"Your feeling?"

"I would wager it is she."

"Both Joanna Brandon and Sally mentioned that their lover spoke Latin. Alice claimed hers was well educated. Can we count on that clue, do you think?" Anxious to find common points, Simon refused to stretch logic too far.

"I could almost say for certain that Derwent does not speak the language," Elizabeth said. "I tried it on him at the de Marcias' and he looked blank as a slate."

"He might pretend knowledge to impress his women," Simon countered. "How would they know if he spoke it well?"

"This is no way to prove anything!" Hugh's frustration exploded from him. "I'll arrest Derwent and see if I can break him."

"But —" Elizabeth stopped when she saw his expression. Neither of them reminded the captain that he'd recently argued against such an action.

"More women may die while we discuss." He rose and stepped to the window, his face grim.

"You're right," Simon agreed. "You have worked behind the scenes long enough. Someone may come forward with information that will help us, whether the killer is Derwent or someone else. If we learn nothing, I can still work secretly."

Elizabeth took breath to say something then chose not to. Hugh did not need reminding that she, too, worked covertly on the matter.

Hugh bowed a farewell to Elizabeth. "Walk with me, Simon." Simon took his leave, his eyes promising to keep her informed.

But there were no disclosures as they left the castle, Hugh walking beside his horse dejectedly. He did not want to talk, wanted only silent company, it seemed. Simon did not have to be told the cause of his mood. If he arrested the wrong man, his job and therefore his livelihood was in jeopardy. If he arrested no one, another woman might die. Henry's letter gave him the authority, but if he was wrong, they both knew the king was capable of denying knowledge of what Bellows had planned. Henry was nothing if not good at shifting blame.

They descended the slope from the castle to the village, ignoring the peaceful, wide view of the city below them and the village up ahead. Sheep and cattle called intermittently across the hillside, but otherwise the area was quiet. "I could have him brought in today and question him in the morning," Hugh finally said, half to himself. "It does them good to spend a night thinking."

Simon shivered, remembering Wat's cell and the smells within it. Of course Derwent would fare better, being of high birth. He would be held in the Tower of London, where there were apartments and servants and green lawns to walk upon for exercise. Still, its grimness was depressing. Derwent would not thank the man who put him there.

"I must do something," Hugh muttered. "I want nothing more than to capture this monster, but . . ." He left his thought unfinished. Both of them understood the consequences if he chose his next step wrongly.

A dog ran out at them, barking frantically, and the owner called it back to her. She was pitifully ugly, her face disfigured through some accident of birth so that there appeared to be no bones beneath the skin. Simon felt his chest tighten with pity for her as they passed on.

"Have you noticed that all the victims are described by those who knew them as surpassingly beautiful?"

"That's true, but what does it mean?"

"And he keeps the heads."

Hugh made no answer. Simon did not know himself where his line of thought led, so he said no more. Surely the heads were not kept like prizes, for their beauty would soon fade once they were lifeless. What did it mean?

"I've never asked, Hugh, but do you have a wife?"

Hugh smiled grimly, following the thought. "No. But I have a widowed sister for whom I am mostly responsible. And her four children. When I think of that madman and what he does to women, I think what I'd feel if someone did that to Bridget." The large head swung widely side to side. "He must be stopped."

Simon agreed, but the matter might soon be out of their hands. Pray God Hugh was right in arresting Derwent and could make him confess. That seemed the only way out.

After some consideration, Hugh decided Derwent's arrest could wait one more day. If past practice continued, there was no murder imminent. Either the man was sated for a while after a killing or he had enough cunning to lie low during the hue and cry that followed his crimes. He decided to find Pemberton and question him.

Part of his reasoning, if he was truthful

with himself, was that Pemberton was less important to the world than Derwent. Questioning Guy would offend no large, high-ranking family, and he might learn more about Alice LaFont, the guests that Princess Mary had entertained at Christmastide, and Sir Anthony Derwent, since they seemed to travel in similar circles.

Understanding Pemberton's sort, Hugh knew he was likely to be found at the tabling dens, places where men could carouse and gamble at their ease. Pemberton and his ilk rarely rose before eleven, then spent hours idling in such places until it was evening and time for the social activities at which they excelled. Elizabeth might believe that Guy had reformed, but it took more than words to show real change. Hugh had little use for such popinjays, and he meant to squeeze this one until he learned something worthwhile.

The place was dark, even at midday, and the clientele mostly drabbers, those who spent too much time at low pursuits. There was a low murmur to the place that never ceased, but occasional shouts and laughter erupted loudly as well. Hugh entered to sneers and turned heads; no welcome for authority here. At a table sat several well-dressed young men, and he looked for Guy among them. They paid him little mind, being absorbed in dicing. Pemberton was not present, but Robin Brandon sat in the center of the group. He recognized several of the others as well. Some were young, the sons of wealthy men who had little purpose in life until their fathers died and they took up the duties of landowners. Others were hangers-on, as Pemberton was, men with little or no income who entertained themselves on the goodwill of others. It must be galling, although none of the young men present looked put-upon.

Watching each roll of the dice eagerly, Robin clutched a pint of ale in his right hand while with the left he absently caressed the breasts of a drab who leaned against him. Far too old to be called a maid, she used paint liberally to bring a maiden's blush to her cheeks and counterfeit roses to her lips.

Brandon took a turn at the dice, using the left hand rather than release his liquid refreshment. A shout arose as his numbers showed well, and he slapped the table happily. "A round!" he called. "That roll is worth a drink for every man." The others cheered, the drab moved off to get the drinks, and the dice passed to the next man.

Hugh approached the woman as she poured ale into pewter tankards. "Have you seen Guy Pemberton today?"

Close up the woman looked terrible, and the paint could not hide the pallor beneath. Her eyes sunk in like currants in yesterday's pudding, and her breath raled in her chest. Consumptive, Hugh guessed. She was tired unto exhaustion and did not bother to hide it from a non-paying customer. "Guy don't come no more," she rasped. "Too good fer the likes o' us now he's found a rich girl."

"I see." Hugh glanced again at the table full of crowing drunkards, laughing now at the loss by the next dicer of what amounted to a month's pay for a captain of the guard. Robin Brandon was the loudest of them all. Although he had dark good looks, Hugh found that the man's liquid eyes and full lips called to mind pictures he'd seen of satyrs. How many times had he ordered this man escorted home when his celebrations had become destructive? "What does Brandon think of Guy's new life?"

"Him? Robin cares for nobody but 'imself. Says Guy can go to hell with his little Catholic for all 'e cares." She softened for a moment. "I'd have to say I miss 'im, though. Guy was the only one of this lot that was ever nice to us girls. To the rest we're just dirt," her gaze hardened, "especially that pig. Sir Robert Brandon's the worst villain ever laid hands on me."

She had filled the tray, and with that comment, left Hugh standing by the keg. Just before reaching the table, he saw her take a deep breath, straighten her back, and paste a smile on her face.

"Now, gentlemen, 'ere's a round o' drinks from Sir Robin!" she called. "Such a gentleman as Robin never was, am I right?" A cheer followed, and the woman took her place again next to the man she hated. As Hugh turned to go, she gave him an ironic grimace as Robin's left hand moved back to where it had been when he entered.

CHAPTER
THIRTY-SEVEN

Simon had been home only a few minutes when his mother's head appeared at the loft edge, peering into the section he shared with his brothers. "There's a girl at the door says she must speak with you." Her tone signaled displeasure with the situation. "She's quite pretty, and the way she asked, friendly and familiar, I'd guess you two are well known to each other."

Simon read his mother's mind as if she'd said her thoughts aloud. Part of Mary Maldon's plan for order had to do with his future. Her son would become a physician like his father. She was willing to make the sacrifices necessary for that to happen, and it never occurred to her that either her son's withered arm or his inclination would prevent it. An attractive female might turn the boy's head and addle his mind with thoughts of love and marriage rather than the serious study required to follow in his father's footsteps. Therefore this girl who asked to speak to Simon was the enemy, and Mary used all her powers of disapproval to let it be known.

Mary returned to her churn, and Simon judged her agitation from the chortle of the paddles inside. He knew the story well. She had waited five years for Jacob while he studied at a real university, scrimping and saving every penny to get an education while she stayed at home with her demanding father and her sickly mother. Jacob had passed his examinations and come home to her a true physician, not a mere blood-letter or surgeon, but one who knew all the modern methods of diagnosis and treatment. She was determined to have a second doctor in the family, and now this girl, who might not be willing to wait five years for a husband, came boldly to the front door and asked for Simon, calm as you please.

Ignoring his mother's baleful expression, Simon smiled as he saw that it was Hannah standing shyly in the large room. He at once spoke to set his mother's mind at ease. "Mother, this is Hannah, who works at Hampstead Castle for Her Highness. Hannah, my mother, Mistress Maldon."

Hannah dropped in a perfect curtsey, not too low, but respectful enough for a physician's wife. "Most pleased to meet you. I am sent here on an errand by Her Highness."

Mary Maldon's manner changed instantly from distrust to pride. "Ah, from the princess!" Hurriedly she drew a wooden chair away from the wall and set it before Hannah with a peremptory thump. "Sit! I shall bring refreshment while you tell your news."

Hannah looked as if she might refuse, but Simon gave her a look and she replied sweetly, "You are most kind."

While his mother was out of the room, he asked quickly, "What does the princess need of me?"

"She sent this." Hannah handed him a note written in Elizabeth's perfect hand. Her face showed no knowledge of its news. Probably she did not read it.

Unfolding the note, Simon scanned its contents. His mother returned with cider and some tarts she had refused him not ten minutes before, claiming they were for the evening's dessert. Evidently the princess' messenger rated higher than supper.

"Simon," he read, "after you left I remembered something Pemberton told me. Robin Brandon had a set of nesting boxes such as the ones we have discussed. We have not focused on him thus far, but should you arrange to meet him and see what you can discover? E."

Robin Brandon. What did they know of the man? He was debauched, he was wealthy, what more? Robin had ruined Guy's tasseled cloak, according to Isabella. What if it was not in a drunken brawl, but in the process of murder? Simon could barely make polite responses to the remarks made by his mother and Hannah, so anxious was he to begin the search for Brandon.

With all the delicacy of a bullock, his mother was investigating Hannah's background. She seemed satisfied with the answers, although he thought he detected some irony in the girl's tone. She knew where such questions led. He wondered if Elizabeth had intentionally sent her with the message. Was his fascination with Hannah known to everyone at Hampstead? There was no sense fretting. He was attracted to her, and if the Princess Royal of England and his mother both approved of a courtship, their way would be blessed indeed.

Twenty minutes later Simon was on his way east, his mother's objections ringing in his ears. He would miss supper, he would not get to Islington and back before nightfall, he would catch his death in the night air. She could not argue with a princess, however, and let him go.

It was after six when Simon neared the Brandon house, an impressive structure of yellow stone with wings curving to the northeast and southwest in matched splendor. On the way he had devised a plan of entry. He would show the note that Elizabeth had sent and claim that it was for Robin. Once inside, he would conceal the note and take a different tack. All he had to worry about was meeting a servant who could read, but that was not likely.

The plan would have worked. The man who answered at the back entrance only glanced at the note. His hands were black and he smelled of grease from polishing boots. The young master was not at home, he said, was not expected until late. From the look on the servant's face Simon gathered disapproval, although he clearly thought himself expressionless. "Where might I find him? My lady's missive is important."

At the word lady, the man's face positively twitched. Simon wished he had a penny, for he guessed there was no loyalty for Master Robin in this servant. As it was he was left standing on the doorstep with a curt negative. He turned and retraced his steps, wondering where to turn now.

So preoccupied was he that it took several moments for him to notice someone calling, "Simon!" Turning, he scanned the crowd of people heading homeward in the fading sunlight. Once more he heard it, and then a form separated itself from the throng and headed toward him: Calkin. The young soldier approached with a friendly grin on his freckled face. "What brings you out here, some female?"

"No." Briefly Simon told Calkin of his plan to see Robin Brandon.

Calkin looked pleased with himself. "It's no trick to find young Brandon this time of day. He'll be just up the road at the Old Bag o' Bones. He generally has a few pints there before he starts on the real night's drinking." A sneer revealed what he thought of Brandon.

"How should I approach him?"

"If you buy him a drink, that'll make him your friend for as long as you can stand him," Calkin sniffed. Seeing Simon's look of dismay, he asked, "You have no money, lad?"

"No, I did not think to need any."

"Here, then." Pulling some coins from his purse, Calkin pressed them into Simon's hand. "The Captain will repay me if you discover something of interest," he said, slapping his shoulder cordially.

They walked on together, Calkin explaining his own presence. "My mother lives not far from here, near the Moorgate. I spent the afternoon seeking the captain and Gooderich but did not find them. At St. James I heard they went to arrest Derwent at his home, but he was not to be found. I know not where they went afterward."

"Derwent is missing? Has he had advance warning and taken flight to avoid arrest?"

"Just as likely he went hawking or for a boat ride on the Thames. We will know tomorrow, when he either returns or does not." As he spoke Simon wondered how a man got so many freckles and whether he minded them. He thought they gave a friendly look to the face.

Calkin stopped walking and faced Simon. "I have been wondering about something. Do you remember how you commented that the heels of Alice LaFont's slippers were scuffed from her feet dragging along the stone pathway?"

"Yes."

"When you pointed that out, I noticed something else. On the bottom of her shoe was an odd design, like something had been scratched into the leather. It meant nothing to me, and I decided they must be random marks made from everyday wear. But at the latest murder scene, I noticed similar marks on the sole of the lady's shoe. I doubt chance could create two such marks that look somewhat like letters. I wish I had seen the others' shoes to know if it is common to all." Calkin rubbed his nose, already sunburnt and peeling from days spent outside.

Simon's interest quickened. "Can you show me what the figures looked like?"

"I can try." Calkin stepped to the side of the street and smoothed spot in the dirt with his foot. "One looked like an A. I learned enough of letters to know that. The other . . ." Bending, he sketched two figures into the soft ground, frowned at the second, and added another line. "Something like that, I think."

Simon gazed at the figure as understanding dawned: the letter A and the omega. Alpha and omega, the beginning and the end. And two victims had these letters traced onto their shoes. What did it mean?

"The first and last letters of the Greek alphabet, signifying God, the beginning and the end of everything."

"Yes, I've heard that at services often enough." Calkin slapped at an insect buzzing around his head. "So the killer thinks he's God?"

"Or doing God's work, making things right somehow." It fit with their theory, but what was corrected by killing women? Simon thanked Calkin, complimenting his memory.

"Glad to help, lad," he said offhandedly. "Such things stay in my mind, like a picture. But I will take my leave now. It will do your disguise no good to be seen with a guardsman, and I am due at St. James. There is the place." With that Calkin moved on, leaving Simon staring at the figures drawn in the dirt. Finally, he scrubbed them away with his foot and continued toward the Bag o' Bones Inn. The sign above the door depicted just that, a bag from which spilled various bones.

Inside, Simon waited while his eyes adjusted to the change in light. The June evening grew slightly dim outside, but it was much darker here. The ceiling was low, with heavy beams across it supported by columns spaced around the room. The wood was black with age and smoke from the fireplace that took up one whole wall. Even the fire seemed somehow dim.

The inhabitants held no light, either. Surly

faces turned toward Simon, a sea of brown and gray skin and beards. Silence fell as he entered and was judged by mute observance. His footsteps sounded loud in its interruption. Squaring his shoulders, he approached the innkeeper, seated and at his ease beside the fire. "A pint, please," he said with as much firmness as he could muster. The man looked him over once and then moved to comply with no great enthusiasm. As he waited, Simon glanced about the room. Most of the men had gone back to their drinks, deeming him no prospect for entertainment. Taking in their appearances, he dismissed those nearby as too old or too poorly dressed to be Brandon.

Just as the landlord handed the pint to him, Simon noticed a man seated at a table in a corner even darker than the rest of the room. He was about twenty-five years old, well dressed though disheveled at the moment, and strikingly handsome except for a day's growth of black beard and a loose-lipped expression. He alone had paid no attention to Simon's entrance into the room, being absorbed in a game of Patience.

"Pour one for the gentleman in the corner," Simon ordered and placed a coin in the man's hand. The man complied, drawing a glass of port from a barrel behind him.

With both drinks Simon headed to the corner table.

"I took the liberty, sir, of bringing you refreshment, since I noticed your glass was almost empty."

The man looked up at Simon, or at least as far as the drink in his hand. Beginning with the tabling den and the ale he'd drunk there, Robin had left his companions for some serious drinking before evening came, and now he was almost comatose. His hand shook as it hovered over the table, and the placement of new cards on the rows was accomplished slowly, with great concentration and frequent misses. The interesting thing about Brandon to those who knew him was that he would revive and become almost manic when evening festivities began, showing no signs of the stupor he evinced at the moment. The problem was that one never knew whether his mania would take the form of wild exuberance or furious anger.

"I thank you, young sir," he slurred. When Simon did not set the drink down, Brandon thought hard about what to do. Realizing through the haze of drink the proper course, he managed, "Sit down, sit down, lad."

Simon sat in the chair opposite and placed the port before Brandon. "You are, I believe,

Robert Brandon the younger. Am I correct?"

"Robin. Your servant." Brandon's eyes never reached Simon's face. He picked up the glass as soon as his hand was away, taking a long drink and sighing with satisfaction. His gaze returned to the cards before him, forgetting his guest.

"My employer recently met one Guy Pemberton, with whom I believe you are acquainted."

The brain fuddled with alcohol fought to make the connection. "Guy? Yes, of course. Good man, Guy. At least he was until he met that girl." His tone implied that females in general were bad enough, one was beyond belief.

"Isabella de Marcia?"

"The very one." Finally, Brandon looked at him with the squint-eyed gaze of one whose eyes can no longer focus clearly. "She anything to you? Sister or somewhat?"

"No."

"Then I say blast her to hell. Guy was a merry companion, willing and eager for a night's adventure, and then he met that girl. Now he needs must do this for Isabella and cannot do that because of Isabella. As if one woman is different from the others." Another long swallow of wine followed this statement.

Brandon stared at his cards. Swords, cups, and staves lay on the table before him. In his hand he held a ten of coin that had no place to be played. Without hesitation he slid it into the deck and continued the game. Simon changed the subject. "I have come on another matter. Guy spoke of a set of three cunning nesting boxes that you possess. My employer has been searching for such a thing for his sister's wedding gift, and he thought you might be willing to sell them."

Brandon's eyes moved up and to the left in an effort of memory and he scratched at his face with the edge of a card. "I had such boxes?"

"Five sided with a heart-shaped latch, he said."

The numbed face showed a glint of recognition. "I have seen them about the house, but it was months ago."

"Did you give them as gifts?"

"I?" He considered the idea as if it were foreign to his nature. "I don't think so, but you must ask Guy. Now he is one for such things. I never saw a man so taken with trappings. If I remember, he had the boxes, not I, but as I said, they are gone now." Brandon gave a belch that made Simon wince when the smell reached him.

"Pemberton had the boxes, not you?"

"Is that not what I said? They were Guy's, not mine."

Simon had a chilling thought. "Did Guy give you a cloak, sir? One with tassels on the front and the hem?"

Brandon squeezed his eyes shut in an attempt to see Simon more clearly. "What's that? A cloak?"

"Yes. With gold tassels for trim."

"He might have, I don't know. Can't recall if he did." Brandon laughed heartily. "Can't remember much right now, eh, lad?" He attempted a comradely cuff on Simon's arm, but it missed almost entirely, barely ruffling his sleeve.

"More likely the other way 'round, though. The fellow is forever borrowing my clothes and only returns half of them. God's eyes! He walks away leaving all manner of clothing that he's borrowed from me, with no thought that I paid good money for 'em." Here he stopped and chuckled so that his whole upper body shook. "Not that I pay, o' course. Scoundrel tailors can wait for it, I say. Should be glad I give 'em my trade."

Brandon's thought wandered for a few seconds. Simon, who had learned a great deal about how to glean information in the last weeks, simply sat quietly and waited. Finally, Brandon sobered for a moment the way the inebriated sometimes do, with overly serious thoughts and careful control of their features, and leaned in confidentially. "Having nothing, you know. That's what it is. He's taken with jewels and fripperies and all because he had nothing as a boy. That's why that girl captured him. Beauty, charm, and best of all, money. That's the charm little Isabella has for Guy. Won't go whoring anymore, won't drink more than a thimbleful —" The sentence trailed off into mumbling and Brandon's chin fell so low that Simon thought it would strike the table.

As Brandon fought unconsciousness, Simon considered this sad excuse for a man. Born to a noble family, blessed with good looks and wealth, he was disgusting: unwashed, unkempt, and unkind. Could he be a murderer? Doubtful. He was too much a sot to plan and carry out the crimes they had seen. Could it be an act? He studied the man's face for signs of pretense. Unaware, Brandon placed another card in the deck that did not play on the columns.

"And she's a damned papist, too," he said suddenly, as if the thought had just occurred to him. "Raised a priest, he was, but I helped him break away. Now he'll be back among them with their black looks and their plots to place the Spaniard on the throne. That sour old maid Mary wrinkles her nose at my company. We need no Spaniards here, I tell you!" He shouted the last, and Simon glanced around to see several men look in their direction. To his relief, the men muttered agreement with the statement. Robin had chosen the tavern well despite his state.

"Are you saying Guy Pemberton was once a priest?"

Brandon smiled drunkenly and finished the glass. "That's what his father sent him to Rome for, you see. They gave him to the Church, to the pope." He said it with venom and sarcasm. "Guy was caught there when old Henry created his own church. The king did not want any of Clement's lackeys in England, so there was poor Guy, a priest meant for a country that rejected the priesthood."

Brandon took another gulp of wine, sloshing it over the rim and wiping his mouth with a sleeve already stained. "When I met him in Rome, Guy was a wrack of a man." He leaned forward with a lop-sided, conspiratorial grin. "He did not tell you this part, did he?"

"No," Simon managed. "Nothing about being a priest."

"They are not so welcome now in England, are they? Oh, he dances attendance on the Princess Mary and she fawns on him, but it means nothing. I went with him to her home once: all papists, every one. I told 'em what I thought of their cursed pope. Didn't like it much, none of 'em."

"And Guy?"

"When I met him, Guy was a wreck of a man," Brandon repeated. "I showed him what life should be. Introduced him to wine and women, things the church had forbidden him. He soon decided that priesthood was not the life he desired."

"He is an apostate?"

"And more." Brandon chuckled, his head nodding in drunken reverie. "Guy took to the adventurer's life like a goose to an old lady's ankles. We had a time of it, I can tell you, along the Mediterranean and right up to London."

"So I've heard."

"We never hurt no one bad." Brandon caught a tone of disgust in Simon's voice. "We only seek adventure." Another belch followed. Brandon's idea of fun was skewed due to his position, which allowed him to take what he wanted and suffer no consequences.

"Since I cannot purchase the boxes from you, sir, I will leave you to your game."

Brandon returned his attention to the cards before him. Rising to leave, Simon stepped directly into a man approaching Brandon's table. Caught off balance, his foot struck the leg and he fell forward, forcing the man to catch him or fall as well. Strong hands gripped his arms and set him back on his feet. "Your pardon, sir, I did not look where I was going," he said, embarrassed.

"Think nothing of it, lad." Looking into a face almost as handsome as Brandon's and a good deal more aware, Simon tensed. Where had he seen this man before? As memory did its work, he quickly lowered his face. It was Guy Pemberton! Simon hurried off, his nerves jangling. He forced himself to walk naturally, but he expected at any moment to be grabbed from behind. *Calm down,* he told himself. *He does not know what you know.* Still, Simon was fearful, and the back of his neck tingled as if expecting a blow. He'd just come face to face with the man who'd killed six women, and his expression of horrified recognition might have betrayed him.

440

Guy stood looking after the boy for a moment, then joined Brandon. "Robin, how goes it?"

The drunkard had missed the incident. "Well met, Guy." He made as if to rise, but it was too much of an effort and he fell back into the chair clumsily.

"Your father asked me to make you presentable for the countess' banquet tonight. Who was the lad?"

"What lad?"

"The one who left just now. With the withered arm."

Brandon had not noticed that either. "There was a boy from some friend of yours. Wanted some silver boxes." Brandon shrugged. "I told him I have no such boxes."

"He said he knew me?"

"Yes. Was the little rogue lying?" Brandon looked up with a vague spark of interest.

Pemberton looked in the direction that Simon had disappeared for a moment. "I know the boy. He is, if I deduce correctly, an acquaintance of my sister Margot."

Chapter
Thirty-Eight

Simon looked behind a dozen times before
he convinced himself that Pemberton was
not following. He tried to think reasonably.
The man did not know him, did not know
where to find him even if Brandon mentioned Simon's lie. Brandon might not even
remember in his present, it seemed usual,
state. He was probably safe, but he had to
find Hugh.

Pemberton had lied about the boxes. They
had been in his possession, not Brandon's.
He was an apostate priest, a man once
devoted to God now turned to a life of
hedonism. He was connected to Alice
LaFont by his own admission and to Joanna
Brandon through his friend Robin. A man
in a cloak like his had frequented the
Shambles, where Mathilda had died, and
Winchester close, where Therese's body was
found. Hugh was about to arrest the wrong
man while the killer sat drinking in the Bag

o' Bones. Simon set off at a trot, conserving his energy since he had a long way to go. Twenty minutes later he approached the gatehouse at St. James, where two guardsmen practiced with a sparthe, hitting a wooden target with regular thuds.

"The captain is not here, lad. Won't be back until morning, they say." The man waited while his companion retrieved the long-handled battle ax from the target.

"Is he at his home, then?"

"No, he went to find someone." He threw the sparthe in an easy motion, hitting the target dead center. "He was not happy about it, for the fellow was not in the city and he had to go find him."

Derwent! Hugh was on the wrong errand and Pemberton, where was he? "Might I see Yeoman Calkin or Gooderich?"

"Gooderich is with the captain; Calkin is Yeoman Bed-Goer tonight, so he may not be disturbed." Simon knew Calkin would be part of the ceremonial bed-making for the king and then guard the chamber through the night. Dare he try to tell this man who did not know him the whole story? Would a mere yeoman take it upon himself to arrest a nobleman, however impoverished, on Simon's say-so? He thought not and turned away. It must wait until tomorrow.

From across the narrow street, God's Instrument on Earth watched the boy go, noting disappointment in his demeanor. Good, he had found no one to tell his story to. Now it was simply a matter of intercepting him before he reached home. Evening was rapidly changing to night, with shadows lengthening all along the street. Choosing a route that led north in an arc, the man spurred his horse onward. He would find an alley where the boy was sure to pass. There. As he came back onto Fleet Street, he saw Simon trudging along with his head down, lost in thought. He glanced around. Crowds on the street had thinned to almost nothing as people went inside to their suppers.

An alleyway opened to the left of where Simon would pass. The pursuer ducked inside and found it deserted. *God is good,* he thought as he waited. He was alpha and omega: the beginning and the end, chosen to be judge over all the earth. It was obvious that his quarry was of Satan. The withered arm was a clear sign. Dark forces plotted to interfere with the completion of God's work, but they had underestimated him. When the boy was almost past the alley, God's Instrument stepped out and smote him with all the force of righteousness. Then for the second time that night, he caught the boy's weight in his strong arms.

The princess spent the evening at St. James with her father and stepmother. Henry had had two days of relative ease, and the three royal children had been called to dine with him. She and Margot returned to Hampstead, the coach Henry had provided for their return noisily making its way through the darkness. Margot, who did not enjoy spending time in the king's presence, was even quieter than usual. She probably thought him a cousin to Beelzebub himself. Holding on to a strap that saved her from some of the jouncing, Elizabeth wondered what Simon had done about her note. Was Brandon the monster they sought? From all accounts he was a despicable man.

When they reached Hampstead and entered the castle, she was still wondering. "Margot, do you know Robin Brandon?" she asked as the woman helped her out of her cloak.

The woman stiffened visibly. "He is not a man that Your Highness should wish to know or know about," she answered in a harsh voice, sounding exactly like Princess

Mary had at the mention of Brandon's name.

"I wondered if he ever wore your brother's cloak."

"From whence comes all this interest in Guy's cloak?" Margot's voice turned sharp and she put a pale hand to her head as if it ached. "Can a man not receive a gift without all manner of questions?"

Something in her voice made Elizabeth take note. "What is it, Margot? You are upset."

"I am not! It is all these questions about the cloak. It is but a garment, Highness."

"Exactly so, and yet you are shaking."

Elizabeth saw a tear roll down the pale cheek, but Margot brushed it away defiantly. "Such a coil over a silly thing! He meant no harm by it, Your Highness. He tried to save my feelings and that is all of it, I assure you."

"I make no sense of what you say. Explain your meaning clearly."

Margot stopped, a confused look on her face. "Why, Sir George's cloak, Highness. It was Guy who wore it and got it dirty. He could have told me the truth, but he didn't want to admit he'd ruined the one I made for him. Knowing there was another like it, he took Sir George's from the peg in the entry."

"Guy ruined the cloak? He didn't lend it to Brandon?"

Her face showed both shame and displeasure. "No, he admits he ruined it in a fight, so he took Sir George's. He would have put it back himself, I am certain, but I noticed it was the wrong one. Mine had finer stitches than Bess can make, for her eyes are poor." A touch of pride showed even in this confession. She smoothed the garments as she hung them on pegs beside the one now under discussion. "All the same, I made him put it back. I was ashamed to admit what I knew when this one was discovered with mud around the bottom." Margot shook her head in self-reprimand, touching a tassel absently. "I should have looked to it myself and cleaned the hem. No one would have known it was gone."

Elizabeth had a sudden sense of foreboding. Guy had lied to Isabella about what happened to his cloak. Guy was the man who had waited for Alice. Could he also have been the man waiting for Mathilda Harrison? Pen Brook had thought the man was taller and thinner than Sir George. In addition, the woman in Winchester, near Therese's house, had described the same tasseled cloak.

Guy had lied. He had not given Robin the

garment. Had it been ruined during the last, desperate struggles of one of the six dead women? Was it bloodstained so that he did not dare let his sister see it? Had he stolen Sir George's similar cloak to forestall questions? There was fear in Margot's eyes. She had suspicions but was afraid to face them.

Elizabeth's mind raced ahead. Margot had supported her brother, probably given him whatever money she could spare. He was familiar with the castle and grounds. "How often did Guy come here?"

The woman hesitated, but the spirit was gone from her and she answered truthfully. "More frequently of late. He had begun to see Brandon's true nature and at times could not bear to associate with the man. When the weather warmed, he sometimes slept in the stable." She reached out as if to touch Elizabeth's arm but made no contact. "He wanted to be able to think his own thoughts."

And have no one know how he looked when he returned from a murderous rampage.

"How did he enter the grounds? The gate was locked."

Margot turned away, leaning against the doorframe for support and resting her forehead on its hard smoothness. "I unlocked the garden gate after dark." Her voice was almost inaudible. "He would signal me with lights that I could see from my bedroom window, two torches, one above the other." Her eyes begged for understanding. "He needed sometimes to leave Brandon's house, to escape from the evil influence of the man. I thought if he could break away —" Margot stopped. "And it is working. He met Isabella and saw a new path opening before him. Not to be someone's minion, as he is to Robin Brandon, but to be a man of respect and . . . prosperity." The last word trailed away. She knew in her heart that it was wealth that attracted Guy.

Elizabeth forestalled further explanation with a question. "So he stayed in my stable. Might he keep some of his things there?"

Devoid of the stiff pride that had sustained her for so long, Margot said blankly, "He hasn't much of his own, but once I saw a leather bag when I let him in."

"Bring a torch."

Margot's face made one mute plea against the command, but she turned quickly and went to obey. Elizabeth hurried up the stairs to Sir George's apartments. The old knight had been dressed for bed but pulled on a night robe before opening the door to find the princess there. The smell of cumin hung on him, liniment for his aches and pains. "Come with me," she ordered. "We must search the stables."

Noting her expression, Blakewell asked no questions. He pulled on soft boots and followed Elizabeth back down the stairs to where Margot stood, a bunch of rushes tipped in pitch in one hand. They hurried to the stable, Sir George in the lead. He collected two servants on the way and lit the torches from the entry lamps. Elizabeth followed closely. Margot hung behind them, unwilling to go on but unable to go back. As soon as they left the main building, one of Hugh's guardsmen approached. Elizabeth briefly explained that they sought evidence in Alice's murder and he joined them, sword drawn.

The stable smelled strongly of old hay and bird droppings. A few horses were gathered at one end. Sir George stopped uncertainly beside them, but Elizabeth paid no attention as she took a torch from one of the servants and proceeded in the opposite direction, where shelves had been built to hold tack and supplies. Most of them were empty, since Hampstead needed only a few horses. Along the bottom were closed shelves made of rough lumber with crude rope fasteners. She began opening doors with one hand, and seeing her purpose, Sir George did the same. In the section on the left end sat a large leather bag such as travelers might carry on a short trip. Blakewell pulled it from its place with a "Here!" Elizabeth stood frozen, knowing what she gazed upon. Margot's face showed confusion. Sir George pulled the bag's laces free and opened it. His expression changed from curious to confused and finally to horrified as he took in the bag's condition.

"It is drenched in blood," he said wonderingly. "The thing is lined with waxed cloth and rags, all soaked in gore. Gloves and a knife as well."

The Guardsman spied something else in the dark space. "Look." He pulled out a small cloth bag and emptied its contents into his hand. Stones glowed softly in the torchlight: pins, rings, amulets, and rosaries. The remains of Mary's lost property.

Behind where the bag had been was the cloak and, folded neatly alongside it, several robes of black, brown, and white, like those of the different orders of nuns once seen in England. All the things Guy Pemberton needed for mayhem he had kept in her stable. Elizabeth pulled out the cloak, unrolling it to reveal its bedraggled state, the inside stiff, the tassels oddly tinged with brown.

Amazement showed on Sir George's face and confusion on that of the guardsman. "People here were used to seeing him come and go, even you," she told Blakewell. "With Margot's help, Guy entered early in the morning and hid the evidence of his crimes. But now that the gate is guarded he could not retrieve his things, so he stole Ninian's bag at my sister's, as he stole her jewelry."

Sir George was at sea. "Pemberton stole from the Princess Mary?"

"He also took your cloak to hide the ruin of his own, but Margot noticed the difference and made him put it back. He's probably using one of Robin's of late. But where is his new hiding place?"

Suddenly Margot fell to her knees with a shriek, tears streaming down her face. Clasping her hands together before her, she prayed in desperate tones, *"Mater Dolorosa, Miserere. Non nobis, Domine." Sorrowful Mary, be merciful. God, not us.*

"Highness?" Sir George asked gently, still unsure of what it all meant.

"Alice's killer is Guy Pemberton. He has killed five women that we know of."

"God be merciful." Unaware, he echoed Margot's plea.

"We must find Captain Bellows." Elizabeth turned to the Guardsman beside her.

"I'll go myself." The young soldier disappeared with a quick bow.

Elizabeth moved to Margot, who still prayed but in mumbled, half-connected phrases. "You must go to bed now. There is no more you can do here."

The once iron-controlled woman was now hysterical. "My brother! They will kill him!"

The princess did not answer but put an arm around the other woman's shoulders. Margot leaned heavily on the girl for whom she was caretaker, speaking in a voice very unlike her, wistful and soft. "He was a bright boy, meant to be a priest. My father sent him to Rome for the finest training. Then Father died and there was no money. Later there was not even a humble place for a priest in England." She stopped, her voice regaining some of its old righteous indignation. "It drove him mad, this nation's loss of faith."

As Margot's words spilled out, Elizabeth led her toward the castle, comforting the older woman as if she were the adult.

"He was a good boy, so good to me when we were children. When my father wanted him to go to the Church, he went willingly. In those days it seemed the best thing. The king was Defender of the Faith, and my brother's career would have been advanced, having studied in Rome. But then there was no place for him, do you understand? No place!" She sobbed out words, trying futilely to excuse the deaths of five women.

She was interrupted by a knocking at the gate. Both women jumped, set on edge by the night's revelations. As they came up the path, a guard stood before the opened peephole. "It's the physician's wife, Your Highness. She wonders if you know where Simon might be. He came not home to-night."

CHAPTER
THIRTY-NINE

The young guardsman arrived at St. James as Hugh and Gooderich stabled their exhausted horses. They had finally located Derwent at the home of his friend, Sir Edward Carleton, only to find that Sir Edward could account for Derwent's whereabouts for the entire night of Constance Maillot's death. The two had sat up with a mare that was foaling and in trouble, taking turns rubbing her down and keeping her calm. Derwent had come back today since the two shared interest in the colt.

Hugh had been careful not to make any charges he could not substantiate, but he did tell Derwent of his lover's death once the man's alibi was established. Derwent was shocked at the news. "Poor Connie." He shook his light curls regretfully. "What happened?"

"She was murdered, Your Lordship."

"Murdered! Recently a boy on the street

warned that she was in danger. How did he know?"

Hugh chose not to answer that. "Do you know of any other man that the lady —" How did one phrase it delicately? "— spent time with?"

Derwent giggled just as Simon had described. "Connie and I 'spent time' together, as you say, quite pleasantly. But of late she had found someone new." He pouted, a childish pose for a man full grown. "Someone of intelligence, she said. As if that was what a woman like Connie needs. Uh, needed." He remembered himself and took a more serious tone. "She never said who it was, but I was ready to move on as well. Despite Milady's stunning looks, there are willing women enough, no need to pine after one who is no longer convivial." He giggled again, and Hugh understood Constance's need to "move on." That sound became more irritating each time one heard it.

Hugh and Gooderich returned to St. James ready for their beds and a day off and found themselves riding apace to Hampstead instead. Hugh took a few minutes to find a replacement for Calkin, judging he might be needed for more important duty than

Yeoman Bed-goer this night.

Elizabeth met them at the gate, frantic, with Sir George behind her. "Simon's missing," she said as Hugh slid from the horse's back. "He went to question Robin Brandon and never returned home. Oh, Hugh, I sent him there!"

Hugh could not help but notice the princess' use of his name for the first time, but then his mind grasped the import of her words.

"The killer is Guy Pemberton. We found the bag he uses to carry the heads." Elizabeth winced as she said it. "Margot admitted that he is a priest."

"Guy?" Gooderich contradicted her without thinking. "Not possible. He's a regular —" he stopped himself, blushing in the torchlight. "He's no priest."

"He became apostate, and I think it turned his mind. Part of him enjoys the wild life he leads, but the other —"

"The other suffers because he deserted the service of God," Hugh finished.

"So he kills women?" Sir George was skeptical.

"Women of loose morals. He resents the lust they arouse in him."

"And he returns them to the church," Elizabeth explained. "He makes love to them in Latin, gives them presents, and tempts them into affairs, promising that they will someday be together. Then he kills them and gives them to God, offering them in place of himself. He makes them nuns, in his diseased mind, with robes and rosaries."

"Brides of Christ," Gooderich concluded. "But why take the heads?"

"Simon thought it had to do with their extraordinary beauty," Hugh turned his horse around, its hooves echoing against the stone of the gateway. "We can't stand here trying to figure it out. Simon is in danger."

"If he is following Pemberton, he cannot get word to us," Gooderich said hopefully.

"Pray God it is that." Elizabeth closed her eyes for a moment, her expression somber.

"Is there any way to know where Pemberton might be?" Hugh mounted, though his horse smelled strongly of sweat and its head drooped with weariness.

"Before I sent her inside I asked Margot to remember everything Guy ever said about particular places." The princess' gray eyes saddened, making her look older than her years. "I fear for her sanity, but she did remember one thing. As a boy Guy loved their home in Baycross, near the Charter

House, now sold to pay the family's debts. They had their own chapel on the grounds, which sat off by itself, away from the other dwellings. Guy told her that he sometimes goes to the old chapel to be alone."

"Baycross is east of here, in Clerkenwell. You may have saved Simon's life, Highness." Hugh turned to the young man who had ridden to find him. "Get four men and meet us at the Alden Crossing. Bring two fresh horses." The man left and he turned to the princess. "Highness, go inside with Hannah and await word from me. I will send with all speed when I learn anything."

Elizabeth knew better than to argue, although she longed to go along, to assure that everything possible was done for Simon. *One day I shall,* she vowed. *They won't always be able to tell me what to do, God willing.* For now she must trust Hugh, as she knew she could.

After they had assured that both gates at Hampstead were guarded, the two exhausted Guardsmen rode off at a gallop for Baycross. On the way Hugh prayed for two things: that Margot was right about her brother's whereabouts and that Simon was still alive when they found him.

Simon awoke to complete darkness and a

cold, hard surface. Lifting his head caused a sharp pain just below the left ear. Probing the spot, he felt a huge lump that jolted him again as his fingers found it. He was still for a few moments, trying to remember what had happened. Hugh had been gone from St. James, and he had started for home. That was the last he remembered. Gingerly, he tried moving: first his legs, which obeyed his brain's command with no problem. His arms too worked; only his head was a problem. Pain radiated from the lump behind his ear down his neck and into one shoulder. Feeling for the knife at his belt, he found nothing. Rising painfully to his knees, he searched the area around him. He knelt before a rough wood door that was fastened shut on the other side.

A second, more careful exploration of his injury led Simon to conclude that he had been struck from behind. It was unlikely that he could have fallen and struck that spot. Slowly thoughts formed and began to make sense. He remembered Brandon's face across the wooden table, recalled bumping into Guy Pemberton as he left the inn. He had been followed, attacked, and brought here. The next question was why? Or more realistically, why was he still alive?

With a shiver, Simon recalled the headless

body of Alice LaFont discovered only a few weeks before. Panic rose and he felt the familiar tightness in his chest that inhibited breathing. *Calm down,* he admonished himself. *If you are still alive, there is hope. There will be a chance for escape, and you must be prepared.* At this his breathing eased, a sort of calm returned, and he began planning how to live through this nightmare. A starting point was to explore the room in which he found himself.

He found it was painful but not impossible to stand erect. Pacing the room off, he guessed it to be about eight feet square, with high shelves against the walls on the two sides at angles to the doorway. The door was rough planks but tightly made, the floor stone. Feeling past the shelves, he found that two of the walls were stone and therefore exterior, while the other two were brick, probably added later to form a storage area. On the shelves were several items covered with dust. Handling them in the darkness he distinguished two candlesticks, one broken; a chalice, dented; a metal plate, rusty; and some paper that smelled of mold. It seemed he was in a chapel, but where, and again, why?

A noise outside the door caused him to jump, stifling a cry as pain again knifed through his neck and shoulder. Someone was moving around outside his prison. Something heavy was dragged into place, then someone made repeated trips to and fro. As the steps led away they were quick, but as they returned they were slower. The person was carrying things from one place to another. Twice Simon heard the solid sound of something heavy set into place on a wooden surface. There was a pause then, and he concluded that whoever it was had gone. Just as he began to breathe more easily the sound of chanting began, a single voice intoning the mass for the dead.

Listening with deepening dread, Simon recognized the voice, the same voice he had heard — how much earlier? Hours? Days? The low-pitched, well-modulated tones rose and fell in practiced repetition of the phrases of the mass. How did it tally? The man thought himself a priest and yet had earned the reputation of a blackguard. Did he believe that killing women would restore the purity of his own soul? Taking care to be quiet, Simon explored the room again, this time for a weapon.

The robed figure knelt, praying quietly once he'd recited the mass for his saints. Guidance from heaven was needed, for he did not know how to handle this new situation. God's plan was no longer clear, for the boy did not fit. Why had this Simon been allowed to discover his secret? He knelt silently for a long time on the cold stone floor, ignoring the discomfort in his knees and waiting for revelation.

The return of his priestly self always brought peace, although Guy could not complete his work without his other half. The Tempter searched out and arranged the sacrifices necessary for purification, weak women too sinful to resist his power. The Priest made them pure again by separating them from their sinful bodies, leaving the corrupt, lifeless parts for burial as brides of Christ. In doing so he restored to England the lost orders: the Carmelites, the Franciscans, the Dominicans, and all the rest. The heads he anointed with oil and dedicated to God, restoring them to Eternal Life.

His prayer for guidance concerned the boy now locked in the chapel storeroom. What had Simon Maldon to do with either the Tempter or the Priest? Guy had made fools of them all, convinced even the Whore's Bastard that he was the charming gallant, but now the boy had discovered his secret and threatened his mission. Why was he here?

Finally, an answer came, as clearly as if someone next to him had whispered it. The boy was a gift from God, sent to lead him to the most suitable sacrifice of all! Jubilant, the Priest, for that was what Pemberton truly considered himself, rose and went to see if the boy had regained consciousness.

Simon heard his captor coming, but he had found no weapon, formulated no plan. Worse, his head refused to work properly. He kept losing track of thoughts, even important ones. As the door opened, Guy Pemberton appeared dimly, the candle he carried illuminating features as perfect as one of Raphael's saints. He was dressed in a robe of brown, coarsely woven cloth, and sandals showed beneath its hem. The expression he wore was exactly the one he'd worn in the tavern, detached friendliness.

"Simon, are you feeling better?"

Simon gazed up, wondering how to deal with the situation. "Why am I here?"

"This is a place where I find peace. It is unlikely that we'll be bothered here." He spoke as if they intended a pleasant evening's visit. Leaning forward, Guy took the leather cord around Simon's neck and pulled the amulet from beneath his tunic. "Interesting piece. I would like to have it, if I may."

Simon obediently pulled the cord over his head, careful to avoid the painful lump, and handed it to Guy, who looped it over his own head, settling it beneath the rough robe. "To bring good fortune, eh?" His tone turned businesslike. "Will you greet the ladies now?" Simon's heart sank with dread. He had all too clear a notion which ladies the madman meant. "Come. They are prepared." He gestured impatiently with his free hand.

Head pounding, Simon left the small storeroom, went down a short corridor as directed, and entered the chapel proper. Guy followed until they were in the main room then stepped ahead, setting the candle on a heavy oak table that had only three legs. The missing one had been replaced with a stick, fragile and ridiculous as companion to three stout, elaborately carved originals. But then the candle's light illuminated the tabletop, and he forgot everything else.

CHAPTER
FORTY

On the old, broken altar sat six large jars
made of heavy glass such as alchemists used
for their experiments. The glass was thick
and poorly made, with air bubbles and
variation in surface smoothness visible even
in the dim light. Each jar's mouth was
covered with waxed cloth tied on with a
leather thong. It wasn't a tight seal, and the
smell of olive oil lingered in the old chapel.
Inside the jars, the heads of the five murdered women faced various directions, as if
they searched the room for something or
someone. The eyes no longer saw but stared
blankly ahead. Hair floating around the
white faces varied in shade from blond to
deep brown.

"I have wondered," Guy said idly, "if I
should find a redhead, having none. I had
decided it is a vanity. God does not notice
the hue." His face became thoughtful. "Of
course, a redhead would not be rejected as

an offering, as long as she is young and beautiful."

"You killed them." It wasn't the right thing to say, but it came out anyway. He looked at Alice LaFont, whose doll-like eyes seemed directed at him but empty, like a blind woman's.

"God needed them for His purposes. Women are weak and often lead men astray, as the first woman did Adam. The tempter called to these women, and they came, not as Peter, James, and John came to Christ, but to the Evil One, who despoiled their bodies until they were useful only as sacrifices." His voice sounded sad at what he perceived to be the women's failure of their final test.

He surveyed his collection with a critical eye. "Impressive, are they not?" He introduced them to Simon in an eerie parody of gallantry, putting a hand on the top of the jar as if to caress the woman within. "This is my first saint, Therese. Appealing, but untrue of heart. She had a lover, not the kind her trade demands, but a man who possessed her affection. I confess it made me angry, but there the idea of my redemption was born, for Therese belongs now only to God and to me. I made her a votary of the order of Augustine, who are known for their chastity."

"Where do the robes come from?"

"A certain lady asked me to procure, secretly, of course, priests' robes from the king's storehouse for her confessor's use. She knew where they were kept and thought they should be put to their proper use. Once I found the warehouse, I took a few from each sect. The idea was growing inside me even then, although God had not revealed it to me fully."

Simon tried to look interested, tried to ignore the heads before them.

Moving down the line of jars, Guy indicated a second head. "This is pretty Mathilda, also a whore. Her death helped me to work out the method, for I found that if the tempter promises false women a bright future, they are easily persuaded to secrecy and silence."

Another step forward. "This is Joanna. As time passed I found the tempter needed more challenging targets. After all, anyone can kill a slut, and no one cares. A nobleman's daughter, however, is a worthy goal. Joanna was easily debauched, so young, so corrupt. I first met her at Robin's home. While I had promised the whores an easier life, the prospect of marriage convinced Joanna to keep our affair secret. She was most willing, as was Alice." He moved on, his scandals rasping against the stone floor. "I had almost forgotten her after she left the Court, but there she was when I visited Margot. Still lovely, still willing for a bit of fun." His face hardened. "Another candidate for God's justice."

He regained his chatty air as he tenderly touched the next jar. "This is Sally. I visited the Derwents briefly in May, and her beauty caught my eye. When I saw how easily she was corrupted, I knew she should be sacrificed as well." Calmly he absolved himself of all responsibility for murder.

"And finally Constance, an ironic name for one so free with her favors. I met her through Derwent as well when she tired of his superficial charm and sought adventure." He regarded the still faintly recognizable woman Simon had tried unsuccessfully to warn. "I gave her eternity."

Proudly Guy swept a hand outward to indicate all the jars. "Beautiful faces, now dedicated to God. They say that Satan was the most beautiful of the angels before he fell. Each of those you see here was Satan's child, fallen from Grace. I gave them eternity, gave them back to God, so their beauty is once again complete."

Simon could have mentioned that some

of them were beginning to look positively rotted, but he kept silent. Guy surveyed the jars, brushing away a fly that landed on the nearest. It moved to the next, but he seemed not to notice. "My collection is only half complete. There must be twelve in all, as Christ had twelve apostles. When the twelve are found and purified, God will destroy the heretic king, who even now suffers the pains of hell for his crimes, and return England to the true church."

Guy clearly believed it was his destiny to see Henry's fall. He bent his head for a moment in meditation and spoke as if to himself, although loud enough that Simon heard him, revealing his tortured soul. "Once my work is done, I will not play the part of the tempter again, will not feel the deadly sins that have tortured me for so long. Purified by service to God, I will vouchsafe England's return to faith." At this he lapsed into silence, his face expressing exaltation.

Simon forced his mind away from the horror and considered his situation. The hour was late. There would be a search for him. He must delay whatever this madman intended long enough to escape. Once out of the chapel, he might be able to outrun Guy and find help. If only his head didn't throb so! He tried to frame his next question as if truly interested. "Why did these women have to die? Are we not all sinners before God?"

Apparently pleased at Simon's interest, Guy explained. "Martyrs build the church. John the Baptist's head was sacrificed to pave the way for Christ's work on Earth. To return the church to the Mary of this age, saints are required. With the rebirth of faith, Mary Tudor will rule. She will bear the son the world awaits."

Simon tried to see the situation from Pemberton's twisted point of view. Devout Mary, strong in her convictions and dedicated to the Catholic Church, was his solution to the world's confusion, despite the fact that at thirty, she was old to begin bearing children. "Mary must rule England, for the sake of all the souls now in perdition, my parents and all the others." He closed his eyes. "Think of the souls lost in these last twelve years, while England has been without grace."

Able to finally put words to his thoughts, Guy obviously could not stop himself. "When I met Robin Brandon in Rome, I had long been wracked with indecision. All my life I had trained for the church, but there was no place in it for me when I was ready. Who cared about an orphaned son of English parents? I found a place in an Italian household, but I had no patience for the daily dullness."

Guy's voice had become thinner, less substantial, his face pained in the faint candlelight. "Robin and I met by chance and discovered that we had grown up not a mile from each other. I believe he found it entertaining to introduce a young priest to the vices of the world and observe as my training was stripped away." He touched his robe reverently, feeling its rough texture. "Whatever debauchery we found together at night, I always attended mass in the morning. It was as if I were two people, even then."

Simon put together the pieces of the story, sensing that it could be told because the hearer was not intended to live to retell it. Guy had separated his lewd self from the virtuous one, and that division allowed him to be charming and serene while carrying out unbelievably bloody deeds.

"Eventually I left Rome. Robin and I traveled for some months and finally returned to England. What pain I suffered then!" He raised his hands before the altar, almost invisible in the blackness outside the candlelight. "Here my parents raised me in the faith, and here my father prayed each day for England after Henry's ruination of the true church." He clasped outstretched hands in a pantomime of desperate orison. "I felt the pull of my vows much more strongly than I had in Rome, where I was nothing."

Guy seemed to remember Simon then, for he leaned close, breathing the heat of his madness onto his victim as he ranted. "I know my purpose now." His eyes glowed with a double fire, the reflection of the candlelight in their depths, and the ardor of the fanatic. "Every soul in England needs me, whether aware of it or not." With that he returned to the matter at hand, the disposal of Simon Maldon. "It is too early for my work to end. I have more to do. You are a trial on my way to Golgotha, but God expects that I will prevail."

"How do you know what must be done?"

"The dreams began when I returned to England. Standing before the judgment of God, I saw myself riven into two men. One of them was God's tempter, encouraging the sin that I myself was so guilty of. But the other! The other shone in heaven as God's redeeming tool, the priest, bringing the people back to faith." His handsome face lit with anticipation. "The two persons will become one again when England is one with the church."

"What if it is not God who asks this of you? What if it is Satan who demands the murder of helpless women?"

Guy's head twitched in denial. "I feared that Satan had taken me at first, and I despaired. But then I met the Princess Mary at her home at Kimbolton. Knowing the gulf between my reputation and my families' intention for me, she took my hands in hers and told me that I must help this nation find the way back to God. Like my sister Margot, she made no secret of her disappointment in me. I felt the pull of her words, reminding me that I was devoted to the service of God, but how could I serve Him in a place where He is denied true worship? There is need for both my incarnations, the tempter and the priest."

A poor young man of impoverished nobility, the lure of Robin's wealth had strained the youthful priest's scruples unto breaking. Only by this mad bargain with God was he able to go on, immersing half of himself in vice and seduction, believing that it could be purified through the work of the other.

Guy had lost the thread of his narrative, falling into a trancelike state. Making his decision quickly, Simon dodged past him and fled down the corridor to the room where he had been imprisoned. It had a stout door, and he closed it behind him just as his captor, confused at the unexpected direction his flight had taken, appeared at the end of the passageway. Quickly Simon pulled on the shelf he had explored earlier, bringing it down in front of the door. Setting his back against the shelf he wedged it against the door, bracing his feet against the opposite wall and pushing with all the strength in his legs to hold it in place.

Guy pounded frantically on the heavy door, shouting and calling curses down on the boy. He could get little force behind his effort in the narrow passage, however, and the door held. Finally he stopped, exhausted, and was silent for a time. When his voice came again, it was friendly and calm, but all the more eerie for that.

"It does not matter, lad. God's purpose is accomplished in any case. You cannot escape, and your absence allows me access to a magnificent sacrifice."

Simon didn't follow for a few seconds, still shaken from the chase and the assault on the door, but Guy gleefully explained. "After all, how long can that sickly boy live? My next gift will assist the true princess to the throne. Her way will be easier without a troublesome Protestant in the background, tempting revolt." The voice receded as Simon grasped the import of his words.

"Wait! Wait! You must listen!"

It was no use. Guy's hurried footsteps echoed down the stones. With great effort Simon pushed the heavy wooden shelf away from the door, but it was now locked. He sank to the cold floor in despair, knowing that the killer had chosen as his next victim Elizabeth herself. Unlike the others, she would not be caught by his charm. She would be tricked into his grasp by the use of Simon's name and the amulet that she had last seen around his neck.

CHAPTER
FORTY-ONE

Because of the lateness of the hour, the soldier at Hampstead's gate was surprised to see a woman approaching from the castle. Swathed in a dark cape, her face almost glowed in the torchlight, so pale was she. Recognizing her as one of Elizabeth's ladies, he greeted her politely.

"How now, lady? Up late, are you not?"

"Her Highness has sent me on an errand. She is sleepless and desires me to fetch a potion."

The guard was doubtful. After the hubbub of earlier events, the princess was sending this woman out alone on an errand? "Should you not take someone with you, a manservant with a stout cudgel?" A guard could not leave his post, but he was reluctant to see this woman leave the safety of the castle.

"My escort has gone out the garden gate. He meant to pick up a torch and a spade to use as a weapon should he need it."

The guard smiled his relief and opened the gate for her.

Margot moved away from the gate uncertainly as it shut behind her. Now where? She had poured the posset she'd been given out the window and then paced her tiny room for almost an hour. Glancing at the road outside Hampstead's wall by chance, she'd discerned two unmoving torches shining in the night, one above the other.

In a trice she had made her decision. Whatever he was, Guy was her brother, her blood, and the only one left to her in this world. What he had done, if what they said was true, he had done in some strange way for his church, which was also hers. The least she could do was warn him. He must leave England, start anew somewhere, in France or even Spain.

Yes, that was it. The Princess Mary would help him to get a place with His Majesty of Spain, a staunch Catholic. There he would not be tempted to stray from his vows but would be appreciated for his devotion to his faith, and — please God — overcome his weaknesses of the flesh.

Now she stood uncertainly, not knowing how to go about finding Guy. Deep night engulfed her, and few sounds carried to her ears. An owl, that sentry of birds, called out its inane question, but no one answered. Bellows and his men had gone to the chapel. She cursed her own weakness in telling the princess about that, but her spirit had been momentarily crushed at the sight of the bloody cape and the sickening mess in the leather bag. Had Guy really killed silly, childlike Alice?

Shaking herself mentally before she fell into despair again, Margot straightened her spine and took firm control of her emotions. What's done is done, and cannot be undone. Now she must save her brother from further sin, get him away from the things that had brought on his madness. But where to look for him?

"Margot," a voice spoke behind her, and she turned to see Guy's angelic face.

Hugh and the soldiers approached their destination at Baycross cautiously, but there was no movement outside the house. The night was far advanced, yet light shone from within. Hugh signaled a halt and scanned the area as the horses snuffed and shook their heads, rattling their harnesses, impatient to either go on or be rid of their burdens. "I'll let them know what we're about," he told the others quietly. "I would have no one firing arrows into our backs thinking we're thieves." He dismounted and went to the door of a rambling half-timbered house, knocking with a gloved fist. An elderly servant answered, his face showing surprise to see the guardsmen.

"Welcome to you all. How may I assist the king's men at this hour?"

"We seek a fugitive who may be hiding in the chapel on these lands. Where is the place?"

The servant looked befuddled. "The chapel? A fugitive in our chapel?"

Hugh's impatience strained courtesy. "Where is it?"

"At the bottom of the hill, beside the river. You'll be guided by the sound of the water. Shall I send for torches?"

"Yes, if you please, but unlit. We will approach quietly, for he may have a prisoner."

The man gasped. So much excitement had not come to Baywick in decades. Sending a boy, he soon provided several pitch-dipped rushes and saw the guardsmen on their way. As they retreated the old man muttered to himself, "I suppose they meant the present chapel, of course, not the old one." Then he shut the door against the evil vapors of night.

The chapel loomed in the night, silent and

dark. With gestures Hugh sent two men to the back and set two outside the door in case the man should get by him and Calkin. Checking the windows, he found they were fixed and provided no exit. No light shone from within, but they moved silently anyway, opening the wooden door slowly to stifle any squeak it might make. No sound came from inside.

Stationing themselves in the small apse, they signaled to Gooderich, who quickly lit a torch and brought it. They entered the chapel itself but nothing moved, nothing seemed out of place. Hugh sniffed but could detect no odor of humanity, only the closed-in smell of places unheated and largely uninhabited. Gooderich moved down the center aisle, shining his torch between the benches.

Calkin lit a second torch from the first and went down one side and up onto the chancel. Finding a door at the back, he called out, "Here." Hugh hurried to it and together they broke the flimsy lock that held the door. Thrusting the torch inside, Calkin lit the way for Hugh, who burst into the small room. Nothing. It held what riches the chapel offered, communion pieces, candlesticks, and other church supplies. Well kept and neat, the place showed no sign of anything unusual. Hugh nevertheless ordered a thorough search of the chapel and the close. They found no sign of Simon or Guy Pemberton.

Elizabeth paced the solar, though the room had long since gone damp with the evening chill. It galled her to be female, young, and royal so that she was not allowed to do the thing she wanted most right now: find her friend.

A rustle in the passageway caused her to look up. Bess stood in the doorway, her brown eyes concerned. "My husband says that Alice's murderer has been identified."

"Yes." Elizabeth saw Bess' relief.

"I knew Sir George had not done such a terrible thing," Bess massaged her own forehead absently, allowing the tense muscles to relax somewhat. "He is not a bad man, Your Highness, nor even a bad husband. Only a man, after all." With that she went on to the bed that her husband did not share.

Elizabeth idly strummed a lute that lay on a side table. *Passion is a powerful force, making us both gods and fools. We instruct our minds, train our bodies, but we too seldom control our emotions. Father's mistakes came at times when his heart overruled his keen mind, when what he wanted took precedence over everything else. If ever I am queen, neither love nor lust will overrule my country's need. Ever.*

Once again her reverie was interrupted. The serving girl Hannah, who caused Simon to blush whenever she came near, hovered in the doorway, her face anxious. She had evidently heard something of the night's terrors. "Come in, and I will tell you what I know."

In a few minutes Elizabeth had laid the tale out for the girl, who bit her lip and went pale but did not cry. "Oh, Your Highness, I hope he is found safe."

Elizabeth noticed her distress despite her own worry. "You are fond of him?"

"Yes, Your Highness."

"Have you told him?"

The pretty head lowered and she pulled on a heavy curl that lay on her shoulder. "No, Your Highness."

"Why not?"

"He is very educated, Simon is. When a man can speak with princesses and kings, why would he notice me?"

Elizabeth, for all her youth, grasped the irony of the situation. Hannah thought herself ignorant and therefore below Simon, while Simon thought himself maimed and therefore unworthy of her. "Promise me that you will speak to him of your feelings when you see him next."

She looked up, aghast. "Is that not the man's place?"

"Trust me in this, Hannah. Simon has as much wit and courage as any man, but he has neither the wit nor the courage to speak his heart to you unless you lead the way."

Hannah fought back her tears. "I will do as you say . . . when I see him."

The guardsman posted at the garden gate heard a scratching at the wooden door and looked out through the peephole. Darkness prevented his seeing much, but it was a woman on the other side. "Who is it?"

"Margot, of this house," was the answer. "Her Highness sent me to fetch a sleeping potion. My servant and I have just returned." She showed the ring she wore, a Tudor rose that signified a lady of the king's court.

"I did not see you go out," the man said with a frown.

"I left by the main gate, but it is quicker if I return through the garden." The white face twisted in what passed with Margot for a smile. "The princess is distraught and needs her posset."

The young guardsman considered briefly and then opened the gate. Margot came through, her black dress blending into the darkness so that she appeared to be only a pale face floating in the air. Her escort followed, a man in a dark, hooded cape that covered all but his lowered face and sandaled feet.

"I am grateful," Margot began, but her sentence was cut short when the guardsman let out a strangled groan and fell forward. In the torchlight she saw her brother with a bloody knife clasped in his hand. The young man on the ground gave out a sigh as the life left him, and Guy relaxed his arm.

Margot was horrified. She had explained Guy's presence. He could have gone with her, hidden in the stables as she'd planned, and then escaped to Spain when she had arranged things. Instead he had killed again, and the look on his face revealed that he had no compunction about the deed. She had not truly believed that her brother could kill without mercy until this minute, but her disbelief had caused the death of this young man. She spoke in a hoarse whisper.

"Guy. Guy, darling, you must listen to me. You are unwell. We must find a doctor as soon as may be. I will speak to the princess, to both of them. They will see that you are given the best of care." She was babbling and knew it, but she had let him inside, into the castle where Elizabeth sat waiting, unaware of the danger that approached. She had thought to help her brother. She knew now that he had other plans.

She had to call out, to warn Elizabeth. As quickly as he had dispatched the guardsman, Guy read her intention and did the same to her, raising the knife and slashing down a second time. Margot's white face twisted with pain and shock. She tried to scream, but her heart had been pierced, its beating stopped by the blade Guy had taken from Simon only a short while earlier.

CHAPTER
FORTY-TWO

Simon had explored his prison for a means of escape three times without success when he heard someone in the passage. Retreating to a corner, he picked up a candlestick too short and stout to be much use. There was scratching at the door, steps retreating, steps again coming near. Finally, the latch lifted and the door swung open.

Not daring to breathe lest he give away his position, Simon waited, listening for a sound that would tell him his captor was near. He was surprised to hear a very different, high-pitched voice call out, "Master Simon, are you there?"

In amazement he replied, "Pen? Penitence Brook?"

A cackle of joy answered him. "Oh, Master Simon, I did not know but what that man had killed you."

Simon rose from his corner and approached the doorway. Together the two groped their way down the passage and through the chapel while Pen explained his presence. "I was told to watch over ye, me and some others as well, so when I saw you on the street, I followed. I was some way back when the man pulled you into the alley, and when I got to it, he had you before him on the saddle, limp as an old rag. He covered you with his cloak, but I knew he'd done you harm. I followed as best I could — lost him once, but an old woman said she'd seen a man with a sick boy and pointed the way. I found him again and trailed him here, where he hid his horse in the trees and carried you inside this place."

They passed the rickety table. Simon's hand touched one of the jars and he pulled his hand away as if bitten. It was too dark to see them, but he imagined the women's faces and the memory spurred him on, stumbling over benches as he hurried out of that place. Pen, unaware of what lay inside the chapel, kept up his account.

"Then came the worst part. I was told to go for help should you need it, but I feared leaving. What if the man took you somewhere else or killed you before I could return? Oh, Master Simon, a lack-wit such as I was never meant to make such choices! I am a simple man, and it near drove me mad trying to decide. In the end I saw him mount his horse and leave, and I decided I would take a look for myself."

They were outside now, and Simon could see Pen's elf-like face dimly. "And grateful I am that you made that choice, Pen. I must hurry to Hampstead Castle now, and you must stay here and watch the door. I do not think the man will return tonight, but if he does, go quickly to Hugh Bellows of the king's guard and tell him to come here. Do you know the way to Hampstead?"

"I do not, but we are near to the east gate of the city. Turn right on the road you'll find as you walk that way." He pointed.

"Good, there will be stables at the gate, and I have great need of a horse."

Outside Baycross Chapel, the seven guardsmen mounted their horses dejectedly, Hugh and Calkin once again feeling the weariness of the long day behind them. It was beginning to lighten to a new day. Would Simon Maldon see it? Hugh was not optimistic. As they turned their horses' heads back toward St. James, Calkin said, "A pleasant chapel, that. Fairly new, do you think?"

"I suppose." Hugh's tired mind tried to get around Calkin's purpose. The man noticed everything.

"I'm thinking it hasn't been there for long. There's no moss on the rock, no squeak in the wood."

Hugh's eyes widened. "They've built a new chapel! Where might the old one be, the one Guy would remember?" Surveying the landscape, the men tried to identify buildings looming in the grayness. The chapel they had just left sat on the bank of the small river. Off to their right and up the rise was the main dwelling of the estate. Around it stood outbuildings, flat-roofed, huddling structures. Behind the house and to the left was a copse of trees. Perhaps there, please God.

They had to be more careful now, since light was dawning. Tying the horses, they moved quickly into the small wood and spread out in a line, peering through the dimness still prevailing there. Finally, a man on the left whistled softly and pointed ahead. Hugh could not see it for a few more steps, but then a shape appeared before him. It was a half-ruined church, the roof in the front third burned black and fragile from a fire. Its walls were green with moss, the windows nailed over with boards. There seemed to be only one door, intact but gaping open. Motioning for the men to surround the place, Hugh once more stepped to the door, Calkin behind him. There was movement inside and they froze, tensed and ready. To the surprise of everyone involved, Penitence Brook emerged from the chapel. Seeing Hugh and six guardsmen, arrows at the ready, Pen flashed his toothless grin and raised both hands in surrender. "Good morning, Captain," he said cheerfully.

For reasons not entirely clear even to herself, Elizabeth told Hannah the whole story of the murders, filling in all that Simon had left out. Hannah took it in quietly, her eyes showing her grasp of the nuances: Henry's dread of these crimes, even Elizabeth's own struggle with the inevitable comparison to her mother's death.

"This is an evil man, Your Highness," she said when Elizabeth finished. "If he taunts your father he is wrong. The king does as he must, but he does not kill lightly, nor take trophies to gloat over." Elizabeth was somewhat comforted to know that Hannah saw the difference between two situations, despite the fact that headless corpses were the result.

After that each surrendered to her own thoughts. As night wore on, they dozed fitfully, neither willing to give in to sleep entirely. They were instantly alert when footsteps sounded outside the room, and Cook appeared in the doorway.

"Your Highness, a guardsman at the kitchen door says there is a lad just inside the garden gate, badly wounded. It is the one with the crippled arm, and they believe he will not live long." Her voice shook as she told it. Cook had grown fond of the physician's boy, who listened to her complaints of aches and pains and brought her medicines to relieve them. The handsome young guardsman who had come to the back door had been very gentle, but he made it clear that Simon was dying. If the princess wanted to see him, it must be soon. "We have sent for help," he said sadly, "but he has lost a great deal of blood."

Cook now reached out a hand toward Elizabeth. "He gave me this." She held out the fleur-de-lis amulet Simon had worn the last time she saw him. "He says to be quick. The boy can barely speak."

"I must go to him," Elizabeth said. "At the very least he can be avenged." Hannah, of another mind, simply breathed a prayer that the guardsman was wrong. "We will follow quickly," Elizabeth told Cook, who bowed and went off.

As the old woman returned to the kitchen, she wondered if she should venture out to see the dying boy. The damp air was hard on her bones, though. A blow to the side of her head sent her to the stone floor like a polled ox. The man who had delivered the "message" bent and picked the old woman up under the arms, dragging her into the pantry. When he turned, a rent in the back of his tunic could be seen, the blood smeared around it still wet. Once he had the cook's body out of sight he considered her head for a moment but stopped himself with a stern mental reprimand. She was not an acceptable sacrifice. He must hurry so he could be in place and ready when the one he wanted appeared.

Elizabeth and Hannah were having what would have been an argument if they had been equals. Instead it was merely Hannah's attempt to make the princess use caution. "It could be a trick," she insisted for the third time.

"The guards are Hugh's trusted men," Elizabeth rejoined. "They block entry at both gates, which are locked. The walls cannot be scaled without a ladder, which would be seen. We are safe inside this place, drab as it is."

Hannah's thoughts ran ahead and she abruptly changed course. "We will need protection against the night air and light to see our way. Do you, Highness, go to the storeroom for a torch, and I will fetch warm cloaks." Elizabeth, glad the girl had given up the debate, agreed.

A few minutes later the back door opened and a slight female form stepped from its light into the graying dawn, closing the door with a firm click. The cloak he remembered. She had worn it at Isabella de Marcia's home the day he met her. Her head was bent as she watched her steps on the dim path. The tempter followed her through the garden, reveling in his success at drawing her out. He had feared she would bring an escort or a companion, and he would have had much more to do. As it was, he might complete his night's work here, in this familiar place. He wished he could see the red hair that would soon be his, but the hood covered it.

The figure reached the garden wall, stopped, and looked about uncertainly. There was no wounded Simon Maldon. In fact, there was no one at all, since Guy had dragged the two bodies outside the wall. Finally, seeing that the gate was open and unguarded, the girl whirled about, suspicious and frightened. That was good. Springing from his hiding place, the tempter put a hand over her mouth, stopping her scream. "I have waited for you, princess," he told her softly. "I will save England, and you must do your part."

She fought him with all her strength, and the hood fell away as she struggled. Brown curls spilled out, and he almost released his grip in surprise. It was not Elizabeth he had captured. The girl sensed his loosened grip and pulled away slightly, but he had already recovered himself. In furious disappointment, he flung the girl to one side, releasing her momentarily. As she fought to keep her balance, he caught her a blow on the head that sent her to the ground with a sharp cry of pain. There she lay still, and he saw her face. One of Elizabeth's servants had tricked him with the cloak. She was not the sacrifice he had come for, but he could see in the half light that she was beautiful. His plan was foiled, but he had no time for delay. She would make a fine addition to the apostles, a worthy sacrifice, and the night would not be wasted.

Simon approached the castle from the north side, its back. He'd had little trouble stealing a horse from the east gate guardhouse while the grooms snored in their bunks. Another time he might have marveled at the nonchalance with which he had carried out a theft that could bring him the same penalty he had seen exacted on the streets not a month ago. It simply didn't matter what happened to him now. He had to stop Guy Pemberton from reaching the princess. He would worry about consequences later.

Taking every shortcut he could find, Simon crossed private lands and outran several barking dogs to reach Hampstead's walls. He intended to enter the main gate, alerting the guardsmen as he did, but as he rounded the wall he saw something that chilled his blood. The garden gate stood open. Worse, something lay outside the wall that should not be there. Rags? Sliding from the horse's bare back, he stepped closer and recoiled at the sight and smell of death. The body of a young man in only his under-tunic slumped against the stone wall. A second one lay beside it, that of a woman. He bent to make out her face — Margot. He had thought her face could be no paler, but the pallor of death gave it the sheen and color of the finest wax. From her chest protruded the knife that Guy had taken from him a few hours earlier.

A noise from inside diverted his attention. It had sounded like a scream of pain, cut off quickly. With no delay Simon entered the garden.

There was fog, just as there had been that other morning, when he had discovered the headless body of Alice LaFont. The hairs on his neck stood up and his chest tightened. Danger seemed to surround him, and he forced back an urge to retreat, to back out of the gate and go for help. If the killer was indeed here in the garden, and if he had a victim, help would come too late, might be too late already. Calming himself as he had before he faced some medical trial for his father, Simon moved off to the left of the gate, circling toward the back of the castle.

A shout came at some distance, from the direction of the main gate. "Clifton, are you there?"

The guards! They had heard the cry too and were coming this way. "Here!" he answered. "It is Simon Maldon! There is danger at the garden gate!" There was low-voiced discussion as the leader directed his men. They would search the garden, they would rescue him and whoever else was in danger; they would end the nightmare.

Movement to his right caught his eye and he turned quickly. A flash of dark fabric moved past his field of vision and was gone, and it took a moment for his brain to interpret what he'd seen. A man in a cloak had gone out the gate, carrying something wrapped in blue. In a trice he identified the wrapping — Elizabeth's cloak. Guy had the princess! Was she dead? Without further thought he reacted, rushing after the figure to the arched entrance. Guy threw the limp body over the saddle and mounted the horse that Simon had left conveniently waiting outside the gate. He looked back to see the youth standing frozen to the spot. "Not the red-haired one," he called back, "but God has provided." Simon uttered a moan of protest, for Hannah's dark hair tumbled from beneath the hood.

Voices behind him were closer now. The guardsmen would arrive in a few seconds. Guy wheeled the horse around and kicked its sides viciously. Responding to the command, the horse bolted ahead. He would escape in the time it took to return to the main gate and mount a posse.

With unconscious decision, Simon turned to the body of Margot beside him. Pulling his knife from her chest, he hefted, aimed, and threw it, perfectly, accurately, and with malice, at the retreating Guy Pemberton. He watched as the figure on horseback stiffened, arched, and fell. The horse whinnied once in confusion, trotted on for a moment, and then slowed its pace. The form slung across the saddle, no longer held in place, slid to the ground.

CHAPTER
FORTY-THREE

Simon was already running toward Hannah
when the guardsmen appeared at the gate
and shouted at him to halt. "It is Simon!"
he called back, continuing toward his goal.
"I've got to see to Hannah!"

He paused at the still form of Pemberton,
sparing only a glance to assure that he was
dead. Glassy, staring eyes confirmed it. As
he approached, Hannah rolled over and
opened her eyes. Seeing him standing over
her, she smiled and then winced, rubbing
her jaw with the back of a hand. "Simon?"
He bent to her, and she sat up groggily.

"You are safe now."

"Simon, two things I must tell you."

"Shh, you must not talk. I'll send for my
father, and he'll see if you're hurt."

"Two things," she repeated. "First, the
door to the storeroom closed of its own accord. There must have been a draft."

Simon felt sick. She was out of her head,

rambling.

"Second," she continued, "she told me I must be the one to begin it, so I will tell you now. I find you most appealing." With that Hannah closed her eyes, but there was a smile on her face, and she nestled herself against Simon's shoulder. After some contemplation, a smile brightened his face as well, and that was how Hugh found him a few seconds later. It was enough to grate on a man's nerves, having ridden his horse half to death all night only to find the little weasel safe and grinning like an idiot.

"Why did you not come looking for me, then?" Elizabeth growled the next afternoon when Hannah was deemed well enough to answer the princess' questions.

"I thought you had gone out before me, and I went quickly to catch up with you," Hannah said serenely, her green eyes wide with an attempt to look honest.

"Wearing my cloak." Hannah said nothing, and after a pause, Elizabeth continued. "You swear you have no idea how the storeroom door slammed shut and locked me inside?"

"Your Highness, I swear to you that I did not touch that door," Hannah said firmly. It was true. She had used a broom handle to push the door closed in case the princess looked behind her.

Elizabeth was not convinced, but she had no choice but to accept the girl's oath. Simon, who until then had tried to be inconspicuous, now changed the subject.

"What account will we give of the night's events?"

There were four of them now: Simon, Elizabeth, Hannah, and Hugh, and each knew that they must be careful and in complete agreement about what was said concerning the deaths at Elizabeth's home. The king would be furious, to be sure, but at least Hugh could assure him that the danger was over. Pen had showed Hugh alone the grisly evidence in the chapel, and he had had Calkin dispose of it discreetly so as to cause no further distress to the families involved. Guy was dead, as was Margot and a young guardsman. Happily, Cook was alive and would recover.

Many people knew bits and pieces, but only four now living knew all of it. Hugh summed it up: "Guy Pemberton's mind was unbalanced, and he killed several women who had been his mistresses. He came here last night to see his sister and killed her after she tried to persuade him to turn himself in. He was killed when guardsmen discovered him trying to break into the princess' garden." It was best for all concerned if no one else knew that Guy had actually entered the grounds even with guards posted everywhere.

Simon cleared up the last remaining questions, explaining Guy's belief that he had been chosen to redeem England for Catholicism. "Fanatics," Elizabeth commented with a shudder. "They make my skin crawl. Would that the world could allow each person to decide his own philosophy."

Simon had recovered his sense of humor enough to tease her. "Ah, an enlightened princess," he emoted. "She would rule with justice, and be loved by all."

Elizabeth glared at him. "She will never rule at all, Master Maldon, and it is dangerous to speak of it, even among friends." He accepted the reprimand with lowered head. This princess could never cease in her vigilance to remain outside politics or her life might be forfeit. Softening her gaze, she continued. "My father has sent word that I am to be moved to the country for the summer months. I leave Hampstead next week."

He was surprised at the news but told himself he should not be. It had been only a matter of time until their relationship ended. Elizabeth would return to her friends, her governess Kat, and her tutors, who would hopefully find her Greek much improved. He would stay on in Hampstead, once more only the physician's crippled son.

His eye caught Hannah's then, and she looked at him directly and smiled before lowering her eyes demurely. His life was not going to return to the way it was before, because Hannah was part of it now. She would stay on at Hampstead, and they would see each other often.

Hugh rose to go. "Your Highness, I will report what we have agreed upon to His Majesty." Their story might satisfy Henry, but he grew more unpredictable every day. He might be proud of his daughter's courage and wit, but they dared not take the chance that he would blame them all for the danger she had faced.

"Simon, Hannah, you have done well, and I applaud your courage and your quick thinking." Here his glance rested just a shade too long on Hannah's and she blushed. "Simon, if ever you need me, send word, and if you visit the Welsh Guard, we will gladly share our bread with you."

No one had told Elizabeth how Pemberton had died; she was aware only that he was killed as he rode away with Hannah as captive. Simon wasn't sure how he felt about the fact that he had slain another human being, but logic told him there had been no other option.

"Thank you, Captain. I will remember your invitation."

With a formal bow to the princess, Hugh left. Hannah, sensing the mood, invented a pressing errand and left with Hugh. Simon and Elizabeth remained silent for a few moments then caught each other's eye and laughed.

"We did well, Simon Maldon."

"We did, Highness." After a moment's pause he added, "It is the first time in my life that I have felt adequate, even valuable."

"I felt the same. We gathered bits of information here and there, we took the pieces of information and fitted and refitted until they made sense, and we used that sense to bring a murderer to justice, for death is certainly justice in this case. What better result of education can there be than to right a wrong in this way?"

Simon grimaced. "It's almost a pity that it's over. Of course I want no more killing, but —"

"I know exactly what you mean. You now go back to being a physician's assistant, and I return to my life as an extraneous, useless heir."

He tried to brighten their leave-taking somewhat. "Actually, I have chosen a new path as a result of this experience. I find I like mixing medicines and such, and have asked my father to apprentice me to an apothecary. The work benefits people but does not involve actual treatment, so my squeamishness will be no detriment. I have some background through work with my father, so I may succeed even though I begin late."

"I am glad to hear it. I shall remember that there is a friend to call on for physic when I am the oldest princess extant."

"You may yet rule," he said, speaking his heart at what he felt would be their last meeting. "And if you do, you will be the greatest ruler this land has ever had."

"Thank you, Simon Maldon." She blushed a little as, with a last bow, he left her to her future.

The chance to rule is not likely. She turned and looked out the window at the garden she had transformed — a "renaissance," the French called it.

England, if I were to rule, I would give myself to the task wholeheartedly. Nothing is too much to offer. I would strive for peace, both within and without, and I would work to make my nation secure and respected throughout the world. I would find men like Simon, men of integrity and dedication, to help me, and in the end everyone would be forced to admit that I had done my best to make England a jewel among nations.

At home that evening Simon's reading was interrupted by his mother's strident call. "Someone to speak with you!"

Descending the ladder from the loft, he saw the cause of his mother's angry tone. A girl waited on the doorstep, but she was no Hannah. This one had the look of the streets and an eye as bold as any sailor's. Her dress showed far too much of her figure, and there was paint on her cheeks. He heard his mother's muttered threat about driving the woman off with her broom, and he hastened to intervene. "It must be important, Mother, or she wouldn't have come all the way up here from —" He dared not say the Shambles, but she had that look. "— from town."

His mother glared once more and moved off as Simon went outside to meet the woman. She was young but trained in the art of seduction. "I'm Lottie," she purred.

"I am Simon," he answered a little too formally. "What brings you here, Lottie?"

"A certain man who is friend to us both,"

she said conspiratorially. Noting her light hair, he remembered Daisy's comment that Peto preferred blondes. "He says he's glad the luck worked for you."

Simon fingered the fleur-de-lis that again hung around his neck. "Tell him I am glad as well, and I thank him for his help." He knew that Peto the Pope had sent Pen to watch over him. "Is he . . . well?"

"Him?" She tossed her head carelessly. "He's always well. Nothing can touch him, nothing at all. He says I'm to offer you . . . whatever you like." The girl eyed him, measuring the strength in his shoulders. She didn't seem to notice the weak arm.

Simon's face reddened and his heart beat faster, mostly from imagining the reaction of his mother to the offer if she'd heard it. "No, but I thank you." The girl looked surprised, then vaguely angry. "I have someone," he explained, "a sweetheart."

"Oh," she said, mollified. "Then I'll be off. He says if ever you need him, send that —" she indicated the amulet that once more hung about his neck — "with a messenger, and he'll find you."

"Please give him my thanks." Simon returned inside, where his mother still fumed over the visit she was sure would disgrace her home forever. "And what did that little piece of filth want?" she demanded.

"She brought a message from a friend," Simon replied. He had gained an odd collection of them over the past weeks: an outlaw, a maidservant, a captain, and a princess. He could not help but wonder what came next.

ABOUT THE AUTHOR

Peg Herring is a writer of plays, mysteries, and romance who once taught high school language arts and history. In her spare time she travels with her husband of many decades, gardens, directs choral groups, and works to keep her hundred-year-old home from crumbling away.

The employees of Thorndike Press hope you have enjoyed this Large Print book. All our Thorndike, Wheeler, and Kennebec Large Print titles are designed for easy reading, and all our books are made to last. Other Thorndike Press Large Print books are available at your library, through selected bookstores, or directly from us.

For information about titles, please call:
(800) 223-1244

or visit our Web site at:
http://gale.cengage.com/thorndike

To share your comments, please write:
Publisher
Thorndike Press
295 Kennedy Memorial Drive
Waterville, ME 04901